PAMELA G. BAKER

Message Sent Through Time

By
Pamela G. Baker

Chapter 1

I'd always believed Newton's linear time theory until I entered this museum house at the end of my cul-de-sac. Here, in the grand ballroom, with its tall, arched windows lining one wall and the polished hardwood floor, the air belonged to a bygone era as if I'd traversed time in the wrong direction. The people with me represented the present. The time periods seemed to collide.

A dozen of my neighbors sat in a ring of metal folding chairs quarreling about whether to fight our annexation into the city of New Hope. I stayed quiet because my boyfriend, Todd, owned the house we lived in.

Todd. I didn't know how to handle his mood swings these last few months—when he was home, which wasn't often. Had I stayed because I liked his neighborhood so much, especially this museum? The rest of the twenty-some homes on the street were all built in the past ten years, starting around 1999. I liked our modern house, but the dichotomy of the neighborhood appealed to me more. Too bad I didn't have a ring on my finger. If we did break up, I'd have to move. What was I thinking? Todd had only been stressed about work. We'd be fine.

"Cassandra." The woman next to me poked me in the shoulder.

Startled, I turned to her, unable to remember her name. Todd and I always referred to her as Red because she colored her short, choppy hair hazard-light red, the most unnatural color I could imagine. "What?"

Red chuckled. "Sam just asked if anyone knew of engineering openings, here or in Atlanta. I thought that would get your attention."

So, this person whose name I couldn't remember, knew my name and what I did for a living. How embarrassing. I shook my head. "No. I can't think of any."

She winked. "Maybe that hunk of a brother you live with can?"

Mrs. Miller from down the street frowned. "He's not her brother."

When Todd and I attended our first homeowners' association meeting, Mrs. Miller had made it clear she didn't approve of mixed-race relationships or "living in sin."

"I know." Red leaned in, nodded toward our eavesdropper, and snickered. "Do you think she felt more comfortable in this house when it was new?"

Mrs. Miller stood and looked down her nose at me. "The meeting is over. Where have you been?" She glanced around at the crown molding and period wallpaper with its gold diamond pattern on a cream background. "Back in 1870?"

I stretched my legs out, crossed my ankles, and tilted my gaze toward her. "Maybe." Despite the folding chairs, this room, with its elegant rug, gold-colored drapes, and elaborate chandelier, made me feel like I was attending a ball.

Red sighed. "I always loved this house. Being able to see it from my front porch is the main reason I bought mine."

Mrs. Miller stepped toward the foyer doorway and glared at us. "Adam wants to lock up, so you'd better get a move on."

I forced myself out of my chair, not wanting to head back to an empty house. Todd had worked late all week. Straggling behind my neighbors, I said goodnight to Adam, the museum curator, and followed Red through the foyer, down the three steps of the wrap-around porch, and onto the street.

She peeled off at her house, the second one on the left, and I continued to Todd's, the next one down. His silver Prius sat in the driveway. I quickened my pace. It was only eight o'clock. He was an hour early.

"Todd?" I opened the front door and closed it behind me. Calling out his name, I strode through the living room, den, and kitchen. Not bothering to check the two small bedrooms or the master, I trotted upstairs to the bonus room he used as an office and knocked on the closed door.

"I'll be out in a few." He sounded irritated.

Few what? Minutes? Hours? Days? I listened at the door, but only heard clicks on the keyboard. Resigned to another evening alone, I trudged downstairs to the kitchen to fix myself cold cereal for supper.

Todd shuffled in as I set down my spoon. He slumped into his seat across the corner from me, and laid his head in his palms, elbows on the table.

I touched his shoulder, and he tensed. Had I done something wrong or had something awful happened? "Are you all right?"

He turned his head from side to side and cleared his throat.

Was he sick? I hurried to the sink and back, then handed him a glass of water.

He sipped, keeping his gaze focused straight ahead.

My pulse rate rose at the grimace on his face. He and I hadn't spent much time together in the past month and when we had, we'd squabbled about his frequent absences. I suspected he hadn't been spending all his time at work. "What's wrong?"

"It's over." He set his glass down with a bang and a splash.

My initial reaction was to go pack, but before I left the room, I clenched my fists and whirled around. "Look, if you

3

want out, you're going to have to talk about it first. You can't ignore me for months and then tell me to leave!"

He jumped up, eyes wide, head cocked. After a moment, his expression softened. "Oh, baby. That's not what I meant." He pulled me into an embrace and stroked my hair. "I'm sorry. I haven't been around much lately. Well, that's about to change 'cause it's not going to happen."

"What?" I peered at him.

He backed away. "My project. They cut my funding. Right when I need..." He shook his head. "They told me to focus on my other research."

He sat at the table and dropped his head in his hands.

I leaned toward him. "Maybe you can work on it here, in your spare time. I could help."

"No." He wiped his brow with his sleeve. "It's over. Please don't ask about it."

"All right." I sighed, carried my bowl to the sink, and slipped out of the room.

~

I hummed an upbeat tune as I approached the coffee station in the breakroom.

"You're in a good mood this morning." My lab tech lifted her cup in salute and stepped out of the way. "First time I've seen a smile on your face in a while."

I scoffed as I reached for the pot and poured the nectar I craved.

"Is it because Todd has more time now?"

I tilted up one corner of my mouth and replaced the carafe. "Maybe." Todd had been home early enough to eat dinner together all week. Our relationship was back on track – or so I hoped. Todd's defeat at his failed project still hung over us.

She leaned in. "Have you heard about William Garcia? He's still missing. Hasn't been seen since last Friday."

I narrowed my eyes. All I knew was a twenty-five-year-old

engineer hadn't shown up for work on Monday. It wasn't the first time, but normally they stumbled in bleary-eyed later in the day. "That's odd."

"Do you think it has anything to do with Todd's project being shut down?" She whispered.

"Why would it? He doesn't work with Todd." I stirred my coffee and strode back to my lab, aware of inquisitive glances from my coworkers. Could William's disappearance be connected to Todd's project? Nah. Had to be a coincidence.

~

I cradled my coffee mug in my hands, savoring the aroma wafting into the crisp air. Today was the first day since last spring, it was cool enough to sit on our back deck.

Todd closed the kitchen door and sat next to me on the picnic table, feet on the bench.

I nudged his shoulder. "I'm looking forward to our outing today. Been awhile."

He lowered his head. "About that…"

I slumped. "No."

The doorbell rang a long shrill tone. He slid forward. "I'll get it."

They leaned on the bell, the way someone had a half-hour before.

I set down my mug and jumped off the table. "You got it last time. Is it the same person?"

He hopped down. "How would I know?"

I raced through the house.

As I opened the front door, Todd slid in front of me.

I caught a glimpse of a short, thin, blonde woman, her ponytail hanging out of a baseball cap.

"Who's she?" I stood on tiptoes, but couldn't see over Todd.

"A business associate." Her tone was low and scratchy.

"Cassandra." Todd faced me and placed both hands on my

shoulders. "I'll handle this."

I pressed my lips together and stomped back through the house to the deck. I'd either have to go zip-lining by myself or wait for another day. Ugh. My coffee was cold. While I heated it up, I stole into the living room to see if Todd was still at the front door. He and the blonde woman were arguing. Too bad I couldn't understand what they said. Had he been seeing her on the side? Did I know him as well as I thought? I shuddered.

After the other woman left, Todd holed up in his office the rest of the weekend.

To work through my stress, I ran five miles later that morning and the next day.

When I arrived home after work on Monday, I had to wait for a large, unmarked white van to pull out of the driveway. What was that about? I hurried inside and caught Todd before he disappeared into his office.

"Hey, did you get some kind of delivery?"

Todd shifted from foot to foot. "Yeah. Equipment for my project. Thought I'd work on it here."

"Can I help?"

He studied the floor. "Maybe." He gave me a quick peck on the cheek and headed upstairs.

I steeled myself for lots of alone time.

~

Three weeks later, on a Thursday night, Todd sank into the easy chair in our bedroom.

I peered over my book as I leaned against the headboard, wearing the oversized t-shirt I slept in most nights. I'd cooked a steak dinner for us. He'd gobbled it in about ten minutes and spent the rest of the evening in his office-turned-lab.

He glanced in my direction, then rubbed his face with the palm of his hand. "Sorry, I got caught up in my project."

"The one you won't tell me about?" I pursed my lips.

He exhaled. "Cassandra. You know I can't. Not yet."

I leaned toward him. "When you brought it home, I hoped you wanted my help."

He closed his eyes and shook his head. "It's for your protection."

His closed expression meant he wouldn't expound on why I'd be in danger if I knew about his project. "Fine." I plopped my book on the nightstand, switched out the light, and curled up on my side.

Todd padded to the bathroom and closed the door.

If it had been earlier in the day, I might have pressed the issue.

~

My alarm blared. Ugh. Six a.m. I reached for the snooze button, but turned it off instead. I hauled myself out of bed and stumbled around to the bathroom to get ready for my run. Todd's side of the bed looked exactly like it had when I'd made it up yesterday.

After completing my morning hygiene routine, I dressed in my training shorts and sports bra, and donned a headband to keep my chin-length curls from falling into my face. I marched upstairs to his lab. Bracing myself for the confrontation I should have instigated last night, I opened the door without knocking first.

"Todd, we need—" Not expecting the room to be dark, I hit the light switch. His computer desk occupied most of the space next to the wall on my right, a mini-fridge sat next to it, and an old pinball game stood in the far corner. His mystery machine jutted out from the wall to my left, about a yard from the window. Its blank display contrasted with the shiny stainless-steel handles on either side of the rectangular platform.

"Great!" I threw up my hands and let them drop to my side.

The sound of a car door closing caught my attention. I crossed the room, careful to step around the treadmill-like apparatus, and looked out the window, just in time to watch

Todd start his car. I whirled around and ran to catch him but plowed into the machine, hit the nearest rail with my hip, and caught myself with my hand on the opposite bar.

"Stupid machine!" I rubbed my hip and stepped back. "Stealing my boyfriend, and I don't even know what you do."

Too late to catch Todd, I stepped onto the brushed-metal platform. It didn't have a belt like a treadmill would, so why did it need railings on either side? I inspected the blank screen on the opposite end from the opening. Despite touching it and pressing what I thought was an ON button, the display stayed blank. I banged my hand against the panel. Nice Cassandra. Way to be an adult. I stepped back. A low tone emanated from the display. It sounded like a whistle, changing from low frequency to high and keeping my attention focused on the brightening panel.

The platform shook, adding a rumble to the noise. I grabbed both rails and hung on tight while I searched the newly illuminated display panel. So many numbers and gauges but no way to turn it off. The apparatus vibrated faster and the whistle changed into a shriek. I could barely think, let alone see anything useful on the unfamiliar display.

I tried to back off but a powerful force kept my hands and feet in place. It couldn't have been centripetal because the machine was shaking, not spinning.

The lights in the room flickered. I closed my eyes for a moment and swallowed hard. A mist enveloped me. I clung to the rails as the fog grew thicker. My hands cramped on the bars, and my knees buckled. The mist muffled the cacophony of sound. My heart hammered in my chest. What was this thing?

My right hand fought the pressure and grappled on the edges of the display panel for an OFF switch. The machine tipped, negating the force that had been holding me in. I clung to the rail as long as I could, but my hands were sweaty. As I slid off, pain shot up the skin on the outside of my leg.

The mist evaporated, replaced by sunlight so bright I closed my eyes. I landed on my bottom with a thud and shielded my head with my arms, expecting the machine to fall on me. Silence.

Chapter 2

"Ma, come quick!"

The young boy's voice penetrated my brain fog. I kept my eyes closed against the sunshine. The damp grass under me and a gentle breeze flowing over chilled me. A dank odor I associated with the woods accosted my nose. How had I fallen off Todd's machine and landed on the ground?

A rustle followed by soft footsteps caught my attention.

"Ma, there she is. She fell out of the sky!"

My eyes flew open. I blinked to adjust to the brightness, and the unfamiliar surroundings. This couldn't be happening.

The boy ran to a woman in a long drab-colored gown with one of those bell skirts like they wore to balls in the mid-nineteenth century. The youngster wore short pants with cuffs at the knees and a button-down shirt.

Had to be a dream. I pinched myself. "Wake up." My surroundings stayed the same, but my heartrate accelerated.

I glanced around to get my bearings. Dust from the dirt road not far away floated in front of me. Across the road lay more fields and woods in the distance. To my left, more countryside. To my right the boy argued with his mother. Did I want to talk to them or not? They might be able to help me, but they might be figments of my imagination. I took a deep breath and let it out slowly. Panicking would do me no good. I needed information.

I struggled to my knees, noticing a few bruises, and feeling some pain in my right hip and leg. Closer inspection revealed a scratch from the outside of my ankle as far up my leg as I could see. Blood seeped out near the bottom, but not enough to need a bandage. I still wore the running gear I had put on that morning. Could I have fallen while I was running and blacked out? No. I wouldn't have left the house without my phone.

Out of the corner of my eye, I caught a glimpse of a building behind the mother and son. The large white farmhouse our homeowners' association met in stood at the end of the dirt road, but all the rest of the houses, including Todd's, had vanished.

I bounced up and headed toward the house which had been built in the late eighteen-hundreds and kept furnished the same as when it was new. Nathaniel Bridger, the original owner hadn't had a family and left it to the town. It was the only familiar building in view, so I marched past the woman and the boy, and continued toward the front door.

"Wait, miss, do you need any help?" The woman held her hands over her son's eyes. A strand of her dark brown hair escaped the bun at the nape of her neck.

"No, I'm good." I picked up my pace.

She ran and caught my arm. When I turned around, the boy peeked at me. The woman gave him a warning glance, and he looked away.

She fixed her stony brown eyes on me. "My lands. You can use some clothes. Let me help."

"No. I'm okay." The house seemed to pull me toward it as if it was the key to my predicament. I needed to be in that dwelling for this—whatever it was—to be over, so I could go back to my real life. I didn't want to be late for work on a Friday.

I marched up the steps onto the wraparound porch I'd always admired. When I walked in the front door, I expected to see the little registration desk in the entryway. It wasn't there, but the staircase across the square foyer, the pocket doors leading to rooms on either side, and the hallway going toward the back of the house looked exactly the same. The cream wallpaper with the gold diamond pattern was even there. Except the colors were more vibrant.

My breath caught in my throat. This couldn't be the museum. I turned to leave, but the woman and her son blocked the doorway.

She stood, one hand on her hip, her other index finger pointed at me. "You can't walk into someone's home without being invited."

"I'm so sorry. Is it yours?" I backed farther into the foyer but stopped when heavy footsteps approached from the adjacent room. A tall, solidly built man, maybe a little older than me, filled the doorway of the small parlor.

"It's mine." He stared straight through me for a split second then averted his gaze.

I shivered under his disdain. Goosebumps appeared on my arms, and a knot a formed in my gut.

He turned toward the woman and tilted his head in my direction. "Lera, who's this?"

Lera shrugged. "Caleb found her down the road a piece."

"She fell out of the sky. I swear, Uncle Nate." Caleb ran to the man and stopped short of plowing into him. He shifted from foot to foot and glanced at me every few seconds.

"I'm sorry." I stepped back and studied my running shoes. "It's just that I thought I knew this house. You see, there's one exactly like it on my street." I shook my head and looked up at him. "Well, maybe not exactly. It's over a hundred years old."

He took a deep breath and clenched his fists at his sides. "This house was built to my own plan and finished last year. I doubt there's another like it. But I accept your apology." His voice had softened but he still didn't meet my eyes.

Nate went down on one knee and placed his hands on the

boy's shoulders. "Now, Caleb, calm down and tell me what you saw."

Could I make my escape? I glanced at the door, but Lera blocked it.

"I was walking down the road toward the berry patch, and—"

"Caleb." Lera pursed her lips.

"Okay, I was running ahead of Ma, but I still saw it." He glanced at his mother, his cheeks pink and his eyes flashing. "She was in this shiny box thing in the sky. Then it disappeared." He rushed toward me and waved his arms. "And she fell to the ground. I swear she wasn't near a tree or nuthin'."

Lera stepped toward her son. "Caleb, the sun must have been in your eyes."

Caleb studied his shoes and kept his mouth shut.

Lera leaned toward Nate. "What are we going to do about her?"

When she moved from the doorway, I would have run, but I didn't know where to go. Plus, I felt a little self-conscious without a shirt on over my sports bra, especially compared to their costumes. I meant to tell them they were the ones who were dressed funny, but I didn't get the chance.

"What's your name?" Nate gazed over my shoulder. He could have been asking someone else except he already knew Lera and Caleb.

I wanted to tell him he was being rude, and it was none of his business, but I had entered his house without being invited. I took a breath. "Cassandra McPherson."

"I'm Nate Bridger."

My eyes went wide. Could this be the original owner? What if…No, not possible. He had to be a descendant.

He gave me a curt nod. "I don't know any McPhersons from around here."

"Enough introductions." Lera took hold of my arm. "We

need to get Miss McPherson dressed before anyone else sees her."

Before I could protest, they whisked me up the stairs and sent Caleb home, but only after making him swear he wouldn't tell anyone about me.

Caleb ran off and then back before we got to the landing. "Do you want me to bring Grandma to help?"

"No!" Lera and Nate said in unison.

Lera smoothed her skirt and exhaled. "Tell Grandma that Uncle Nate needed my help this morning. I might not make it home in time for dinner."

Were they going to keep me here indefinitely? No. Convinced I'd wake up soon, I allowed them to lead me into one of the guest rooms. The cream-colored wallpaper with vines and rosebuds, dark wood moldings, and four poster bed were the same as when I'd last visited this room. Even the wooden rocking chair sat by the window. But now everything looked new.

"Miss McPherson." Lera stood next to Nate near the hallway. "Make yourself at home, and I'll find you something more suitable to wear."

I smiled, and wandered around the room, pretending to notice everything except Nate and Lera talking about me. Nate glanced at me several times, but every time I tried to meet his eyes, he'd avert them. You'd think he'd never seen anyone in shorts and a bra-top before. It would be interesting to watch him at the beach.

"Did you look around to see where she could have come from? A carriage or something?" Nate kept his volume low.

"Yes, but I didn't see anything," Lera whispered. "When Caleb pointed her out, she was lying in the grass, quite a ways from the road."

"She couldn't have fallen from a great height. She's not hurt bad enough." He glanced at me. "She didn't hit her head, did she?"

My hand flew to the back of my head. "No, I don't think so."

Nate nodded at Lera. "We should clean that scrape."

"I'll see to that." Lera tilted her head toward me. "But we need to figure out what to do with her."

"We can't let her walk around looking like that." He flung his open palm in my direction.

"You don't like what she's wearing?" She grinned. "You're having a hard time keeping your eyes off her."

He shifted his weight. "It's a little . . . distracting. Find her something decent to wear."

"I'll have to go home for that." She raised her eyebrows. "Unless you want her to wear something of yours?"

He shook his head. "Go to a friend's house." He paced into the hallway and back. "No, keep as few people involved as possible, at least till we know who she is. Take some money out of the jar in the kitchen and go into town and buy something. I'll keep her here."

"I bet you will." She giggled and left the room.

He followed her out the door and closed it. "I'll stay right here." He paused. "Hurry."

"Before you do something you'll regret?" She giggled again.

"Take Prince and don't bother with the carriage," he called. "You can make it in half the time."

Until the door closed, it had been like watching a movie. Though I knew they were talking about me, I wasn't involved. Now, it was all too real. I glanced out the window, trapped by a stranger in the museum house down the street from mine. Only, it wasn't a museum, and my street didn't exist. This had to be a nightmare.

"Ma'am." He could have said it several times before it registered.

"Sir?" I raised my voice, so he could hear me.

"Do you know how you got here?"

"No." What else could I say?

I wandered around the room. I should've used the time to think, to come up with a plan, but I couldn't get my mind to focus. It was the same old problem. Whenever I had to wait in line or in a doctor's office, I would try to make plans, or think through a problem with one of my work projects. Unfortunately, I wouldn't be able to get my mind off the fact I was waiting.

But what was I waiting for? Were they going to give me clothes and send me on my way? Or did they have other plans? They hadn't mistreated me, but they shut me in here. Nate acted embarrassed to be in the same room with me. At least I hadn't fallen into the hands of a psycho killer or something. When this was over, I intended to stop watching so many thrillers.

Who were Nate and Lera? Nate's real name could be Nathaniel, and he had the same last name as the original owner. He could be a descendant, but I had always thought there weren't any. Nathaniel Bridger left the house to the city as a museum because he died without heirs. And what was Lera's relationship to Nate? Caleb had called Nate 'uncle.' They could be siblings, but they didn't look anything alike. Could she be his sister-in-law?

Nate's voice interrupted my thoughts. "What do you remember?"

"Lots of things." I paced in front of the door.

He huffed out his breath. "I mean about this morning."

"Nothing between being annoyed with my boyfriend and landing in the field." He wouldn't believe me if I told him what really happened. I wasn't sure I believed it myself.

"Boyfriend?" He sounded confused.

"His name is Todd James."

"Who?" He paused. "I don't know anyone by that name. Does he live in town?"

"That depends. What town is this?"

"New Hope."

I plopped onto the four-poster bed. The last time I sat there, I'd had to step over the velvet-covered rope that separated the entryway from the rest of the room. I shuddered then took a deep breath.

"Miss McPherson? Did you hear me?"

"It's Cassandra." I pressed my thumb and index finger on the bridge of my nose. "Give me a minute to process this."

He raised his voice. "Miss McPherson, does Mr. James live in New Hope, Georgia?"

I glanced out the window. "We both do. We live down the street from a house like this one. Have for over a year."

"Impossible."

"What do you mean, impossible?" I jumped off the bed and sailed to the door. "I should know where I've lived for the past year."

He cleared his throat. "We know most everyone in town. Do you live closer to Atlanta?"

"We both work in Atlanta, but we live in New Hope."

He hesitated for a second. "What do you do?"

"We're engineers. Well, Todd's more of a pure scientist. He's into research and development. I design and test integrated circuits." I paced in front of the door. "You don't seem to think much of me, but I'm highly respected at work. That's how I met Todd. He was impressed when I won an award and came to my office to ask me out. Todd's brilliant. He's got loads of patents. He's been working on something secret lately. That's why I was upset."

I took a breath, expecting some sort of reply from the other side of the door, but none came. I closed my eyes and slumped onto the bed. Had I said too much?

Nate stayed quiet for a long time, an hour maybe. My internal clock is normally precise, but under the circumstances, I didn't trust it. I wanted to peek out to see if he was still there but didn't want him to catch me.

My mind waffled between trying to wake up from this nightmare and a horrifying suspicion I had found out what Todd's machine did and that it worked.

Chapter 3

When I brushed my leg against the bedpost, the physical pain reminded me of my scratch. Having no idea how long it would take for Lera to get back, I needed to do something if only to distract my thoughts.

"Mr. Bridger?"

Scrambling noises. "Yes?" His voice came from head height.

"Do you think you could get me something to wash off this scrape?"

"Yes. Sorry." Floorboards creaked as he started down the hall. "Don't go anywhere."

I rolled my eyes. Where would I go?

Nate knocked. "Miss McPherson."

I hurried to the door and opened it.

Without even a glance in my direction, he handed me a metal bowl of water with a cloth in it.

"Thank you."

He pulled the door closed, and slid down it, landing with a thunk.

Having not experienced behavior like that since grade school, I giggled despite the circumstances. I set the basin on the stand and stood in front of the window to pat the wet cloth on my scrape. To get the lower part of my leg, I sat on the edge of the rocking chair. After I'd cleaned out as much of the scratch that I could see, I leaned back in the rocker and gazed out the window, visualizing what my view should be.

I pictured the upscale suburban street, lined with large houses built to different floor plans. None were quite as grand as this house at the end of the road, the only one on the cul-de-sac. My brain filled in the correct images, and I lulled myself into believing I was just down the street and would be able to go home soon. I sat there in a semi-awake state for another long stretch of time. Voices in the hallway startled me.

"Lera, thank God you're back," Nate said. "I think she's delirious. I'll get Uncle Ed."

"What about her scratches?"

"I took care of that."

"You did?" Lera sounded shocked.

"I supplied the means. She may need help."

The door opened, and Lera strutted in laden with garments. It looked like she'd brought enough clothes for a week. She held up each piece and showed it to me as if it was the prettiest thing she'd ever seen. It was a while before I realized I was supposed to wear them all at once. My eyes went wide, but it didn't faze her. She kept holding up garments calling them petticoats, crinolines, and other terms I'd never heard.

"Sunday at preachin' we learned about the golden rule. You know, do unto others? Well, I just took that to heart this morning. I bought all the things I would want someone to buy for me. The best they had. Nate can afford it." She looked like a schoolgirl, holding the dress up to herself and flouncing around in front of the mirror.

When she nearly knocked the water bowl off the stand, she stopped and caught it before it could slosh over the side. "Oh, I forgot about that scrape. Let me see it."

She laid the dress on the bed, picked up the cloth, and wrung it as she squatted down to inspect my leg. "You got most of it, except right here." She rubbed the top of my thigh.

I jumped and let out a yelp. "I can do it." I reached for the cloth.

"No, let me." She held it away from me. "You can't see the whole thing, and we need to make sure we get all the dirt out of it. I should have done this earlier." She patted my thigh with the wet cloth.

I hissed in pain.

"I'm sorry." She stifled a giggle. "It's not funny. It's just that Nate was too bent on getting clothes for you."

I put my hands on my hips. "What's his problem?"

"What's yours? Waltzing in here in next to nothing and wondering why a bachelor can't keep his eyes off you." She pulled me over to the mirror. "Look at yourself."

I shrugged. "So?"

"You have the best figure, prettiest complexion, and whitest teeth I've ever seen. Once your hair grows out, you'll be the most gorgeous woman in town. Maybe even in Atlanta."

"What's wrong with my hair?" I fingered the short curls.

"Oh, strawberry blonde is a lovely color. I wouldn't mind having curls either, but it's not the style, now, is it?"

"It isn't?" Having spent most of my time pursuing intellectual goals, I had never worried about my appearance, but I didn't think I was that out of touch. Then I remembered Lera wasn't exactly with the times either, unless . . . no, impossible.

I slid to the floor. This couldn't be real.

Lera gathered a few of the lighter white cotton garments from the bed. "I think we'd better get you dressed. Stand up and take off whatever that is, unless you want to wear these over?"

I shook my head and did as she told me. I donned a light cotton shirt-like thing and sat down to take off my sneakers.

Lera circled around them then picked one up and inspected it. "Mind if I try this on? I got you some shoes."

"No. Go ahead." I slipped off my shorts and pulled on

something she called a petticoat. "Hey, is this a joke, or are we going to a costume party?" I forced a laugh.

She stared at me, then stepped down on the sneaker. Her eyes widened and she cocked her head. Lera put the other sneaker on, pranced around the room, and then stopped, leaned toward me, and gazed into my eyes, as if she was trying to read my mind.

My expression was intentionally blank. A war waged inside me, and I didn't want it to show on my face. The intellectual part of me wanted to find out if my suspicions were correct, but the practical side just wanted to go home.

"I know one thing." She backed up a step. "You ain't, I mean, aren't from around here. I never seen—" She blinked. "I mean, I never saw anything like this before. I feel like I could run all day in these."

She pranced again, but a knock on the door interrupted her.

"She ready yet? Uncle Ed's here," Nate said.

"Shoot." She rushed toward me. "Give us a few more minutes."

"All right. Bring her down to the parlor when she's ready."

"That'll be a while," I said under my breath.

She helped me with the rest of the clothing, including a few pieces that looked like they had steel rods. She finished with a pretty, light-blue bodice and light-blue and dark-blue plaid overskirt. I gazed into the mirror. Was that me?

She handed me a pair of what she called everyday boots. I glanced down at my running shoes on her feet. "You might want to change your own shoes."

"Oh, you're right." She ambled toward the bed. "I wish I didn't have to."

I sat on the bed to put on the boots and nearly fell over when my skirt popped up.

Lera laughed. "You have to be careful when you sit." She stood over me. "You might want to practice before you go downstairs."

She showed me how to lift the hoop when I sat. There was an art to it. She helped me with my shoes. When she took off my sneakers, I slid them under the bed along with my shorts and bra, hoping to get them later.

We promenaded out the door, down the hall, and down the stairs, Lera in the lead and me following several feet behind. Even at that distance, I had a hard time keeping my skirt from bumping hers. At least my personal space wouldn't be invaded today.

As we entered the parlor, both men stood. Nate looked me over and then raised his eyebrows at Lera. She smiled and sashayed toward the fireplace. He must have guessed how much money she'd spent.

Nate grinned and turned his attention to me. "Miss McPherson. You look lovely." He addressed me with direct eye contact for the first time. He kept my hand in his until his taller, thinner companion cleared his throat. "Miss McPherson, this is my uncle, Ed Gardner."

"Pleased to meet you." Ed waved his arm toward a seating arrangement near the window. "Shall we sit?"

He led me to a wingback chair and took the one across from it. Nate and Lera left the room.

"Now, Miss McPherson, Nate tells me you have some gaps in your memory." He repeated the few facts I'd told Lera and Nate.

I nodded.

Ed narrowed his dark eyes at me. "The last place you remember. Tell me about it." He leaned back, making a steeple out of his fingers.

I shrugged. "I was in my boyfriend's lab."

He raised his eyebrows. "Describe it for me, please."

"I don't spend much time in there." I glanced over his shoulder at the window. "It's his office. He's got a few computers and some of his experiments."

He leaned forward clasping his hands in front of him. "Computers?"

"You know, PCs. He's probably got the highest speed processors—" I stopped mid-sentence reminding myself to be careful about what information I divulged. "Who are you anyway?" Annoyance sounded in my voice.

He sat up straight. "Nate told you. I'm his uncle."

"So why are you asking me about the lab?" I squinted. "I thought you were a doctor."

"No. I work the farm with Nate." He waved his arm. "Folks around here think of me as a doctor."

"Do you live here?"

"I live down the road out back, in Nate's grandparents' house. The one my wife grew up in."

I leaned forward. "So, you married Nate's aunt?"

He nodded. "Now, why—"

"Who's Lera? Is she a maid or something?" I glanced at the closed door to the dining room.

"No, she's my daughter-in-law. She and Caleb moved in with us when my son—" He looked down. "John…died."

I lowered my voice. "I'm sorry to hear that."

"Thank you. But it was nearly two years ago." He shifted in his seat. "Why were you there this morning?"

"Excuse me?" Oh, he was back to his line of questioning. Maybe if I answered, I'd trigger a memory, something that could help me get home. "I was trying to find my boyfriend."

"I assume you didn't."

"I did, but he was driving away."

He rested an elbow on the chair arm. "What happened next?"

I blinked. "I'm not sure."

"What's the next thing you remember?"

"Landing on the ground and hearing Caleb call his mother."

Okay, so I couldn't tell him the whole story. I felt embarrassed about messing with Todd's machine, and I didn't think he'd buy the part about the mist and the room disappearing.

He stood and stepped toward the fireplace, tapping his finger on his chin. "Are you sure you haven't been here before?"

"No!" I jumped up and pressed my fingers to my temples. "I just told you, I'm not sure of anything."

"I see." He placed his hand on my arm and guided me to sit next to him on the sofa. He let go but stayed close and locked eyes with me. "Do you remember anything between seeing your boyfriend drive away and hearing Caleb?"

"No." I heaved a sigh. "Why are you asking me all these questions?"

He glanced away. "I'm sorry. I thought I might be able to help—with your memory problem."

"If you want to help me, you can stop this charade, get me some real clothes, and get me back to New Hope, Georgia."

"You're already there. About four miles out." He leaned back, still watching me.

"No, I couldn't be." But Nate had told me that earlier. I squeezed the bridge of my nose. "Is there another house like this one in town?"

"No."

"About how many people live here?"

"Just Nate."

I huffed. "I meant, in town."

"Round about four hundred." He stood, walked toward the window, and peered out. "Miss McPherson. Do you know what year it is?"

"There must be two New Hopes, because my town has at least twelve thousand people. It's been growing—"

My head throbbed. I looked at the floor, hands on my cheeks, as if, by holding my head in place I could keep it from spinning. "What year is it?" I kept my voice low.

Lera rushed in and knelt beside me. "Are you all right, honey?"

I lifted my head, hoping I didn't look as bad as I felt. No wonder they thought I was ill. It was a polite way of saying crazy.

"I'm fine. I think I'm just hungry. I'm not sure when I ate last." I smiled, trying to lighten my tone. I glanced at Ed, hoping he'd tell me the year, but he gazed out the window.

Lera helped me up. "We've got a nice dinner all ready for you." She led me into the dining room and settled me into a chair on the long side of the table.

Ed followed us. "Lera, would you mind going home and telling Mattie that I'll be eating here?"

"Sure. I already told Nate what I thought you should do." She glanced at me before returning her attention to Ed. "I'll tell Miss Mattie that Nate needed you."

"Too late." Nate entered the dining room from the opposite doorway.

Outside, horse hooves and wheels came to a stop, followed by quick footsteps on the ground and then on wood. A short, medium-framed lady glided into the room and stood in the doorway.

"Good morning." She smiled so wide she sucked all the air out of the room. "What's the occasion, Nate?" She glanced at me as she stepped toward him. "If I'd known you had a guest I would have gladly come to help." Her syrupy voice almost made me gag.

"Hello, Aunt Mattie." Nate gave her a peck on the cheek. "Why don't you join us?"

"Well, I should be getting dinner at our house. I just came to find Lera." She hesitated and turned toward the younger woman. "Caleb said you'd be home by dinner time."

"I'm sorry, Ma'am." Lera pulled out a chair. "Caleb got mixed up, but I'm sure Lydia can manage their dinner. It's just her, Mark, and Caleb since the rest of us will be eating here."

"Yes, join us, Dear." Ed rushed over to her.

"I'll get another place setting. I'm sure we'll have enough." Lera hurried out of the room.

All the deference to Nate's aunt made me even more nervous. Could this day get any weirder?

"I didn't mean to crash your party." Mattie pursed her lips.

"It's not a party." Nate approached me and held his arm out toward his aunt. "We found Miss McPherson this morning. Cassandra McPherson, this is my Aunt Mattie, Mattie Gardner."

"Hello." I started to rise from my chair.

"Don't get up on my account." Mattie nodded toward me. "I'm pleased to make your acquaintance." She squinted at Nate. "What do you mean you found her?"

Lera breezed in with the place setting. "Miss Mattie, as soon as we got here this morning, Caleb told me he heard a carriage on the road, the one at the front of the house." She placed the plate. "Then he said he heard a loud noise. Well, you know Caleb. So, I let him talk, not paying him much mind. He kept on and on, saying it sounded like a crash and maybe we should go check. When he said someone could have been hurt—" She placed the last utensil on the table. "I'm sorry. I can finish my story while we're eating."

Mattie gestured for Nate to take the seat at one end of the table while Ed sat at the other end. Lera and Mattie sat next to each other, opposite me.

Mattie nodded at her nephew. "Nate, would you do the honors?"

I had no idea what she meant until everyone bowed their heads, and Nate prayed. He was much more verbose while talking to God than to me. It gave me time to study my dinner companions. Nate, immediately to my right, was rugged looking, with straggly, light-brown, collar-length hair. He wasn't handsome by any stretch of the imagination, but he wasn't ugly either. I liked his deep voice, but I couldn't relate to what he was saying.

Mattie sat directly across from me. She was short, a little plump, probably in her late forties. Her hair was dark brown, with just a touch of gray, worn back in a tight bun at the nape of her neck. The bun was the only thing she had in common with Lera, who was at least twenty years younger with lots of natural color in her face and excitement in her eyes. Lera flashed me a conspiratorial smile. What did she and I have to conspire about? She must have thought Nate was ending his prayer because she closed her eyes again.

I hazarded a quick glance at Ed. He was slightly taller than Nate, had wiry, graying hair, dark eyes, and dark skin. He looked to be in his early fifties.

Nate finished his prayer, and Lera launched into her story. While I listened, I ate some kind of meat, lima beans, and corn.

"As I was saying, Caleb was pestering me so much, I sent him home."

Mattie patted Lera's hand. "That's fine dear. I can handle Caleb."

"After a while, Nate and I got to wondering if Caleb had heard something. We walked down the road and saw Miss McPherson." Lera glanced at me. "May we call you Cassandra?"

I nodded, but she'd turned back toward Mattie.

Lera waved her hand. "Cassandra was standing in the middle of the road looking around like she was lost. She told us the carriage driver dropped her at the house, but she didn't think it was the right one, so she started walking back toward town."

"Where was she supposed to be?" Mattie asked.

"That's what I'm getting to." Lera's eyes sparkled as she smiled. "She was supposed to be right here. But having never been here before and not quite remembering why she was coming, she didn't know."

Nate watched Lera as if he was hanging on every word to

make sure he got the story straight. So far, Mattie seemed to be buying it.

Mattie bobbed her head toward me. "How did you know she was supposed to be here?"

"I didn't, but Nate recognized her. Too bad she didn't recognize him." Lera leaned toward her mother-in-law. "Miss Mattie, this is Nate's fiancée."

I choked, but managed to cover it with a cough.

Mattie frowned. "But her name was Margaret McEvers."

Nate stared at Lera, his eyes as big as saucers.

Lera touched Mattie's shoulder. "You and I know that, but Cassandra doesn't remember."

Everyone stared at me.

My stomach knotted, and all I could do was shrug.

"Wait, Lera." Nate half stood, leaning toward her.

Lera raised her palm. "Now, Nate, Miss Mattie should know the whole story. Maybe she can help."

Lera turned toward Mattie. "The best we can piece together is that Margaret, I mean, Cassandra was on her way here to marry Nate last summer." She gestured toward me as if I was a prize on a game show. "She got off the train and hired a carriage to come here. She must have had an accident while she was still in Atlanta. She was in the hospital for a while and couldn't remember her name or where she was going. Finally, a week ago, she found Nate's address in her bag and decided to come, thinking maybe she could get her memory back."

"No, Lera." Nate pushed back from the table.

"I know, Nate, dear." Lera placed her hand on her heart. "You don't want to embarrass Cassandra, but I'm sure she doesn't want the whole town to continue to think she jilted you. Do you Cassandra?" She smiled at me, her eyes challenging me to disagree.

"What?" I was surprised to be addressed. Hadn't I been watching a horror flick? I glanced at Nate and then Ed hoping they'd come to my rescue.

Nate stood next to his aunt. "Look, Aunt Mattie, we were just trying to figure out how we could help her."

"You could've come to me." Mattie peered at her husband.

Ed placed his palms on the table. "That was the next thing I was going to do, right after I examined her."

Mattie glanced at the table and then at Ed, her eyebrows raised. "After dinner?"

"My stomach was growling." I grinned, trying to lighten the tension.

"I did ask her some questions." Ed leaned forward. "As far as I can tell, she's physically healthy, but has some gaps in her memory."

"To include thinking she's someone else?" Mattie threw Ed the side-eye. "Where did Cassandra come from?" She looked at me. "I mean the name."

"Oh!" Lera waved her hands. "Someone at the hospital mentioned that name and she thought it sounded familiar. She decided to use it until she remembers more."

I studied Mattie's face, but from her mild expression, I couldn't tell if she believed Lera or not.

"I think there's been some trauma, whether it was physical or emotional, I'm not sure," Ed said. "I want to observe her for a while, so with your concurrence of course, I propose that Cassandra stay with us."

"I agree." Mattie bobbed her head. "And you, Nate, can come courting her proper." That honeyed voice reappeared. "You can get to know each other all over again."

Nate sucked in a breath.

Mattie peered at her husband. "How long do you think it'll take to get her memory back?"

"I don't know." Ed narrowed his eyes. "Why?"

Mattie lifted her chin. "I'd like to know when to set the date, that's all."

"Date?" Nate furrowed his brow.

Mattie smiled. "For the wedding, of course."

Chapter 4

No way could I get married here. Where did that machine go? Shouldn't Todd have already come back for me? Could I have broken it?

"Cassandra?" Lera raised her voice.

"I'm sorry." I forced myself to relax my white-knuckled grip on the edge of the table. "What did you say?"

Mattie stood. "Cassandra, why don't you let me take you home to get settled?" She ambled toward me. "Lera can clean up here. Do you have any belongings to pack?"

I nodded. My running clothes lay under the bed upstairs.

Wide-eyed, Lera shook her head.

I changed my nod to a shake. "No, Ma'am."

"Just call me Miss Mattie. Everyone does." She patted my hand. "We'll get along fine. I'm sure you'll be back to yourself in no time."

She led me out the back door to the carriage and helped me up onto the seat. "Nate, now you come to supper tonight and you and Cassandra can chat on the porch after."

"Yes, do come." I wanted to add, "So I can tell you there's no way I'm going to marry you," but thought that to be impolitic considering my present circumstances.

What would I do if Mattie didn't take me in? It's not like I could go out and get an engineering job. What kind of work did women do back then—now? For the first time in my life, I wished I'd paid more attention in history class.

Mattie snapped the reins. The carriage jerked forward, and I grabbed ahold of my seat.

She smiled. "So, Cassie. You don't mind if I call you Cassie, do you?"

I shook my head. Until today, I'd always insisted on Cassandra but why argue?

"It seems to fit you better. You definitely don't look like a Margaret." She leaned toward me. "But I don't look like a Matilda either."

I shook my head again, glancing around for anything familiar, hoping to see Todd. As Mattie guided the horse down the path that led away from the back of the house, I tried to picture what this would have looked like just a few hours ago in my time. We'd be crossing our back yard. I blinked, half expecting to see the house I shared with Todd.

"So where do your parents live?" Mattie broke into my reverie.

"My father lives in D.C. and my mother in New York." I clamped my lips together at my gaff.

Mattie frowned and glanced at me. "I thought you were from Savannah?"

"Yes. I lived with my aunt after my parents' divorce." What an awful lie. I needed to keep my mind on the present to avoid more mistakes.

Mattie stopped the carriage and pierced me with her gaze. "Margaret's parents aren't divorced. Who are you?"

I swallowed. "Cassandra McPherson."

"So why are you posing as Margaret?" She took a breath and narrowed her eyes at me. "Did Lera make that up?"

I nodded then shook my head. I didn't want to get Lera in trouble with her mother-in-law.

"Um, I think she assumed it when I just showed up." I

shrugged. "I'm not sure how I got here. I do have some memory gaps."

"You remembered your parents quick enough." She pursed her lips.

"I'm only missing a short time this morning. Just before I met Caleb."

She raised one eyebrow. "What about having Nate's address in your purse?"

"Lera did make up that part. To explain." I winced, hoping I wasn't getting Lera in trouble.

"So where are you from?" For the first time, she sounded annoyed.

"Atlanta." Technically, it wasn't a lie. I had lived there during college and for a year after.

Mattie squinted at me, seeming to study me. After an uncomfortable silence, she turned her attention back to the horse and snapped the reins. The carriage continued down the road. "You are welcome to stay with us as long as you need to." She lifted her chin. "As long as you respect the rules."

Mattie snapped the reins again, and the horse trotted faster. I held on tighter.

After a moment of silence, she cleared her throat. "We'd better stick to Lera's story." One corner of her mouth tilted up. "It'll keep Highland's niece away from Nate, anyway."

Interesting. I hoped she'd say more but it wasn't my business.

We pulled up to a modest-sized house I'd never seen. Mattie hopped down and hurried around the carriage in time to help me. I didn't know how she managed in those clothes, but her gown wasn't quite as large as mine. As I landed, I stumbled. Mattie caught me and kept me upright. I resolved to ask about getting a more functional wardrobe—as soon as I could get up the courage.

A young boy about Caleb's age, but with a complexion like

34

Todd's, came running. Mattie handed him the reins asking him to take care of the horse and put the carriage in the shed. They didn't still have slaves, did they? Too bad we'd gotten interrupted before Ed could tell me what year it was.

"That was Jacob. He's the son of our tenants." She pointed to an unpainted wood cabin, not far from the main house. "That's where Ed and I lived until Nate's pa died and Nate asked us to move into the family house. This is where I grew up. I was so pleased to be able to move back." She led the way up the porch steps. "Not pleased for the reason, mind you."

"Of course," I murmured, though it wouldn't have mattered if I'd said nothing.

Mattie, several steps ahead of me, chatted about the house. From the distance and direction, we'd traveled, we should be in the new subdivision with the starter homes.

I followed Mattie up the steps to the wide porch, through the front door, and into a foyer. She showed me the ladies' parlor to the left and the gentleman's parlor to the right. Both rooms were much smaller than those at Nate's. She led me through the ladies' parlor to the dining room, where a teenaged girl was clearing the table.

"Lydia, come here and meet Miss Cassie."

Lydia set down the plates, hurried over to me, and performed a quick curtsy, flipping her long brown hair behind her shoulders.

"Cassie, this is my youngest, Lydia."

"Nice to meet you, Ma'am." Lydia glanced at her feet.

I nodded. "Same—"

"Well, go on and finish with the dishes." Mattie waved her arm toward the door next to the sideboard. "We've got a lot to do this afternoon. I'll take Cassie up to your room."

Mattie led me through a third doorway into the central hall and up the stairs. "I hope you don't mind sharing."

"No, that's fine." Did I have a choice? "I hope Lydia

35

doesn't mind."

"Oh, no. She's been missing her sister, Sarah, ever since she got married. It's been three months. Such a lovely wedding. And everyone told us not to have it in December. The weather was beautiful that day. Why wait for June when you're in love, right?"

"I wouldn't know."

Mattie stopped on the landing and looked down at me, hands on her hips. "What about Nate?"

"What?" I studied her serious expression. She acted like she believed I was Nate's fiancée. Had I entered the Twilight Zone?

She grinned, a twinkle in her eye. "You're going to have to do better than that if you want people to believe your story."

"Lera's story." I squinted at her. "So, you're not going to tell Nate and Lera that you know?"

"No, let them think they've put one over on me. I'm sure they'll figure it out in due time." She led me up the few steps to the landing and down the hall to my room.

Mattie sauntered inside and pointed to the bed in the near corner. "Make yourself at home. I'll have Lera bring in some things for you to borrow until we can find your bag or get you some more clothes." She waved her hand toward the other bed. "Lydia's things would be too small, but Lera's close to your size. The skirts will have to be shortened of course."

I'd loved to have borrowed Lydia's clothes. She wore a blouse and a full skirt to her ankles without any kind of hoop under it. I leaned against the doorjamb and glanced around, having no idea how to respond to Mattie or anyone else I'd met today.

"Why don't you rest?" Mattie ambled toward the door. "You've had a hard day. Lydia and I'll be downstairs if you need anything. We'll call you when Nate gets here." She wiggled her fingers at me as she disappeared behind the closing door.

I sat on my bed and my skirt popped up again. How was I

supposed to rest in this getup?

I managed to get myself off the bed and hitch my skirt up so it wouldn't injure me before I sat back down. From the edge of the bed, I surveyed the room with one glance. It was simple but pretty – two twin beds on opposite walls at one end of the room and a dresser and small wardrobe at the other end of the room, with a window in the center opposite the door. Next to the window stood a small desk and between the beds a small table held a ceramic basin. Brushes and combs lay on the table and a mirror graced the wall above it. The curtains were yellow and the bedspreads were white with yellow trim, giving the room a cheerful look.

I could have ended up in worse places, but shouldn't be here at all. I lay back, wishing I could go to sleep and wake up in my own bed.

Think, Cassandra. What happened? How could I have gone back in time? If only Ed hadn't asked me what year it was, I might still think this was a dream or a hoax. I took a deep breath.

What did I know about Todd's machine? Not much, since he'd kept it a secret. If I'd known, I wouldn't be in this mess. Why didn't he tell me?

But if I'd been building a time machine, I wouldn't have told me, either.

I closed my eyes and took a few deep breaths, holding and letting them out on counts of eight. Given my awkward position and the contraption I wore, I relaxed about as much as possible.

Someone knocked on the door. Before I could ask who was there, Lera barged in. She grinned as she closed the door and leaned against it. "Cassie, I hope Mattie didn't bore you too—" Her brow furrowed. "You poor thing."

She trotted over and reached for me. "Here, stand up and I'll help you undress. You can't rest in this. Mattie didn't offer to help?"

"No."

37

"Well, she probably had something on her mind."

"I can think of a few things." I struggled to my feet. "Thank you for buying me the clothes. The dress is really pretty."

"Don't you worry about that." She loosened my bodice lacing.

"But do you think I could wear something a little more sensible, at least around the house?" I bit my lip.

"What do you mean?" She finished with the lacing and peered at me.

"Less material and no metal or bone or whatever."

"You'd attract quite a bit of attention if you did that." She waved her hand. "But you'll attract attention whatever you do. Being Nate's missing fiancée and all."

I stuck up my index finger. "About that."

"You don't have to thank me. It was the good Lord. I was prayin' about how we could help you and that idea popped into my head." She smiled and lifted her chin. "Killed two birds with one stone."

"Oh?" I cocked my head.

"Why sure." She took the overskirt off and started with the hoop. "This way, no one will be snickering behind Nate's back thinking his girl jilted him. You were hurt and couldn't get here. They'll understand that."

"Yes, but it wasn't me." I breathed in deeply. It felt good to get that bell-shaped thing off me. I could deal with the rest if I had to. "Wait, what about Margaret? Does Nate know what really happened to her?"

She scoffed. "She married someone else and moved to New York. I guess she couldn't wait for Nate to finish the house."

"That's too bad." I sat on the bed. "But if everyone knows, how are—"

She waved her hand across her face. "Oh, most of the town thinks it's just a rumor. Nate and I are the only ones that know for sure."

She sat on Lydia's bed and leaned toward me. "He hasn't been the same since. At first, he was worried. Thought something bad had happened to her. Then, when he got the letter, he was devastated. He hasn't even looked at another girl since. It's been several months."

"No one deserves that." I gazed past her toward the window. "But I can't be his fiancée."

"You don't really have to be engaged to him. Just play at trying to remember him. See what happens." She patted my arm and stood.

I peered up at her. "Why are you doing all this?"

"Because the Lord told me to. Why else?" She showed me her signature sly grin, then turned toward the door. "When you're ready to get dressed for dinner, holler down. I'll come help." She glided through the door and closed it.

I settled into the pillow. How did she move so gracefully in that outfit? Unless I could figure out a way to get myself home, I would have to learn. Why was this happening? Tears bubbled to the surface. I wiped my eyes and took a deep breath. A pity party wouldn't help. I needed to be analytical. Focus on getting home.

I pulled myself off the bed, walked to the little desk next to the window, and stared out at the green fields. I could look for Todd, but I'd have to get to town. I wasn't sure what people would think of me making eye contact with every black man that looked to be in his early thirties, but I didn't care. I had to find him. Wait, if he could come back for me, wouldn't he have come to the same moment I did? He should already have found me. My skin prickled, and I shuddered. I took a deep breath and let it out slowly. Concentrate on the solution. Quash the fear.

Searching for Todd wasn't a good enough plan. I needed to either find his time machine or build one of my own. If only I knew something about it.

Maybe I did. I sat at the desk and dredged up every memory of Todd's project. That blonde woman had shown up two days before his equipment had. Was she involved? How could I have been so oblivious?

My lab assistant had insinuated Todd had something to do with William Garcia going missing. They had never found him. It happened right before they cut Todd's funding. My breath caught.

If Todd had sent someone time traveling and couldn't get them back. . . I gasped. It felt harder to breathe than when I wore the corset.

I stood and paced the room between the dresser and the window peering out each time. I don't know why. The view revealed the same green lawn with woods in the distance every time I looked. At the other end of the room, I'd gaze in the mirror. Already, I looked like a stranger.

Not that I studied myself often. Normally, in the morning, I would put on enough makeup to be presentable, finger-comb my curls, and not think about my appearance until the next morning.

As I paced, I planned. Each glance in the mirror showed more determination on my face. At least, that's what I hoped. The alternative was panic. I intended to look for Todd everywhere I went, investigate Nate's house for any remnants of the time machine, and listen for any clues. I would have liked to build my own time machine, but how could I do it here—without equipment—when even in my time I wouldn't know where to start?

I was probably on my fifteenth trip across the room, wringing my hands as I went, when I heard a knock. Before I could answer, the door opened.

Lera strolled in. "I told you to holler down for me when you were ready to get up. You must not have taken much of a nap."

"How did you know I was up?"

"I could hear you. For someone so little you have a heavy step. 'Course, I was in the parlor right underneath this room." She glanced at the open door. "What's the problem? You sound like you're mad at something, or someone."

I bit my lip. "I'm a little anxious."

She leaned toward me. "What really happened? Did someone just drop you and run off?"

I stepped back. "I don't know. I don't remember anything before hearing Caleb." I took a shaky breath. "That's what I'm anxious about."

She sighed. "You're here now. We'll just have to make the best of it. Let me help you back into your clothes." She picked up the corset.

"About that. What if I just put on the top and the over skirt without that corset and hoop thingy?" I conjured my best puppy dog expression. "I just can't move in those."

"I wish I could oblige but Mattie would have a fit." She frowned. "And, you'd be tripping over the skirt."

"I might be able to handle the corset, but I can't wear that hoop thing." I pointed to the object I detested on Lydia's bed.

"You'll have to. Tonight." She put it back on me.

I grimaced until she was finished.

She patted my shoulder. "Tomorrow, we'll see what we can do. Maybe we can find a smaller skirt, or take this one up or something. Can you sew?"

I shook my head.

"Well, I could teach you."

"Maybe there's something else you could teach me right now." I leaned toward her and lowered my voice. "Could you tell me where the bathroom is and how to use it in this getup?"

She stood with her hands on her hips and stared at me. "We only take baths on Saturday unless there's a big party in the middle of the week. Why would you take a bath in that?"

"No, I mean the toilet. I need to use the toilet."

She lowered her head but kept her eyes on mine.

"I have to pee." I winced at how loud my voice sounded.

She let out a breath. "Oh, why didn't you say so? The privy

is out by the cow shed. I'll show you."

On our way through the house Lera murmured under her breath, "She sure ain't from around here. Maybe from another country?"

I couldn't help feeling the same way about everyone else. She led me out the back door and turned left onto a wooden walkway between the house and the kitchen. The museum curator had told me that separating the kitchen was common in this era to lessen the threat of fires.

We stepped down into the yard, and passed two cows and a garden toward a small wooden structure I'd only seen in movies. I pinched my nose to avoid the stink. "How am I supposed to get this dress into that little space?"

She giggled and opened the door. "Use both hands."

Chapter 5

When I peered around the partially open kitchen door, Lera and Lydia stopped chatting.

"Hi, Cassie." Lera picked up a pile of cloth and hurried to me. "Put this on and come help."

I stepped into the room and held up my hands. "Is there a sink?" I couldn't think about doing anything until I'd washed my hands. After my experience in the outhouse, I wanted to bathe my whole body and clean parts of my dress. I worried that I'd brought the foul odor from the tiny building with me, but Lydia and Lera didn't so much as wrinkle their noses.

Lydia led me to a corner of the room. "Miss Cassie, you can wash here." She waved her hand in front of a basin of clean water, then pointed toward the back door of the kitchen. "We have a well, right outside. It's real convenient." She glanced over her shoulder. "Of course, Nate has water pumped straight into his kitchen and water closet. Wind power."

"That's nice." I forced a smile. What could be less convenient than lowering a bucket down and cranking the handle to winch it back up? I probably didn't want to know. As I washed my hands, I glanced out the window and realized Todd wouldn't think to come here. He'd search Nate's house. I had to find a way to get back there soon. Maybe I could inquire about the wind power. They hadn't mentioned it at the museum, and I found it intriguing.

As I turned from the sink, Lera stood in my way holding that large piece of cloth. I nearly used it for a towel before I realized it was an apron, the largest one I'd ever seen. Lera tied it around me.

They set me to kneading bread. Lera explained they usually did that earlier in the day, but with all the excitement, they were a bit behind. She showed me how to fold the dough and then stretch it. She repeated the maneuver several times before I got the hang of it. Lera chatted while she worked, but Lydia stayed quiet. Was she angry about having to share her room? Though I didn't expect to be here long, it wouldn't do to be inconsiderate of my roommate. Finally, Lera took some gingerbread, hot out of the oven, into the pantry.

I cleared my throat. "Lydia, I wanted to thank you for letting me share your room. I'll try to be a good roommate."

"You're welcome?" She furrowed her brow.

I had no idea what I'd said to confuse her. Deciding not to speak unless it was necessary, I stayed quiet until I thought the dough was ready. Then I asked Lydia what I should do with it.

She took the dough and with karate-like movements, folded it into a loaf, and put it in a pan. Next time I'd ask her to do it in slow motion.

"Thank you." I hurried back to the sink to wash my hands.

"That's a real pretty dress." Lydia opened the door under the wood-stove and slid the bread in. "Lera's had her eye on one like it for a while now. She's hoping to get it in a few weeks."

"Is she saving money or something?" I glanced at her, while I shook my hands and reached for a towel.

"No, she can't wear anything that bright yet." She trudged back to the worktable.

Lera breezed into the room. "I will be buying a dress like it in four days and nineteen hours."

As I finished drying my hands, I frowned and tilted my

head.

"That's when my mourning will be up." She glanced behind her and stepped toward me. "If it were up to me, I would already be wearing dresses like it." She fingered the sash hanging from my waist. "But, in deference to my in-laws, I've worn drab colors for nearly two years."

"That's when your husband died?" He could have been killed in the war. If he was, it would clue me in on the current year. "How did it happen?"

Lera wandered toward the worktable. "He fell off a horse."

Lydia scowled at her.

Lera picked up a rag and strode toward me, her lips pursed. "We think." She took a breath and huffed it out. "He went riding late one night. We found him the next morning in the woods." She touched my arm. "It looked like the horse had stepped on him." She dipped the rag into the sink and wrang it. "We didn't find the beast until late that day."

"How awful." I touched her shoulder, but she stepped away. "I'm so sorry for you."

Lera stuck her chin in the air. "Thank you, but Caleb and I are fine." She glided to the worktable and wiped it with the damp rag. "Mattie and Ed took us in, told us we could stay as long as we needed to." She held onto the towel and marched to the other room in the kitchen building.

Lydia nodded at me, continuing to add ingredients to a metal bowl. "John was the oldest. He and Lera lived in the small house, the one we're renting out now. Our tenants, the Joneses, have a small plot of land they farm. We also hire them and others from time to time. Pa, Nate, and Mark, my other brother, can't work this much land by themselves."

I wandered to the table. "It's all one farm?"

"Yes." Lydia wiped her brow with her wrist. "Nate owns it, but Pa owns this house and the land surrounding it." She picked up a wooden spoon and stirred the liquid in the bowl. "And Mark will have a piece of land in a few years, when he turns twenty-one."

Lera bustled into the room and dropped the towel on the table. "It's time to go in and help Miss Mattie with the needlework for the bazaar." She sashayed to me. "Lydia can handle what little there is to do here." Before Lydia could complain, Lera took my apron off me, hung it on a hook, and guided me out the door.

She chatted all the way through the house, not giving me the chance to ask what a bazaar was. It didn't seem to matter that I wasn't paying attention to her. That probably couldn't be said about Mattie. I didn't look forward to spending more time alone with her and felt relieved when Lera led me into the ladies' parlor, perched on an ornate chair, and picked up her needlework.

I settled on a velvet covered bench, the only vacant seat in the small room, and watched their fingers fly, needles flashing up and down through the material. At first, they asked me questions, but after I answered in as few words as possible, they conversed with each other.

I tried to listen to avoid surprises and for any helpful information but couldn't keep my mind from wandering. Was the missing engineer still here? Did I dare ask if they knew a William Garcia?

Mattie glanced at the beautiful grandfather clock in the corner and declared it was time to start supper. It might be better to wait and ask Nate or Ed anyway.

I helped with supper as much as I could without getting in their way. We had it ready and on the table for a good half hour before the men got home. By the time they walked in, Mattie stood in the doorway with her hands on her hips, tapping her foot. Why was she so upset? Todd usually came home four or five hours late, if at all.

"Sorry, Aunt Mattie." Nate stared at me. "I kept them late

because I didn't get to work until after dinner."

I glanced at the floor. "I guess that was my fault."

"Nonsense." Mattie led Nate toward the table, motioning for everyone to sit. She ushered me to the seat beside Nate. "You did the right thing, coming to us." She patted me on the shoulder. "Don't you worry."

Ed said grace. I closed my eyes and bowed my head, not wanting to get caught again. I didn't think Lera would say anything, but I wasn't sure I liked her conspiratorial look during the mid-day meal.

The conversation revolved around the farm and the community, the church bazaar being the most popular subject. It sounded kind of like a country fair. I looked forward to it, if only to look for Todd or his assistant, though he'd never mentioned one. All I had was a name. If only I knew what William Garcia looked like or when I could get to town. They'd said the bazaar would be on Saturday, but I didn't dare ask what day of the week it was, so I tuned back into their conversation.

Toward the end of supper, Mark teased Lydia about an apron she was making for the bazaar. "You'll never finish that in two days."

I figured it must be Wednesday. It had been a Friday when I'd left, but that wouldn't matter.

When Mattie and Lera began clearing the table, I stood and gathered my silverware.

Mattie stopped with one plate in her hand. "You've helped enough for today, Cassie." She handed the plate to Lydia and stepped toward her nephew. "Nate, why don't you take her out on the porch for a while?"

Nate dropped his napkin on the table, stood, and closed the short gap between us. He guided me through the parlor, outside onto the porch, and ushered me to a chair before I could ask about walking to his place.

We sat in the first two wooden chairs lined up to the left of the door and gazed out across the open field at the clear night sky. My knees bounced up and down under my crinolines while I stole glances at him. His focus stayed on the stars, and he kept his face neutral. Should I ask if he knew a William Garcia or not? Wait, even if Garcia had traveled back, I had no idea to what year.

Nate's voice broke my contemplation. "Have you remembered anything?"

I pursed my lips. "You're not starting to think I am your fiancée, are you?"

"I know you're not." He took a breath and dropped his shoulders. "But you are suffering some sort of memory loss or something, aren't you?"

"Or something." I fiddled with my sash.

"Are you from Europe?"

"No." I squinted at him. "Where did you get that idea?"

He shrugged. "I understand your words but not the way you use them, sometimes."

"This place seems pretty foreign to me, too." I focused on the porch railing.

He peered at me for a moment. "Ask me any questions you need to. We'll have lots of time together."

Instead of asking about William Garcia, I stuck with something I thought might be safe. "How long are you going to court me? That is the term Mattie used, isn't it?"

"Yes, it is." He turned his head toward the porch rail.

"Well?" I leaned toward him, trying to see his expression in the dimming light.

He sat up straight and looked at me. "I don't know. As long as I can."

I pulled back and squinted. "Why?"

He blew out a breath. "If Aunt Mattie likes you, the only thing that's going to stop me from courting you is the wedding."

Chapter 6

"Wedding?" I jumped up and fell toward Nate.

He caught me. "Whoa. You're not used to those clothes, are you?"

"Is it that obvious?" My face heated.

He nodded as he steadied me on the chair. Then he sat and continued to look at me through narrowed eyes.

Better say something. "Nate, thank you for all your help earlier. I don't know what I would have done."

"You'd probably be in jail for indecent exposure." He thumped the arm of his chair with his knuckles and glanced at me. "Where you're from, do you walk around like that in public?"

"Yes and no."

He raised one eyebrow.

"I wear that outfit to go jogging in the park or to the gym. I wouldn't wear it to a store or work or anything. But I've seen people in stores with less on." I couldn't keep myself from babbling. At least I hadn't used words he didn't understand. But did he know what a gym was?

"What do you do…for work?"

"I told you I'm a…oh." I couldn't say engineer. He had a whole different meaning for that word. They didn't even use electricity, yet. What kind of jobs did women have here?

"Teacher." It was the only thing I could think of.

He squinted at me. "I thought you worked on a train."

"I traveled on a train." I coughed and shifted in my chair. "I'm not sure what I told you earlier."

"That makes two of us." His eyes bore into mine.

I focused on my sash, fiddling with it. "I was confused. Lera's story isn't a total fabrication. I do have some memory loss."

"Where were you just before Caleb found you?" He leaned closer.

I pulled away as much as I could. "I can't remember."

"You told me you were in town, that you'd lived here for a year with your boyfriend."

"I must have been mistaken." I threw my hand up, brushing his face. "I can't remember now. Maybe it was a town name that sounded like New Hope."

He leaned back and gazed out toward the field. "I think you were more truthful earlier."

I turned away so he couldn't see the hurt on my face. How dare he accuse me of lying?

Of course I was, but he wouldn't believe me if I told the truth. Why did it bother me so much? I had never worried about what acquaintances thought of me before.

"Cassie, I didn't mean to accuse you." He softened his voice. "I think you know what happened. You just don't want to tell me."

I looked him in the eye. "I don't know what happened."

He sighed and slumped in his chair.

I didn't want to disappoint him. "But I have a theory."

"Tell me." He leaned toward me and clasped my hand.

I glanced at the rough wooden planks of the porch. "You wouldn't believe me."

He withdrew his hand. "I don't believe what you just told me. What's the difference?"

I stuck one finger in the air. "First, promise me you won't put me in an insane asylum."

His brow furrowed.

I kept a serious expression on my face. "Promise?"

He nodded. "I promise."

"Promise that you won't tell anyone, especially Lera."

He turned away from me for a moment, giving me the side eye. "If you don't trust anyone else, why trust me?"

"You're right. I shouldn't tell you." I placed both hands in my lap.

He stood, paced the length of the porch and back, and stopped in front of me. "I promise not to tell anyone."

I stood and looked up to meet his gaze. "How do I know I can trust you?"

He pursed his lips. "I could have had you sent to jail, or just thrown you out this morning." He stepped back. "It would have been a lot easier."

Why hadn't he thrown me out?

He held his hand out, almost touching my shoulder. "But I felt I had an obligation to help you. Still do."

I narrowed my eyes. "Why?"

"You landed on my property." He let his arm drop to his side and a smile crept across his face. "Besides, I wouldn't want embarrassing stories circulating about my intended, would I?"

"You have a point." I smiled but only for a moment. "All right, I'll tell you." I settled in my chair, and he sat next to me. I took a deep breath. Here goes.

"You two have been out here for ages." Lera sauntered out the door. "You must be getting on right well." She flashed me her conspiratorial grin. "You've remembered him at least a little. I can see it in your face."

Nate wagged a finger at her. "Don't start believing your—"

Lera pointed to Mattie at the door.

Nate clamped his mouth shut, appearing even more

annoyed than when I'd arrived.

I shrugged, relieved. Lera had given me time to think about whether or not to tell Nate my real predicament.

Mattie set down a tray of apple pie on a low table at the other end of the porch and Ed followed with a porcelain coffee pot and cups.

"I thought it would be fun to have dessert out here tonight." Mattie clapped her hands together. "It's such a beautiful evening. Got to take advantage of the good weather before it starts getting too hot."

Nate and I stayed where we were and accepted a piece of pie from Lydia. It was the first thing I'd actually tasted all day.

"I don't think I've ever had better apple pie." I glanced around wondering who'd made it.

"Why, thank you." Mattie beamed.

I didn't remember seeing Mattie in the kitchen all day, but if Lydia or Lera made the pie, their expressions didn't give them away.

"Mattie always did make the best pies." Ed set down his empty plate. "That's one of the first things I liked about her." He grinned.

She smacked him on the shoulder. "Mr. Gardner, you know you married me for my money and not my baking."

My eyes flew open wide, and I held my breath.

Everyone else laughed.

Lera began talking about people I didn't know.

My mind wandered, and I caught myself watching Mattie and Ed. They sat on a wooden porch swing, holding hands, even after being married at least twenty-five years, maybe longer. Envy made my face feel warm, and I switched my mental energy into keeping my expression as blank as possible.

"Why do you think someone would steal a quilt?" Lera's question caught my attention. "It was a family heirloom. Why would anyone else want it?" Lera tossed her hands up and let them drop in her lap.

"Are they sure it was stolen?" Mattie squinted at her daughter-in-law. "Something like that could have been placed in storage somewhere." She glanced at Ed. "We've lost track of things that way."

Lera leaned toward Mattie. "Well, Sally insisted she'd put it in her cedar chest when she got engaged."

"Wasn't that nearly two years ago?" Mattie smoothed her skirt.

"Yes. She remembered there were several others who had things go missing about that time." Lera pointed her whole hand toward the field.

"It could be a coincidence." Ed slapped his hands on his thighs and stood.

Lera and Mattie scoffed.

"Well, it could." Ed raised his hand. "There's no proof, and it was a while ago."

"True." Lera picked up her mug. "And all the things that went missing were just ordinary items. You can get them anywhere."

"What things were stolen?" I'd investigate anything these people considered out of the ordinary even if it did happen two years ago. That could be two days ago to someone from my time.

Lera shooed away a fly. "Oh, things like lanterns and candlesticks. The Goddards lost a stack of books and a map of their property."

Some of those things could help a time traveler stuck here without anyone to stay with.

"That's curious." Nate stood. "Hopefully, it's in the past." He pulled out his pocket watch. "Folks, it's getting late. I need to get in a full day's work tomorrow." He tipped his wide-brimmed wool hat and headed for the front steps.

Mattie stood in his way and stared at him.

"Thank you for supper. I enjoyed it." Nate stepped to the

side.

Mattie slid in front of him and bobbed her head toward me.

Nate slumped and turned back to me.

Mattie hustled the rest of the family into the house, but she watched from the doorway.

A lump formed in my throat. What was this strange dance all about?

"Cassie, I had a nice time. I'm glad you're here." Nate glanced at Mattie who nodded. He took my hand in his, leaned down, and kissed it.

I froze with my mouth hanging open.

He dropped my hand, picked up a lantern, and hurried off the porch toward his horse.

I watched him until he'd moved too far into the darkness to see more than the lantern. Remembering Nathanial Bridger had been the owner of the museum house confused me. This Nate was very different from the old bachelor who kept his house like a shrine even though he wouldn't allow anyone other than his aunt to enter. Could I trust this young Nate?

"I see there's still a spark between you two." Mattie smiled at me from the open doorway.

"It's more like something new." I blinked, staying in my chair. Was Mattie pretending just for Lera's sake? "I don't remember him."

Lera rushed out of the house toward me. "You will. You'll see." She placed her hand on the back of my chair.

"He's a smart one, my Nate. He's taking it slow." Mattie nodded toward me. "Waiting for you to fall in love with him again."

Mattie and Lera helped me up and escorted me inside in silence. When we were halfway upstairs, Mattie stopped and glanced down at me. "I would have expected him to call you Margaret by mistake."

Was she trying to make Lera squirm?

"Why would he?" Lera landed on the step behind me. "You said it yourself, Miss Mattie. Nate's a smart one."

Mattie smiled and continued upstairs.

Lera and I let out a breath and exchanged a wide-eyed glance.

The corners of Mattie's mouth curved up slightly. She must be enjoying her charade.

Lera covered in her usual way, by changing the subject. "Cassie, if you need any help with your dress, I'm sure Lydia would be glad to assist you. I would, but I have to go see to Caleb. I sent him to bed an hour ago, but he usually won't go to sleep until I tuck him in."

"I'll be fine," I said, with more confidence than I felt.

When I entered Lydia's room, I wondered what I was going to wear to bed.

"Hi Cassie." Lydia leaned over and lit an oil lamp that sat on the stand between the beds. She wore a long shirt very similar to one of the layers I had on.

I greeted her, sat down on the bed, and tried to take off my shoes but I couldn't reach my feet.

"Okay, this skirt is going to have to come off first." I took the overskirt off, but couldn't undo the hoop. Lera had put the thing on me and I wasn't sure how it fastened.

"It's called a crinoline." Lydia stared at me, leaning against the headboard.

"It's a pain in the butt, if you ask me." Oops. I covered my mouth with my hand.

Lydia smiled. "Come here." She stretched out her arm and curled her fingers toward herself.

I obeyed, willing to do anything to free myself from that contraption. She untied the strings at my waist and loosened it enough for it to drop to the floor. I stepped out of it, flung it in the corner of the room, and did a little freedom dance. I took off everything except the long chemise, folded them as neatly as I could, and climbed into bed.

"I've heard people complain about crinolines but you really hate them." She sat cross legged on her bed.

"I do." I wanted to tell her that out of all the things to hate, like no indoor plumbing, no electricity, no television, radio, or computers, that costume was the thing I loathed most. I kept that to myself.

Lydia cocked her head. "Can I ask you a question?"

"You just did." I grinned.

She grimaced then bowed her head.

"I'm sorry, force of habit." I held my breath until she looked up. "Of course, you can ask me a question." I figured she'd ask where I came from, and I planned to tell her I didn't know.

"Are you really going to marry my cousin?"

"No." I sucked in air then coughed. She was Mattie's daughter. I didn't know if Mattie's charade extended to Lydia. I glanced at the ceiling. "Well, if I get my memory back, or we get closer, I guess so."

She squinted at me. "Where's the engagement ring?"

A lump formed in my throat. "Uh, I don't know. I must have lost it in the accident."

"Maybe, it got stolen!" She jumped off the bed and mimed a fight with an imaginary foe. With her right hand, she ripped a non-existent ring off her left.

I tapped my fingers into my palm in polite applause.

She took a slight bow and sat on the bed. "Do you remember what it looked like?"

"Let me see." I squinted and took my time. "It had a diamond."

She shook her head.

"I think." I closed my eyes for a second. "Maybe not."

"Wrong. It was my grandmother's ring." She hurried to the dresser, pulled something out of the bottom drawer, and bounded over to me. "It looked like this." She showed me a beautiful white gold band with three emeralds in the center, flanked by two slightly smaller sapphires. "Margaret sent it back to Nate by post. He gave it to me."

"Does your mom know?" I searched her face.

She wrinkled her nose. "Of course not." She sat on the edge of my bed. "It would kill her if she thought someone had broken off an engagement to her favorite nephew."

"Isn't Nate worried that she'll find it?" I examined the ring.

She scoffed. "It's more likely she'd find it if Nate kept it."

I cocked my head. "That doesn't make sense."

"That's my mother." She giggled as she stood and wandered around the room. "Ma has always worried about Nate. She sort of adopted him when his mother died. She goes over there to help him with his house at least three times a week, even though he has a hired maid that comes in twice a week." She halted mid-stride. "We suspect Ma is there to snoop, rather than to clean."

I narrowed my eyes. "If she snoops in Nate's house, what makes you think she doesn't here?"

"Lera." She clutched the bedpost. One corner of her lips quirked upward.

I leaned back and scrunched my face. "Why?"

"Ma tried going through Lera's things once and got caught. They had a huge ruckus, worse than Lera and John's fight the night he died." Lydia clamped her mouth shut.

She took a deep breath and resumed her stroll. "Well, after Ma and Lera's argument, it got quiet for the better part of an hour. When they came out of the room, they were both calm with stony looks on their faces. Lera told me later that they had come to an understanding and that Ma would not be entering our rooms, Lera's, Caleb's or mine and Sarah's unless we were there."

I squinted at her. "When did that happen?"

She glanced away. "After Lera moved back here, so a few weeks after John died. Ma turned her attentions to Nate after that." She sat on her bed and glanced at the ceiling. "Of course, Mark is always complaining about her snooping in his room. He wasn't part of Lera's deal. I know Ma's been in here a few times, but I don't think she stays long enough to do more than scan the room."

I leaned toward her. "What are you going to do if she finds the ring?"

"Here." She handed it to me. "Put it on."

"How do I explain why I wasn't wearing it earlier?" I slipped the ring on my finger, amazed at how well it fit.

"I'm sure you and Lera can think of something." She smiled, reached over to the vanity between the beds, and extinguished the flame in the oil lamp.

I tried to sleep, but thoughts of home kept tugging at me. I missed my friends, my job—my life. I missed Todd, too, but I was used to that. I fumed at him and myself. If I hadn't been so insecure about us and his project, I'd be in my own bed right now. I'd probably be alone, but at least I could go to the bathroom without walking outside or using the chamber pot. I wrinkled my nose. Why had I let my mind go there? It was going to be a long night.

Chapter 7

I woke up to a knock on the door, followed immediately by Lera barging in. Someone should teach her the purpose of knocking.

She breezed across the room. "You're not even awake yet? Lydia's already downstairs."

"I'm awake now." I dragged myself to a sitting position. My head throbbed like I had a hangover, despite the fact there was no liquor in anything I ate or drank last night.

She gathered my clothes. "Here, I thought you might need some help."

I stretched my hand out in front of my face. "I'm not wearing that hoop thing. If we can't shorten the dress so I can wear it alone, then find me something else." Where was this boldness coming from?

She stopped and glared at me, still holding my clothes. "Haven't you ever heard beggars can't be choosers?" She stepped toward me, shaking her head. "Honestly, all I've done for you is try to help and this is the thanks I get."

I cringed. "I'm sorry. I was rude." I hauled myself out of bed, resigned to the awful crinoline. "I'm so not a morning person," I mumbled.

Lera stood next to the bed, holding up the overskirt to form a barrier between us. "And this was the prettiest dress in the store. In order to wear it without the hoop we'd have to shorten it so much, most of the pattern in the skirt would be cut off." She clicked her tongue. "I just couldn't do that." She lowered the dress and peered at me through thick eyelashes, her lips curved into a sly smile. "You understand, don't you?"

At first, I thought she was politely turning me down, but then I read her expression. I sat on the edge of the bed, crossed my legs, and showed her my conspiratorial grin. "Lera, I'll make a deal with you. If you find me something I can wear without the hoop, you can have that dress."

She stared down her nose at me for so long I thought I'd made a mistake. When I was about to take it back, she flashed her wicked smile. "I knew I was going to like you. I'll be back in a minute." She sauntered out of the room carrying all my clothes except the chemise I had on and the corset she left on the dresser.

What else could I do but go back to bed?

It seemed like the moment I'd drifted back to sleep, Lera barged in, not bothering to knock this time. She carried a white shirt and charcoal gray jacket with a charcoal gray skirt to match. I let her help me into it. She provided a stiff slip to go under it making it full but nothing like that hoop.

I strolled across the room to the mirror and admired my image. "This, I might be able to handle." I smiled at Lera's reflection in the mirror. "Thank you."

She bobbed a curtsey. "You'll need a few more things. Maybe we can go to the store when we're in town on Saturday."

"That would be great." I swirled around and frowned. "But you were right, I don't have any money."

One corner of her mouth tilted upward. "I still have some leftover from yesterday." She ushered me out the door.

Lera knew what she wanted and how to get it. I couldn't knock her, though. I'd gotten what I wanted, at least for the moment.

When I entered the dining room, Mattie stood next to the

sideboard, her back to me, but everyone else must have eaten and left. As the door clicked shut, she laid something down and pivoted toward me. "I heard about your deal with Lera." She pursed her lips. "You shouldn't have given away such a beautiful dress."

"That's all right. I wasn't attached to it."

"That's what she told me." Mattie bobbed her head toward me. "That gray one does suit you."

"Thank you, I like it." I twirled without knocking anything over, or myself off balance.

She led me to the only space at the table with no dirty dishes. I settled in, and she placed a loaded plate in front of me. She sat next to me and talked while I ate pancakes, eggs, and sausage. It was far more breakfast than I was used to, but I was hungrier than normal.

"You don't know anything about New Hope, do you?" Mattie waited until I shook my head. "Well, it's so different than when I was little. My parents bought all our land when the town only had fifty people. Now, the population is over four hundred."

Lydia entered and cleared the table.

Mattie ignored her and went right on with her monologue. "It's always been one of the more prosperous towns in the South." She waved her hands as she spoke. "Even though we were one of the first to stop the practice of slavery. Long before it was forced upon us. And the war never reached us."

I tilted my head, then remembered New Hope was west of Atlanta. "Good thing Sherman headed east." It was one of the few things I recalled from History class.

"We sent money and men to help start the rebuilding of Atlanta, though." She leaned back and rested her palms on her lap.

The sudden silence felt awkward. "That's nice to hear." I set my fork down on my empty plate, pulled back from the table, and followed Lydia toward the kitchen with my dishes.

Mattie stopped me with a hand on my arm. "Let Lydia get that."

"Please, let me at least clean up after myself." I stepped away. "I want to pull my weight around here."

She hesitated and squinted at me.

I kept myself from wincing at my use of a slang phrase.

"You will." She resumed her previous demeanor. "I have something else for you to do right now." She set my dishes on the sideboard and guided me out to the carriage where Lera joined us.

Though I hoped we were on the way to town so I could look for Todd, I didn't relish another carriage ride. The first one had been short but scary, and I had no idea how long this one would be. At least in this outfit, I could get into the carriage by myself.

Mattie settled next to me while Lera sat in the front and grabbed the reins. She talked about Caleb, the farm, and her friends in town, glancing over her shoulder at Mattie and me as she drove. Mattie let her talk. Maybe that was part of their understanding. I was surprised I could hear her at all over the clatter of the wheels and the horses' hooves on the dirt roads, but the carriage was rather small.

Toward the end of the ride, Mattie patted my hand. "I'm glad you put your ring back on."

Lera sucked in air and glanced at my finger. "I'm sure she was wearing it yesterday, Miss Mattie. You must not have noticed."

"No, I looked. She wasn't wearing one." Mattie lifted my hand. "I figured she'd taken it off because she couldn't remember who'd given it to her."

"Oh, well. I thought for sure I saw it," Lera muttered.

"You are both right." I pulled my hand away and rested it in my lap to still the shaking. "I was wearing it part of the day, but I took it off when I kneaded the dough for the bread. I forgot to put it back on until last night."

Mattie seemed satisfied with that explanation, and Lera flashed me a look of respect.

I'd have to start a journal to keep my facts straight. Maybe I should tell Lera that Mattie knew I wasn't Margaret. No, I should stay out of their relationship.

Lera stopped the carriage at the first house on the outskirts of town. My hope of being able to look for Todd was dashed when we went straight to the door. We called on Mrs. Hodges, a stout little woman even shorter than Mattie.

Mattie introduced me as Nate's lost fiancée and recited the whole story about the accident and amnesia. In her version, I wasn't sure if it was an accident or a robbery. I'd ended up in an Atlanta hospital with nothing except the clothes I was wearing.

Mrs. Hodges acted highly sympathetic and delighted in repeating the story to the four other women who stopped by. During the storytelling, we worked on a quilt for the bazaar. I suspected the real reason for the visit was to introduce me to the elite of the women's circle before the big unveiling at the bazaar, but I let them think I believed the main purpose was the quilt.

Following Mattie's example, I got the hang of the stitching quickly. The rest of the morning I sewed and listened for any information that might help me locate Todd or his assistant. Because Nate and I were the main topic of conversation, I didn't get much.

Lera spent quite a bit of time in the next room talking to Ida, Mrs. Hodges' granddaughter. Ida was in her early twenties and still single. They giggled together like they were both school girls.

On my way back from the privy, I caught Ida by herself. Frustrated at not being able to do much about my situation, I took a risk. "Ida, do you know anyone in town named William Garcia?"

She glanced behind her and shook her head.

I stepped toward her. "Todd James?"

She frowned and shook her head again. "I'm sorry."

I sighed. "I guess my memory for names isn't very reliable." I forced a smile and hurried back to the quilting, hoping I hadn't started any gossip I couldn't handle.

For the rest of the visit, I made my number one priority to not say anything I'd regret later. I stayed quiet, polite, and diligent.

On the way back in the carriage, Mattie announced that every lady in the room agreed that Nate had made a good choice.

I thanked her, resolved to get back to my own time before I ended up married.

For the rest of the day, I stayed with Lera and Lydia as much as I could. Mattie seemed like a very nice lady, but the way everyone else deferred to her made me uneasy. Even the ladies at Mrs. Hodges' treated her like the unofficial town mayor.

Nate didn't appear until supper time, but I thought about him all afternoon, obsessing about what to say when he asked me again how I'd gotten here.

After supper, without prodding from Mattie, Nate asked if I would like to go for a walk. I didn't want to tell him my story, but I couldn't refuse his invitation. Not with Mattie nodding her approval.

He held out his arm, and I clasped his elbow as we strolled outside and down the path toward his house.

Nate glanced at me. "So how was Mrs. Hodges' quilting bee?"

"I can't tell you. I've wrestled with this all day, and I decided I needed to wait until I have proof."

He pulled his head back and furrowed his brow.

When his question finally registered, my face heated. Could I be any more of an idiot?

He scowled. "Oh, you're talking about last night."

I winced. "Yes, I'm sorry. That's what I was expecting." If

I'd only listened enough to answer his real question, I could have stalled for quite some time. I tried anyway. "Mrs. Hodges is nice. Mattie told me I made a good impression. They all think you and I are a great match." I smiled sweetly.

His expression softened and a grin appeared for a second. "You keep that up and you and I are going to end up married."

I glanced at the trees on the edge of the dirt path. "Don't worry. It won't come to that."

He leaned toward me. "What are you planning?"

I lifted my chin. "I promise I'll be gone before any wedding. You and I can just keep stalling until I can get out of here."

"If you leave me, it'll break Aunt Mattie's heart." He sounded like he was joking, but I couldn't be sure.

I looked up at him. "Then, you break up with me."

"I can't do that. I made a promise." He gazed straight ahead and his tone was gravelly.

I pursed my lips. "You made a promise to Margaret, not me."

He planted his feet and stared straight at me. "But Aunt Mattie thinks it was to you." He glanced skyward. "But I'm talking about the one I made to God."

I peered at him. Unfortunately, it was twilight and he blended into the shadows. "A promise about me?"

He shifted his weight. "Not specifically, but about taking care of the people around me and doing God's will."

"Hmm." Resuming our stroll, I tried not to show my surprise. I knew people who had made promises to God, but it was always in times of horrific stress, and they never bothered to keep them.

The back of Nate's house came into view.

"It's a beautiful house. I've never seen it from this direction." I held my breath. Had I said too much?

"Thanks." He slowed his pace. "Sometimes I wish I'd never

built it."

I adjusted my gait to match his. "Why?"

He gazed at the house. "Don't need it. Not without a family of my own."

"You could move the rest of the family in. There's plenty of room."

He blew out a breath. "I tried. Aunt Mattie wouldn't hear of it. She still thinks I'll get married and raise my own family." He shook his head. "She's attached to the house she grew up in, anyway."

I kept myself from pointing out that most of his decisions had something to do with Mattie.

When we approached the carriage house, we turned back and he reached for my hand. He pulled it up and fingered the ring, looking closely at it. "Nice. Did Lydia give you this?"

I nodded. "You don't mind?"

He shrugged. "Goes with Lera's story." He held my hand as we strolled toward Mattie's. "So how are we going to break the engagement?"

The perfect solution popped into my head. "We'll let Mattie do it."

He scoffed. "She adores you so far. How are you going to manage that?"

"I'm going to find Todd."

"Your boyfriend. I'd almost forgotten about him." He picked up the pace. "So, tell me about Todd. Maybe I can help you find him."

"Let's see. He's quite handsome, early thirties, close cropped black hair, dark brown eyes, medium brown complexion—"

"Todd's a negro?"

"Yes." I held up my index finger. "But if you do find him, don't use that word."

He stopped and stared at me for a few seconds. "Finding

Todd will most definitely break our engagement."

~

The next morning passed in a flurry of activity. I wondered where I'd gotten the idea the pace was slower in the nineteenth century. Publications were the only media, but news could still travel fast, especially if Lera was involved. As we worked, I learned who was getting married, who was expecting, and how many kids they already had. She knew that three people had been arrested for drunk and disorderly conduct, and of a couple who was having trouble in their marriage. I kept my ears open for word about a new black man in town, but that was the only thing she didn't mention.

After dinner, on my way back from the outhouse, I glanced at the cabin Mattie rented out. A solid dark-skinned woman carrying a basket approached the front door. Mattie's tenant, Mrs. Jones? I ran over to her.

"Mrs. Jones, do you need any help with that?"

"No, thank you." She turned away and opened the door.

I stopped short of the entryway. "Mrs. Jones, I'm Cassie McPherson. I'm staying with the Gardners."

She stepped inside and started to shut the door.

I wrapped my fingers around the edge, keeping it open a sliver. "Please, I have a friend you might know. I just want to get a message to him."

"I wouldn't know any of your friends." She opened the door wider and stared at me.

I stepped back a few paces. "Do you know Todd James? He might have visited here a few times."

She shook her head, then frowned. "I know Maurice James. He's got three sons, but none named Todd." She tutted. "What kind of name is that?"

I stepped forward. "What does Maurice look like?"

"I'm sorry. I've got too much to do to stand around. Good day." She shut the door tight.

"Thanks," I yelled, not knowing if she'd heard me or not. It was probably a good thing if she hadn't heard the sarcasm in my voice. I hurried back to the house, hoping I hadn't upset the landlord-tenant relationship.

Nate came for supper again, but this time we stayed on the porch and had dessert with the rest of the family. He told Mattie I was a teacher, and I almost denied it without thinking.

Lera saved me. "Cassie, why didn't you tell us? We could use help teaching Caleb."

"Doesn't he go to school?" But he'd been home since I'd been here.

"Not anymore!" Caleb's face revealed a wide grin, cherry pie crumbs at the corner of his mouth.

Lera scowled at him. "We had to pull him out."

"The teacher told us she couldn't do anything with him." Mattie smoothed her skirt. "I think she was overwhelmed."

Ed set down his coffee mug. "There are over forty kids in the class, all different ages, and only one teacher." He mussed Caleb's hair. "I've been trying to work with him in my spare time."

Lera draped her arm around Caleb's shoulder. "But by the time Ed gets in from the fields, Caleb is already too tired."

"I told you, Ed, that you could take some time off in the early afternoon," Nate said.

Ed pushed back the brim of his cap. "Too much to get done right now."

"This summer we'll have to take a break in the afternoon anyway." Nate stood and stretched. "It'll be too hot to work."

"You can't expect Caleb to go to school in the summer," Lera said.

I took a deep breath. "I can work with him. Tell me what level he's on and we can start tomorrow."

"Oh, not tomorrow, Cassie." Mattie leaned toward me. "Tomorrow is Saturday."

"The bazaar!" Caleb jumped up.

"Monday then," I said.

Everyone agreed, except Caleb, who pouted. How long would it take them to figure out that I wasn't really a teacher?

Nate glanced at Mattie, then gave me a quick peck on my hand. "I need to get going. Night." He waved to the rest of them.

"Don't forget to pick us up bright and early tomorrow." Mattie patted the arm of her rocker. "Lera and I are running a booth in the morning, so we'll need to get there before it starts."

I furrowed my brow. Why would we need to wait for Nate? An image of the carriage house at the museum flashed into my mind. Nate had a large wagon all of us could fit in.

"I'll be here." Nate stood next to the porch rail. "Cassie and I can watch Caleb if you like."

"No need. Caleb and I have some things to attend to tomorrow." Ed winked at the boy.

"You and Cassie just take the day to enjoy yourselves." Mattie rocked forward. "You work too hard, Nate."

Mattie had settled the matter, as usual. It's a good thing she's a beneficent ruler.

Chapter 8

I woke up with hope in my heart or at least on my mind. Something big would happen today; I could feel it. I'd find Todd, and he'd take me home. I'd promise not to bug him about working late and be happy with my life. No, he'd stop working on the time machine, and we'd both promise to make each other a priority. Maybe we could even travel back to the days before he started working on that stupid project.

I hopped out of bed and dressed in my gray outfit. Mattie was alone in the kitchen when I arrived, so I helped her make breakfast, humming 'Whistle While You Work.'

"You're in a good mood." She glanced at me. "You must be excited about spending the day with Nate."

I nodded, stopping myself from telling her I'd be going home.

Nate arrived for breakfast, and we all ate together. I listened to the excited chatter around me, stealing glances at Nate. Every time I looked his direction, he turned his head, as if he didn't want me to catch him staring.

"We'd better get going." Mattie rose and picked up several plates and serving dishes.

Everyone followed and cleared the table in one trip, then scattered, leaving me with Mattie and Ed.

"We'll wash up later." Mattie wiped her hands on her apron

and flung it off.

"Can't wait to get there?" Ed offered Mattie his arm.

Mattie smiled and patted Ed's hand. "I'm looking forward to it. I hope Miss Jenny comes and sees Nate with Cassie."

Ed chuckled and guided her outside.

I followed them to the wagon, where Nate hitched up the mules.

Everyone except Mark piled into the wagon. I would have preferred to sit in the back with my eyes closed, but since Nate drove, they expected me to sit on the seat with him. At least I hadn't had to ride a horse. I would avoid that as long as possible, preferring conveyances that don't have minds of their own. What was I thinking? I'd be going home today and wouldn't have to worry about it.

As we set out, Mark took the lead in a smaller carriage pulled by one horse.

After surviving the hour-long jostling on uneven dirt roads, I had to stay in the cart another several minutes until we got to the other end of main street and detoured around the blocked off section in front of the church. Nate parked the wagon behind the church, and we carried Mattie's stuff to the front where the ladies were putting out their wares on the tables that lined both sides of the street.

We set down Mattie's bundles on a long slab of wood resting on sawhorses. Lydia, Ed, and Caleb wandered off. Lera pulled out a bright blue cloth to drape over the table.

Nate checked his pocket watch. "It'll be an hour before they open."

Mattie glanced up at him. "Go show her around town."

Nate grinned and held his arm out for me.

I accepted, hoping to spot Todd.

We strolled down Mainstreet in a comfortable silence. The two of us were quiet, but the people setting up at the bazaar clattered and chattered. Mainstreet teemed with people.

I scanned all the faces we passed.

Nate leaned in close. "Looking for Todd?"

I nodded.

Each time we spied a black man, Nate looked at me, and I shook my head. In the first hour, we repeated our little dance over a dozen times. I tried to stay calm, reminding myself what I knew in my heart. I'd be home by nightfall.

Soon after the bazaar opened, Nate and I wandered in. Everyone gawked at us. Had they heard that Nate's fiancée was finally here? It could have also been my short hair or the diameter of my dress, less than a third the size of everyone else's. I didn't care on either account.

Nate greeted acquaintances and chatted for a few minutes here and there, introducing me as his fiancée. If anyone asked us about a date for the wedding, we both said we hadn't yet set one. One man quipped that he'd ask Miss Mattie. I laughed at the joke, but only to be polite.

Around noon, we bought some plates of fried chicken and coleslaw and sat at the only table available.

A medium-framed man with dark slicked-back hair approached. "May we join you?" He extended one arm toward a pretty blonde woman.

Nate set his plate down and stuck out his hand to shake. "Sure. Pastor Kelley. Mrs. Kelley."

Pastor Kelley shook Nate's hand and glanced at me.

"Oh, this is Cassandra McPherson." Nate bit his lip. "She's new in town. Staying with Aunt Mattie."

Mrs. Kelley set her plate on the table and grasped my hand in both of hers. "Just call me Nell. I'm glad to make your acquaintance."

"Likewise." I smiled and studied her expression. From the twinkle in her eye, she must have heard I was Nate's fiancée, but did she know it was a ruse?

Pastor Kelley said grace, and then we conversed as we ate.

The pastor and Nate talked about business and local politics. I didn't pay much attention to the conversation as I surreptitiously searched for Todd. The only black men I saw were working at the refreshment stand and none looked anything like my boyfriend.

Mrs. Kelley clanked her fork on her clean plate. "Are you two enjoying your day?"

"Yes. I've never been to anything like this." I feigned interest. "What are you raising money for?"

"Missions projects." Mrs. Kelley beamed. "This town's been so blessed we've been supporting another church farther south. And a small percentage will go to a missionary friend of ours out west." She hesitated and peered at me as if she expected a reply.

Not knowing what to say, I glanced at Nate.

Mrs. Kelley leaned toward me. "What church did you attend in Savannah?"

"Oh, uh." I tried to buy time. I had no idea of any church names. "I'm not sure."

Nell sat up straight and frowned at Nate.

"Uh, she has some memory loss." Nate placed his hand behind my back not quite touching me.

"I think I went to a Lutheran church." I stared at the puffy white clouds as if I was trying to remember. "No. That one was in Washington."

She narrowed her eyes.

I tapped my fingers on the table. "I have family there."

She continued to barrage me with pointed questions about my past and what church traditions I was used to.

When I'd had enough, I plunked my palms on the table. "All right, I've only been to church once and that was to attend the funeral of a friend of my parents. It was in Washington, D.C."

Why did I care if they thought I'd lied? What was the worst

thing that could happen? The pastor might be disgusted with me and go off and tell Mattie that her nephew was engaged to a heathen. Fine with me.

Mrs. Kelley glanced at her husband and then smiled at me, a gleam in her eye.

My pulse quickened, and I feared she would pounce any moment. I turned to Nate for help, but he sat with his head bowed and hands folded in his lap.

The pastor followed Nate's lead.

Mrs. Kelley placed her palms on the table and leaned in. "Have you ever heard about Jesus?"

I scoffed. "Of course, I've heard of Jesus."

"Do you know Him?" Her voice softened.

I shook my head. "How could I know someone who lived two thousand years ago?"

She blinked. "Not quite two thousand."

Oops. "Close."

Mrs. Kelley's blue eyes pierced mine. "What do you know about him?"

I shrugged. "Um, He was born in a stable and He performed miracles, I think."

"Anything else?"

I glanced at Nate, but he still had his head bowed. "He died on a cross. That's about all I know." I faced Nell Kelley and pressed my hands on the table to keep from wringing them. "I'm sorry. I've never read much of the Bible. I'm not sure I've read any."

She pulled out a small leather-bound book, flipped the pages to a marked spot and began reading. "Romans 3:23, For all have sinned and come short of the glory of God." She gazed at me. "Do you understand that?"

I shifted in my seat and nodded.

She turned the page. "Romans 6:23, For the wages of sin is death; but the gift of God is eternal life through Jesus Christ our

Lord." She raised her head. "Do you understand?"

My stomach knotted, and I shook my head.

She closed the book, her finger keeping her place. "Everyone is appointed to die—"

"I get that part." I studied my hands as I squeezed them together. "Everyone sins. Everyone dies. It's the rest I don't understand."

She smiled and opened the Bible. "That's the best part. Let me continue. Romans 5:8, But God commendeth his love toward us, in that, while we were yet sinners, Christ died for us."

I had a fleeting thought that the time would be better spent looking for Todd, but she peered at me with such passion in her eyes, I couldn't look away.

"Verse 9. Much more then, being now justified by his blood, we shall be saved from wrath through him."

I leaned toward her but her words stopped penetrating my conscious mind. Why did this woman continue to babble at me?

She closed the Bible, sat up, and smiled.

I cocked my head. What had I missed?

She reached her hand out, palm up. "You see, God is offering everyone a free gift. You can escape death and live with Him in Heaven. All you have to do is accept the gift."

I squinted at her. "How do I do that?"

She flipped the pages of the well-worn Bible. "Romans 10:9. That if thou shalt confess with thy mouth the Lord Jesus, and shalt believe in thine heart that God hath raised him from the dead, thou shalt be saved."

I squirmed and glanced at Nate who hadn't changed position. Was he praying for me?

"All it takes is a simple prayer. I can help." She covered my hand with hers.

I pulled my hands into my lap. I'd had people try to force religion on me before. That turned me off more than anything. "I'm not sure. I'll think about it."

Nate raised his head and opened his eyes, his lips set in a thin line.

"But, Miss McPherson, you need to make a decision today." Mrs. Kelley leaned over the small table and touched my upper arm. "You never know—"

"When she's ready." Nate flashed her a steely look.

Pastor Kelley stood and placed his hands on his wife's shoulders. "Thank you for listening."

Mrs. Kelley pursed her lips then smiled. "It's been nice meeting you."

Pastor Kelley nodded toward me. "We'll be praying for you." They picked up their plates and left.

Nate and I stared at each other for a moment. I broke eye contact and pushed a small bit of coleslaw around on my plate.

Nate clasped my hand. "Cassie, will you go to church with me tomorrow?"

"Yes. I'd like that." I'd be expected to go anyway. Still, it was nice to be asked.

Nate and I took our dishes back to the vendor and browsed the sales tables. I recognized the quilt I'd worked on and the doilies Mattie had made.

Nate tugged my arm.

I twirled to look at him and tilted my head.

He ushered me out of the sales area. We wound through the crowds, then he picked up his pace.

Nate leaned toward me and whispered, "My friend, Martin, is back there. If he catches up to us, just follow my lead."

I frowned.

"He's the one who introduced me to Margaret."

Chapter 9

We hurried down Mainstreet. When we neared the general store, we glanced toward the church. Martin turned back toward the festivities.

I heaved a sigh of relief and smiled.

Nate's jaw clenched. "We've only postponed the inevitable, I'm afraid." Nate pulled the store door open.

"We'll have some time to think of what to say." I gawked as we stepped inside. It was bigger than I expected. A counter stood to our right, with candy displayed at one side, shelves of canned and dry goods behind it, and a pickle barrel on the end.

Nate ushered me straight back to the dry goods section. "You're going to need another dress and undergarments. Pick out anything you like. It's on me." He hurried to the other side of the store before I could protest.

Because I was going home that day, I wouldn't need anything, but I couldn't tell him that. Lera could probably use anything Nate bought me, anyway. I ambled around, inspecting blouses and skirts, not confident about what to choose. What was the sizing like? Could I try anything on? I took a deep breath and willed myself to stay calm.

"Cassie, there you are. I saw you leaving the bazaar." Lera's voice projected to the back of the store. "I told Nate to wait for me so I could help you." She strode toward me.

"Hi, Lera." I hid my relief. "I could have managed, but now that you're here, what do you think of this?" I held up a blouse.

Lera shook her head and found something more suitable. She picked out another whole set of clothes minus the hoop and a piece of cotton fabric. "With this, I'll make you another slip."

After wrapping my purchase, the store keeper handed Nate a package about the size and shape of a cigar box. Nate paid the bill, lifted my package and his, and the three of us strolled toward the bazaar. We hadn't taken more than a few steps when Lera nearly bumped into a young woman dressed in a frilly light green gown and carrying a white parasol.

The girl stepped back, checked that her blonde ringlets were still in place and glowered at me.

"Pardon me." Lera stepped away from the blonde.

"Oh, It's just as much my fault, Mrs. Gardner." The woman peered at Lera then back at me.

"Where are my manners?" Lera held her hand out toward me. "Miss Jenny Highland, meet Miss Cassie McPherson."

Nate tucked my hand in the crook of his elbow. "My fiancée."

I glanced from Nate to Jenny.

She wrinkled her brow. "It's so nice to make your acquaintance." Her icy tone didn't match her statement.

"How is your uncle?" Lera drew her attention from me.

"He's well." Her smile didn't reach her eyes. "He's been so kind as to offer me refuge here for a spell. He's even agreed to spend weekends here to keep me company until he comes for the summer."

Lera offered a small curtsey. "We'll be pleased to see more of Mr. Highland." She bobbed her head. "And you. I hope you'll enjoy your stay here. Do accompany us to the bazaar. You'll get to meet nearly everyone in town. You couldn't have had time to meet many people yet."

"Thank you kindly, but I don't want to intrude." She

glanced at Nate and me, then smiled at Lera. "And, I'm in need of supplies. But it was nice seeing you again." She hurried past us into the store.

I raised my eyebrows.

Nate and Lera stifled giggles as they ushered me down the street.

"What was that all about?" I shifted my gaze from Lera to Nate.

"Thank you, Lera. I now see the true worth in your story." Nate laughed out loud.

Lera stopped giggling. "Don't laugh too much. You'll still have to deal with her."

"Yes, but at least she won't get any romantic ideas." He shook his head.

"Would someone tell me what's going on?" I stopped in the street near the church, hand on my hip.

"Later." Nate left me with Lera while he jogged with our packages to wagon.

Lera whispered in my ear, "Jenny met Nate last week and made it very clear she was interested in him. Positively gave Nate the shivers. Even made me a little uncomfortable." Lera chuckled. "The funny part is she says she moved here to escape an unwanted admirer."

I rolled my eyes. "Talk about irony."

Lera squinted at me then giggled as she ushered me back to the crowd. She introduced me to several young women who were talking to Mrs. Hodges' granddaughter, Ida.

I listened to them chat and glanced around. Where was Todd? He should have found me by now.

Lera leaned toward me. "Starting to like him, aren't you?"

Oh, she thought I was looking for Nate. I nodded. It wouldn't hurt to let her think she'd successfully played matchmaker. I was a little surprised she didn't want Nate for herself. Unless she'd done the same thing with him that she'd done with the dress, given him to me in hopes of getting him back. No, that didn't make sense, but then I couldn't understand any of these people.

Without a word, Lera pulled me away from the group and hurried toward Nate. Before I could utter a question, she turned and pointed her head. I followed her gaze and saw Martin right behind us.

Nate met us and started to lead me away.

"Why are you avoiding me, Nate?" Martin's footsteps sounded behind us. "I just wanted to congratulate you. I heard your fiancée finally arrived."

We stopped and about-faced.

A short, thin man about my age gaped at us. "That's not Margaret."

Nate squeezed my hand and lifted his chin toward Martin. "But you're not surprised, are you?"

Martin shrugged. "She could have changed her mind."

"And divorced the man she married in New York?" Nate stared straight at his friend. "Look, Martin. Cassie is my fiancée. Aunt Mattie never met Margaret, so Lera made up the story to try to save face a little."

Martin stared at me for a long moment. "Where did you two meet?"

"In my house," Nate blurted.

Martin's eyebrows rose.

"Lera introduced us." He waved his arm toward the crowd where Lera stood. "She met Cassie on the road to Atlanta." He stepped toward Martin. "Please don't tell anyone."

Martin hesitated but then a slow smile spread across his face. "For you, I'll keep my mouth shut. Congratulations." He kissed my hand and slapped Nate on the back. "How about a drink to celebrate?"

I was ready for one, but Nate shook his head.

Martin grinned. "Oh, pardon me. I haven't been home in a

while."

I narrowed my eyes.

Martin tilted his head toward me. "He's sworn off the booze. Heard he quit cold turkey about a month after Margaret's failed appearance."

Nate lowered his voice. "It was beginning to be a problem. I'll tell you about it later."

Like I cared. Either Nate was starting to believe the charade or he was a good actor.

Lera came back with her friend, Ida, and they spirited Martin away. Good. I wasn't sure I liked him, even if he was Nate's friend.

Nate guided me out of the churchyard, and we wandered off by ourselves down a wooded path. As we left, I pointed out Mark strolling hand in hand with a girl. "Mark has a girlfriend?"

"I believe he has several." He snapped a twig off a branch that hung over the path.

"He's cute. He probably does. I would expect you to have a lot of girlfriends, too." I clapped my hand over my mouth.

Nate pulled his arm away from mine and kept his gaze straight ahead. "There were a lot of girls interested in me before Margaret. I didn't even realize it until I came back from Savannah, engaged."

"What about since it was broken?" I peered at his profile.

"I'm not interested." He followed the path as it curved around a tree.

I strolled with him, but he didn't offer his arm again.

"You saw. That's one of the benefits of this charade." One corner of his mouth turned up. "Keeps the young ladies from getting romantic ideas about me."

I raised my eyebrows. "Jenny?"

He nodded. "She's one. Mattie's been getting visits from several young ladies. She says they're hoping to see me." He exhaled. "One of them is Emily's sister."

"Emily?"

"Mark's girlfriend."

"Oh." I pictured the young girl with the ponytail I'd seen with Mark. "You know you shouldn't close yourself off." I glanced up at him. "And I'm not sure I'm comfortable being used as an excuse." I wanted to tell him that I'd been hurt before, too. That you just had to keep trying. But I could tell by his set jaw that I'd already said enough.

He veered off the path, sat on a large rock, and patted the space next to him.

I settled in and watched him.

He stared at the trees. "Cassie, I know you don't want to tell me, but I have to ask. How did you get here?"

"I've already told you. I don't know." I lifted off the rock. "Maybe we should go back to town and look for Todd."

He held his arm out in front of me. "Do you have any idea where he'd be?"

"No." I sat and glanced at him. "Where would black men hang out?"

He narrowed his eyes and let his hand fall to his lap. "Hang out?"

I shrugged. "You know, sit around and tell stories."

"Oh." He shook his head. "Places I can't take you."

I stood and paced in front of him. "Great. We've got to find him or I'll be stuck here."

"Is that so bad?"

I faced him. "I don't want to take your charity forever."

"Don't worry. Aunt Mattie will have you earning your keep soon." He chuckled.

I pursed my lips and stared at him.

"Why won't you tell me how you got here?"

"Because you wouldn't believe me." I lowered my head. "You already think I'm crazy."

"That was the first day. You hit your head when you fell."

He stood and reached toward me. "That's what Ed says happened."

"Ed's not a doctor. He told me." I stepped back.

"Not by trade, but he knows a lot about medicine." He turned toward the path. "Most folks in town come to Ed before they go to the doctor."

I squinted. "Why? Because he gives free advice?"

He faced me. "Because he's proven a lot of what the doctors do doesn't work."

"Like what?"

He sat on the rock, picking up a twig that had fallen on it.

I sat next to him, ready for his story.

"When John was little, he had a fever. The doctor said to sweat it out of him. He put him in a warm room and laid blankets on him. His fever got worse." He twirled the twig in his hands as he talked. "Ed took the blankets off and bathed him in a tub of lukewarm water. His fever went down. Mattie's done that ever since. She says she's never seen a fever go down so fast."

My mother did that. I remembered her saying it was a new idea when her mother was little. My grandmother was born at least forty years after this time. My eyes widened and I lowered my head to hide it. Maybe Ed knew more than he let on. "Do you know where Ed learned it?"

He shrugged. "He says most of what he knows is just common sense."

"Does he know a lot about other things, too?" I studied Nate's face.

He gave me a crooked smile. "Yes. He's certainly helped me a lot with the farm."

"How?" I stared at his hands trying to hide my growing suspicion.

"Aw, I don't think you're really interested." He threw down the twig. "You just don't want to answer my question."

I closed my eyes. "I can't."

"I don't believe that." He kept his voice low but sounded annoyed.

My eyes snapped open and I turned away, my arms folded across my chest. "You don't believe me? I'm the one that shouldn't believe a word you say. You or Lera."

"What do you mean?" He touched my shoulder.

I faced him, my arms still folded. "I've seen you two tell bald-faced lies without blinking. How can I believe you?"

"I've only lied to protect Mattie and Lera." He looked past me.

"You and Lera were made for each other." I stood, fists at my sides, and strode a few paces. "I'm surprised she's not after you yourself." I threw him a side-eye. "Oh, I forgot, she's still in mourning."

He sat with his arms around one knee, a smirk on his face. "Why would you care?"

"I don't." I swiveled away from him. The silence got to me and I snuck a few peeks.

He lowered his leg and leaned forward. "I suspect that when Lera's mourning period is up, she'll be keeping company with one Mr. Simon Highland."

"Jenny's uncle?" I whirled around and narrowed my eyes. "How do you know that?"

"He's asked about her. Seeing as he's the richest man in town, I know she'll be interested."

"Is that why she said you'd still have to deal with Jenny?"

He nodded.

Jenny had mentioned that her uncle was spending weekends here. "Does he even live here?"

"Yes, but only about half the year." He glanced at the sky. "He's a merchant in Atlanta. Makes enough money there that he can vacation here for five or six months." Nate raised his eyebrows. "That's how the story goes. He didn't start summering here until a few years ago."

"It sounds like you're skeptical of Mr. Highland. Are you going to tell Lera?"

He peered at me. "Do you think she'd listen?"

"Is he good looking as well as rich?"

He shrugged. "He's fair, for someone in his early forties."

A grin escaped my lips. "She won't listen."

He maintained eye contact as he stood. "I agree." He bit his lip and laid both hands on my shoulders. "I'll listen. Anytime you want to tell me what's going on." He held out his arm for me, and we strolled down the path toward the bazaar.

I considered it. Nate was the most level-headed of any of them. Though, Ed might be a good person to talk to. But could I trust him? Where did he get all the medical and farming knowledge? Could he have met Todd's assistant? Maybe not, because if he did know about time travelers, he'd certainly know I was one. Still, I'd like to find out what he knew.

A whiff of fried chicken brought me out of my reverie. "Nate, where did Ed and Caleb go today? I haven't seen them since we pulled in."

"I suspect they went fishing this morning. This afternoon, Ed planned to get the planting supplies loaded in the wagon."

"But there won't be room for us." I hate it when I whine.

He glanced at me as we emerged from the woods. "So?"

I furrowed my brow. "But where will we ride?"

"Who said you'd be riding?" He smirked.

My eyes went wide. I opened my mouth to speak, but what could I say?

Nate chuckled. "That's why Mark drove the carriage this morning. You ladies will be riding home with him, while Ed, Caleb, and I haul the supplies."

"You start planting soon?" Hiding my relief, I peeked at him as we neared the bazaar, both slowing our gait.

"First thing Monday morning." He frowned. "We should have started today."

I squinted. "Why didn't you?"

He pointed to the ladies still selling their wares in front of the church.

Mattie had insisted we all attend the bazaar. No point in mentioning how he always did her bidding.

Ed and Caleb waved to us as they sauntered toward the wagon with fishing poles over their shoulders.

Nate led me to Mattie. "Hey, Aunt Mattie. I need to help Ed load the wagon. Would you keep Cassie company for a while?"

At least he didn't say, "Watch Cassie." Did they think I'd break if they left me alone?

"I'd be delighted." Mattie led me behind her table. "I haven't seen you all day. Have you been enjoying yourself?"

"Oh, yes." I smiled as I watched Nate lope toward the wagon. I'd had a good time despite not finding Todd or his assistant. "I met so many people. I'll never be able to remember their names."

"Don't worry. You'll remember them in time. I need to help clean up a little." She motioned for me to fold the white tablecloth she'd placed on the wood plank next to Lera's blue one. "I don't have to pack anything up because all my handiwork sold."

"Cool. I mean that's wonderful."

She flashed me a curious look.

"Did the quilt sell?"

"Oh yes, and for a good price too. Thank you for your help." She handed me one edge of the tablecloth to help her fold.

Whew. She didn't press me about saying, "cool," in the wrong context.

Mattie stacked the cloth in her basket, and took my hand in both of hers. "I know everything will work out between you and Nate. You already seem like one of the family." She patted my hand. "It took me a lot longer to feel that way about Lera."

What had she meant by that?

Mattie approached Mrs. Hodges and helped her pack items that hadn't sold. I followed behind her, but she was so efficient, I ended up just listening to all the ladies' chatter, thankful she hadn't waited for a response from me. What could I say? I couldn't tell her that Nate was helping me find my boyfriend. I nearly giggled imagining her reaction if she knew Todd would be helping me get back to the twenty-first century. Self-conscious, I glanced around, but nobody seemed to notice any unexpected expressions on my face.

Mattie covered the last basket she'd packed and bid goodbye to Mrs. Hodges. She stepped toward me. "Cassie, can you help me round up everyone?"

"I can try."

"I'll get Mark. You bring Lera and Lydia and meet me at the carriage." She hurried toward the church.

I trudged off to the last place I'd seen Lydia and Lera and spotted them with a group of young women at the other corner of the yard. Knowing it would take Mattie a while to find Mark and drag him away from his girl, I took my time.

Fear had been niggling at me most of the afternoon, but now my pulse raced. My glance darted around the area where different groups of people mingled. Where was Todd? Had I been wrong about going home tonight?

Mattie raised her arm and waved from the church steps, then headed around to the back where Mark had parked the carriage.

I picked up my pace and called to Lera and Lydia. "Miss Mattie's ready to go. She said to meet her at the carriage."

Before I'd gotten close enough to hear any of their conversation, they stopped talking and glared at me.

"Sorry to interrupt. I didn't mean to be rude." I strode toward the church, glancing around. Would Todd sweep in at the last minute?

"Wait." Lera fell into step with me. "We're sorry, too. I just didn't want the day to end. I know you were only the messenger."

When we approached the rear of the church, Mattie stood at the carriage by herself.

Lera glanced at me. "Have you seen Mark today?"

I nodded in Mattie's direction. "Yeah, but not recently. He was with his girl, down near the woods."

Lera's face got tight. "Do you know who she was?"

I shook my head.

Lydia jogged to catch up with us. "What did she look like?"

"Short, thin, blonde hair, tied back but not in a bun."

Lydia sucked in air. "That sounds like Emily Wilson. I knew he liked her." She tapped her forehead. "Why didn't I think of that?"

"Yeah, Nate called her Emily." I peered at her. "What's the problem?"

"Emily's mother took her home a short while ago." Lera stopped walking and lowered her voice. "She has red spots on her face. Her mother admitted she'd had a fever off and on for the past few days. But Emily had wanted to come today so badly that she'd let her." She clenched her jaw. "Now we've probably all been exposed. Especially Mark."

I stood opposite Lydia and Lera. "Measles?"

They nodded.

I exhaled. It was only measles. My eyes went wide. It wasn't *only measles* back then. Or rather, now.

Lera, Lydia, and I turned toward Mattie but stood and watched as Ed and Mark approached the carriage. Ed and Mattie conversed briefly, worried expressions on their faces, then Mattie took Mark into the carriage. As we approached, Ed stopped us. "Have any of you had the measles?"

We all shook our heads no. I remembered I'd been immunized, but I didn't think they'd believe me, and it was too late to change my no to a yes.

"Mark's been exposed." Ed wiped his brow with a handkerchief. "He has a slight fever already, so we're afraid he'll come down with them. Mattie's had them, so she's going to take Mark home. The rest of us will move into Nate's."

Nate stopped the wagon and Caleb hopped out. "We get to stay with Nate?"

"Yes, but there'll be a lot of work to do." Lera brushed dirt off her son's shirt. "You'll have to do your part."

"I can stay with Mattie and help her." Nate stepped off the wagon. "I've had the measles."

Ed clapped Nate on the shoulder. "No. Mattie said she can take care of Mark. She doesn't want you or me distracted from the planting. We'll need to hire someone to take Mark's place as it is."

"We can all help." What was I thinking?

"The only help Mattie will accept is toting things back and forth. Nate should do that," Ed said.

"We can cook their meals, and Nate can take them," Lera said.

"Good." Ed lifted Caleb onto the wagon seat. "We'll all go to Nate's, and then Nate can ride down to get some of our clothes. Mattie said she'd have them ready on the porch." He lowered his voice. "Thankfully, Mark's been spending a lot more time with Emily than he has with the family."

Nate frowned. "Are you all right, Ed?"

"Yeah, I never thought I'd hear myself say that." Ed snorted as he tightened the ropes holding supplies on the wagon.

Nate helped me up on the seat between him and Caleb. Ed, Lera, and Lydia squeezed in with the cargo.

During the ride I dwelled on my predicament. Knowing I couldn't get measles wasn't much solace. There were plenty of other diseases I could catch. I could die before I got home, if I ever got home. Todd hadn't shown up, and it didn't look like I'd get back into town for a while. Even if I did, he probably wouldn't be there. Could he tell where, or when I'd gone? Even if he did know, the way things had been going, I wasn't positive he would come back after me. How could I have been so wrong this morning?

As we jostled the four miles to Nate's house, I watched the sun set and my hopes of getting home tonight fade. We would be at Nate's house, though. Maybe Todd would come there, or I'd find the time machine. Somehow, I would find my way home.

Chapter 10

When we arrived at Nate's everyone sprang into action. Nate and Ed, with Caleb trying to help, unloaded the wagon. Lera brought in my package and Nate's, no doubt wondering what was in the latter.

After a quick dinner made from odds and ends out of Nate's pantry, Nate took part of the meal to Mattie. I helped Lydia and Lera clear the table and wash the dishes. Lera handed me the last plate to dry. "We'll do the washing on Monday." She turned to me. "At least you have something new to wear tomorrow." She dried her hands on her apron and marched toward the house. I followed, not knowing what else to do.

Lera crossed the breezeway to the main house. "At least we don't have to move the bathtub."

"And we don't have to lug hot water either." Lydia opened the back door.

I squinted. "What are you talking about?"

"We have to get ready for church tomorrow." Lera paused in the mudroom. "Do you want the first bath? Lydia started heating the water when we got here so it should be ready by now."

"What do you mean you don't have to lug water?" I followed her through to the dining room.

"Oh, Nate has the most modern house ever." Lydia passed

us, and headed into the small parlor. "You saw the pipes in the kitchen. He has pipes into his water closet too, and a windmill pump that pumps the water to the attic." She stopped and waved her arms from the direction of the kitchen to the upstairs. "The water flows from there through the pipes to the water closet. It's heated in the kitchen."

"Oh, I've never heard of that." Normally, I'd want to know exactly how it worked, but now, I just wanted to use it. I let them lead me to the water closet. On the way, I picked up my parcel of clothes. A clean night shirt would be nice.

As we reached the landing between floors, I asked, "Which rooms are we using?"

"I don't think Nate cares." Lera made the u-turn and continued up to the second floor. "There are three extra rooms."

"Four," I replied without thinking.

"Three, unless you want to sleep on the floor," Lera said.

"He never furnished the master bedroom." Lydia jogged to the second floor and pointed toward the large room over the parlor and dining room. "He was waiting for Margaret."

"You mean Cassie, dear." Lera smiled.

Lydia rolled her eyes. "Mama's not here, Lera. You don't have to keep pretending."

Lera squinted at her. "How did you know?"

"Who do you think gave her the ring?" Lydia stood by the railing and looked down at Lera.

"Nate?" Lera tilted her head.

Lydia beamed. "Nate gave it to me after Margaret sent it back."

Lera blew out a breath and sagged onto the top step. "Who else knows?"

Lydia shrugged. "No one that I know of."

"Martin." I joined Lydia at the railing. "He introduced Nate to Margaret. But he doesn't know the whole truth. Nate told him we really are engaged."

Lera stood, pressed her skirt with her hands, and took a deep breath. "Cassie, you and Lydia will have to share. Caleb and I can share that one." She pointed to the room on the side opposite the master and toward the rear, the only room with two beds. "Nate's using the one right in front of us. I don't think Ed will care so why don't you two pick which room you want?"

Lydia shrugged so I picked the room between Nate's and the bathroom, the one they'd brought me to when I'd arrived. My shorts and track shoes were in there. If it wasn't already dark, I would have gone running. At least I knew I'd get a bath.

Lera walked around toward the closet on the back hallway to get bed linens. Lydia showed me the water closet, which was one room I'd never been inside. The museum kept the door open but they had a chain across so you could only look in, and the door wouldn't open wide enough to crawl through. I'd never seen the end of the tub with the shower head attached. It was a crude pull-string, but better than I'd expected.

Lydia puffed out her chest. "I bet you've never seen one of those before, have you?"

I curled my lips under. "No. Not like that one."

"This is a shower." She turned the taps and pulled the string. Water gushed out until she let go. "It's the only one in town that I know of. Pa told me Nate always uses it, and sometimes he and Mark take showers after they come in from the fields."

"Pretty cool." I winced at my gaff.

"No, it's hot water." She kneeled and put the plug in the drain. "Do you need any help?" Without waiting for an answer, she showed me how to adjust the taps to get a good temperature.

I tested the water. It was hotter than I expected. Sometime I'd ask where Nate got the idea for the shower.

Lydia showed me the small closet where the towels were kept, and then led me back to the bathroom, talking non-stop about the plumbing. She showed me the soap and what to use to wash my hair. It smelled like alcohol.

"I don't need any help with this dress." I hoped she would get the hint and leave. To my surprise, she did.

I got undressed, and sank into the tub. I closed my eyes and tried to imagine I was in my own bathroom. It didn't work. This plumbing indicated a time-traveler had been here before me. But who was it, and how could I find out?

When I started to wrinkle, I tried to create a lather with the harsh soap Lydia had given me, and washed myself the best I could. Then I stood up, rinsed off in the shower, and washed my hair. I tugged the canvas curtain bunched at the back of the tub around to the front. Only one side of the tub was against the wall, so the curtain had to cover both ends as well as the other side. I turned the faucets on and pulled the string. The water was cold at first and shot out so fast I jumped. I slipped but caught myself on the shower curtain. It tore before I managed to let go and grab the shower pipe to steady myself. Whew. The tear in the curtain was small. I hadn't done irreparable damage.

"Cassie, are you all right?" Lydia yelled from the hallway.

"I'm fine. Got caught off guard by the force of the shower," I called. "I'll be out soon."

Bracing myself, I pulled the string again. I'd used pull-string showers before, but they were usually not much better than a trickle. With this one, it wouldn't take me long to rinse my hair.

After I finished, I wrapped the towel around me and started to open the door before I remembered where I was. Should I dress in the water closet, or wrap myself in the towel and run down the hall to my room, the next door to the left? The only room to the right was the unfurnished master bedroom, so nobody would be coming from that direction.

The bathroom was a little moist, and I wanted a chance to dry off before I dressed. Plus, I didn't want to keep Lydia waiting any longer. "Lydia, is anyone else upstairs?"

"No. Why?"

"I'm coming out." I ran past her with my towel wrapped around me, carrying my dry-goods package.

She snickered as she took my place in the water closet. She wore a robe. I should have purchased one.

Before I could get to our room, footsteps sounded on the stairs. I ran in and pulled the door closed with so much force that when it slammed to a stop, I kept going. I landed on my bottom in the center of the room, still holding the doorknob, my towel no longer wrapped around me, and my package on top of me.

"So much for not breaking anything." I pushed the package to the floor.

"Are you all right?" Nate called from outside the door.

"I'm fine, but I don't think your door is."

"Hold on. I'll get it open."

"No!"

"You want to be locked in?"

"I need to get dressed first." I tore open my package and searched frantically for the night shirt.

"I have to get some tools. I'll be back in a few minutes."

"Oh, okay." I felt underdressed in the nightshirt but I wasn't sure why. Nate had already seen me wearing less. I hung the new skirt and jacket in the wardrobe and set aside the slip material. At the bottom of the pile, I found a plain white cotton robe. Lera must have slipped it in.

I donned the robe and sat in the rocking chair in the corner of the room. For the first time in four days, I felt clean and comfortable. I leaned back and allowed myself to relax. My thoughts drifted over the past few days. I'd arrived here penniless and with very little clothing. These people took me in and treated me like family. No, they treated me like a guest, instead of the freeloader that I was.

It could have been a lot worse. I could have landed in total wilderness, or been found by people not nearly as nice. I shuddered. Even though much of the time I'd been miserable, I couldn't help but feel that someone had been watching over me the last few days. Nate would say it was God. Could he be right?

Whether it was God, or chance, I needed to thank Nate and the others, as soon as I could get out of the room. I peered out the window, but it was so dark, all I could see was my ghostlike reflection. I rubbed my arms and rocked back in the chair. How long would it take Nate to get me out of here? Glancing at the door didn't produce Nate any quicker. Neither did pacing back and forth from the door to the window. I stopped near the door and took deep breaths, and letting them out slowly. Finally heavy footsteps sounded on the stairs, followed by a clank of a tool against the door hardware.

When the door opened, I ran to Nate and wrapped my arms around his waist.

"What, don't like to be locked in?" He extricated himself from my embrace, and glanced around probably making sure no one saw us.

"I'm sorry." I stepped back and lowered my head. "I'm also sorry about the doorknob."

Nate shrugged and picked it up off the floor. "I'll tighten it this time." He followed me into the room leaving the door open and motioned for me to take a seat in the rocker.

"I'll fix it shortly, but I wanted to give you this first." He knelt next to my chair and held out the small package he'd purchased at the general store.

I leaned back. "That's for me?"

He grinned. "Go ahead. Open it."

I tore open the paper revealing a black leather-bound book with the words 'Holy Bible' on the front. Flipping through it, I noticed it was the King James Version.

"Thank you." I meant it.

"I thought you should have one of your own."

"I appreciate it." I looked him in the eye and swallowed.

"Nate, I realized tonight that I should have thanked you earlier. You and your family. You've been very good to me. I took you for granted."

He narrowed his eyes. "Why tonight?"

I let out a breath. "I'm not sure. I guess I finally had a chance to think. I found this." I pinched a piece of the robe I wore. "I didn't even know we'd bought it, but Lera must have slipped it in. Sometimes she irritates me, but she can be helpful too."

He chuckled. "That's a good description of everyone." He stood and kissed me on the top of the head. "But it's perfect for Lera." He walked toward the door and replaced the doorknob.

I opened the Bible and started reading. The least I could do was use his gift. Not that I had anything else to do.

I didn't get very far before Lydia and Lera came in wanting to know what was going on. Nate filled them in as he finished reattaching the knob.

Lera flashed her sly smile. "Too bad it didn't break with both of you in the room."

My face heated.

Nate rolled his eyes.

I hid my smile when I realized that in my world, Lera would fit right in.

Nate and Lera discussed the details about who would take meals to Mattie and Mark and take care of the rest of the chores.

My eyes opened wide at the mention of Lydia's brother. "How is Mark? I'm so sorry, I spaced it." It took every ounce of my will not to clamp my hand over my mouth.

Nate squinted at me. "He has a fever, but he's not feeling bad yet."

"Well, even if he's not feeling bad, he should be in bed." Lera stuck her hand up, palm out. "I know, Ed has helped a lot of people, but I still hold to some of the old ways."

"So, what do you think she should do, sweat him?" Lydia

sat on the bed.

"No, but he should stay in bed unless he's in the bath." Lera put one hand on her hip.

I kept my mouth shut, glad they hadn't picked up on my slip of the tongue.

Lera went off to get Caleb out of the tub, and Lydia left to get our linens. A patchwork quilt covered the bed, so I hadn't noticed there were no sheets underneath. When they had both left the room, Nate strolled to my chair, bent down on one knee, and peered at me. "What does spaced mean?"

I bit my lip. "I was hoping no one caught that." It took a moment to come up with an answer. "I'm not sure exactly. I tend to use it when I have so much else on my mind that I forget something important."

He nodded and stood.

"I felt bad that I'd forgotten to ask about Mark. I realize this could be serious."

"I know." He headed toward the door, then turned back. "Good night, Cassie." He closed the door behind him. A moment later, the door to the next room opened and closed.

Lydia returned with the linens, and I helped her make our bed. As I placed the Bible on the nightstand, I flipped it open to an inscription on the inside cover. It read: To Cassie, From Nate, April 2, 1870. I shivered as I climbed into bed.

Chapter 11

The sun streamed through the slats in the shutters. I blinked sleep out of my eyes, unsure of where I was. One glance at Lydia, curled up and breathing slowly beside me, reminded me. With the sun that high, it had to be at least eight. Why was the house so quiet? Since it took about an hour to get to town, the church service must start late.

As much as I wanted to go into town, I wasn't looking forward to the carriage ride. I much preferred my Camry, but even that wouldn't be a great ride on these roads. I rolled over away from Lydia and the window. Why couldn't I go back to sleep and wake up in my own bed? Why had I thought I'd be going home yesterday? We'd moved to Nate's, but I hadn't gotten any closer to home. Or had I?

I'd always been drawn to this house. There might be something here that could help. I planned to investigate every cranny while we were here. I would also talk to Ed and find out if he'd met Todd's assistant.

Footsteps sounded in the hall followed by knocks on more than one door.

"Time to get up," Lera called. "We have to leave early to drop off Mattie and Mark's breakfast."

Lydia and I dragged ourselves out of bed and dressed. She paid me a compliment on my new frock which was similar to the gray one but pale yellow, with little rosebuds on it. I had never thought to wear anything that feminine before, preferring navy and black pants, with dark or bright-colored button-down shirts.

It was time to start earning my keep, so I followed Lydia to the kitchen to help with breakfast. During the meal, everyone made polite conversation, but it was strained, and worry showed on their faces. I hoped Mark wouldn't get too sick. I was glad to be living in Nate's house, but not for that reason.

After clearing the table and gathering cloaks and Bibles, we loaded everyone and breakfast into the larger wagon. Nate and Ed must have hitched up the team while the rest of us were cleaning the kitchen.

Nate helped me into the front seat between him and Caleb and the others took the back seat which hadn't been there the day before. I did a double-take.

Nate laughed. "It was in the barn. We can take it off when we don't need it."

We bumped our way to Mattie's. When we arrived, Nate hopped out, took the breakfast tray from Ed, and hurried to the back door.

Mattie accepted the tray, and shooed him away.

He strode to the wagon, eyes focused on the ground, mouth held in a straight line.

"How bad is it?" Ed asked.

"He woke Mattie up at around two this morning." Nate approached the wagon still looking down. "His fever's been pretty high since then and neither of them got much sleep."

Ed started to jump out of the wagon, but Nate held his hand up. "She'd have my hide if I let you stay." He stepped back. "Mattie can handle it herself. She told me to make sure the rest of the family gets to church."

Ed hopped down from the back seat.

Nate stood in his way.

Ed stared at Nate. "That's my son. The only one I have

left."

I glanced at Lydia and cringed, old feelings I thought were long buried coming to the surface.

Nate held Ed with both hands on his shoulders and looked him in the eye. "There's nothing you can do except catch measles. Do you really want to add to the workload?"

"Pa, come on back." Lydia patted the seat next to her.

Nate and Ed froze for a long moment. Finally, Ed nodded and Nate let go. Ed settled onto the wagon seat close to Lydia, and draped his arm around her. "Now don't you go gettin' sick."

We pulled out, so I couldn't hear Lydia's reply over the sound of the horses' hooves, but I felt better. At least Ed wasn't favoring Mark like I had feared.

When we arrived, I hopped down without assistance, thankful I wasn't wearing a crinoline. Lera and Caleb led the way into the church, followed by Ed, Lydia, Nate, and me. It was a modestly-sized room with ten sets of pews on each side of the main aisle. We reached ours, the second one on the left, and Nate waited for me, leaving him the aisle seat.

I estimated there was seating for around one-hundred-twenty-five to a hundred and fifty. The pews were dark wood, both the backs and the benches. I'd experienced less comfortable seating before, but only at football games and political rallies.

I scanned the room and recognized many of the people I'd met the day before. They nodded or whispered good morning. The platform had a podium in the center and a piano to our left, but nobody occupied the bench.

Pastor Kelley took his place at the lectern. "It seems too quiet in here without Miss Mattie."

There were nods and murmurs of consent. Mattie must've talked as much here as she did at home.

The pastor gripped both edges of the podium. "I'm sure she'll be back in no time. Please keep her and Mark in your prayers along with the whole Wilson family. Emily and her two younger brothers have the measles as well. I'm sure there are other ailments and different problems that we don't know about. And lest we forget, it's planting season. Shall we pray?"

As he led the congregation in a prayer, I looked around. I should have had my eyes closed, but I felt too uncomfortable. Besides, I needed to take every opportunity to look for Todd. But I wouldn't find him here. There wasn't even a tanned face in the crowd. Nobody watched me, so I lowered my head and tried to concentrate on the prayer. It was a lot like my new Bible, almost a different language.

He prayed for practical things, like healing but the end of the prayer caught my attention. He asked for God's presence to be in that place and for the Holy Spirit to speak to each one in the room. I rubbed my arms trying not to shiver. I'd always thought of God as far away, out in the heavens. That is, when I thought about God at all.

After the prayer, the pastor smiled and raised his arm, palm up. "Our first Hymn will be 'O Worship the King.' We're going to have to make up for not having a pianist or a pastor with perfect pitch. But I'm sure we can make a joyful noise."

There were a few titters of laughter while we rose to sing. I'd heard better, but I couldn't complain because I was just as off-key as everyone else. During the hymn, it finally dawned on me; Mattie was the pianist.

After the first verse, I paid attention to the words. The second verse seemed to back up my notion of God as a judge watching us from a distance, but the third painted a different picture. It brought back the feeling I'd had the night before, of being watched over, protected. The last verse reminded me of Mark and all of us who could get sick. Knowing most everyone felt concerned, I glanced around and saw confidence, strength, or peace on their faces.

As we sang the last stanza, Pastor Kelley furrowed his brow and gazed toward the front doors. A few at a time, the congregation stopped singing and turned around.

The doors stood open and bright sunlight streamed in forming a silhouette in the shape of a large man holding his hat and shifting from foot to foot. "I hate to interrupt, Pastor, but the Wiley's barn is on fire."

Most of the men in the room, including Nate and Ed, stampeded out the door. Lera stood behind Caleb, both arms fastened around him while he struggled to break free.

Pastor Kelley hurried down the center aisle. "Ladies, please pray. That will be our service for today." He took off his robe, handed it to his wife, and dashed for the door.

With few exceptions, the ladies stayed in their seats and prayed. One young woman stood and started to follow the men, but some older women stopped her. Lera led Lydia, Caleb, and me out the side door of the church.

"Come on." Lera waved her arm toward the woods. "We can walk to the Wiley's and pick up a wagon to make a water run. The men will be too busy fighting the fire."

Lydia and Caleb took off after her without a word.

I planted my feet. "We were told to stay and pray."

"That's funny." Lera glanced over her shoulder. "I didn't think you prayed."

She had me there. They didn't stop, so I followed Lydia, staying a few paces behind. "Who are the Wileys?"

"They are an old couple," Lydia said. "They don't come to church anymore. Ma and the other ladies look in on them from time to time. Yesterday, Anna told me Mr. Wiley was sick."

Caleb stopped and pointed at smoke and flames licking up over the trees in front of us. "It looks like they're gonna lose their barn."

"I just hope they don't lose the house too," Lera muttered. She took Caleb's hand and led us out of the woods into a clearing with a small house and a burning barn on the opposite side.

Several wagonloads of buckets stood between the house and the barn. Men and a few women made a daisy chain handing buckets of water to each other, the last person dousing the flames, or trying to, at least. With all the water sloshing on the people, not enough made it to the fire. They had managed to keep it away from the house but weren't making much progress putting it out.

Lera held her hand in front of her forehead, like a salute, and scanned the clearing. "Do you see Ed or Nate?"

"No. Our wagon isn't here, either." Lydia strode toward the action. "They're probably on their way."

Spotting some black men making their own chain on the other side of the fire, I wandered in that direction. I tried to scan their faces for Todd without anyone noticing. I was partially successful. No one noticed.

Searching the crowd, I found Lera, Caleb, and Lydia heading toward the well where the buckets were being refilled. I circled around all the workers, making sure Todd wasn't there and started toward Lera. I may as well help.

Another wagon approached. Nate and Ed drove in with a full load, but not buckets of water. There were several men and what looked like a large canvas pillow. Ed attached a hose to it and aimed the nozzle at the fire. Nate and several others pressed on the edges of the canvas generating a spray with enough volume to put out the fire with just the contents of the bag. Pretty clever.

Lydia ran to her father and gushed over the contraption, as did everyone else. His fire extinguisher must have been something new.

As everyone congratulated Ed, I stood next to what was left of the barn and watched Nate search through the rubble.

He picked up a kerosene lantern that was laying on its side. "This could have been the culprit."

An old lady limped over to him. "That's impossible. We

haven't been in the barn in days. Even if one of us left a lantern in there, it would have burned out before this morning."

"I'll show this to the sheriff, Mrs. Wiley." Nate looked up and locked eyes with me.

He strode toward me, his face turning red. "What are you doing here?" His voice was quiet but with an edge, and he took me by the arm and lead me toward the wagon. "You should know better. You could have gotten hurt or killed. Well, what do you have to say for yourself?" He draped his arm over the edge of the buckboard.

"I followed Lera and Lydia." I studied my boots and tried not to sound guilty.

"What about Caleb?"

"He came, too."

He raised my chin with his index finger. "So, where are they?"

I spotted them close to the house and nodded in that direction. "Over there. And I didn't get close to the fire. It was out before I got there."

He grunted and leaned against the wagon, still red-faced but a bit calmer.

To distract him, I asked, "Do you have any idea who would deliberately set that fire?"

"Ideas, yes. Proof, no." He narrowed his eyes. "How did you know?"

"I heard what Mrs. Wiley said. There haven't been any storms lately. I can't think of any other ways it could have started." I nibbled the corner of my lip. "Unless someone was camping out in their barn."

"That's an interesting thought." He pulled on his chin. "But you are the only newcomer in town lately—at least that I know of."

"Ask Lera to make sure." I peered at him.

His shoulders relaxed and the corner of his mouth turned

up. "I'll do that."

I let myself smile, too, but only for a moment.

The rest of the family trooped to the wagon. Nate cleared his throat and helped me onto the seat.

On our way back to the house, we rode through town. When we approached the church, a lady stood in the road waving for us to stop. I groaned, sure there was another emergency.

We pulled over and five women handed us food to take to Mattie and Mark. Mrs. Hodges, the spokesperson for the group, asked how they were and told us to inform Mattie they were praying. Ed and Lydia graciously accepted the pots and casserole dishes and thanked the ladies.

On the ride to Mattie's, I resolved to find time alone to investigate Nate's house. When we stopped, Lera and Lydia handed two of the dishes off to Nate. After he'd disappeared into the house, I raised my eyebrows at Lera.

Lera huffed. "Well, the two of them can't eat all that food before it goes bad."

"This way, we can all rest up for tomorrow," Ed said.

That sounded ominous, but I didn't want to think about tomorrow. I had an agenda for today.

In stony silence, Nate hurried to the wagon and climbed on. He flicked the reins to start the team before Ed could jump off. No one said anything until we reached Nate's house.

"This town needs a real fire hose not my jerry-rigged one," Ed said as we climbed out of the wagon. "Better yet, a fire department. Have men ready. We wasted a lot of time going to get the hose."

Nate unhitched one of the mules. "Your hose worked though. And storing one at Fremont's was a good idea."

"Yeah, if we'd had to come all the way back here, they might have lost the house, too." Ed accepted the soup pot from Lydia allowing her to climb down. Then he handed back the pot. "That reminds me. We need to repair the bag and get it back there soon. Still, if we had a fire department in town, we might have saved the barn."

"You're right." Nate turned to me. "We're doing better than most, but this town's too small to support a fire department."

"I don't think we have enough fires for that, do we?" Lera remained seated, holding one of the dishes.

Ed reached for her casserole. "Maybe not, but we don't have that many crimes either, and the county has a sheriff's department."

"Other than those thefts that started year before last." Nate finished unhitching the team. He and Ed led them to the barn. Caleb followed asking questions about the fire and the contraption they'd used to put it out.

Lydia handed me a pot of stew, and I trailed her and Lera into the kitchen, each of them carrying a casserole dish.

"Why didn't Ed ask about Mark?" I wondered aloud.

Lera stopped and glanced over her shoulder, causing me to bump into Lydia who'd also stopped short. "He didn't need to." Lera scowled. "Didn't you see the look on Nate's face?" She gave me a curt nod and continued into the kitchen.

I bit my lip. Mark must be the same or worse.

"At least dinner will be easy." Lydia put both the casseroles in the wood burning oven and stoked the fire.

I set the pot on top of it. "Are we going to eat all this for dinner?"

Lera peeked in the pot. "Put that in the root cellar. We'll heat it up for supper."

I did as I was told. We set the table, then went into the sitting room and lounged while the food heated. It was the first time I'd seen Lera or Lydia sit still. I'm not sure how long we waited because I dozed off.

Caleb bounded in, waking me. Lera told him to go outside until dinner. He dashed out the front door toward the side of the house that used to contain an old tire swing. I assumed it was still there, or rather, already there and probably new.

Nate and Ed strolled in from the dining room. Ed eased himself into the big wing chair across from Lydia and Nate sat between Lera and me on the sofa.

Lera leaned forward and nudged Nate. "So, are you going to apologize to her?"

Both Nate and I turned our heads toward her. Was he as confused as I was?

"Who?" Nate asked.

"You." Lera nodded first at him and then at me. "For yelling at her at the fire. You didn't think we saw that, did you?"

"I didn't yell." He leaned back against the sofa.

"Your version." She shot me her sly grin.

My cheeks warmed. "You don't need to apologize."

"Oh, let him," Lera said.

"Okay, I'm sorry." Nate turned toward Lera. "Are you happy, now?"

"Thrilled." Lera leaned back flinging her arms over her head. "Scared ya, didn't she?"

"How soon will dinner be ready?" I asked.

"That's a good question," Nate said.

Lera lowered her arms. "It depends on how hot you like it."

I stood. "Maybe we ought to check."

Lydia jumped up and hurried toward the door. "I'll do it."

One avenue of escape had eluded me. I sat on the edge of the sofa and glanced at Nate. "Were you saying something about someone new in town? Other than me?"

"Yes." He shifted toward his cousin. "Lera, do you know?"

She narrowed her eyes. "Why?"

"It's a theory. Someone was in the Wiley's barn." Nate tapped his fingers on his thighs. "We thought they might be staying there."

"There's no one new in town except Jenny." Lera gazed at the ceiling. "I don't know about you, but if I could live in a mansion, I don't think I'd be camping out in the Wiley's barn." She sat up straight and gasped. "Maybe the same person responsible for things going missing is back." Her eyes went wide. "Maybe it's a phantom."

"Well, someone must have been in there and left that lantern burning." I crossed my arms over my chest.

Lera waved one arm. "You are forgetting the obvious. One of the Wiley's could have left it there and forgotten. They're both ancient."

"Anything could have knocked it over and caused the fire." Ed leveled a piercing stare at me.

Case closed. I slumped, upset that Lera didn't know of anyone new in town and wary of approaching Ed. So much for at least part of my afternoon plan.

Chapter 12

After dinner, I helped Lydia clean up while Lera went outside with Caleb. I didn't mind the work. What I did mind was losing track of Ed. I'd planned to follow him out of the dining room and corner him as soon as possible, but I couldn't refuse to help. With only one thing on my mind, I didn't make very good company for Lydia. At least I gave her a rare opportunity to talk.

"After we finish, we've got the rest of the afternoon free." Lydia stacked the plates in the cupboard. "Do you want me to show you around the house? It's so modern, it's amazing."

"Yes." I handed her a cup to dry. "I'd love to see it." I knew the house better than she could guess, but there were subtle differences and rooms the museum didn't have open that I wanted to explore.

Lydia led me out of the kitchen to an adjacent room. It was slightly smaller than the kitchen, with two work surfaces, several large wash tubs, and a strange machine that looked like a wringer with a crank on it.

"This is the washroom." Lydia pointed to the machine in the middle. "That is the newest washing machine there is."

"Oh, nice." I attempted to sound impressed. "I take it I'll be sick of this room by sundown tomorrow?"

Lydia laughed. "Won't we all? Normally, we hire help on wash day, but Mrs. Jones will be working for Ma tomorrow."

"Mrs. Jones?" I squinted at her.

"They rent the old house next to ours." Lydia headed outside.

"I know that. I'm surprised she works for your ma." I stayed put, hoping she'd feel freer to talk here than in the main house where we might be overheard.

She stopped in the doorway and faced me. "She works for Nate two days a week and for us one or two days. Nate hires Mr. Jones and the boys when he needs them. They have their own plot of land that they work, too. Have you met her?"

"We weren't introduced, but we did have a conversation, sort of." I inspected the washing machine.

Lydia giggled. "Mrs. Jones doesn't talk much, but she's a good worker."

"What's Mrs. Jones' first name?"

She cleared her throat and lifted her chin. "As far as we're concerned, it's Mrs." A slow smile spread across her face.

I chuckled then my breath caught. "Did the Joneses used to be slaves?"

"Yes, but not ours." Lydia stepped back into the room. "We never owned slaves. Well, at least my parents never did. Ma's parents had a few, but Pa refused. He always worked his part of the farm by himself or with hired help." She took a breath and gazed over my shoulder. "He never got as wealthy as Ma's family, but we're well enough off. Nate's father freed all his slaves a few years before he died." Lydia smiled and met my eyes. "I like to think Pa was responsible for that."

Before I had time to mull over any of this new information, she motioned toward the main house. We left the wash room and crossed the breezeway to the back door. As she opened it, she hesitated. "Come to think of it, not very many people in this town owned slaves. We sent delegates to some meetings saying that it was possible to make a decent living without them. That was years before the war." She pushed the door all the way open and ushered me through into a small room with a work table, cabinets, and a bench, work shoes lined up under it. She shut the door tight. "We call this the pantry."

I smirked. "I thought you were only fourteen."

She lifted her chin. "I'll be fifteen next month."

"How do you know so much?" When I was her age, I didn't bother tracking anything other than ninth grade gossip.

She shrugged as she walked through the pantry and opened the door to the dining room. "I listen to Pa and read as much as I can get my hands on." She stopped beside the large central table and waved her hand toward it. "Nate bought all new furniture when the house was finished. Some of the rooms were empty for quite a while. This one was the first to be furnished, other than the kitchen."

"It's lovely." I ran my fingers over the intricate carving on the mahogany china cabinet. "Did Nate pick out the furniture?"

"He and Pa bought and made the stuff for the kitchen and water closet. Ma and Lera picked out the rest, as well as the paint colors and wall paper."

"What about you?"

"They didn't ask my opinion much. I spent more time watching the construction and the plumbing. That's more interesting." Lydia's eyes lit up.

I could relate. I admired beautiful rooms, but I would have no idea where to begin decorating one.

She led me toward the front of the house to a small parlor they called the sitting room. Since that was the space we'd occupied earlier, Lydia only pointed out the fireplace and the bay window. Apparently, the fireplace had the most modern flue they could get, making it the safest in the county. Good to know given the fire earlier.

We crossed the foyer to the main parlor which was the same size as the dining room and sitting room on the opposite side. De ja vu washed over me. The only thing missing from this room was an oval of twenty metal folding chairs. How was it possible that was less than a week ago?

I shivered, but Lydia had already started upstairs. Why tour the upstairs? I was intimately acquainted with the bathroom and our room, and the other bedrooms were occupied. The hallway upstairs was square, surrounding the staircase. At the top of the stairs, Lydia turned left and led me past our room and the water closet into the master bedroom.

As soon as we entered the dark space, she opened the wooden shutters on the nearest window, revealing a bare room with a lovely hardwood floor and butter yellow walls. "This room is the same size as the both the dining room and sitting room." Her face fell. "It's a shame not to use it."

I nodded. "Maybe he'll meet someone."

"We can hope." She opened a door on my right and led me into a large walk-in closet. "Have you ever seen anything like it?" She waved her arm at the racks on three walls. "Ma, Lera, and I could all hang our gowns and crinolines in there and still have room left over."

"Margaret must have had a lot of gowns." Todd's house had two closets that large, but I couldn't tell her.

We traveled down the hall past our room to the other side where Lera and Ed's rooms were. Lydia passed Ed's door, commenting that his room was similar to ours. The last door belonged to Lera and Caleb. We peeked in. It was larger than ours and had one double bed and a single.

"That's supposed to be the nursery." Lydia closed the door, then pointed to two narrower doors on the back wall. She turned the knob on the first one but it wouldn't budge. "Hmm, these are just storage rooms. I wonder why this one's locked."

Curious, I tried the next one. The door opened to a small space lined with near-empty shelves. A few sets of linens lay there but most of them had probably been used the night before. A broom stood in the corner.

"That's just the linen closet." Lydia closed the door. "The other closet used to be full of books. It has a trap door to the attic."

I pivoted toward a steep stairway behind me going up to another floor. "Isn't that the way up to the attic?"

"No." She smirked as she climbed the first step. "But I'll show you where it does go."

I followed her to the center of a medium sized chamber with slanted walls on the front. Much of it was empty but the front wall was lined with antique toys on either side of a window seat. I gulped. They weren't antiques to Lydia.

"These were all Nate's toys. His father saved them and Nate stored them up here until he has a child of his own." She crossed the bare wood floor, glanced out the window and whirled to face me. "Won't this be the best play room?"

I nodded, holding back tears. I turned away and pretended to inspect a horse figurine. For the first time, I truly grasped the connection between the man I was getting to know and the one I'd read about at the museum. Nathaniel Bridger never married. He'd left the house to the town because he didn't have any heirs. I'd always thought it was a sad story, but I had been detached from it, from Nate. I took it for granted it was the only way we would have the museum.

Now that I knew him, I didn't care so much whether the house would be left to the town. Nate's family was more important. Did it have to be that way? Did he have to remain a bachelor? I sighed. Yesterday, he told me he wasn't interested in getting married any more. That was his choice.

I sat on the window seat and gazed out at the front lawn, and dirt road through the fields, the trees in the distance. "Do you mind if I stay here a while? I like this view. It's peaceful."

"It is," Lydia said. "I'll go find Caleb. Lera can probably use a hand with him by now."

"Don't you ever rest?"

"Yes, you saw me before dinner." I could hear the smile in her voice.

Lydia was much more mature than any fourteen-year-old I'd ever met. Of course, I hadn't met any since I was in high school.

I waited for my tears to dry while looking out the window at the near perfect spring day. Caleb ran toward the house. Lera chased him, nearly catching him. Lydia should be able to find them easily. The two ran in and out of my view for quite a while. Where was Lydia? Ed approached Lera and held a short conversation. Then he waved at me, and I waved back.

I stood, planning to go downstairs and talk to Ed, but one of the toys caught my eye. It was a little tin jack-in-the-box. When I cranked the handle, an ugly clown face popped out. I gasped. Kids growing up in this time couldn't be wimps.

This room was one of the closed portions of the museum, but some of these toys were displayed in the room Lera and Caleb shared. I recognized a few wooden animals and a cart on wheels. There was a hobby horse in the corner. Too bad they'd never be played with again. Better not think about that right now.

I headed toward the stairs, but a door at the back of the room caught my attention. That must be the attic Lydia mentioned. I'd never seen a two-story storage room before. I tried the knob but it didn't budge. Must be something valuable in there. Was it locked because of me?

Turning toward the stairway, I jumped when I found myself face to face with Ed.

"Didn't mean to startle you, Miss." He lowered his head.

"It doesn't take much. I was just heading downstairs." I hesitated. This was a good time to ask my questions, but my mind went blank.

"Do you mind staying a few minutes?" Ed blocked the stairs. "I'd like a word with you."

"Sure." I backed up.

He walked over to the window seat and motioned for me to sit. I complied and he pulled a crate from the corner and perched on it.

"Nate tells me you're looking for Todd James." He didn't waste any time.

"Yes. Do you know anything about Todd?"

"I've met him."

"When!" I jumped, nearly bashing my head on the slanted ceiling.

"It was a while ago." He placed a hand on my shoulder guiding me to sit. "The only thing I can promise is that I'll keep an eye open for him."

"He was here?" I studied his face.

His dark eyes gleamed and his brow furrowed, but he appeared to focus his attention past me. Was he afraid to make eye contact? "The last time I saw Todd was in Atlanta." He glanced behind him.

"That makes sense, I guess. He works in Atlanta." I took a chance. "Do you know anything about Todd's inventions?" I leaned forward. "Did he tell you anything about how he got here? I mean, to Atlanta."

"Cassie, how did you get here?" Ed frowned. Now his eyes locked onto mine.

I straightened up. "You're working for Nate, aren't you?"

"Why?" He blinked. "Has he been asking you?"

I rolled my eyes. "Don't tell me you didn't know."

"The only thing he told me was that you were looking for Todd James." He ran his hand through his black hair.

I narrowed my eyes. "Why would Nate tell you I was looking for my boyfriend when you are supposed to think he and I are engaged?"

Ed grinned. "He didn't tell me Todd was your boyfriend."

"Oh." I slumped.

"I knew you weren't Margaret anyway." Ed snorted. "Oh,

Nate's attracted to you, but anyone with eyes can see that you two had never met before." He stood and turned away. "Cassie, what year were you born?"

"Nineteen eighty-two." My hands flew to my mouth.

"I knew it." Ed whirled around and stared down at me.

"Uh, no. Eighteen-eighty." What year was it again? "I mean eighteen forty-two."

"Nice try. So, you're twenty-eight. It must have been twenty-ten when you left, also?" He sat on the crate.

"Ha-ha." I slapped my thigh. "That's funny. No, I said the wrong year. My memory is spotty."

He kept eye contact. "Your memory is fine. It's just full of things that haven't happened yet."

I wanted to look away, but I kept my gaze on him hoping to see the truth in his expression. "How do you know that? Why would anyone here believe that? Why do you?"

He lowered his head.

"You're Todd's assistant!" I hopped up and paced around him. "Why didn't I recognize you? You recognized me, didn't you?"

He stood and faced me. "I wasn't his assistant. Just a friend. And I didn't know who you were until a moment ago when you said he was your boyfriend."

"But you were the one who was missing?" I squinted at him. That guy was younger than me. "You can't be William Garcia."

He nodded. "Been here for thirty years."

"Oh!" My hand flew to cover my mouth.

"William Edgar Garcia." He shrugged. "I didn't change it all that much."

I frowned. "Why didn't you tell me?"

He sat on the crate and exhaled. "I wasn't sure I could trust you."

I plopped onto the window seat. "I don't understand."

He pulled a handkerchief from his pocket and wiped his brow. "Before you showed up, I suspected there was another time-traveler."

I tilted my head. "Why?"

"All the thefts." He shifted his weight. "Common household items now, but in twenty-ten, antiques."

My jaw dropped. "You think someone was stealing things and taking them back to our time to sell as antiques?"

"More likely, hiding them and going back to dig them up." He slipped the handkerchief back into his pocket. "If they took them back, the items wouldn't pass authenticity tests."

"I get it." I swallowed. Could there be another of us? It didn't matter. "Ed, do you know how to get back?"

He shook his head. "Maybe the other time-traveler could help."

My breath caught. I leaned forward, pressing my hands into my thighs. "That's why I've been looking for Todd, hoping he'd come back after me."

He pursed his lips. "I think someone else came. Todd's not the kind to steal."

I straightened. "He stole the time machine. He moved it to his house when the company cut the funding."

He slapped his thigh. "That's how you ended up on Nate's property!"

He might have started to trust me, but then his face clouded.

I peered out the window. Lera, Caleb, and Nate played in the front yard. Where was Lydia?

"Cassie, did you ever go back to an earlier time?"

I whipped around to find him standing, staring down at me. I shook my head. "No."

"Why did you come here?"

"It was an accident!" I hopped up, balling my hands into fists at my sides. "Do you think I'm an idiot? I wouldn't time-travel on purpose with no way of getting back." I gritted my teeth so hard, my jaw started to ache. What a time for my TMJ to flare up. I rubbed my face. "I suppose there isn't any aspirin?"

He shook his head.

My head throbbed. I needed to get out of here. "That road in the front. You don't use it much. Does anyone?" I glanced out the window.

"Only when we go to Atlanta. It connects to the main road. That's why we put it in."

"I have another couple of hours before I need to help with supper, don't I?"

He nodded.

"Good. I'll be back." I started down the stairs but stopped mid-way. "You're not going to tell anyone are you? About me?"

He raised his eyebrows. "And let them think I'm crazy, too?"

"Good point." I hurried down to my room, dropped onto my hands and knees, and reached under the bed. My running clothes were right where I'd left them. I changed out of my dress and multiple layers of underclothes and donned the shorts and sports bra. After tying my shoelaces, I grabbed my robe to avoid parading through the house half naked. When I reached the road, I hung the robe over a fence post.

I stretched my calves. It had been a while, and they were tight. My whole body felt tight. I planned to run the mile to the main road and back and then walk halfway and back. If I felt like it, I might go farther.

As I ran, thoughts swirled through my brain. Ed was good. He'd gotten more information out of me than I had out of him. Also, he'd avoided telling me why he'd come. What was he hiding? Maybe I could find out something from Lera or Lydia. Where was Lydia? At least she wasn't here. I reveled in being alone on the road.

I ran faster, and the thoughts in my head settled a little. This was the first day in nearly a week that I'd been alone longer than it took to use the necessary, and the first time I'd been running. The wind whipped through my short curls and the sun kissed my temples. Endorphins kicked in, and I ran faster. Too bad I didn't have a stopwatch. This could be my best mile ever, beating my nine-minute average. Maybe not. Time may seem to go faster because I was alone. What was time, anyway?

I made it to the main road without seeing anyone, turned around, and raced back. I ran the second mile just as fast and felt so good, I planned to continue back to the main road. When the house came into view, either Nate or Ed, I couldn't tell which, walked toward the road. I jogged the opposite direction.

Before long, footsteps sounded behind me. I picked up my pace. I had the better shoes, but he hadn't already run two miles. I kept my gait as steady as possible. If he caught up with me, I'd feign ignorance and make him think this was part of my workout. He would catch me eventually because I'd have to head back. So why was he still running?

"Cassie!" Nate closed in on me.

Was he afraid I wasn't coming back? I didn't have any place else to go.

I pretended not to hear him, continuing toward the intersection about a hundred yards away.

Nate pulled up next to me. "Where you going?"

"Just out running. Needed the fresh air." I nodded at the crossroad. "I'm turning around up there." I sprinted to the end of the road, then turned back and slowed to a jog.

He fell into step with me. Neither of us spoke until we made it a quarter of the way back and slowed to a walk.

I huffed. "I ran over three miles. I guess I should walk the rest of the way."

He stared straight ahead instead of right at me, though he'd glanced in my direction a few times, always with a scowl. At least he hadn't yelled at me.

"I needed that." I shook my arms. "I've been feeling cooped

up. My muscles are all tight."

"Aren't they going to get tighter?"

"When I get back, I'll stretch." I should have brought a towel to wipe off all the sweat.

As if he read my mind, Nate produced a clean handkerchief and handed it to me.

"Thanks." I took it and patted my forehead and the nape of my neck.

About three quarters of the way back, I looked to my right, remembering where Todd's house had been or would be. Led by intuition, I veered off the road. Maybe, in this field, there was proof. Part of the machine could still be there, hidden in the tall grass. Who knew what good that would do me? Still, I couldn't keep myself from looking.

"Cassie, where are you going?" Nate sounded annoyed.

"This is where I landed the other day," I said, as if he should have known.

"So?"

"Maybe there are clues." I bent at the waist and scanned the field. "I hadn't thought to look around."

"Don't you think you should change first and come back later."

"It'll be dark soon. This won't take long." I knelt and searched the grass with my hands.

Nate stood behind me and cleared his throat.

"My robe is on the fence post at the end of the road."

Nate took off before I finished the sentence. Seconds later, he helped me into my robe, his head turned away from me.

I hid my smile as I continued my search. Grass rustled ahead of me, and I looked up, almost bumping heads with Nate. We crawled around on all fours for several minutes.

"What are we looking for?"

"I don't know." I shrugged. "Something that doesn't belong here."

"Something like this?" He held a silver-colored screw with a jagged edge.

I took it, lifted my robe, and matched it up against the scrape on my right leg. It was healing but not so fast that I wouldn't be able to tell if it matched the screw. Except that I couldn't see it because it was on the outside of my thigh.

Without thinking, I opened my robe. "Nate, can you tell if this screw could have done this?"

He glanced around, either looking for someone who could take his place, or making sure no one was watching. Then he took the screw and placed it against the scrape. "Ouch. That must have hurt."

"I've had worse," I said. "So could the screw have made it?"

"Looks like it." He let the robe fall back over my leg. "So where did this come from?"

I thought fast. "It must have fallen off of whatever vehicle dropped me."

He scratched his head. "This is pretty far off the road."

I shrugged. "Where did you find it?"

He pointed about two feet to my left and I moved to search the area more thoroughly. He continued hunting a few paces away until the sun went down far enough that we couldn't see.

"I don't think we're going to find anything else." Nate reached his hand down toward me.

I let him help me up. "Thanks for the assistance." We strolled back to the house. "Lera said we only take baths once a week, but do you mind if I shower before supper?"

"Go right ahead." Nate handed me the screw.

I trotted into the house and upstairs to my room. It would be better to stretch there. Feeling relieved to find the room empty, I deposited the screw in one of my drawers, pulled off the robe, leaned against the bed post, and stretched my calves. When the door opened, I jumped. I must have been deep in thought because I should have heard Lydia's footsteps.

She looked just as startled as I was, even a little guilty as she hid her hands behind her back. Maybe she did act like a fourteen-year-old after all.

"Oh, you're busy. I'll come back later." She backed up.

"Don't be silly. This is your room, too." I held onto the bedpost and continued stretching, craning my neck to see what she held behind her.

She stood facing me, whether it was to keep me from seeing the object or because she was curious about me, I'm not sure.

"What are you doing?" Her head tilted to one side.

I kept an eye on her. "Stretching. I've been out running."

"In that?" She pointed at me. The book she'd held dropped to the floor.

"Yes. Where have you been?"

"Here." She picked up the book and plopped on the bed, shoving the thin volume under her. "Did anyone see you?"

"Just Nate." I grabbed my ankle to stretch my thigh behind me.

"It's a good thing Ma didn't." She examined my shoes and bra a little closer. "You would have been marching down the aisle this evening, wedding clothes or not."

My face heated. "So, how was Caleb this afternoon?"

She shrugged one shoulder. "He's Caleb, same as always."

She wasn't going to own up to her deception easily. I pointed to the book she half sat on. "What's that?"

"Oh, it's only a book I found in the sitting room."

"Can I see it?"

"It's not all that interesting." She placed her hand on the edge of it. "It's my family's history. It stops with my mother's generation."

I stepped toward the door. "Okay, I'm going to take a shower."

She stood. "Wait, you took a bath yesterday."

"So? I just went running. I need another one."

"But—"

"Nate told me I could." I waited a beat and when she didn't say anything, I exited the room, grabbed a towel from the linen closet, and entered the bathroom. I wished I could shave my legs, but the only razor I'd seen was a straight razor. It would be safer to let it grow.

While I showered, I couldn't help wondering where Lydia had been. Why did she tell me she was going to find Caleb if she only planned to get a book from the sitting room? It was the only bookcase I remembered, but she'd also said there were books in the locked closet.

I shook those thoughts out of my head. It wasn't any of my business. I dried off as thoroughly as I could in the steaming room, put on my robe and peeked out the door. The coast was clear and I hurried to my room without incident. Lydia was gone. Yay for privacy.

As soon as I'd dressed, I went downstairs looking for Lydia, planning to apologize for my curiosity about the book. She wasn't in the sitting room or the dining room, so I left the main house enroute to the kitchen.

Nate exited the barn and strode toward me. "Cassie, I won't be here for supper. I'm going to spend some time with Mattie."

I headed his direction. "Okay, tell her I hope Mark will be feeling better soon."

"Thanks. What Aunt Mattie really wants is prayer." He stopped as I approached him and put his hand on my shoulder. "Have you thought about what Mrs. Kelley said yesterday?"

I hesitated, trying to gather my thoughts on all that scripture she'd thrown at me.

Nate dropped his hand to his side. "I'm sorry. I didn't mean to push."

"You didn't." I peered at him. "I've been thinking about a lot of things. I'm confused."

"If you have any questions, you can ask me. I'm sure the others wouldn't mind either." A smile grew on his lips. "Of course, depending on who you ask, you might get more confused."

I raised my eyebrows. "Lera?"

He snapped his fingers and pointed at me as if to say, "Bingo." He stepped back. "I probably shouldn't have offered now though. I won't see you much this week. Maybe at supper."

"Aren't you coming in for dinner?" So far, he and Ed had always come in for the mid-day meal.

"No, we'll pack something to take with us." He shifted his hat from one hand to the other. "We don't want to waste time. We're trying to get three fields done this week."

I nodded, but I had no idea how big the fields were or how many they had.

"I'd better get going." He took another step and donned his hat. "I want to get back, so I can get to sleep early."

"Oh, yeah. I'm sorry I delayed you."

"Don't be." He tipped his hat toward me.

I couldn't help but smile.

Supper that night was simple and short. It seemed everyone had one thing in mind: getting to bed early. I went up to the room with Lydia and got ready, but felt too wired to sleep. Not wanting to keep Lydia awake, I went down to the sitting room. On my way out the door, I picked up the Bible Nate had given me. At least, I could entertain some of the ideas the pastor's wife had mentioned. It might even make me sleepy.

I lit one of the gas lamps in the sitting room and sat in the closest chair. Wishing for electric light, I started where I'd left off the previous evening in Genesis. It wasn't long before I started flipping pages and reading pieces here and there, finally opening to the page that read 'New Testament.' I vaguely recalled hearing something about how it was more relevant.

I started reading Mathew, but after a few verses, skipped to chapter two. I didn't understand everything, but I kept reading, getting more revved up than sleepy. Some of Jesus' teachings seemed hard, but I never questioned his authority. Somehow, I knew this book was true, and Jesus was real. Now, if I could only figure out what to do about it.

In chapter seven a few verses jumped out at me. "Ask, and it shall be given you; seek, and ye shall find; knock, and it shall be opened unto you: For every one that asketh receiveth; and he that seeketh findeth; and to him that knocketh it shall be opened."

I closed the Bible over my finger and laid it in my lap. "Okay, Lord, I'm taking you at your word. I'm asking. Please help me get home."

"Cassie?" Nate padded from the dining room toward me, evidently having just gotten home from Mattie's.

My eyes went wide. "What are you doing up so late?"

He knelt beside my chair. No, it was more like he sank. His eyes were dull, weary, his brow furrowed and his mouth was set in a straight line.

"Is it Mark?"

"Both."

My hand flew to my chest. "Oh, no, Mattie's sick now?"

"No, just tired. I think she's a little lonely, too, but she won't admit it." He snapped his head toward me. "And don't even try to go down there."

"I know." I peered at him. "So how bad is it?"

"His fever is pretty high. That's why Aunt Mattie's so worried. She thought he had a few days before it would get this bad."

I closed my Bible. "Well, let me know if there's anything I can do."

"Pray."

"Yeah, well, I'm not very good at that." I stood, tucking my Bible under my arm. "I think it's about time for bed."

"You're right. I have to get up early tomorrow." He rose to his feet and extinguished the gas lamp. "I'll be right behind you." He held his lantern to the side allowing me to see.

"Thanks." I walked toward the stairs.

"Keep reading, Cassie," he said softly in my ear.

As I climbed the stairs, looking straight ahead, feeling Nate's presence behind me, I clutched the Bible tighter.

Chapter 13

Lydia whipped my blanket off and pulled my arm. "Come on, Cassie, we need your help this morning."

"What?" I squinted at her as I grabbed the blanket and curled it toward my chin. "We have to start the wash before sunup?"

"We'll do that later." She wrestled the blanket from me. "We have to get breakfast for everyone. Nate will take some to Mattie. And we'll put up something for their dinner."

I struggled to sit up. "Okay, but why couldn't we do the dinner thing yesterday?"

"Because yesterday was Sunday." She rolled her eyes, dropped my underclothes on the bed, and stood next to the door tapping her foot.

I still didn't understand, but I dragged myself out of bed

and let Lydia help me with my corset.

"I'll leave you to finish dressing." Lydia hurried into the hallway.

My favorite gray dress was in the wash, so I donned the new one.

Though I'd heard more noise than usual, I was unprepared for what I saw when I arrived downstairs. I rushed through the dining room, which was full of men, most of whom I'd never seen before. When I entered the kitchen, Lera had their breakfast ready.

Lydia and I carried it in and set the trays on the sideboard, then Lydia pulled me out of the way. We watched as the group descended on the food and devoured it.

Nate had hired a motley crew. Some of them looked like they'd been working non-stop their whole lives, and some seemed to have never done a day's work. One or two looked like children, but they all had adult appetites. Of course, none even remotely resembled Todd.

We brought in so much food I wondered how economical it was to hire these guys. That was Nate's problem. With any luck, I would be long gone by the harvest when I assumed he'd need them again.

While the hired-hands ate, Lydia, Lera, and I packed food for Mattie and a huge dinner of bread, fried chicken, cold potatoes, and corn bread. None of this food had been made yesterday.

"Lera, what time did you get up this morning?"

"Four." She placed a loaf of bread wrapped in cloth in the already full basket, set it aside, and started another.

"Why didn't you get me up to help you?" I wrapped a hunk of pork in a linen towel.

"Nate asked us not to. He said you were up late last night."

"So was he." I glanced at her. "He was up at four?"

"Don't worry about him. He'll be fine." Lera wiped her

brow with the back of her wrist.

I wasn't worried, but Lera probably heard what she expected.

After the men left, we sat at the worktable in the kitchen and ate what little there was left.

After gobbling my eggs and bread, I took a sip of strong tea. "Are we going to need to go into town for supplies?"

Lera popped the last small piece of biscuit in her mouth, chewed, and swallowed. "We've got enough for the week in the cellar."

I cocked my head. "Are we feeding the masses every morning this week?"

Lydia and Lera both nodded and, in unison, picked up their empty plates and took them to the sink.

"Does everyone who hires workers feed them?" I followed them with my plate.

Lydia picked up some cups and utensils from the worktable. "No, but we have as long as I can remember."

"Your pa started it." Lera leaned against the sink. "I remember when I was about Caleb's age, I used to—" She stopped abruptly and hustled us through our morning chores. We cleaned up the kitchen and dining room, then rounded up clothes to wash.

Despite the washing machine, if you could call it that, I don't think I've ever worked so hard in all my life. We boiled water, poured the large pots into the washtubs, soaked clothes, and rubbed them with harsh soap. And that was before we rinsed them and cranked them through the wringer. When we carried the heavy clothes outside and hung them on the clotheslines, I envied Lera. She didn't have to stretch quite as far as Lydia and I did to reach.

By noon, I felt more wrung out than the wash. My hands were already red and sore. I trudged into the kitchen and plopped in a chair. Lydia and Lera found food and placed it on the table, but I was too tired to even look at it.

"You'd better eat something, Cassie," Lera said. "The day's only half over."

I couldn't muster the strength to eat and talk, so I pulled a chicken leg out of the bowl, and gnawed on it, aware that Lera and Lydia were chatting. It took me a while to tune into their conversation.

"Your pa was a little odd when he first came here," Lera said. "So?"

"I don't know." Lydia waved her fork. "It got me thinking. He never talks about his past."

"Of course, he does. He talks about you, Mark, and Sarah when you were little all the time." Lera lowered her head. "He even talks about John."

Lydia rolled her eyes. "I mean he doesn't talk about anything before here. He says he came from Atlanta but nothing before that." She lowered her voice. "He doesn't have any family."

My skin prickled. "What brought this up?"

Lydia turned toward me. "Anna Dennis told me that everyone is comparing you with Pa, remembering how odd he was when he first came here."

"Odd? They think I'm odd?" I sat up straighter. Better to focus their attention on myself than Ed.

Lera reached across the table and patted my hand. "It's only that you have different habits. Your hair and refusing to wear crinolines."

I bent down, and looked at their dresses under the table. "I don't see you two wearing them today."

"You have a point." Lera cleared her throat. "But we wouldn't be seen in public without them."

"I don't know. The dining room was public this morning," I said, unable to resist.

"That's why I stayed in the kitchen." Lera stood and cleared the table, signaling the end of the conversation.

I remained seated as long as possible. When they both stared at me on their way out to the washroom, I hauled myself off the chair. I longed for a hot soak but Lera and Lydia wouldn't stand for me bathing three days in a row.

After checking the laundry out on the line, Lera announced that we needed to do some baking in preparation for supper that night and dinner the next day. They left me to fold the few linens and undergarments that were already dry. I'd done fairly well with the washing machine, so they probably thought it was safe to leave me alone in the laundry room. I was relieved not to be left alone in the kitchen. I was afraid of the oven. It wasn't only the food I feared I'd burn.

It was nice to finally have a bit of time to myself, even if I was still working. At least I could let my mind drift. I didn't mind manual labor, but I wasn't used to this much. I couldn't wait to get back and tell my friends how hard life had been for our ancestors and how good we had it. They probably wouldn't believe me, though, unless they experienced it for themselves.

I finished folding the last shirt and delivered the clothes and linens to the appropriate rooms, then returned to the kitchen. The house seemed unusually quiet.

I leaned on the doorframe. "Where's Caleb?"

"He's with Pa." Lydia continued to roll out a pie crust. "He's been wanting to go every year. This time Pa finally said yes."

"I hope he don't get in the way." Lera blew a strand of hair out of her face as she muscled a wooden spoon in a large metal bowl.

"He won't. Pa knows what to do with him." Lydia glanced over at Lera. "He used to take Mark and John when they were eight."

"I'm sorry." I stepped toward Lera. "I just remembered you had asked me to tutor Caleb."

"I did, didn't I?" Lera dumped out the contents of her bowl and began kneading dough. "I'd forgotten he was going to work today." A corner of her mouth turned up. "I still want you to teach him. He might even be here tomorrow."

Lydia transferred the pie crust to a pan. "I think Caleb will want to go back out the rest of the week."

"I'm sure he will." Lera folded the dough over. "But, will Ed want him?" She peered at me. "Cassie, how is the wash coming?"

"It's done." I followed Lera's gaze and shuffled to the sink to start washing dishes.

It was past sundown when the men came home. We already had supper on the table. Nate looked tired, but not quite as grim as the night before. During supper, I caught him studying me. Did I look worse? When he got up from the table, he picked up his plate and headed for the kitchen.

"Leave that and go to bed," Lera said.

Nate turned around, still holding his plate. "I need to go check on Aunt Mattie and Mark."

Ed stepped toward Nate. "I'm sure they're all right. You need your sleep."

"I'll be fine." Nate set his plate down and left out the back door.

"He can't go by himself." Lera stood. "He'll fall asleep." She helped me out of my chair and pulled me by the arm out back. We caught up with Nate at the barn.

"Take Cassie with you, Nate." Lera stepped behind me. "You'll need the company to keep you awake."

"She'll fall asleep before I will." Nate stopped, one hand on the barn door.

"It'll keep you from staying too long. Mattie won't let her in." She let go of my arm.

"Can't argue with you, there." Nate slid the doors apart. "Come on, Cassie."

I didn't even get a say in it? But without enough energy to argue, I followed Nate into the barn. Instead of hitching a mule to the wagon, he saddled a large white horse. "Cassie, this is Mr. Ed."

I snorted. "Ed named him, didn't he?" As soon as it left my mouth, I wished I could take it back.

"How'd you know?" He narrowed his eyes, as he led Mr. Ed out into the yard.

I winced. Think fast, Cassie. "Uh. Naming the horse after himself?" That was lame.

He shook his head. "I'm not sure why, but he thought it was hilarious."

I kept my mouth shut as Nate mounted and helped me up behind him.

Glad my skirt was large enough for me to ride astride, I held onto Nate for dear life. I'd never be able to ride sidesaddle. Thankfully, the horse walked most of the way. After the initial fear subsided, I leaned against Nate and relaxed enough to almost fall asleep.

When we reached Mattie's, Nate dismounted and took a package out of the saddle bag. "Wait here. I'll be just a minute."

"Uh, no. I think I need to wait there." I pointed to the ground.

Nate chuckled and helped me down. He tied Mr. Ed to the porch rail, and I sat on the step. I gazed at the clear sky and tried to remember the last time I'd seen so many stars. Probably not ever at Todd's. Too much light from the city.

What had I been doing last Monday? That is, the last Monday I was home, which would have been more than a week ago. I had worked late and gotten home after Todd for once. He was in his lab, and we didn't talk much. I'd been upset that whole last week. When I made it home, things were going to be a lot different.

"Hi, Cassie," Mattie said.

I stood and twirled around. "How's Mark?"

Mattie stood in the doorway, her expression somber. "About the same." Her eyes nearly closed. "Keep praying."

I nodded, but I couldn't tell her I would.

Nate gave her a quick hug, and dipped his head toward me as he crossed the porch. He mounted Mr. Ed, pulled me up behind him, and signaled the horse to walk.

I leaned in. "How's Mattie?"

"Strong. She'll make it."

"I wish I could pray." Did I say that?

"You will." He sounded a little too certain for my taste.

The next thing I knew, Nate lifted me off the horse. "We're here."

"I'm sorry." I rubbed my eyes. "I was supposed to keep you awake."

He winked. "Mr. Ed knows the way."

I watched while he unsaddled, and brushed Mr. Ed, then led him back to his stall. Why didn't I go to my room? We didn't talk and I wasn't any help with the horse. Nate took my arm and led me into the house and up the stairs. We both said, "Good night," as we opened our room doors then stepped inside. I undressed in the dark, left my clothes on the floor, and rolled into bed. I think I was asleep before my head hit the pillow.

I slept the sleep of the dead and the next morning, I wished I was. Every muscle in my body ached. I wanted to stay in bed, but I knew the best thing to do for muscle pain was to keep moving. Not to mention the fact that I didn't have a choice. Lera kept me busy that day and the rest of the week.

We cooked and baked, spun, wove, and sewed. Well, I didn't do all of that, but I either helped or tried to learn. We dusted, beat rugs, swept floors, washed dishes, gathered eggs, and made butter. That last chore is misleading. It sounds simple.

I'd never thought about where butter came from or how much work went into it. We started by milking the cow. That was a feat in itself, but the worst part was after the cream was separated into the churn. It took hours of pumping the handle and my muscles were still sore from wash day. Any spare minute I had, I spent looking for anything that could be part of the time machine. I made excuses to go to the barn and the carriage house but never had enough time to search properly.

On Thursday, Caleb had finally had enough of planting and stayed home. Either that, or Ed and Nate had had enough of him. I helped Lydia and Lera in the kitchen during the morning, but in the afternoon, I gave Caleb his first lesson.

Thinking it would give my sore muscles a break, I looked forward to it. Silly me. They didn't have any text books, so I used a few of the books from the sitting room. I had asked Lera how far he'd gotten in school. After she'd answered first grade, I realized I didn't remember what skill level that was, and it might not be the same now as when I was in school.

I'd start by assessing his reading skill. The easiest book I could find was The Last of the Mohicans. I'd never read it, but I'd seen the movie. I tried to get Caleb interested by describing a few of the scenes.

Caleb scowled. "If you know the story, why do you want me to read it to you?"

"Because I want to see how much you can read." I placed my finger under the first word. It didn't take me long to figure out why he was reluctant. He was able to read three words out of the first paragraph. Undaunted, I asked him to continue. It took forever to get through the first page and I had to tell him most of the words.

"How about I read to you and you follow along?"

He slumped.

"Hasn't anyone ever read to you?"

He shook his head slowly, then stopped, his eyes wide. "Gramps used to once in a while."

I squinted. "Your mom never read to you when you were

little?"

"No, Ma'am." He lowered his head.

As much as Lera doted on him, it seemed strange to me that she'd never read to him. But had I ever seen her read anything?

Putting that worry at the back of my mind, I read the first chapter to him and tried to get him to follow along. It was a shame he didn't seem interested in books. Reading had been one of my favorite pastimes, but that had been in high school. When was the last time I'd read for pleasure?

That didn't work. It was time to try something else. I asked him to count for me. He scrunched his face and hesitated. At first, I thought it was for the same reason he didn't want to read. When he finally complied, he counted to a hundred by ones, faster than I would have. Then, he counted by twos, fives, and he threw in threes for good measure.

"Okay, hot shot." I smiled.

He cocked his head.

"Let's see how good you are at arithmetic. What is thirty-four plus twenty-five?"

"Fifty-nine." No hesitation.

"I'm impressed." I followed that with several harder addition and subtraction questions and he got them all right. He got most of the multiplication questions right also, but he wasn't as good at division. That was fine. I was pretty sure division was higher than first grade level. Multiplication, too.

When I pulled out the slate, our lesson went downhill fast. It seemed Caleb was a whiz with numbers as long as they were in his head. He couldn't recognize the written versions.

At least I knew where he stood. Caleb needed to learn to read and write, and I would have to start from the beginning. Because he had a natural affinity for numbers, I'd start there.

By the end of the afternoon, Caleb could write the numbers one through five. I felt like I'd accomplished something.

"Good job." I erased the slate.

He beamed up at me.

"Now, Caleb." I set down the slate and stood. "We'll come back to arithmetic tomorrow, but only after we've worked on reading and writing."

His face fell, and he seemed to wilt.

How to fix this? "I'm sorry, Caleb, but you need to learn how to read. I'll try to think of a way to make it more fun, like math." I didn't have the foggiest idea how I was going to do that, but he smiled, sort of.

While I washed dishes after supper, the light bulb went on in my head. Alone in the kitchen, I'd been letting my mind wander. Instead of thinking about the time machine, I'd drifted back to my own schooling and hit on the perfect solution to my tutoring issue. It was brilliant, something most kids hate but I had liked, and Caleb would love. I set my mind to work, thinking of word problems that I could write out for him to read. I'd tell him it was math.

"You must have had a good day," Nate said.

I jumped and whirled around to see him standing just inside the kitchen, leaning on the door jamb. "How long have you been there?"

"Just long enough to see you smile." He stepped closer. "That's a rare occasion. Mind if I ask why?"

"You can ask anything you like. It doesn't mean you'll get an answer." I snapped a towel in his direction and hung it on a peg.

He stepped back and chuckled. "Well, then. Would you like to ride down to Mattie's with me tonight?"

I sauntered closer to him. "This would make four in a row. People might talk."

"Oh, go with him." Lera barged in from the wash room. "Stop puttin' on airs."

At first, I thought she was joking but the stern expression on her face indicated otherwise. I flashed Nate a look that said,

"What's her problem?" as I joined him.

He shrugged and held his elbow out for me. "So, what were you smiling about?"

I linked arms and strolled toward Mr. Ed, already saddled, and tied to a hitching post near the barn. "Oh, I figured out how I'm going to teach Caleb to read." Still nervous around the large animal, I tried to concentrate on the conversation and not the impending ride.

Nate mounted Mr. Ed and reached toward me. "How?"

I peered up at him. "Did you know Caleb was really good at arithmetic?"

"I knew he could count." Nate pulled me up behind him.

I was still none too graceful. Now if I could have worn pants, it might have been different. "He can add and subtract two and three-digit numbers, but only in his head."

"Really?" Nate nudged Mr. Ed to a walk.

"Yeah, he can't read though, not even numbers, but that's how I'm going to teach him. Word problems. Now, all I have to do is write some. Do you want to help?"

"No, thanks. I hated those." He laughed, and I stuck my tongue out at him. Too bad he couldn't see me.

When we got to Mattie's, I waited on the step as I had all week, savoring the few minutes to just sit and be alone.

Nate came out, and Mattie waved from the door again.

"How is he?" I called.

"His fever is down a little, and the spots have come out. He's miserable, but he'll live." She smiled and this time it reached her eyes.

I stood and waved. "Say hi for us, and tell him not to scratch."

"Do you want to walk a bit?" Nate asked.

"That would be good for me. I'm still a little sore."

We strolled toward Nate's, Mr. Ed in tow.

"Have you done any more reading?" Nate glanced at me.

"We didn't do much at all today because Caleb and I were both so frustrated—" I stopped when Nate placed his hands in a T shape. He must have picked up the time-out signal from Ed.

"No, I meant in the Bible."

"Oh. I haven't had much of a chance. I think I read a little the night before last, but I'm not sure much sank in. I'm not used to the language."

He furrowed his brow. "It's in English."

"I meant the writing style. It's a bit formal."

He nodded. "Well, if you have any questions. . ."

"I don't know what to ask, yet." I glanced up at him and felt relieved to see him gaze straight ahead, not watching the confused expression on my face. "So, the week's almost over. Are you going to have to work on Saturday?"

"Looks like it." He pushed a tree branch out of the way. "Maybe only half the day. We'll have more to do next week, but we should be able to get it all done about mid-week."

"Then what?" A breeze caught my skirt and it fluttered around my legs.

"Then we'll have other work to do. We'll put in a garden a little later, but Mattie and Lera will do most of that." He glanced at me, showing his tired eyes in the twilight. "There's always something, but it won't be quite as long hours. That is until fall."

"Harvest?" I tilted my head toward him.

"Yep, but that's a good thing. At least it has been since I've been farming."

I furrowed my brow. "What do you mean?"

"My pa told me we haven't had a bad harvest since Ed got here. Most of the other farmers think I'm due one." He grinned.

"You don't seem worried."

"Don't hold to superstition." He lifted his chin. "Besides, we've had so many good years we could handle one bad one."

"Not if you let Lera spend your money." I showed him my cheesy grin.

He raised his eyebrows. "I've only done that where you're concerned."

I slapped him on the shoulder. "Now you're accusing me of spending too much money?"

He stepped back, grimaced, and rubbed his shoulder.

I bit my lip. "I didn't mean to hit you hard."

He glared at me for a few seconds. I expected him to chastise me, but it was still just light enough that I could see a smile slowly build from his lips to the twinkle in his eye. "Scared ya, didn't I?"

"All right." I smacked his shoulder again, harder this time.

He held up his palms. "Truce."

I narrowed my eyes at him for a few seconds. "Okay. Truce."

He smiled and held his hand out for me to grasp.

When was the last time I'd held hands with anyone? I didn't pass up the opportunity. We strolled in silence. His warmth flowed from my fingers throughout my body. When we entered the barn, he dropped my hand to unsaddle and get Mr. Ed back in his stall. I shivered. Not due to physical cold, but a realization that I had dropped my guard with Nate. I still didn't know if I could trust him, especially if he found out where I came from and decided I was crazy.

Still, I waited for him and we entered the house via the back door. As we scraped dirt off our shoes, Lera and Lydia's excited voices emanated from the next room. I opened the dining room door and peered in. Lera bustled from one end of the room to the other, into the sitting room and back again, pointing as she talked and waving a towel around as she pointed. Lydia followed, taking notes on Caleb's slate.

As soon as we entered, Lera marched toward us. "There you are. I'm sorry I didn't get your blessing, but Ed told me it would be all right. The messenger was waiting so I told him yes and sent him on his way." She took a breath and headed back into the small parlor.

Nate tagged along after her. "My blessing for what?" He touched her arm and she stopped.

"Oh, Mr. Highland sent a messenger with his calling card." Lera turned and waved her hand toward an envelope on the end table. "He asked if it would be possible to call on me on Saturday afternoon. I sent back an invitation to tea. I hope that's all right."

With all the extra work, I hoped he'd say no, but there'd be no living with Lera if he did.

Nate rubbed his chin with his thumb and index finger.

Lera twisted a towel, and shifted from foot to foot. "I know I've only been out of mourning for a few days, but he's only coming to tea."

Nate let her squirm for a few more seconds. Then he winked. "It's fine with me."

"You're in a mood tonight." Lera slapped him lightly with her towel. "You could have just said yes in the first place." She continued muttering as she hurried through the foyer into the large parlor.

"That must have been the problem earlier." I leaned toward Nate and whispered. "She was expecting the card, and it was late."

Nate grinned and nodded. "You might want to go to bed, soon. It looks like you're going to be busy tomorrow."

"It's your house. You could tell her she doesn't need to redecorate." I sat in the chair by the fireplace.

"I'm inclined to let her do whatever she needs to in order to land Mr. Highland." He crossed in front of me and sat in the chair closer to the window.

"I'm in," I said. A long term, constant dose of Lera might be a little much. I would be leaving, but Nate wouldn't, and he'd be stuck with Lera until she re-married.

Nate cocked his head.

What did I say this time? I needed to think before I spoke, especially around Nate.

~

The next day started early and ended late with way too much work in between. After feeding the workers, we moved furniture and cleaned everything in sight. And we did it to the cadence of a drill sergeant. Lera kept me moving faster than I do when I run. At least I burned a lot of calories.

After an early dinner, Lera and Lydia brought several dresses in various stages of completion into the sitting room.

"Where'd you get those?" I nodded toward the multi-colored garments in their arms.

"Nate brought them from Mattie's." Lera draped two dresses over the sofa. "I've been working on them in my spare time. Now, I need to get one finished by tomorrow."

"Tomorrow?" I gasped. "There's not enough time."

"We have a sewing machine." Lera seemed unconcerned. She and Lydia continued to unpack the dresses and inspect each one.

Why had she been working on more than one at a time? No way would I ask her.

Lera held up a gorgeous pale-yellow gown. It looked beautiful against her olive complexion and dark brown hair.

"That one." I rushed over to her. "It's stunning."

"It still needs a lot of work," Lydia said.

"That color is so perfect for you." I touched the silky fabric. "You'll get it done. I'll help."

"Thank you, Cassie." Lera's face lit up.

~

Lera looked radiant the next afternoon when she was ready for tea with Mr. Highland a whole hour early. She paced and twisted a towel, putting it down temporarily to position tea cups just perfectly and fuss with the table cloth on the cart and the doilies on the end tables. She'd debated using the more formal parlor, but in the end, she'd decided the sitting room didn't seem as presumptuous.

"Lera, why don't you just sit and relax. Read a book or something." Exhausted, that's all I wanted to do.

"That's a good idea." Lydia entered from the dining room. "I think I'm going to rest a while." She hurried toward the stairs.

"Me, too." I followed her. Luckily, Lera was either too preoccupied or nervous to notice. She'd kept us busy since Thursday evening. Yesterday, I'd managed to squeeze in an hour of tutoring Caleb, but the rest of the day Lera filled with preparations for the tea. We'd still been working when Nate and Ed got home, and they'd had to wait for supper. Nate had visited Mattie while he waited. My annoyance at not being able to go with him, surprised me.

Lydia and I entered our room and collapsed onto the bed.

"I hope this works quickly, because I can't go through much more of it." I propped my head up with one hand, elbow resting on the pillow.

Lydia lifted herself up on both forearms and narrowed her eyes at me. "You know what's going on?"

"Yeah, she's trying to reel in her man, isn't she?"

"Sure, but I didn't think you'd know." She sat up and leaned against the head board, staring at the ceiling.

"Why wouldn't I?" I sat up, hands on my hips.

"No reason." She studied the ruffle on her skirt.

I sighed. "Nate told me."

"Aha, I was right." She peered at me. "You don't do things like that where you come from, do you?"

I leaned forward into a stretch. "You mean, try to act better than we are to impress someone?" I sat up. "Of course, we do. At least some of us do."

She narrowed her eyes. "But you don't?"

"I wouldn't go to all this trouble." A memory popped into my mind. "Well, once, I liked this guy at work and I made sure that he got notice of an award I earned." I leaned into a side stretch. "I hacked into my boss's email account and added Todd's address to the group list."

Lydia leapt off the bed.

I gasped and sat up straight. "I mean, I made sure his address was on the list the secretary used. The boss wouldn't realize." I must have looked like a deer caught in the headlights.

"You worked?" Her eyes were wide and her voice sounded breathy. "Where?"

I blinked. "Atlanta."

She bent toward me. "What did you do?"

"Oh, just office work." I leaned back, resting my weight on my hands, hoping my nonchalance would distract her from my earlier flub.

"What's email?" She cocked her head.

"What?" I waved my hand in front of my face. "Oh, I must have been talking too fast. I'm sure I said the mail." Had she bought it?

She relaxed her posture, but didn't change her thoughtful expression. "How long did you work?"

"Several years."

"So why don't you go back there?" She took a step toward the window.

"It's not that simple. I don't have the money." I hauled myself off the bed and walked past her to the window hoping to see Simon's carriage out front, but all was quiet.

"Nate would give it to you." She stood next to me. "Unless...you're starting to like him, aren't you?"

"What?" Was I starting to like Nate? I looked away, afraid my expression would give away how I was feeling. I didn't want Lydia to know before I did.

"You've been spending a lot of time together. What do you talk about when you take your rides to Ma's?"

"I don't know, just stuff." I faced her and crossed my arms

over my chest. "And if I could go home right now, I wouldn't hesitate."

She nodded knowingly, which in a fourteen-year-old was quite irritating.

I pushed past her and flopped back onto the bed. We stayed silent, and I had nearly dozed off when carriage wheels sounded on the gravel at the front of the house. I groaned.

"You'd better go." Lydia nudged me. "She wanted you to answer the door, like we rehearsed."

I pushed myself off the bed wishing I could trade places with Lydia for the afternoon. She was able to lay low, but I was supposed to help serve. Caleb had been sent out with the men. I wasn't sure when they were getting back, but I wouldn't put it past Nate to show up during the tea.

That thought propelled me down the stairs. I envisioned the irritated expression on Lera's face when Nate, Ed, and Caleb barged in on her tea party. By the time I got downstairs, I probably wore a goofy smile. I opened the door to an older, rounder, and shorter gentleman than I expected. He stood next to Jenny, his niece whom we'd met in town. Mr. Highland still had a full head of graying brown hair and a handsome face.

He tipped his hat. "Miss Cassie, I presume. I'm Simon Highland. Lovely to make your acquaintance."

I opened the door wider and led them in. "Likewise." We entered the sitting room where Lera was waiting.

"My dear, what a vision you are." Highland took her hand in his and held it for a second before he kissed it.

"Why, thank you, Mr. Highland." Lera fluttered her eyelashes. "You're too kind, I'm sure."

I rolled my eyes, keeping my face averted so they wouldn't see me.

"Do call me Simon. You already know my niece, Jenny."

Lera sat on the sofa and patted the space next to her. He settled a hand's breadth away. That left Jenny and me in the two wingback chairs we'd placed in the grouping that morning.

As soon as I'd taken a seat, Lera asked me to get the tea. I bit my tongue, pasted on a polite smile, and left the room. Their lively chatter accompanied me all the way to the dining room and back.

I bent to lift the tray of scones off the bottom shelf of the tea cart and started to place them on the low table but at Lera's prompting, offered them first to Simon and then to Jenny and Lera. Before I set them down, I grabbed one. Lera poured my tea.

She and Simon were a good match. They could both talk without taking a breath. Jenny inserted a comment here and there. It was too much work for me, so I sipped and nibbled.

Simon glanced in my direction so often, I squirmed.

When I was in the middle of my second scone, he turned to me. "Cassie, you don't mind if I call you that do you? Of course you don't. Cassie, you're awfully quiet. Where are you from?"

My eyes went wide as I racked my brain trying to remember Lera's story. I continued chewing, stalling for time, and looked at her for help.

"Why, I thought I told you, Simon." Lera set her cup on the table. "She's from Savannah."

I swallowed. "Yeah, I mean yes." I gazed at the serving cart. "You see, I was in an accident and my memory isn't … all there."

"I'm sorry to hear that." Simon leaned toward me, his expression somber.

Out of the corner of my eye, I caught Jenny's raised eyebrows. Maybe I fooled one of them. The expression on Jenny's face triggered a memory. No, she just looked familiar. Maybe she'd raised her eyebrows the day we bumped into her in town.

Simon kept his focus on me. Lera answered most of his questions and deftly steered the conversation back to something else, only to have Simon ask me another question. Though she didn't show it, Lera had to be irritated. What could I do? I hadn't done anything to encourage him.

When the men entered from the foyer, I jumped up, ran to Nate, and threw my arms around him.

He chuckled and hugged me back.

I pulled away and turned my head, my face feeling warm.

Nate stood next to me at the edge of the sitting room while Lera introduced Caleb and then sent him outside.

Ed shooed Caleb out the door.

Nate strode over and shook hands with Simon.

Jenny cleared her throat and stared at Nate.

Simon glanced at her. "You've been introduced to Mr. Gardner and Mr. Bridger haven't you, Jenny?"

"Mr. Bridger, yes." She ambled over and stood in front of Ed as he approached.

Simon stretched his open palm toward Ed. "Jenny, meet Mr. Ed Gardner, Lera's father-in-law."

"Pleasure." Jenny curtseyed.

Ed bowed. "Likewise." He squinted at Jenny. Are you sure we haven't already met? You look familiar."

Jenny laughed and shook her head. "I get that all the time. I must look like a lot of people."

Something seemed off about Jenny, but it could be my unfamiliarity with this lifestyle.

Ed glanced at the furniture grouping. "It doesn't look like there's enough places for us, Nate."

"I guess we'll have to get cleaned up and then help with supper. You will stay, won't you?" Nate nodded at Simon.

Lera's face lit up, and she sidled up to her beau. "Of course they will."

"Thank you for the invitation." Simon smiled at Lera. They returned to their seats, and Jenny joined their conversation.

I felt happy to sit, sip tea, and let the talk float over my head.

When Nate and Ed returned, Lydia accompanied them. She sailed through the room without a word. I rose and followed her.

"Cassie, please stay." Ed stood behind the sofa.

"No, Ed. You've been working all day. You and Nate stay and join the party. I'll help Lydia with supper." I pushed Ed into my seat and hurried to the kitchen.

"I'll help." Nate jogged after me to the kitchen. He closed the door and leaned against it, grinning. "Missed me, huh?"

"Simon's been paying way too much attention to me." My eyes darted toward Lydia at the woodstove.

"Not surprising." Nate walked toward the shelves. "I never liked Simon."

I followed him. "So why did you invite him to supper?"

He shrugged. "For Lera."

Lydia surveyed the shelves. "The more time he and Lera spend together, the faster he proposes."

"So you hope." I moved to allow Nate and Lydia more room to work.

"Lera, too." Lydia gathered several jars and cloth-wrapped packages in her apron and strode toward the center of the kitchen.

She deposited an armload of food on the worktable. We sliced cold cuts and bread and made a salad. Nate helped us pour all the condiments into fancy little glass dishes. There were relishes, and mustards, and things I'd never seen before.

After we had everything prepared, Nate took his gold watch out of his pocket. "How long do you think we can stay in here before they get suspicious?"

"I don't know. That depends on how well their conversation is going." Lydia cracked open the kitchen door and stuck her head out. "Pa's there, so we probably have at least a half hour before they notice."

"They probably won't be hungry for a while." I sat in one

of the chairs at the worktable, my hand over my belly.

Nate squinted at me.

I chuckled. "Maybe that's just me; they didn't eat as many scones as I did."

Nate and Lydia laughed. Nate sat next to me and put his feet up on the stool beside him. Lydia sat across from us.

"So, how's the courting going?" Nate asked.

"Lera seems to be having a good time," I said.

"I hope this works out for her." Lydia bit her lip.

Nate eyed Lydia. "What do you think about Mr. Highland?"

Lydia scoffed. "I'm only fourteen. What do I know?"

Nate and I both laughed.

"What?" Lydia lifted her chin.

"You can read people like books," Nate said.

Lydia eyed Nate and then me as if she was sizing us up before she spoke.

I nodded my encouragement.

"I don't like Highland, but there's no talking Lera out of this." She let out a breath. "Like Ma says, the only thing we can do is pray."

I snickered at the sarcasm in her voice.

Nate reached toward me and Lydia. "Okay, let's do."

My eyes flew open, and my jaw dropped, but I let Nate take my hand.

Lydia rolled her eyes, but completed the circle by clasping my hand on top of the worktable.

Nate prayed for God's blessings on Lera and for wisdom and safety. He also prayed for Simon and Jenny.

It would have never occurred to me to pray for someone I didn't like.

We took our time carrying the food to the dining room. When we finally gathered for supper, I listened and watched. Ed, Lera, and Simon steered the conversation during the meal. Lera fawned over Simon. Lydia and Nate answered when they were asked a direct question. Ed stole glances at Jenny.

Jenny was quieter than she'd been earlier, and she seemed to be watching both Ed and me. Why?

Ed had asked if he'd met her, and she looked familiar to me, too. I coughed to cover my gasp. Could we have met her in twenty-ten?

Chapter 14

I bounced along next to Nate on the front seat of the wagon without squinting. This was a first. A glance over my shoulder revealed dark clouds rolling in from behind. "It looks like it's going to rain soon."

"We'll get there before it does. But I'm afraid we'll be driving back in it." Nate flicked the reins.

At least I wouldn't have to sit through the service with wet clothes and hair. I studied the rest of the family. Ed and Lydia sat with stoic expressions, Caleb fidgeted as usual, but Lera sat on the edge of her seat, twisting her handkerchief, and biting her lip.

"Does Simon usually attend church when he's in town?" I leaned toward Nate, making sure Lera couldn't hear me.

"That's where she met him."

Nate parked the wagon in the side yard of the church, and Lera stepped down much more gracefully than I had when I'd worn that blue dress. Her eyes scanned the crowd as we approached the church. Just before we entered, she broke ranks.

Lera hurried toward Simon and Jenny. "Why, Simon, it's nice to see you again so soon."

"Good morning, my dear." Simon covered her hands with his. "I'm glad I caught you before the service. I've had a change in plans. I know I mentioned a picnic next week, but I remembered last night that I won't be able to visit next

151

weekend." He nodded toward Nate. "Would you and your family like to come to a picnic today?"

"We'd love to, wouldn't we?" Lera trained those big brown eyes on Nate.

Nate peered at the cloud cover. "It doesn't look like good weather for a picnic."

Simon patted Lera's hand. "It's all taken care of. We'll have it inside."

Nate shook Simon's hand. "In that case, thank you."

Lera smiled and exhaled.

"I can't promise we'll be able to stay long." Nate pointed his hand toward the dark clouds. "Looks like the roads could get muddy this afternoon."

"We understand." Jenny flashed a grin at Ed. "Too bad we can't control the weather."

"I think today is perfect timing for rain." Ed gave Jenny the side-eye and entered the sanctuary.

Jenny glared at him, but I may have been the only one who noticed.

After we were seated in our pew, Lydia leaned toward me and whispered, "Funny, Jenny wasn't here last week, but today she's here with Simon."

I cupped the side of my mouth with my hand. "We'll probably only see her in church when Simon's here."

Lera narrowed her eyes at us, her finger in front of her lips.

If I didn't feel I was expected to, I might not come. When the singing started, I changed my mind. Maybe I would, just to get out of the house. It was about the only entertainment available. I never realized how much I took technology for granted. If these people wanted to hear music, they had to either play or sing or find someone else who could. And I'd fought my mom about practicing for my piano lessons.

Why hadn't I thought about that before? I could have taken Mattie's place today if I'd had time to practice. But I hadn't had a free minute anyway, except last Sunday afternoon. Was it even acceptable to practice on a Sunday?

~

Simon, Lera, and Jenny rode in Simon's glossy black closed carriage, leading us to his house. I sat next to Nate in the front seat of his buckboard, with Ed, Caleb, and Lydia in the seat behind us. We turned down a winding tree-lined lane. The wind blew the new leaves on the trees, reminding me of the impending storm.

When the house came into view, I gasped. It could have been Twelve Oaks from *Gone with the Wind*. This house wasn't still standing in my time. What happened to it?

Simon, playing the gracious host, led us into the foyer, kissing the ladies' hands and shaking the men's. He shook Caleb's whole body.

We entered a foyer the size of a small ballroom, with an elegant staircase winding upward opposite of the front double doors. After depositing hats and wraps with the doorman, Simon toured us through two formal parlors, one on each side of the foyer, and a dining room toward the back of the house.

He led us into a large sitting room with furniture pushed to the edges lining the wall. A tablecloth containing a platter of sandwiches, and an array of pickles and other vegetables and fruits that couldn't have been fresh this early in the year, lay on the floor. A young girl wearing an apron and a cap over her black braids scurried out the door at other end of the room. How many servants did Simon have? This house looked twice the size of Nate's, so it would take a lot more work to keep up even if it didn't have inhabitants most of the year. And the picnic spread was too lavish for one person to have prepared it this morning.

Lera surveyed the picnic and then smiled at Simon. "How quaint."

I could think of a few less than flattering words for it. If we were going to eat inside, I would prefer to do it at a table, or at least in a sitting room chair.

Lera and Lydia settled on the floor in their crinolines. They were more graceful than I would be in my full skirt minus the hoop. Nate helped me sit, and Ed looked rather uncomfortable assisting Jenny, who wore a smug smile.

During the meal, I glanced in her direction as often as possible without drawing attention. Why did she make Ed squirm? Why did she look so familiar and yet, unfamiliar to me? I must have seen her before but someplace totally different. Was Jenny the other time-traveler Ed suspected? She couldn't be. She was Highland's niece.

"Cassie." Nate tapped me on my shoulder.

My eyes darted toward Nate and then in the direction he nodded. "Oh, excuse me."

"How do you like our town?" Simon gestured toward his niece. "Do you find it as boring as Jenny, here?"

"Oh, no. It's not boring at all." Lera kept me too busy to be bored. Plus, I spent any free time I had trying to figure out how to get home.

"So that's why you were a million miles away, just now?" Jenny flashed me a sly smile.

"I'm sorry." I yawned. "I didn't get much sleep last night."

Jenny stared at me for a second then snapped her head toward a serving girl and refused the piece of poundcake she'd been offered.

Why did Jenny seem so interested in me and Ed? As I accepted my cake, I shook the thought out of my head.

Because of the weather, we prepared to leave sooner than would be socially acceptable otherwise. I didn't mind.

On our way out, Simon gave each of us a hand-engraved card. "I want to personally introduce my niece to the town. What better way than to hold a ball."

The invitation indicated the party would be on Saturday in two weeks.

Simon shook Ed's hand. "Will Mattie be able to attend?"

"That depends on Mark." Ed stepped toward the door. "I know she'd love to come, but she won't leave Mark if he's still sick." He heaved a sigh. "And she won't let anyone else tend to him."

"He should be better by then." Lera waved her invitation, a wide smile on her face. "She told Nate this morning, his fever's coming down."

Lydia scowled, probably because she was too young to attend. I might want to avoid her for a while.

Simon opened the door. A light rain fell and a large mass of dark clouds hovered to the west. "You're welcome to stay until the storm passes."

"No, thank you." Nate stepped onto the porch and donned his hat. "It looks like it'll last a while. We'll try to outrun it."

Nobody argued. Lera was probably the only one who wanted to stay with Simon and Jenny, but she rarely went against Nate. We trooped out to the wagon. Nate drove in a different direction from the way we came.

Ed leaned forward from the back seat. "You taking the shortcut?"

"Thought we could outrun it this way." Nate spoke up to be heard over the wind.

"What if we don't?" Lera held her hat on with one hand.

Nate pointed to the ominous cloud "If that gets to us before we get home, we'll get stuck. It won't matter if we're on the main road or not."

"But, if we're on the main road, it'll be easier to get out." Ed bobbed his head toward Nate.

Lydia tapped Nate on the shoulder. "Ma always says to stay on the main roads in bad weather."

Nate clenched his jaw. "Aunt Mattie's not here."

"The shortcut roads are going to get impassable faster than the main roads," Ed said.

"I know that, Ed." Nate turned to me. "The shortcut is about three miles, versus five on the main roads. Do you have an opinion?"

I shook my head, surprised he was even thinking about doing something Mattie advised against. The last thing I wanted was to get involved in a family power struggle. With an irritated look on his face and a loud sigh, Nate headed back into town.

We made it the mile northwest into New Hope and about a mile, out of the four northeast to Nate's farm before the storm hit. The roads were even ruttier than normal. The wagon bumped and tipped more with each minute of the torrential downpour. I hated to think of what the shortcut would have been like.

We jounced along another mile before the road paralleled a creek and now it was soggy. Nate tried to steer the horses around the puddles, but it was impossible to miss them all. Mud splattered up at us. In the front seat, Nate, Caleb, and I got it worse than the others. Caleb giggled and squirmed next to me.

I was wiping a splatter of mud out of my eye when we came to a full stop. The horses strained, but the wagon wouldn't budge.

"Everybody out." Nate swung his legs over and hopped down.

I didn't protest. We probably should have unloaded when we'd approached the creek. After Nate helped me down, I stood off to the side and Ed and Nate assumed positions behind the wagon.

"Lydia, get up on the seat and drive the team." Ed waved his arm toward the rest of us. "Everyone else, push."

Lera headed toward the wagon, so I followed. I didn't know how much help I'd be, but I was already a muddy mess.

We pushed for what seemed like an eternity—about ten minutes. That wagon wouldn't budge.

Finally, Nate and Ed stopped and the rest of us waited for directions.

"We'll have to walk home." Nate plodded toward the mules. "We'll pick up the wagon when this dries up."

He and Ed unhitched the team and started leading them home. The rest of us trudged behind them. By the time we made it to Nate's, it was nearly nightfall.

All I wanted was a hot bath, but I didn't dare say anything. Instead, I continued to follow Lydia and Lera as we approached the house from the main road. They veered around toward the back behind the men.

Nate stopped next to the kitchen building. "Why don't you girls go get cleaned up? We'll take care of the mules and dry off as much as we can."

Good plan, but how would we get to the bathroom without messing up the house? The downpour had taken care of most of the mud, but we were dripping. Lera and Lydia let me into the wash room. We took off our shoes, undressed down to one layer, and left the outer clothes on the floor, no doubt for wash day tomorrow. We ran through the kitchen and across the breezeway into the house, giggling all the way upstairs.

We stopped in front of the bathroom, and they looked at me like I should go first.

"I had the first bath last night." My eyes flicked from Lera to Lydia. "One of you go first."

They glanced at each other then ran for towels. Lera made it back first. "I'll bathe and then go get some hot tea and supper ready."

Lydia stepped toward me. "You're really good at getting out of work."

"I didn't get out of much this past week." I opened the door to our room. "Maybe I was just being nice."

"Oh, then you can go next." With a cheesy grin, she entered, stripped off the wet underclothes, and donned her robe.

I shook my head. "You're the sneaky one."

~

157

After I showered and dressed, I went downstairs to help Lera get supper.

She poured me a cup of tea and sat at the worktable.

I slumped into the chair opposite her and sipped the strong beverage. Waiting for it to cool a bit, I held the cup in both hands, enjoying the heat on my fingers and the steam on my face.

"Feels good to warm up after an afternoon like that, doesn't it?" Lera peered at me over her cup.

"It does." I exhaled. "I don't know which was worse, the hour in the wagon or the two it took to walk."

One corner of her mouth turned up. "You don't much like the wagon, do you?"

"Gee, how'd you guess?"

"Thanks for letting me take the first bath." Lera sipped her tea. "And for not complaining this afternoon."

I shrugged. "It's not like that would have helped."

"The same thing happened when Sarah's friend, Missy was with us."

I furrowed my brow. "Sarah?"

"Lydia's sister. She's married."

"Oh, yeah, Mattie told me about her."

She waved her hand in front of her face. "Anyway, you'd have thought it was the end of the world." She set down her cup. "Missy cried and hollered and told Ed that he had to fix the wagon. Nearly refused to walk, but Mattie took her off by herself. I'm not sure what transpired, but you know Miss Mattie." She leaned forward. "Missy trudged through the mud along with the rest of us, but she cried and muttered the whole way." Lera chuckled. "Anyway, thanks for not making things worse." She took another sip of tea. "So how did you like our picnic? You're always so quiet."

"I rarely get a chance to say anything."

She scowled.

I grinned. "No, I put my foot in my mouth less, if it's not open as much."

She nodded, an eager expression on her face, no doubt waiting for my answer.

I took a breath. "I could have done without the sitting on the floor part, but otherwise it was fine." I took the last sip of my tea and set the cup down. Lera poured me another.

She leaned toward me, hands on the table. "What do you think about Simon?"

I blinked. "He's all yours, if that's what you're worried about."

"No, not at all." She sipped her tea. "Well, I was a little yesterday."

"He seemed pre-occupied with me. It made me feel a little weird." I glanced at the doorway. "But, you know, Jenny is worse." I lowered my voice. "I know I've seen her before, but I can't place her. I feel like she's watching me, but I can't seem to catch her at it." Maybe I shouldn't have confided in her, but at least I didn't tell her where I thought I'd seen Jenny.

Lera narrowed her eyes. "Hmm, I haven't paid much attention to Jenny." She leaned back and grinned. "But I know why she's watching you. It was obvious she was after Nate the first time she met him." She held up one finger. "We might have a chance to find out where you've seen her before. I've invited her over on Thursday afternoon, and we'll probably see her on Sunday again." She set down her cup. "Of course, the following week, they'll be getting ready for the ball. Oh, that reminds me, we'll need to start making dresses sometime this week."

"Aren't you going to wear the yellow one?" If I had a gorgeous dress like that, I'd wear it for every special occasion.

"It's more of a day dress." She picked up a dish towel and twisted it.

"On you, it looks like a ball gown."

She flicked the towel at me. "He's already seen me in that

one."

"No one else has." I leaned forward. "And you'll be hard pressed to find a gown that suits you half as well."

Lydia stomped into the room and poured herself a cup of tea. "Talking about the stupid ball already?"

"You only feel that way because you can't go." Lera smirked. "Just wait a year. You won't think it's so stupid."

Lydia glanced around. "I thought you were going to get supper ready."

Lera pushed up from her chair. "I was waiting for you to come down, so I could let the men know the coast was clear."

Lydia turned on her heels, stuck her head out the door, and called out to the guys that the water closet was free.

Lera winked at me, and we started putting together a light supper.

~

After Nate and I returned from taking Mark and Mattie's supper, Lera put Caleb to bed, and Lydia went upstairs with a sulky expression on her face. Nate and I joined Ed in the sitting room. I sat at the piano and opened the hymn book. Nate strolled over and listened while I played a few bars.

"Why didn't you tell us you could play?" He sat on the bench facing away from the piano. "You could have filled in for Mattie."

I shrugged. "I haven't played in years. It would take a lot of practice for me to be good enough to play in church." I played the hymn to prove my point.

"Have you ever heard this tune before?" He swiveled his legs around to face the piano.

"No." I flipped the page of the hymnal. "It's obvious, huh?"

"Why don't you play something you've heard?"

"That gives me the choice of the hymns we sang today and the ones we sang last week. I've never heard any of them played, but at least I would know the tune."

"Sort of." He flipped the pages of the hymnal and set it back on the stand. "I can hum this one."

After listening to Nate, and playing through a few times, it didn't sound too bad. I felt rusty, though. I rested my hands in my lap. "Hopefully, since Mark's doing better, Mattie will be back next week."

"If there's any way possible, Mattie will be in church next Sunday." Ed peered at us over the newssheet he held. "You can count on it."

"Good." I turned around on the bench.

Nate pressed the hymnal open. "But that doesn't mean you should stop practicing."

Chapter 15

I slipped the clothespin over the last petticoat, fastening it to the line, and shielded my eyes against the bright sun. At least it would be a good day to dry all the mud-caked clothing we'd washed this morning. I wasn't looking forward to doing the rest of the laundry in the afternoon.

As we were cleaning up after dinner, Nate pulled me aside. "Cassie, in a couple of hours, Ed and I are going to try to get the wagon out of the rut. I'm going on into town to visit the Wiley's. Would you like to come?"

"Yes." I jumped at the chance even though it meant another buggy ride.

"Good." Nate stepped back. "You might want to get to Caleb's lesson early today."

I smiled and nodded—anything to get me out of laundry.

Caleb acted his usual uncooperative self, but at least I got to sit for most of the two hours. About halfway through the session, I took him outside and let him run for a few minutes.

He could recognize most of the letters and knew what sounds they made but had trouble writing them. He would sound out single words, but if I showed him a paragraph and asked him to read, he became overwhelmed. At one point I wondered if he had dyslexia, but even if I knew for sure, I wouldn't know how to teach him. I felt frustrated at the lack of progress, but I kept plugging.

When Nate appeared in the sitting room, Caleb jumped up. "Can I go, Uncle Nate?"

Fear that Nate would say yes, replaced my relief that Caleb's lesson was over.

"All right, you can help get the wagon out." Nate laid his hand on Caleb's shoulder. "As long as you come back to the house with Grandpa."

Ed and Caleb rode one of the mules, and Nate and I rode the other to the wagon. Ed hopped off the mule and inspected the wheels. "Not damaged."

Nate helped him hitch up the team, then climbed in and drove the wagon out of the rut.

Ed assisted me up to the seat, then he and Caleb took off on foot, but they didn't head back in the direction of the house.

"Where are they going?" I gripped the edge of the seat as the wagon lurched forward.

Nate shrugged. "Don't know. I'm sure they'll be home for supper."

If he wasn't worried about it, neither was I. We rode in silence for a while. I was content sitting instead of working, though staying in the wagon seat was work.

I held on tighter as we turned off the main road. "Nate, why are we going to visit the Wileys?"

"I told Mattie I'd check on them."

"That's right. Lera told me Mattie likes to stop by once in a while to see if they need any help. But the other ladies check on them, too, don't they?"

He nodded, and his lip curled up. "I was hoping to poke around in the remains of the fire, too."

I raised an eyebrow. "A farmer and a detective, huh?"

"Yep." He turned to me, a slow smile growing. "I thought about studying law at one time."

I pulled back to study his expression. "Why didn't you?"

He shrugged one shoulder and peered at the road. "Inherited the farm."

Moments later, Nate veered the wagon onto a path through the woods and stopped at the clearing. "Let's get to work, shall we?" He jumped down, tied the animals to a fence post, and extended his hand for me.

The Wiley's house—much smaller than Nate's or Mattie's—was plain wood, not painted like Nate's. As soon as we stepped onto the porch, Mrs. Wiley opened the door. Had she been waiting for us?

"Good afternoon." She shook Nate's hand and glanced at me. "This must be your intended."

I held my breath.

"Mrs. Wiley." Nate let go of her hand and tipped his head toward me. "This is Cassie McPherson."

I stuck my hand out to shake, but Mrs. Wiley bobbed a slight curtsey. "Pleased to meet you. Do come in."

She ushered us into a medium-sized room that contained a sitting area straight ahead and bedroom furniture in the corner to the left. An aged, balding man rocked in one of the wooden chairs in front of the fireplace. He started to pull himself up from his rocker, but Nate walked over, shook his hand. "Mr. Wiley, this is Cassandra."

Mrs. Wiley shouted my name into his ear and he nodded.

"Pleased to meet you," he said in a shaky voice.

Nate and I sat on an upholstered bench, leaving the other rocking chair for Mrs. Wiley.

"Aunt Mattie sends her regards." Nate leaned forward. "She wants to know how you're doing."

Mrs. Wiley beamed. "Tell her thanks. We're getting along." Her brow furrowed. "Eleanor Hodges came by last week and told us about Mark. How is he?"

"He'll be fine." Nate sat up straight.

Mrs. Wiley asked about each member of Nate's family as

well as half the town. And I'd thought we were checking on her.

When Nate finally had an opening, he said, "We're trying to organize a barn-raising for you, but with planting season—"

"Oh, don't go putting yourself out on our account." Mrs. Wiley raised her palm, then let it drop to her lap. "We haven't housed any animals in that old barn in years. It was mostly used for storage. That's how I know we weren't in there."

"Any ideas who could have been?" Nate peered at her.

She glanced at the ceiling. "That's the hardest part. Wondering what happened."

"Had you seen anyone, or heard anyone around before the fire?" Nate asked.

She shook her head slowly. "No. Why?"

"I thought someone could have been camping out in there." Nate glanced at me. "Was there anything in the barn worth stealing?"

"Not in my opinion." Mrs. Wiley chuckled.

"What was in there?" I asked. Could it be something a time traveler might want?

"Normal things. My spinning wheel and loom. Can't use them anymore." She leaned forward squinting under her glasses. "Can't see well enough." She looked past us. "There were also some old brass candlesticks and several lanterns."

"Do you mind if I poke around out back before we leave?" Nate pressed his hands on his thighs and stood.

She smiled. "Not at all."

We walked through the house to the breezeway between the dining room and kitchen, and descended the steps into the backyard. Nate kept his eyes on the ground until we reached the pile of ashes where the barn used to stand. What was he looking for? All I could see was trampled dirt and grass. It would have been impossible to isolate a foot print.

We sifted through the ashes but I didn't see anything that could be the remains of the items Mrs. Wiley had mentioned.

I sighed. "There's not much left."

"Something's missing." Nate scraped the ashes with a metal fireplace poker.

"Everything's missing." I scoffed. "It all got consumed in the fire. Everything except the lantern that started it."

"And this." He raised the poker. "Didn't Mrs. Wiley say there were other lanterns?"

I nodded.

"And brass candlesticks. They should still be here in some form." Nate raised his eyebrows.

My eyes widened. "Do you think it's the town thief? But wasn't that nearly two years ago?"

He nodded. "The Wiley's haven't been out here lately, so they might not have noticed. No way to know who, though."

If Ed's theory was correct, the thief was a time-traveler, but they might not be here anymore.

"I'll add this to my prayer list." Nate took my hand and led me back to the wagon.

I wished I could plop a worry into a cubby like that and not let it bother me. But Nate didn't have a suspicion of who the thief was, and I couldn't tell him mine. Besides, I didn't know for certain who the time traveler was.

Chapter 16

The big day arrived. Lera got us all up at the crack of dawn so we could get our work done in the morning. After dinner, Lydia tended Caleb, and Lera took a bath while I went to my room and caught up on some reading.

I'd promised Nate I'd try to read the Bible he'd bought me. Having finished Mathew and made it half way through Mark, I wasn't quite sure how much I understood or wanted to. The book open in my lap, I leaned back in the rocking chair and stared at the ceiling. Why hadn't God answered my prayer? I repeated it nearly every night at bedtime, at least when I was conscious long enough. Why was I still here?

I'd searched around the house and grounds but not found any clues other than that mangled screw. Every time we'd gone to town, I'd looked for Todd. Why wouldn't he come back for me? Had I been right that he'd been planning to break up with me? I groaned. What did it matter? It didn't look like I'd ever see him again.

A knock on my door startled me. I hadn't read more than a verse. So much for my promise for that day. Lera asked me to come to her room after I finished my bath. Although I was curious, I took my time in the bathroom.

When I entered Lera's room, she stayed in front of the fireplace fanning her hair. I walked in shaking my newly washed mane, thankful it was still short enough to dry quickly.

I pointed to a metal rod that was stuck into the coals. "Is that a curling iron?"

"Yes." She smiled. "I was hoping we could do each other's hair."

"I could try to help you with yours." I fingered my tight chin-length curls. "But there's not much you can do with mine."

"We'll see about that." She flashed a sly smile.

Already a little nervous about the ball, I didn't need her coming at me with hot metal.

She used a towel to pull the cover off the curling iron, and I helped her do tiny ringlets in the front and a bun in the back with several large curls around it. It suited her better than the simple chignon she usually wore at the nape of her neck.

I stood behind her looking in the mirror. "Lera, you're a real beauty."

"Oh, stop." Her smile lit up her eyes, making her look even more lovely.

She picked up a brush and the hot iron and turned toward me.

I flinched.

"If you keep doing that, you will get burned." She put a hand on her hip and tilted her head. "Haven't you ever used one of these before?"

"No. My hair is naturally curly." I tugged a strand and it snapped back.

"Yes, but it's not very orderly." She checked that it was dry, then used the curling iron. When she finished, I looked in the mirror at someone else. My normally untidy hair was smooth, styled into six ringlets surrounding my head at chin length with tiny curls on each side in the front. My brown eyes were wide and my mouth hung open.

"That's the best I can do with this length. You should let it grow out."

"This is amazing." I preened. "Once I put on the gown, I really won't look like me."

I'd agreed to wear a hoop, but only because my dress was too long to wear without one.

Lydia brought my gown in. She stopped and stared at me with her mouth agape.

I looked her in the eye. "Do you like it or hate it? I can't tell."

She blinked and rushed over to me. "It's beautiful. How?"

"Ask her." I pointed at Lera.

She lounged on the bed filing her nails. "I have my talents."

I stepped into my dress which had a chocolate brown skirt, with tan accents and a tan and brown bodice cut low, but not enough to show cleavage. Lera had told me the fabric was the cheapest one at the store because the color wasn't popular. She agreed it worked for me, though.

~

Nate waited in the foyer, looking dapper in a black suit, as Lera and I descended the stairs. Lera liked to make an entrance. I was happy I'd followed her when Nate locked wide eyes with me and his jaw dropped. What did those commercials say? Priceless.

I smiled and batted my eyelashes.

"I'm certain the two of you will be the loveliest ladies at the ball." Nate held out an arm for each of us but kept his gaze on me.

"Thank you." Lera clutched his elbow. "And you will be one of the most handsome men."

"I agree." I linked arms with him. It was the snappiest patter I could come up with, considering most of my concentration was being used to control the dress.

Nate leaned toward me. "I see you've succumbed to the fashion again."

"Just for the evening." I leaned forward. "Lera begged."

She huffed. "I did not."

"Maybe not with words but with your expressions." I smiled.

She didn't have a comeback.

We walked out the front door, and to my surprise, a hansom cab with a driver waited for us.

"I was expecting the wagon," I said.

"Simon sent this for us. We couldn't be seen going to a ball in the wagon, now, could we?" Lera marched toward the big, black, closed carriage.

I had to admit, it was nicer than our buggies. Nate and I sat in the back seat, facing the driver, and Lera sat in the front, facing us.

"What about Mattie and Ed?" I asked.

"They're taking my carriage," Nate said.

When we pulled up in front of Simon's house, Mattie and Ed stood in the driveway. Mattie appeared tired but happy in her new bright blue gown.

"It's nice to be able to join the living," she whispered to no one in particular. She made eye contact with me. "I mean, it's good to get out and socialize again."

"I understand." I accompanied her toward the house. "The last few weeks had to have been lonely."

"I don't think I would have made it if it hadn't been for Nate." She whispered in my ear, "He's a good man."

"I agree." I sucked in a breath afraid she'd want to set a wedding date. I couldn't get married here. I needed to focus my efforts to get home.

Nate and Ed followed us into Simon's house. The pocket doors stood open, making the foyer and large parlor into one room. The orchestra played from upstairs on the landing and most of guests twirled around the dance floor.

After a few dances, I forgot about my problems. It took all my concentration to follow Nate and not step on his feet. Lucky for me, Nate was a good dancer. As long as Nate was my partner, I enjoyed the party.

Once, his friend Martin cut in. He was short and skinny and expected me to know what I was doing. I felt uncomfortable, but not as much as when I partnered with Simon. His smile looked more like a leer, and he held me closer than I would have thought possible wearing a hoop. I spent most of that dance searching for Nate. When I caught his eye, I silently pleaded for him to save me. He read my expression and took me away from Simon.

"Thank you." I exhaled. "Please don't let anyone else cut in."

He smiled so big his eyes twinkled. "At your service, Miss." He bowed and took me in his arms then waltzed me across the room.

When the orchestra took a break, Nate and I walked over to the buffet table. We were almost at the front of the line when some men from town asked Nate to join them. He looked at me first, but I nodded for him to go.

I wasn't hungry, so I left the line and searched for Mattie. Jenny found me first. She asked if she could speak to me in private and led me to a small library.

As soon as we'd entered the room, she closed the door and whirled around. "Okay, I'll cut right to the chase. I need your help."

I stepped back. "*My* help?"

She leaned against the door, keeping it closed. "Yes, I need you to help me get Simon and Lera together."

I waved my hand, palm up. "How can I do that?"

"Marry Nate."

I shook my head and reached for the doorknob, but she shifted to block me.

"With you married, Simon won't be distracted." Jenny pushed me toward a grouping of leather reading chairs.

I broke away from her and stood, hands on hips. "Did Lera put you up to this?"

"No. Of course not." She motioned for me to have a seat.

"Well, I can't marry Nate. It wouldn't be fair." I started toward the door.

She caught me by the upper arm and whirled me around to face her. "I can tell you have feelings for him."

"I'm not staying here." I broke her hold on my arm. "I'll be going home as soon as I can."

"That's where I can help." She smiled and stepped toward me.

"I doubt it." I snorted and backed up.

She dragged me farther into the room. "You're Todd James' girlfriend, right?"

My jaw dropped. "What?"

The corners of her lips turned up in a sly smile. "I was Todd's assistant."

We stared at each other for a long moment.

"I've got the only way out." She held up a little gadget that resembled a TV remote. "If you don't help me, I'll be happy to let you stay here."

I froze, staring at the rectangular piece of plastic. She had to be the blonde who was hanging around Todd after he stole the time machine. Where was Todd? Didn't Jenny want Nate? Her request didn't make any sense. How could I trust her? Ed might be able to help me figure out what to do.

I pivoted toward the door, but Jenny ran to block my path.

My breath hitched. "If you know how to get back, what are you doing here, and why would you need my help?"

"Playing time-cop." She held up the remote. "This is the only way back. Help me fix the timeline, and I'll take you."

"What does that have to do with Lera and Simon?"

She leaned against the door and sighed. "They are supposed to be married already. I'm trying to keep the timeline from shifting more."

I peered at her. "Send me back now, and I won't be a distraction to Simon."

"I don't want you getting in my way with Todd until I'm done here." She stood up, and spoke through clenched teeth. "Follow orders and you'll get home, unlike my stupid boyfriend."

"There's someone else here from our time!" I threw my arms up in exasperation. By the time my wrist hit my thigh, I realized it wasn't a fourth time-traveler. "Ed?"

She nodded.

"He said he was a friend." I paced a few steps, trying to think. "And I don't remember Todd having an assistant."

She scoffed. "You wouldn't."

I shook my head. "What's that supposed to mean?"

"Nothing you need to know." She turned toward the door.

I stomped my foot, but only to get her attention. "I'm not going to help you until I get some answers. What did you come back to do?"

She glared at me. When I refused to budge, she crossed to the center of the room, plopped into an oversized leather chair, and breathed a heavy sigh. "When I came here, Ed followed me. The timeline changed, and I'm trying to fix it."

I stepped toward her. "So go back to the time just before Ed came."

Jenny rolled her eyes. "It didn't work." She held up the remote. "I'm not sure why." She stuffed it in her bag. "If I can get this thing fixed, I will."

"Wait a minute. If it doesn't work, why should I help?" I stayed between her and the door.

She stood. "I can go back to the point in time after I left, but not before."

My face heated. "Why should I believe you?"

She tapped the bag holding the remote. "I'm your only hope

of going home."

I lifted my chin. "Not if Todd comes after me."

She laughed and sauntered toward the door. "Todd doesn't want anything to do with this part of history."

I backed up, gripped the doorknob, and shook my head. Todd wouldn't leave me here because he didn't like the time period.

She pursed her lips. "He thinks you went back to D.C."

"How?"

She tossed her hair. "You sent him an email."

"You mean you did. Why?" I let go of the doorknob and closed the gap between us.

She stepped back but wouldn't make eye contact. "I don't want him coming here, getting in my way. Besides, I need a place to crash when I'm in twenty-ten."

"Wait." I wagged my finger at her. "Why would Todd think I left him if I didn't take any of my stuff?"

She smirked. "I'll let you know which storage space it's in when I take you back."

I lunged toward her, about to break my personal non-violence policy when crowd noises from the party increased.

She scooted away and opened the door. "It sounds like the men are back. We'll have to finish this later."

Instead of punching Jenny, I stalked past her.

She caught my arm and whispered. "Remember, I'm your only ticket home."

I shook my arm out of her grasp and hurried toward Nate. He took one look at me and asked if I wanted some fresh air. I nodded and we walked out to the courtyard at the side of the house.

We strolled, arm-in-arm, to the back of the garden before either of us spoke. "Pretty night," Nate said.

"Thank you." I glanced at him but couldn't see his expression. "For not asking."

"You're welcome." He cleared his throat. "Do you want to know what my meeting was about?"

"What?" I'd forgotten he'd been summoned.

"The fire at the Wiley's"

I nodded.

"Apparently, the sheriff agrees with me that the fire was a cover up or an accident while the thief was in there. He said there'd been more thefts than we'd heard about and he's afraid it's starting again. He thinks one person is responsible for the thefts and the fire."

"What kinds of things have been stolen?" I wanted to think about anything other than my conversation with Jenny.

"Mostly common items – lanterns, books, clothes, utensils. He asked us if we'd seen anyone suspicious around."

Given Ed's theory that another time-traveler was the thief, Jenny was probably the culprit. I almost told Nate. I trusted him, but he wouldn't believe in time travel, and I still had a niggling fear of ending up in an insane asylum. Also, if I accused Jenny, I'd never get home. But I couldn't do what she wanted, so how much hope did I have anyway?

"Are you all right?" Nate held my arm a bit tighter. "Do you want to sit down?"

I blinked. "No, I'm fine. Is the sheriff going to do anything about the thefts?"

"That's what the meeting was about. He's questioning everyone who's had something stolen and everyone at the fire."

"Wouldn't the person who started the fire have left before anyone else got there?"

"Those were my exact words to the sheriff, but he said he had to start somewhere." Nate slowed his stride and shook his head. "Sheriff Hill is not going to be popular. He's requesting everyone go to the station."

"Will Lera, Lydia, and I have to go?"

"Afraid so. We're all scheduled for Tuesday afternoon."

"I won't be much help." Unless I spilled the beans about Jenny. No, I couldn't do that.

"That probably goes for all of us." He led me toward the lively music emanating from the ballroom. "How about another dance?"

"Okay, but remember you promised not to let anyone cut in, especially Highland."

He offered me his arm as a wide grin spread across his face. "I remember."

I had more fun than I can remember at any other party. I enjoyed Nate's company so much, I forgot about my conversation with Jenny.

It came back to me on the ride home when Lera wouldn't stop singing the praises of Simon Highland, Jenny, and everyone responsible for the ball. Apparently, she'd had a good time and spent a great deal of it with Simon. The one time he had danced with me, I hadn't seen her. Probably, she'd been out of the room.

"Cassie, I invited Simon and Jenny to tea later in the week," Lera said. "Jenny told me you and she had a pleasant conversation. She's looking forward to getting to know you better. Isn't she sweet?"

I clammed up, but it didn't matter. Lera continued chatting while I stewed, all the way to Nate's. Jenny had said we'd finish later. I hadn't the foggiest idea what else she could lay on me. And why hadn't Ed mentioned knowing Jenny? He must have recognized her. Come to think of it, Ed had been avoiding me lately. Did he think I was involved in Jenny's schemes?

At home, I kissed Nate on the cheek, thanked him for the evening and went straight to my room. All I wanted was to go to sleep and wake up back in my own bed, the nightmare over.

I opened the door to our room, and Lydia sprang to a sitting position. "How was the ball?"

"I thought you said it was stupid." I closed the door and began undressing.

"But how did it go?" She knelt on the bed and leaned toward me. "Did Lera make any progress with her beau? How about Ma and Pa? Did they have a good time?"

"Your ma looked beautiful. They seemed to be having a good time, but I didn't spend much time with them or Lera." I fumbled with the hoop.

Lydia hopped off the bed and came to my aid.

I continued to fill her in on the evening. It was the least I could do. "On the way home, all Lera talked about was Simon. I guess she's closing in."

She eyed me. "What did you do?"

"I danced with Nate most of the evening."

"You did?" She pulled the crinoline off me.

I took it from her and stored it in the wardrobe. "Well, he danced, and I tried not to mess him up too much."

She giggled.

I smoothed my chemise. "He's a good dancer."

"I know. He made Ma teach him before he went to Savannah the second time." She ambled toward the bed.

I raised an eyebrow. "After he'd met Margaret?"

She nodded and climbed into bed.

I yawned and sat on the bed. "I'm tired. I'll tell you more about it tomorrow."

"Did you see much of Jenny?"

"Tomorrow." I lay down

"There's something about her I don't like." She leaned against the headboard.

I hit the pillow and rolled over with my back to her.

She got the message and stayed quiet.

I tried to sleep, but Jenny's words kept swirling around in my head. The timeline had changed. Lera and Simon were already supposed to be married. How could Ed coming back have kept Lera from marrying Simon? John! If Ed hadn't come back, Mattie would have either married someone else or stayed single. Either way, Lydia, Mark, John, and Sarah wouldn't have been born. Lera wouldn't be living with the Gardners, and Caleb wouldn't exist. It would only be Nate and Mattie.

"Oh!" My eyes flew open.

"What is it?" Lydia asked.

"Sorry, I must have been dreaming." If only I were. The museum curator had told me that after Nathaniel Bridger had been jilted, he'd invited his spinster Aunt to live with him. That had to have been Mattie. I tossed and turned. If Jenny got the machine fixed…I didn't want to think about it. Hopefully, she wouldn't. I still wanted her to take me home, though.

I fretted for a long while. About the time I thought I'd never sleep again, those first Bible verses came back to me: "Ask, seek, knock."

"Okay, Lord. I'm asking again. Please tell me how to get home. Who should I trust?" I didn't get an immediate answer, but my mind settled enough to allow me to sleep.

The next morning, I rose early excited about going to church. God would answer my prayer. I would pay attention to the service, and everything would be clear. It was a good plan.

Chapter 17

Although we arrived at church early, Jenny and Highland waited out front.

Jenny sauntered over to me. "Cassie, I do believe we didn't get to finish our chat last night. Let's take a little walk." She grabbed my arm and pulled me toward the path into the woods.

I allowed it because I had a few questions for her.

She chatted about the ball until we were out of earshot. Then she stopped and glared at me. "So, are you going to help me or not?"

I narrowed my eyes. "I haven't decided yet. I need more information."

"Don't you want to go home?" She tightened her grip on my arm with one hand and held a drawstring bag containing the remote in front of my face.

"Of course, I do." I wrenched my arm free and rubbed it.

"Then do what I tell you." Her hands quivered, betraying her steady voice.

I glanced at Nate, who stood in front of the church gazing my direction, then lifted my chin. "Answer some questions and I might."

She shrugged.

"Why did you and Ed come here in the first place?" I placed both hands on my hips.

"*We* didn't come. I did." She stepped back and glanced away. "Ed must have followed me."

I narrowed my eyes. "Why didn't he find you here?"

Her lips curved up slightly. "After I traveled here, I reset the year on the machine so Todd wouldn't know where I'd gone." She huffed. "He had strict rules about not changing the past." She pursed her lips. "It seems that Ed managed it without trying."

I pressed my fingers into the bridge of my nose. "So, Ed married Mattie and she had John. Lera married John instead of Simon." I shook my head. "Wait. If you didn't see Ed here, how did you know anything was different?"

"Can't you guess?" She stared at me.

I shook my head.

She let out an exasperated sigh. "I didn't. Not until I got back to our time." She paced a few steps and looked past me. "At first, nothing was different. Then I realized several family members were not only missing, but nobody had ever heard of them."

My stomach knotted. Could my presence here cause people not to exist? I took a deep breath. "When did you figure out what the problem was?"

She fiddled with the strings of her bag. "When I found out Ed was missing. I've tried to fix it ever since." She blew out a breath. "Problem is, I didn't go back far enough the first time, and now it won't let me go to any earlier time. Stupid machine." She shook the bag containing the remote. "Todd won't fix it."

My eyes widened. "You convinced Todd to steal the machine?"

"Yeah, so I could get access to it." She scoffed. "It wasn't that hard. I promised him funding to continue the project."

"How did you get the funding?" From stealing? Good thing I didn't say that.

"My finances are my business." She nodded toward Simon

and Lera having an animated discussion. "We need to get to church soon. Are you going to help me or not?"

"Wait a minute. Send me back today." I leaned toward her. "I promise I won't tell Todd and I won't get in your way."

"Are you crazy?" She took hold of my arm. "Even if I believed you, it wouldn't work. The Gardners and Nate would be searching for you for months." She rolled her eyes. "There wouldn't be any wedding plans for Lera."

"I've only been here a few weeks." I shook my head. "They wouldn't spend that much time."

She put her fists on her hips. "From the way Lera talks," she glanced in Lera's direction, "and rarely stops, Mattie and her family would be looking for me even though we've only met a few times. They've gotten to know you, and they like you." She sighed and let her hands drop to her sides.

Was my own family was looking for me? They might not even know I was missing. If it wasn't November yet, they probably wouldn't.

Jenny stared at me stone faced. "No. Neither of us can go back until this thing is fixed. It'll cause too much of a disturbance."

"Now you figure that out." I stepped toward her, fists clenched at my sides. "Why did you have to come here and meddle in the first place?"

She waved her hand in the air. "To prove Todd's theory. He was too chicken to do it himself."

Todd wasn't perfect but he was brave. I clenched my teeth and stalked past her toward Nate.

She stopped me by grabbing my arm. "Don't pass judgment on me," she said in my ear. "What's your excuse?" She stepped back and let go of my arm. "Tourism, or curiosity?"

I whipped around to face her, clutching my dress to keep from slapping her. In the most controlled voice I could muster, I said, "I got here by accident. I had no idea what the machine was, only that it stole Todd from me. I tripped over the stupid thing and hit the on button." I wouldn't admit to Jenny that I had banged on it out of frustration.

She threw her head back and laughed.

I breathed deeply as I plodded back to Nate. Before I reached him, I managed to force a smile. To my surprise, he didn't ask about Jenny. Instead, he took my arm and ushered me to my seat. We were the first in the church, and we sat quietly by ourselves until the service started. Holding hands with Nate steadied my nerves. My plan from last night made me feel calmer, yet. I would get answers here.

Mattie started the service with a rousing piano solo. She played the hymns well also, and the singing was much improved over the weeks without a pianist. 'Brethren We Have Met to Worship' never sounded so good. I even understood most of it.

Pastor Kelley prayed for several families who were under the weather, the Wileys, and the sheriff. I prayed along until the preacher asked for help for whomever started the fire. My eyes flew open. How could he pray for someone who was causing so much trouble, even if he didn't know who it was?

Pastor Kelley preached on how to discern the will of God. If ever there was a timelier message, I couldn't think of it. I hung on every word he spoke.

My heart pounded as a lightbulb flicked on in my mind. My prayers hadn't been answered because I wasn't thinking about anyone but myself. I certainly hadn't been interested in what God wanted or if there was a reason I was here. When Mrs. Kelley had said everyone was a sinner, I knew it included me. But I had never prayed about that or tried to turn away from it. My chest constricted. Was this conviction or a heart attack?

I closed my eyes. "I know I'm a sinner, and I want your gift to save me from myself. Please help me to follow you."

My muscles relaxed and calm washed over me. I felt a slight squeeze of my hand from Nate.

When I tuned back into the sermon, Pastor Kelley said something about trusting that still small voice. I wanted to leap out of my seat and ask him to repeat the last five minutes or so. Maybe Nate could fill me in later, but then he might ask me why I'd missed it. A knot formed in my stomach. Should I admit the reason I hadn't been paying attention?

Chapter 18

Toward the end of dinner at Mattie and Ed's, Lera nudged Nate.

Nate cleared his throat. "Aunt Mattie, I've been thinking. Why don't we let Lera, Caleb, Lydia, and Cassie stay at my place? It'll make this one much less crowded."

Mattie glanced from me to Nate. "No, now that's your house, yours and Cassie's. You'll want to start off by yourselves."

"Lera, Caleb, and I could move back here after the wedding," Lydia said. "Please, Ma."

"We don't even have a date set," Nate said.

Lera smiled, probably thinking she might get married first.

"I know what this is about." Mattie scanned the table. "Lera wants to entertain Highland and is ashamed to do it here. I'll admit Nate's house is nicer."

I held my breath. I wanted to stay at Nate's, but I didn't want to insult the matriarch of the family.

Mattie peered at Ed. "What will people think?"

"Who cares?" Ed waved his fork. "Most people won't even notice. It's like we're one household anyway."

Nate shrugged. "We could all live at my place. It's big enough, and it would be easier to keep up one house than two."

"No, I'll not have that." Mattie sat up straight and placed

both hands on the table. "I can keep up my own house." She pursed her lips but one corner quirked upward. "Especially with fewer bodies in it."

Lydia smiled and her shoulders lowered. "Thank you, Ma."

Mattie eyed Mark. "So, do you want to move to Nate's, too."

"No, Ma'am." Mark flashed a grin. "Why would I want to live with my sisters and someone else's fiancée?"

"Good boy." Ed patted Mark's shoulder.

I squinted at Ed. Why hadn't he told me who Jenny was? Should I tell him he was probably right about the thefts? Trying out my new faith, I asked the Lord that question.

I didn't get a chance to talk to Ed before we headed back to Nate's. Even so, I was in a considerably better mood than I had been earlier. My predicament was the same, but it didn't seem as hopeless.

~

Arm in arm with Nate, I strolled down the lane in front of the house enjoying the sunshine and the Sunday afternoon respite.

Ed jogged up behind us. "Nate, do you mind if I speak to Cassie?"

We stopped, and Nate nodded. "No, go ahead."

Ed hesitated and jerked his head toward the house.

"Oh." Nate glanced at me. "I'll go take care of the horses." He strode off toward the barn.

Ed and I strolled toward the main road. While waiting for him to begin, I prayed for wisdom.

After three aborted attempts, Ed said, "Cassie, you need to stay away from Jenny."

"I know who she is." I kept my voice low.

He stopped and stared at me.

"Jenny told me." I cocked my head. "Why didn't you?"

He cleared his throat. "I haven't had a chance."

I pursed my lips and narrowed my eyes at him.

He shifted his weight from one foot to the other and stuffed his hands in his pockets. "I wasn't positive about Jenny. And you haven't spent much time with her. Not until this morning."

I leaned toward him. "How could you not recognize her?"

Ed pulled one hand from his pocket and waved it in front of his face. "It's been thirty years!" He exhaled and lowered his voice. "It took me a while to recognize you, too. And you didn't blend in as well."

"Why do you want me to stay away from her?" I shielded my eyes with my hand so I could see his face. "She's my only way home."

"Why are you still here, then?" He looked at the ground.

I took a deep breath. "She wants me to help her do something. She says she'll take me back after it's done."

He slapped his leg. "I knew she was up to something. What does she want you to do?" He offered me his arm.

We ambled down the lane while I laid out the plan to get Lera and Simon together.

A bead of sweat formed on his brow. "I suppose she didn't say why?"

"Just that they were already supposed to be married."

"I meant did she explain why she cared?" He stopped and studied me.

I scoffed. "Of course, not."

We stared at the horizon for a while. A dirt road wound through farmland. How could it be so different from the suburban neighborhood I experienced here a few weeks ago?

I peered at him. "Are you going to try to go back?"

He shook his head. "No, my life is here. I've known that for about twenty-nine years."

I nodded. It made sense. "What do you think I should do?"

He sighed. "You're going to have to make your own decision."

I closed my eyes for a second. "You know, three weeks ago, I wouldn't have given it a thought. I'd have done whatever it took." I blew out a breath. "But now, I want to do the right thing. I shouldn't try to change the timeline any more than I already have."

He placed a hand on my shoulder. "Be careful. I don't trust Jenny."

I shivered. "Was she your girlfriend?"

He set his jaw and strode toward the house.

I hurried to catch him and touched his sleeve.

He stopped and swallowed. "Until she started going after Todd."

"Why did you follow her?" I walked around him to see his expression.

He furrowed his brow. "I didn't think. When she vanished and the machine reappeared, I jumped on it to try to bring her back. Keep her out of trouble."

"Did she get in trouble a lot?"

"All the time." A corner of his mouth quirked up. "Getting her out became second nature." He shook his head. "She never was grateful."

"Well, she hasn't changed." I pivoted to his side and started strolling. "Jenny's mad at you for messing up the timeline."

He kept pace with me. "If she hadn't come, I wouldn't have followed."

"Whatever we do, we have to keep her from getting her remote fixed."

He slowed his gait and glanced at me. "I thought you wanted to go back."

"Right now, she can only go back to a point in time after she initially left. If she gets it fixed, she'll go back to before she left the first time and keep you from coming here. If she does that, Mark, Lydia, and Caleb would cease to exist."

"I doubt that." Ed stopped and gazed off toward his house.

"But, if you hadn't—"

"But I did." He turned toward me. "What's done is done."

"Yes, but you changed history." I rubbed my temple.

He bent his head to within a foot of mine and gazed into my eyes. "Only because God allowed it. Remember, God is in control." He stood up straight. "Jenny won't be able to do anything He doesn't sanction."

His lined face revealed years of trouble and hard work, but his shining eyes declared he'd made peace with his situation. How had he handled all this with nobody to talk to?

"Ed, does anybody else know?" I kept my tone soft.

He backed up a few steps. "About you or me?"

"You."

"Mattie knows. I didn't tell her." He chuckled. "She figured it out."

My eyes widened. "It didn't bother her?"

"She was more upset that I didn't tell her." He glanced at the porch. "But she understood that I didn't think she'd believe me."

I squinted at him. "Has she told anyone else?"

"Not as far as I know, but if she were to tell anyone it would be—"

"Nate."

He nodded confirmation.

"They're as close as they would have been if it were just the two of them." I paced in front of him. "It's almost like part of them knows about the alternate history. We have to keep Jenny from changing it back." I stopped and peered at him.

He exhaled. "Now, you're thinking too much. You're making this too deep."

"Well, isn't it?" I flailed my arm. "I've been giving myself headaches trying to make sense of it. I keep remembering my past, and then go, oh wait, that's the future. It's enough to make your head spin."

"Then do what I did." He laid his hands on my shoulders and gazed into my eyes. "Learn to live in the present."

I stared at him.

He dropped his hands to his sides. "I'll try to help you get home. Whatever you want me to do."

I shook my head. "That's just it. I was hoping you'd know what to do. Can you talk to Jenny?"

"She never listened to me when we were together. What makes you think she will now?" He exhaled. "I can try. I'll be praying for you. You'll know what to do when the time comes." He patted my shoulder. Then he strode toward the barn.

I wandered around the yard. How did Ed cope thirty years ago? He'd been in Atlanta. He must have come here hoping to find Todd. He and Mattie had been married nearly thirty years . . . but he had only been gone a month. I rubbed my forehead again. Why did Todd have to mess with time?

Only one way to handle this. I marched inside and up to my room. After finding my running gear under the bed, I was dressed and out the front door in record time. To warm up, I walked half way to the main road wondering how well I'd do, since I hadn't run in several weeks. The first mile was a little rough, but I sped up for the second.

I kept up a good pace while letting my mind sort itself out. My earlier prayer about what to tell Ed had been answered. He'd opened the door. I thanked God and prayed for continued guidance. "Above all, God, I need to know what to tell Nate. I know I can't marry him unless I decide to stay." Where did that come from? "Please help me get home without causing any heartbreak. Amen."

About a quarter mile from the house, I slowed to a walk, glad no one was around because I'd forgotten my robe. As I approached the porch, the front door opened. Expecting it to be Nate or Lydia, I continued. By the time I saw her, it was too late. Mattie looked straight at me, eyes bugging out. Her hands flew to her mouth.

"I can explain." I stopped and crossed my arms in front of me.

"What's to explain?" Nate appeared in the doorway behind Mattie, towering over her. "Oh." He closed his eyes and sighed.

Mattie turned around, pushed him into the house, and made him stand with his back to me.

"You." Mattie pointed at me. "Go straight to your room and put some clothes on." She smoothed her skirt. "Then come down here so we can talk."

I needed a shower. Though I shouldn't take the time, I could be homeless before the day was out.

While I rinsed, I contemplated stealing the remote from Jenny. No, I had already compromised my morals with all the lying. I couldn't start stealing, too, even if it was something that I should have already been able to use.

When I plodded downstairs wearing my gray jacket and skirt, Nate and Mattie waited for me in the sitting room. At least Mattie appeared a bit calmer.

She motioned for me to take the wing-back chair kitty-corner from the sofa where she and Nate perched. She'd positioned herself between us.

"Nate tells me that is acceptable attire where you come from." She used her honey voice, but there was an edge to it. She sat straight, muscles tensed. "Well, it's not here. You have to learn to play by our rules as long as you are accepting our hospitality. Is that clear?"

"Yes." My voice squeaked.

"Now, at least you had the decency to run on the road no one uses. Thank you for that."

I lowered my head, concentrating on keeping my legs from fidgeting. Saying, "you're welcome" wouldn't help my situation.

She smoothed her skirt. "Under the circumstances, I'm afraid I'll have to insist that you girls and Caleb move back to our house for the time being."

"But they'll blame me." I closed my eyes, hating myself for whining.

"Nevertheless, it's the best thing. Moving day will be tomorrow. It would be today, if it weren't Sunday."

I nodded, but kept my head down like a school girl being chastised in class when someone passed me a note.

"Now, don't look so glum." The honey voice continued as she patted my skirt. "You'll be moving back in here real soon."

I snapped my head up and looked at Nate.

He touched Mattie's shoulder. "Aunt Mattie, can we talk in private?"

She smiled and stood. "Of course, dear. I'll go help Lera in the kitchen." She glided into the dining room.

I sat on the edge of my chair, silent until she was out of the room. "Nate, what did she mean?"

He slid over to the seat Mattie had vacated and clasped my hand in both of his. "She thinks we should get married as soon as possible."

Air whooshed out of my lungs. I wanted to run, but Nate's presence steadied me. Maybe I could get home before the wedding. I took a shaky breath. "When?"

He cleared his throat. "The first week in June."

"That's less than a month. It's too short. I can't possibly get home—" I stopped when I saw the hurt in his eyes. "I mean, we've never really talked about it, except that we both agreed to postpone as long as possible."

He peered at me through soulful brown eyes. "That was almost a month ago. Things have changed since then, haven't they?"

My free hand clenched. "What are you saying?"

He slid off the sofa onto one knee, still holding my hand.

My breath hitched.

"Will you marry me, Cassie?"

I made a little choking sound. I'd waited for those words all my life and the closest I'd gotten was, "I think you should move in with me."

The one time I get the right question it's all wrong. It's not even my lifetime.

I took my time choosing words. "Nate, I know we've gotten close. You'd make a wonderful husband."

"But?" He released my hand, and slid onto the sofa.

I lowered my head. "I can't stay here. I'll be leaving as soon as I can."

"Have you figured out how to get back to your time?"

I jumped out of the chair and whirled to face him, my eyes wide and my jaw slack.

He grinned, his eyes sparkling. "Didn't think I'd believe you, huh?"

"You're right." I perched on the chair, willing my pulse to slow. "How long have you known?"

"I've suspected for a while, but I wasn't sure until today." His smile widened.

"Did you talk to Ed?"

"No. Mattie."

I tilted my head. "Does Mattie know about me?"

"Funny thing about that." Nate glanced toward the dining room, then leaned in and lowered his voice. "Mattie is still pretending she believes you're Margaret. I'm not sure if she knows who you really are." He sat up. "She suspects Jenny of being a time-traveler."

I gasped. "Did she tell you about Ed?"

He nodded. "Is she right about Jenny?"

I exhaled. "Yes. She was the first, and the only one with the mechanism to get home."

I told him as much as I knew for certain, including Jenny's petition for help with Simon and Lera. I left out my suspicion about the thefts. "I hope I haven't misled you. I didn't know how to get home until recently and now I'm at Jenny's mercy."

"I appreciate that." He took my hand in his and rested them on my lap.

We sat in silence for quite a while. Mattie peeked in on us once, but I didn't let on that I'd seen her. How could I have let her see me half dressed? I'd become too complacent. But she never—

"Nate, why was Mattie coming out the front door?" I pulled my hand away from his.

Nate scratched his temple. "She came to get Ed, and Lera asked her to stay for tea. Then suggested we have it on the porch."

"Lera!" I jumped up and stomped toward the kitchen.

Nate caught me, placing himself between me and the door to the dining room. "Don't go making this worse. You know why Lera did it. She wants you off-limits to Simon as soon as possible."

"In my mind I already am." I flashed my ring. "We are engaged."

He frowned. "Officially."

"What does that mean?" I gave him the side-eye.

Nate placed his hands on my upper arms. "Lera knows it isn't real. Maybe she's insecure."

"Yes, but I've told her I have no interest in Simon."

"Look we can argue this all day, but it's not going to change anything." Nate pulled me closer and I sagged against him. He wrapped his arms around me and whispered in my ear, "I still want to marry you and not because of Aunt Mattie."

I wrapped my arms around his waist and squeezed. Did I only want someone to hold onto? "Even though I might leave?"

"Yep. Course, I'm hoping you won't." He pulled me back to the sofa and draped his arm around me. "I have one more question." He took a deep breath.

What else could be that important?

193

"What about Todd?"

"Todd?" I pulled back, taking a second to comprehend. "Oh. I haven't had a chance to talk to him, but he thinks I left him, anyway." I blinked. "I suppose I have." It was the first time I'd admitted it, but I'd been growing away from Todd since before he'd stolen the machine. Lately, he'd become no more than my way home.

I held my hand up, palm out. "Todd's not the problem. It's me." I looked into Nate's shining eyes. "But I'll think about it."

"Do me a favor." He gave my shoulder a gentle squeeze. "Pray about it."

I nodded, about to tell him I could finally pray, not that I'd remembered to since my run.

Caleb bounded in. "Supper's ready early, since we didn't get tea."

"I'm sorry," I said to Caleb's back as he ran ahead of us into the dining room.

During supper, Mattie and Lera started to plan the wedding.

Nate spoke up. "Hold it. We don't even have a date yet."

Lera clicked her tongue. "Well, under the circumstances, I think the sooner the better."

Everyone started talking at once, agreeing or not, I couldn't tell.

Nate held up his hand. "I don't want to hear any more about it until we announce a date." It was the first time he'd countered Mattie.

Ed and Nate kept the conversation off the wedding. I couldn't help smiling. Lera's scheming had backfired on her. She'd have to move back to Mattie's, too.

Chapter 19

I glanced at the clothes hanging on the line as I trudged toward the kitchen. It was the last set, and I'd have to come back tomorrow to take them down. I poured a cup of water from the pitcher on the worktable and slumped into a chair. Because we had to move back to Mattie's today, Lera had insisted we do laundry and cleaning in one day. She and Lydia were upstairs packing, no doubt grumbling about me.

I took a sip of the lukewarm water and made a sour face.

"Here you are," Nate said from the doorway.

I neutralized my expression and smoothed my hair. "Hi."

"Lera and Lydia are ready to leave." He took off his hat and stepped inside. "Would you like to walk with me?"

I smiled. "I'd love to." I could walk a mile anytime to avoid that wagon. And I had to admit, I enjoyed being with Nate. I raised my hand toward him.

He pulled me out of the chair, but kept hold of my hand. "Tired?"

"That's an understatement." I strolled next to him, letting the wagon containing the rest of the crew and our luggage get farther ahead.

"So, how are Caleb's lessons going?" Nate asked.

"Slow, but he's making progress. He loves the word problems." I pursed my lips. "Solving them, not reading them."

"How's he doing with the Bible reading?"

"He's not too interested. I'm learning more though."

"Good." He angled toward me. "Have you tried reading Esther with him?"

"No, we're reading the gospels." I glanced at him. "Why Esther?"

"It's like a mystery story. I enjoyed it when I was his age."

I nodded. "I'll try it, thanks."

He squeezed my hand. "Cassie, I'm glad you've placed your faith in Jesus."

I stopped and stared at him. My hand slipped out of his. "How did you know? I didn't tell anyone."

"Um. You didn't?" He smirked. "Yesterday in church, you whispered. I heard most of your prayer."

"No, I was just thinking it." My head tilted to one side, my eyes getting wider. "Wasn't I?"

He shook his head.

I covered my face with my hands. "I didn't mean to announce it."

He leaned in. "You need to."

I let my hands drop to my sides, but I didn't look up at him. "Give me some time. This is pretty new."

He took my hand in his and we continued down the path. He pointed out different plants and trees and shared stories about growing up there. He talked a lot about John. The two had been close, more like brothers than cousins except John was a few months younger.

"Nate, how much do you know about John's death?"

"It was a tragic accident." He picked up his pace.

"You're sure?" I snuck a peek at his expression.

He worked his jaw, but nodded. Closed off, like everyone else when I brought up John's death. I shuddered. Could one of the time-travelers be the cause?

~

I placed the sheets we'd washed yesterday in the linen closet and turned toward the other closet. The door wasn't flush with the wall. I checked the knob. It was locked, but the door wasn't latched. This was the closet Lydia had been so interested in the day she'd hidden that book from me.

Though no one else was in the house, I scanned the hallway before I pulled the door open and stepped inside. Instead of the large mysterious space I expected, I found a closet with loaded shelves on one side and a ladder to the upstairs level bolted to the opposite wall. I climbed up, pushed up the trap door, and poked my head through the opening, disappointed at finding an empty room. In the lower space, I perused the shelves, surprised to see so much in storage in a new house.

Two stacks of books on a low shelf caught my eye. One had considerably less dust in a rectangular outline. Lydia must have taken a book from the top. I thumbed through the rest to get an idea of the volume she'd hidden. Several were family records and journals. Two had the name Frances Bridger written on the first page. The last date was 1846. She must have been Nate's mom. There were a few others with much earlier dates. Perhaps those were written by Mattie's mother.

I wanted to sit down and read through them, but I knew Lera would flick one of her towels at me if I didn't return soon. We were due in town that afternoon to give our statements about the fire. Afterwards, we planned to visit the Kelleys for tea. Lera would want to make sure we looked our best.

I dusted off the books and returned them to their shelf. As I started to close the door, a knot formed in my stomach. Trusting my gut, I left it the way I found it. If only I could make time to investigate further.

On the way into town, I sat between Lydia and Nate, with Mattie, Ed, and Lera in the back.

"Mark's lucky," Lydia grumbled. "I wish I could stay home with Caleb."

Me too. All the way, I debated about what to tell the Sheriff. Jenny was the thief, but I had no proof, and I couldn't remember seeing Jenny at the fire. Part of me wanted to implicate her anyway, but the part of me that wanted to get home, rejected the idea.

I needn't have worried. When we arrived at the police station, we were told the case had been solved. Ed started to lead us out, but Mattie caught the sheriff's attention as he walked in from the back.

"Sheriff." She hurried toward him, waving. "Good news that the fire was explained. Did it have anything to do with the thefts?"

Sheriff Hill stopped and squinted at her. "Why would you think that?"

Mattie smoothed her skirt. "I thought that's why you were investigating."

"Well." He sighed and pulled us aside. "If you must know—"

"And she must," Nate mumbled under his breath.

I giggled but focused on the Sheriff before I missed anything.

"Eve Wilson confessed to being in the Wiley's barn Sunday morning and leaving a lantern there. She got spooked at a noise and ran."

"What was she doing there?" Ed asked.

"Claimed she was investigating. Wanted to know if anything had been stolen from them." Sheriff Hill shook his head. "She woke up early on account of not sleeping in her own bed." He took a breath. "She was staying with the Wiley's neighbors. Her sister and brother were quarantined."

"Oh yes." Mattie clasped her hands together. "Emily had the measles."

"But why would she want to investigate?" Nate asked.

"Bored and looking for something to do." Sheriff Hill

smiled at Nate. "Then she admitted to trying to impress you."

Nate sighed while the rest of us chuckled.

Lera poked him in the shoulder. "Why am I not surprised?"

Sheriff Hill waved his hand. "At any rate, items were missing but no way to tell when they had been stolen."

Mattie raised an eyebrow. "You closed the case?"

The sheriff nodded.

"Makes sense." She paused and then glanced around at the family all waiting for her. "It's tea time."

Mattie led us down the street toward the little white house next to the church. Mrs. Kelley had the door open before we ascended the porch steps. As the Gardner family filed into the house, Nate stopped on the walkway, clasped my hand and whispered, "How about the last Friday in June?"

"For what?" I whispered back.

He peered at me, and pursed his lips.

I winced. "This isn't just tea, because we happen to be in town, is it?"

"My guess is no."

"Well don't stand there, come in." Mrs. Kelly stood on the top porch step and beckoned.

I plastered on a smile and preceded Nate into the Kelley's small living room. Nate sat next to me on a casual couch, kitty-corner from Mattie and Ed seated on an ornate sofa. Lera and Lydia occupied straight chairs probably pulled in from the dining room.

Mrs. Kelley served tea and the best lemon cookies I'd had in years. I enjoyed the conversation which centered on their western missionary friend. Nobody mentioned weddings. Nate must have been wrong. After accepting a second cup of tea, I sipped it.

Mattie cleared her throat. "We'd like to announce the wedding date soon." She peered at Pastor Kelley. "Do you have an availability the first week of June?"

I choked, nearly spitting out the tea in my mouth. Lera patted my back.

Nate came to my rescue. "Actually, Aunt Mattie, we were thinking the last week in June. It would give you more time to get ready."

I swallowed the tea and nodded, glad Nate had prepared me.

Pastor Kelley exclaimed that the last week in June would be perfect for him. Nate asked for Friday and the date was set.

Now all I had to do was get Lera married first. No pressure. I rolled my eyes at myself. I would need to pray often.

~

News of our wedding was released via Lera and Mrs. Kelley and spread faster than if they had posted it on Facebook. By Thursday, when we attended the monthly quilting bee, everyone shared information about the wedding with details even I didn't know.

Mrs. Hodges told me we were to be married at eleven A.M. at the church, followed by a dinner at Nate's house. There would be a band and dancing on the front lawn, which to hear her tell it, was such a breach of tradition it was scandalous. It sounded like so much fun, I felt sorry I'd miss it.

On Friday, Lera entertained Simon Highland at Nate's house. Lydia and I helped her prepare. Nate had invited all of us to supper, expecting Simon to stay. Jenny wasn't with him and for that I was grateful.

Lydia and I were in the dining room setting the table when Lera squealed. We rushed into the sitting room.

Simon stood from a kneeling position, and Lera hopped around, waving her left hand. She started toward us, went back and hugged Simon, and then ran to us to show us her rock. It was the largest, most ostentatious ruby I'd ever seen. It had small diamonds on each side and small rubies flanking the diamonds. I looked at my ring and smiled. It was much more tasteful.

Lera gazed at the ruby on her outstretched hand, then glanced at me. "I suppose we could set the date for July, since you're getting married in June. But I'm afraid it will be too hot." She wandered around the room, talking about a mid-July date, alternately peeking at Simon and then me.

I let her go on for a while, my smile broadening. "Lera, don't even think about my wedding. Just pick the date you want."

"Are you sure?" Lera peered at me for a second and then turned to her fiancé. "Because, I think Mattie's suggestion of the first week in June would be marvelous. What do you think, Simon?"

He kissed her hand. "I'll be happy to marry you on whatever date you choose. A schedule can always be re-arranged."

Lydia rolled her eyes, and I stifled a giggle.

That gave us three weeks to get Lera's wedding planned and then three more weeks for mine. Mattie was none too happy when she found out, but she coped. In retaliation, she promised to keep Lydia, Lera, me, and Mrs. Jones busy all day, every day.

During the preparation for Lera's wedding, we spent a good deal of time traveling from Mattie's to Simon's house. Lera had permission, and a budget, to redecorate as much as she wanted. At first, I felt nervous around Simon, but he always played the part of a gentleman, and didn't act interested in me other than as Lera's friend. Most of the time, he was either away or in his study.

Jenny inserted herself into the wedding preparations, insisting on making decisions about food and décor, but not doing any of the work. I admired Lera for the way she handled it. Each time Jenny chose something Lera didn't like, Lera would tell the servant in charge what she wanted instead. The servants always followed Lera's instructions. Even though, I needed Jenny to get back home, I wished she'd get out of our way.

A week before the wedding, Jenny entered Simon's small parlor while I arranged wedding gifts on a long table. She picked up a candlestick from a trunk on the floor and plopped it on the table.

I took a deep breath and sidestepped toward her. "Jenny, have you gotten the remote fixed yet?"

She continued arranging packages until I moved closer and asked again.

She leaned in and whispered, "It works well enough to get us back. We still have work to do."

I raised my eyebrows. "Will I get any notice?"

"So you can whisper teary goodbyes?" She snorted. "You haven't been stupid and told Nate, have you?"

"Of course not." I blew a strand of hair off my face. "He figured it out."

She leaned back. "How?"

"Mattie told him about Ed." As I set out gifts, I glanced toward the parlor door, debating whether to tell her Mattie's suspicions about her. On the one hand, I would love to have seen the expression on her face, but I didn't want to alienate her. Dealing with Jenny involved walking a mental tightrope.

Jenny shook her head and gazed at the table full of gifts. "I think we're finished here." She grabbed my arm above the elbow and whispered in my ear, "Keep to the present plan. I'll let you know if I need you to do anything else." She patted the little drawstring bag she always carried the remote in. Did she sleep with it?

Amidst all the wedding preparations, I tried to carve out at least two hours a day for Caleb's instruction. He was progressing, but not very fast. My goal was to at least get him reading on a third-grade level before I left, but he wasn't even close. He was improving faster in math. He'd make a great engineer one day, if I could teach him to read.

I borrowed some books from Ed and showed Caleb pictures

of machines, trains, anything he might be interested in and told him that we could read all about them. He replied that he didn't have to read about them. He could put them together by looking at them. To let him prove it, I scrounged up some parts off toys from Nate's playroom. Caleb assembled a toy tractor in about a minute and then told me which parts were missing.

That evening, Nate took my hand as we walked the path from his house back to Mattie and Ed's.

"Caleb's really good with his hands. I wish I could get him to read." I glanced at Nate. "Why do you think he resists so much?"

He shrugged. "Why should he do something that's hard when everything else comes so easily?"

"Hmm. You have a point. But that doesn't help."

"Give him time. He'll get it."

I stopped. "But I don't have time."

He turned me around to face him, hands on both my shoulders. "How much longer?"

I heaved a sigh. "I'm not sure. She said she had to get Lera and Simon together, but every time I remind her, they're getting married, she puts me off."

We hadn't talked about my leaving since the night he proposed. I took a deep breath and looked him in the eye. "Nate, it might be months from now, or never when Jenny helps me go home, but I'm hoping it's before the wedding."

He removed his hands from my shoulders and stiffened.

I touched his upper arm. "I'm sorry. It's not because of you. You break up with me. Then you won't be embarrassed again when—"

He closed his eyes. "That's not the problem."

"How will Mattie handle it?"

He blinked his eyes open. "She'll be upset, but she'll survive. Like she did with Margaret."

I started walking again, wanting to get back to my room as

soon as possible.

Nate took hold of my arm and stopped me. He closed the gap, turned me to him, and locked eyes with me, those golden-brown eyes shining. I tried to look away, but he cupped my face in both of his large warm hands. He bent down and kissed me, soft and slow. My insides heated and my brain turned to mush. I let the kiss go on much longer than I should have.

I pushed my palms against his chest, and backed up. "You're making this harder than necessary."

Chapter 20

The day dawned warm and muggy. Despite her best efforts, Lera would get July weather for her wedding.

"Well, there's nothing can be done about the weather." Mattie bustled through the kitchen. "We'll have to hope and pray that the flowers don't wilt."

After Lera's performance on the first few outings with Simon, I expected her to be jittery, but she surprised me. The only time she seemed the slightest bit nervous was right before the wedding when Mark came into the bridal suite to escort Mattie downstairs.

Lera squeezed Mattie's hand. "Now you promise to take good care of Caleb. Are you sure two weeks isn't too long? I know I can persuade Simon to shorten the wedding trip if you need me to."

"Of course, I can take care of my only grandchild for two short weeks." Mattie patted Lera's hand and strolled off on Mark's arm.

"You're afraid we'll spoil him." Ed stood with us, waiting to escort Lera down the aisle.

I'd asked Nate a few days before if he thought it was weird that Lera's in-laws were giving her away.

He'd shrugged. "Ed and Mattie are the only parents she has. They expected her to get married again."

"But so soon after she came out of mourning?"

"She mourned John two years. Even Aunt Mattie thinks that's enough," Nate said.

Since the kiss, Nate and I had continued going on our usual stroll after supper as the family expected, but we'd kept the conversation to the events around us and our hands and other body parts to ourselves. I still hoped he'd break up with me, but hadn't dared to broach the subject.

I felt a poke in the middle of my back. Lydia had made her entrance at the top of the stairs and Lera and Ida shooed me out the door. First Lera had roped me into wearing a yellow gown with a crinoline, and then decided to use the staircase as the first part of the aisle. My stomach knotted. I'd practiced several times, but I would be the least graceful. All the way down, I prayed to stay upright. When I reached the foyer, I smiled for the first time, and continued through the open pocket doors to the make-shift altar in the ballroom.

The open door allowed everyone a view of the staircase, making it the perfect place for a stunning bride to make a grand entrance.

Lera had selected a white gown, insisting that white symbolized joy as well as purity. Mattie had helped with her hair. With extra ringlets, it looked better than it had for Simon's ball. Her dress was sleeveless and low cut. It had a fitted lace over silk bodice and the fullest skirt ever. I would have fallen down those stairs in that gown, but Lera glided.

She approached Simon with the widest smile I'd seen on her face. It looked genuine. Was she was marrying him for more than his money?

Simon returned her smile. I didn't recognize the middle-aged men standing with him, probably friends from Atlanta.

Jenny sat in the front row on Simon's side, her face like stone. Why wasn't she happy? Getting Simon and Lera together was the reason she was here, wasn't it?

The ceremony was shorter than I'd expected. They repeated their vows, exchanged rings, and Pastor Kelley pronounced them man and wife. I would have to talk to him before our wedding and get that changed to husband and wife. What was I thinking? Our wedding couldn't happen.

As soon as Lera and Simon walked back down the aisle and welcomed guests to the dining room, Jenny slunk toward the back door.

"Nate, I'll be back in a few." Without waiting for a reply, I followed her toward the shortcut in the woods. Halfway between the house and the privy, I caught up to her. "Jenny, you've done it. They're together."

She glanced over her shoulder without stopping. "So?"

I picked up my pace to keep up with her. "I can go home now, right?"

"I never said that." She passed the privy and veered toward the barn.

I jogged after her. "Yes, you did."

She stopped short and whirled toward me. "I said, if you helped me set things straight, I'd help you get back. We're not finished yet."

"But you said we needed to get them together. It's done."

She clenched her jaw. "I didn't tell you everything."

"What else?" I huffed and stamped my slippered foot.

"I'll tell you when I can." She pushed me into the barn, turned toward the woods, and waved her arms over her head.

"What's that supposed to mean?" I popped my head out of the barn door.

"Stay put until I get back to the house." She patted the bag carrying the remote.

I wanted to chase her and scream, but she held my future in that drawstring bag. Taking deep breaths to calm myself, I stayed in the barn while she jogged toward the house. She must have had more practice than I did with these dresses.

When she stopped short, pivoted, and took a few brisk steps toward the privy, I looked at the house. Some of the party guests milled around on the side lawn. After Jenny went into the privy, I ventured a few steps out of the barn and scanned the edge of the woods, wanting to go investigate, but not quite daring. When the privy door opened, I hurried back inside the barn and waited for Jenny to get close to the house before following her.

By the time I reached the yard, Jenny had left, so I started toward the woods.

Nate found me before I could get far. "Cassie, the music's starting. Do you want to dance?"

I faced him. "Yes, but not now. Jenny was signaling to someone at the edge of the woods."

Nate took my hand. "Lead the way."

"I'll go." I dropped his hand.

"Not without me," he whispered.

One look at his clenched jaw told me I either had to take Nate with me or risk missing whoever was out there. I'd already wasted enough time, so I headed toward the woods with Nate right behind.

On our way across the field behind the garden, I tried to ignore the weeds brushing against my dress and the stink from the privy. Light bounced off something behind a tree. Nate quickened his pace and passed me.

"Any idea what that was?" I asked as we approached the tree-line.

He shook his head and slowed. "Only got a glimpse. Like a flash."

I scanned the cloudless sky. "Not lightning."

He chuckled and headed toward the tree I'd seen the light behind.

We stood in the approximate location and glanced around in opposite directions.

Nate tapped my shoulder. "Look at this." He pointed to

some broken branches and a rectangular spot where the floor vegetation had been compressed.

It was possibly the right size for the time machine. I shivered. Had I missed Todd? My heart sank. "I don't think we're going to find anybody."

Nate offered his arm. "Do you want to go back to the party?"

I forced a smile. "I do, thank you." We linked arms and strolled to the house.

After several dances, Lera and Simon stood at the front door, ready to leave. Lera smiled and waved. "It's your turn next." She tossed her bouquet to me.

The flowers hit me in the chest and my arms flew up to clutch them to me.

Lera giggled. "And I'm taking you up on your offer." She looked at Nate. "She'll be coming here every day to tutor Caleb, so you have two weeks to teach her how to drive or ride." She turned around and sashayed, arm in arm with Simon, out the door to a waiting carriage.

Nate raised his eyebrows at me.

I shook my head. "I'll be walking, thank you."

He chuckled and guided me out to the dance floor.

The remainder of the reception was more fun than Jenny's ball. At least, it should have been because Nate and I danced every dance. I tried to concentrate on the steps and Nate, but Jenny invaded my mind. Who was in the woods? And what were they up to? Is that why she looked angry during the ceremony?

As we danced, I kept track of Jenny. A few times, I caught Ed watching her. When Nate left me to get us some drinks, I approached Ed. "Have you seen her doing anything suspicious?"

"Only acting a little too giddy." Ed lowered his head toward me. "You?"

I filled him in about the mystery person in the woods. He agreed we had no way of knowing if it was Todd and said he'd keep an eye on her. When Nate returned, I tried to forget Jenny. Her story didn't make sense. She said she was trying to keep the timeline from changing, but leaving me here indefinitely would do the opposite. She had to have another motive. Because I couldn't rely on her, I needed a plan to get myself home.

Chapter 21

The next day, on the way home from church, Nate offered me the reins.

I shook my head. "Do you want to endanger all our lives?"

He stopped the team in the middle of the road and pressed the leather into my hand. "You need to learn to drive."

He'd changed his tune since last night. He must have not wanted to argue then. I slumped, then straightened and tried to follow his directions. After Nate helped me get the team going, I tightened up on the reins so much that the mules stopped. I glanced at Nate and then back at the rest of the family, but everyone either shrugged or stifled giggles. I whipped the reins like I'd seen Nate do, but the mules didn't budge.

"See? They know I'm an amateur. They want a real driver." I held the reins out to him.

Nate stuck his hands up. "Try again."

Through many attempts to whip the reins and yell at the mules, we stayed right where we were. Expecting the rest of the family to be annoyed or get out and walk, I glanced over my shoulder to find them smiling and whispering to each other. Well, they didn't have movies or television, so I may as well give them a show.

I stood, whooped as loudly as I could, and snapped the reins hard. The mules jerked to a trot, and I plopped into the seat.

Mattie and Lydia laughed so hard, I feared they would fall off the back seat.

Nate grabbed the reins over my hands and slowed the mules to a decent pace. He held on until I could feel the right tension. When Nate let go, I was able to keep the mules moving.

At our first turnoff, I was tempted to drop the reins and cover my face. I gave Nate a panicked look, and he held them with me until we'd navigated the turn. I drove the rest of the way to Mattie and Ed's.

When we approached the barn, I pulled back on the reins and brought the wagon to a halt. "I got this."

They all laughed. Ed clapped, and everyone joined in.

I stood up and took a bow, but the wagon lurched, and I nearly fell out. Nate was on the ground getting ready to unhitch the mules and stopped them before they took off again. My pride was the only thing hurt.

The rest of the family entered the house, but I waited outside the barn for Nate to finish taking care of the mules.

"You didn't have to do that in front of the whole family." I stood with my arms crossed over my chest as he exited.

He stopped and leaned against the barn. "It turned out all right. You're still going to need a few lessons." He glanced my direction, but stayed several yards from me. "I'll bring the smaller carriage tomorrow afternoon. One of the horses can pull that. It'll be easier."

"I can walk to Highland's and anyplace else I want to go." I left out the part about not being here much longer.

"Just the same, Lera's right. You need to know how to handle a carriage. It wouldn't hurt to know how to ride, either. I should have taught you sooner."

I stuck my palm out between us. "Oh no, don't blame yourself. I have been actively avoiding the horses."

"What for? Riding is faster than the carriage. It's fun, too." He meandered over close to me. "You can feel freer riding than running."

The guy knew how to get my attention.

"About that." I dropped my hand to my side and peered up at him. "Could you get my running gear back from Mattie?"

"Yes." He crossed his arms over his chest and gazed out across the field.

I looked from him to the door. Why was he still standing there?

He grinned at me. "What's it worth to you?"

I narrowed my eyes, torn. I loathed emotional blackmail, but I really wanted to feel that freedom, and it wouldn't happen on a horse. Not for a long time.

I sighed. "What do you want?"

"Go horseback riding with me this afternoon."

My cheeks warmed. "I might not come back."

His face paled. "I thought Jenny had delayed."

I rolled my eyes. "I meant I might not live through the experience."

He laughed, relief flooding his face. "You'll be fine. I'll let you ride Mr. Ed. He likes you."

"What about John? A horse killed him."

Nate's face clouded up. "That was different." He turned away and loped inside.

I followed, hoping he'd forget about the ride.

~

As soon as dinner was over, Nate ushered me out to the barn. He showed me how to saddle his horse and then helped me saddle Mr. Ed.

"Who are you riding today?" I asked. Anything to delay.

Nate patted the mare's dark brown withers. "Mary Ann."

"That's a strange name for a horse."

"That's what I thought, but Ed said it went with the name of the other horse we got that day." He pointed to a reddish-brown mare.

I smirked. "Let me guess. Ginger?"

He glanced at me, his head cocked. "Yeah, how'd you know?"

"It's a long story."

"We've got all afternoon." He helped me up on Mr. Ed. "You can talk while we ride."

Nate mounted his horse and showed me how to press my heels into the animal to get started. I managed to get Mr. Ed going on the first try and side by side, we walked the path toward Nate's. I kept quiet at first, concentrating on staying in the saddle.

"So, where did the horses get their names?" Nate asked.

"Has Ed told you anything about the future?" I hazarded a glance at him.

He squinted at me. "Not much."

I spent the rest of the afternoon explaining radio, movies, television, telephones, and air travel, concentrating on the technologies that he might experience in his lifetime.

We continued past Nate's house out to the lane—Bridger Street in my time—out front. I assumed we'd ride down to the main road and back, but Nate veered off into the pasture. We rode for quite a while, not seeing anything but fields. I stopped my monologue. "Is all this land yours?"

"Yep." Nate sat taller.

"No wonder you have to hire people to help."

Nate bobbed his head toward me. "You haven't gotten to the part about Mr. Ed and Mary Ann."

"They're two different shows." I explained about *Mr. Ed* first. I patted the neck of the horse I rode. "This guy looks a lot like the one in the show, but doesn't sound anything like him."

Nate laughed. "What about Mary Ann?"

"And Ginger." I started to point at him, but kept both hands on the reins. By the time I finished explaining *Gilligan's Island*, the sun kissed the horizon. We were still miles from home. I furrowed my brow at Nate.

He nodded. "We're going to have to trot."

"What?" I cringed.

"You can do it. Dig your heels in a little harder, like this." He accelerated.

Mr. Ed kept up, but it took all my resolve not to pull back on the reins. When we arrived at Nate's, I was sore, and it was dark. Nate took a lantern from the barn, and we started walking the horses toward Mattie's.

"I wish I could stay here tonight." Did I say that out loud?

"I wish you could too." Nate grasped my hand. "I'd let you, but we need to go to Mattie's anyway. She'll worry if we don't."

"See, if we had a phone, we could call her."

He squeezed my hand. "We'll be the first to have one."

I smiled but only for an instant. By the time he could get a phone, I would be gone.

Chapter 22

Caleb finished his math problem, glanced up at me, and then at the pantry door. He'd been fidgeting more than usual this afternoon, maybe because the house was quiet with Lera, Mattie, and Mark all off visiting Emily and her parents.

The back door banged shut, and Caleb dropped his slate on the table and hopped out of his chair.

Ed appeared in the doorway. "Caleb, you ready to go fishing?"

"Yes, sir!" Caleb ran right past Ed, into the pantry.

Ed chuckled. "Nate's coming with us, Cassie. You're welcome to come along."

I smiled to hide my inward shudder. "No thanks. You all go have fun."

"We'll bring fish home for dinner." Ed nodded and left.

I took the opportunity to head toward Nate's house. Exhausted from two weeks of wedding preparations, lessons with Caleb, driving and riding instruction from Nate, and panic, I still couldn't pass up this chance. I'd given up on Jenny taking me home and needed a new plan. From the first day, I'd known Nate's house was the key, but how?

After hurrying down the tree-lined path to Nate's back door, I wandered through the house trying to think. Upstairs in the back hallway, I noticed the closet door I'd left ajar weeks before. Surprised it hadn't been closed, I entered the little space. I picked up one of the journals I'd dusted off, opened to the front, and read about Nate when he was a baby. He was big and healthy and didn't cry much. The center section chronicled his early childhood and led toward his mother's hopes for his future. She prayed he'd grow into a kind, gentle man. I clutched the book to my chest. Her prayers had been answered.

Toward the end of the journal, she'd written a letter to Nate. Did he know about it? I bit my lip. I would never open anyone else's mail, but this wasn't the same, was it? Despite misgivings, I read it. The letter indicated she knew she was going to die. She wrote Nate that she loved him and exhorted him to read his Bible and stay involved with people of faith. He must have read this, probably over and over.

I sighed and placed the book back on the shelf. It would come in handy for someone who truly was going to marry Nate. It was like a message sent through time.

That's it! Why didn't I think of it sooner? The last time I'd come to the museum, Adam, the curator had told me they'd recently found a journal and they would be poking around for more gems.

He'd smiled and shaken his head. "This guy was a real crackpot."

My eyes flew open wide. Ed? But his journal was probably the one that left the dust outline. So maybe they don't have it now and wouldn't be looking. But they weren't looking for anything when they found Ed's, and my visit was after Ed had gone missing. Pressing my fingers to my temples, I trotted downstairs.

At the desk in the sitting room, I pulled out a sheet of paper and a pencil. My hands trembled and I knew I'd never be able to get anything legible out of a fountain pen. But hold it. If I wrote in pencil, would they still be able to read it in a hundred and forty years? Shoot. I dropped the pencil and retrieved a pen, an ink bottle, and a piece of scrap paper to practice.

After several tries, I produced the following note for Todd, written on Nate's good stationery:

> Todd,
> I didn't go to DC. I accidentally used your new invention. Jenny's holding me hostage. 1870. You know where.
> Cassandra June.

And this one for the museum curator:

> Adam Livingston,
> Please give the enclosed note to Todd James, 206, Bridger St. I'm in trouble, and this is the only place I could leave it. I'll explain as soon as I can.
> Cassandra McPherson

I picked up the notes by the edges so as not to smear the ink, and ran upstairs to the closet. Scanning the shelves, I tried to find a place where the notes would stay hidden until Adam could find them.

I folded the notes, Adam's on top, and slid them into one of the journals down the stack. Now, all I had to do was pray that Adam would see them before anyone else did. It was a long shot, but I had done something to help myself. As I strolled the wooded path toward Mattie's, I prayed, "God take me home before the wedding."

~

The next morning while Mattie, Lydia and I sewed in the sitting room, my mind wandered. What would I be doing if I were at home? I would definitely be at work, probably in a meeting. I loathed most meetings. My favorite part of work was spent in the lab, designing circuits, or testing my circuit boards after they had come from the fabrication shop. I missed it, but not as much as I would have expected. I'd been so busy trying to survive here and figure out how to get home, that I hadn't spent much time thinking about being there.

"Penny for your thoughts," Mattie said.

I looked up to find her watching me not sew. How long had I been just sitting? "Nothing. Tired I guess." It was lame but all I could come up with.

She leaned toward me. "You aren't getting cold feet, are you?"

"Oh, no." I pushed my needle through the heavy gray fabric. It wasn't a lie. I'd had cold feet from the beginning.

"You know, the wedding is a week from tomorrow," she said in her cheery voice.

"Is Lera coming back tomorrow or Saturday?" Lydia asked.

"Saturday. Why?" Mattie peered at her daughter.

Lydia shrugged. "Just wondering."

Lydia usually didn't make idle conversation. What was up? When Mattie left the room to tend to something in the kitchen, I seized my opportunity. "Lydia, why so concerned about Lera?"

She stabbed her needle into the linen. "I was hoping when Lera gets here, Jenny will stop coming over every day."

I tilted my head. "I thought you'd been getting along with her."

She snorted. "I've had to. Everyone else scatters when she arrives."

"Well, she always comes during Caleb's lessons or my driving time." I rested the fabric in my lap, a smile forming on my face. "Not that I'm upset. Why don't you like her?"

She narrowed her eyes at me. "You're purposely avoiding her."

I showed her the most innocent expression I could muster.

"She's always asking about you. If your moods have changed suddenly. How busy you are. Stuff like that."

I furrowed my brow. "I'm sure I don't know why."

She rolled her eyes up like she didn't believe me. She had a right not to. But why would Jenny be suspicious of me?

I exhaled. "Well, you're probably right to be wary of her."

Lydia nodded and turned away. I felt relieved that the conversation was over until she whipped her head around again. "Is Jenny from the future, too?"

My hands flew to my mouth, narrowly missing poking my face with the needle. I stuck my needle into the cloth and listened, to make sure Mattie wasn't approaching. "This is getting out of hand."

"I'm right, aren't I?" Her eyes shown bright.

"Yes." I couldn't lie. "Who doesn't know?"

Lydia counted on her fingers. "Lera, Mama, Mark, Sarah, and Caleb."

"At least it's a majority." Resisting telling her she was wrong about her mother, I prayed to know how much I should disclose. I squinted at her. "How did you know?"

She showed me a rare sheepish grin. "Oh, you know, the way you showed up. Your hair, those clothes, the screw you hid in your drawer."

"I'd forgotten about that." I tilted my head. "How did that help you?"

"Nate told me you found it in the spot where you landed. I don't know any vehicle or anything else that would contain anything like that. Too shiny."

I raised an eyebrow. "Did your pa's journal help, too?"

Her face flushed as she made several quick small stitches on the apron. "What's Jenny here for?"

Thankfully, before I could answer, Mattie appeared at the door.

I cleared my throat. "I thought you said she was staying

with Simon. Didn't she have an ardent admirer she wasn't fond of?"

Lydia stared daggers at me until her mother entered the room. Then she busied herself sewing.

"Talking about people behind their backs is gossip, Missy." Mattie focused on Lydia, but I knew she was talking to me as well.

"Yes, Ma'am." Lydia kept her head down, needle flashing.

"We had enough of that when Lera was here." Mattie sat in her wingback chair.

Lydia and I glanced at each other. Lydia rolled her eyes, and I doubled my lips over to keep from laughing.

That afternoon, I told Nate about the incident. He agreed that I shouldn't tell Lydia any more than I had to. Both of us wanted to get a peek at Ed's journal.

I went to bed early and searched for the little book, hoping Lydia had hidden it in our room. After looking in the drawers, wardrobe, and behind the shutters, I'd about given up. I sat on the bed and my eyes wandered to Lydia's side of the room. That lightbulb flashed into my mind. No, she couldn't have stashed it there; it was the obligatory hiding place on every sit-com.

But Lydia didn't know that. I lifted the mattress and uncovered the journal. Of course, I didn't get past the first few lines before floorboards creaked outside the door. I stashed the book where I'd found it and climbed into bed.

The lines I'd read explained why Ed had locked the closet door. The journal was meant for the museum curator to find. It asked him to locate Todd and tell him to get Ed back from 1840. Apparently, Adam hadn't believed Ed's journal. I hadn't mentioned time-travel, so I still had hope that he would deliver my note to Todd.

When Lydia entered, I faked sleep to avoid her questions. In case it was a form of lying, I prayed for forgiveness. I'd been praying more and more, but not getting any answers.

PAMELA G. BAKER

Chapter 23

On Saturday, late morning, a shiny black closed carriage arrived. I veered toward it from the outhouse as Lera exited the cab, a big smile on her face.

She ran to the porch hugged Caleb who clung to her.

I glanced in the cab for Simon, but Lera arrived alone.

Lera pulled out of Caleb's embrace, but held onto his arm. "Simon had some business to attend to in Atlanta." Lera's smile didn't reach her eyes as she bobbed her head toward me. "But he'll be here in time for your wedding, Cassie." She turned back to Caleb. "I couldn't be away from my boy another day." She squeezed him again, and they trotted into the house.

I bit my lip as I ambled down the walkway. Were she and Simon having troubles already? Was that why Jenny was still here? To make sure they stayed together? But Jenny wouldn't know, yet. She hadn't been to the future since the wedding—or had she?

About an hour later, Lera and Caleb took off under protest. Mattie had repeatedly asked Lera to stay until Simon came back, but Lera insisted that Caleb needed to get used to the new house. Lydia and I exchanged knowing glances. Living in the mansion was one of Lera's biggest reasons for getting married.

"I'll come over Wednesday and Thursday to help get ready for the wedding, Miss Mattie." Lera flounced toward me. "I expect to see you Monday afternoon for Caleb's lessons. I'm sure Nate's taught you to drive by now."

I put one hand on my hip. "He has, but I'll be walking."

~

Sunday morning our pew felt too spacious. Mattie played the piano as usual, but Lera and Caleb sat in Simon's pew with Jenny. They all had glum looks on their faces, especially Caleb sandwiched between them, no doubt being held down. I sat in my usual spot between Lydia and Nate. Over the past few weeks, the services had become more informative and comfortable for me. But this morning, I started to squirm as soon as we entered the building. It was the last Sunday before the wedding. I didn't feel right about going through with it, but I couldn't see a way out.

The sermon topic was vows and oaths. The main point was to say what you mean and mean what you say, something I'd always tried to do. I chewed on the thought through the rest of the service, the ride home, and dinner. When Nate and I went for our usual Sunday drive, I couldn't stand it any longer.

"Nate, I don't think I can go through with it." I kept the horse steady as I glanced at him.

"What?" His tone hesitant, he squinted at me.

"The wedding. I mean, after the sermon today. I don't think I can take that vow, knowing I'll be leaving." I bit my lip as I watched him out of the corner of my eye.

He didn't move a muscle except in his face. He closed his eyes and tightened his jaw. I wasn't sure if he was trying to think of something to say or keep himself from saying what was on his mind. Probably the latter.

While I stared at Nate, no one was watching the road. We hit something hard. The carriage popped up and when it landed, I fell on top of Nate. He caught himself just before tumbling out. The horse took off full tilt and Nate had to take over the reins to get the carriage under control. He stopped and got out to check for damage.

"There's a crack in the wheel but it should get us home." He wiped his brow.

I craned my neck. "What did we hit?"

"Probably a rock." He continued to walk around the carriage, checking the wheels.

I covered my face with my hands, rested my elbows on my knees, and shook so hard the carriage rocked. Nate slid in next to me and draped his arm around my shoulders. "Don't worry. I'm sure we didn't leave an animal dead on the road."

I sobbed louder and leaned my head on his shoulder. We stayed there until I stopped crying and could speak. "I'm so sorry. I wasn't paying attention."

He gave me his handkerchief. "It's all right. It could have happened to anyone."

"Don't you see? I don't belong here." I wiped a tear from my eye.

"You're the one who can't see." He leaned back enough to tip my chin up and gaze into my eyes. "You've been here three months. And you've changed all our lives. Caleb is learning to read. Lydia has grown a lot more independent. Ed has started talking about his past." He paused for a few seconds. "I've let myself love someone again."

My breath caught. I felt both thrilled and sick. "No, you can't do that." I shifted my weight off him and faced forward. "Anyone could have taught Caleb to read." My voice shook. "Lydia would have grown independent anyway, and you would have found someone else without me."

But I was wrong. He'd remained a bachelor. I studied the buttons on my shirtwaist.

"I didn't, did I?" He turned me toward him, his hands on my biceps. "That's why the house was a museum. I didn't have a family, right?"

I nodded and pulled away. "But in the history, I knew, you

225

lived with your spinster Aunt. Ed already changed that, so your story might be different without me."

He shook his head, his brow furrowed.

I leaned toward him. "Nate, I have to try to go back. You need to break up with me before the wedding. Use any reason you want."

He faced front and clenched his teeth. "No."

"I don't want to hurt you. It will look like you were jilted twice."

He peered at me through shining eyes. Maybe I was getting through to him. Maybe he'd break up with me for Mattie's sake, at least. I was prepared to agree with any scenario he suggested to break off the engagement.

He took a deep breath. "Jenny's not taking you back any time soon, right?"

"Right."

"If you leave me before the wedding, where will you go?"

He had a point. I didn't know anyone else except Lera. At the thought of staying with her and Simon, I shuddered. I couldn't support myself either. The only thing I was qualified for was teaching, if that, and the town already had a teacher. I had to stay here for Todd to find me or to be close to Jenny. If she did agree to take me back, she certainly wouldn't come looking for me.

"I don't know." I blinked a tear away.

He touched my shoulder. "Cassie, did you ever stop to consider there might have been a reason you were allowed to come here?"

I rolled my eyes. "It was an accident."

"I don't think so." His voice was quiet but firm.

"What do you mean?" I leaned back.

He looked me in the eye. "I think God sent you here."

I snorted.

"I'm serious." He glanced at the sky. "At least God allowed

it, and He's using you." He leaned over toward me. "I've noticed that those blasted crinolines are being worn less and less and the skirts are getting smaller." He grinned. "That's a ministry in itself."

A genuine smile formed on my lips. It must have encouraged him.

He smirked. "And I don't think any of us would have thought to teach Caleb to read using word problems."

"That didn't work all that well." I pursed my lips.

Nate pointed at me. "But it got him started."

"The book of Esther worked better and that was your idea." I dipped my head toward him.

"See? We make a good team." He leaned in closer, swung his arm around me, and squeezed my opposite shoulder. His expression tender, his eyes searched my soul.

I blew out a breath, my eyes still locked with his. "You're not going to let me out of it are you?"

He grinned. "Nope."

I raised my eyebrows. "Even if I'm still bent on leaving when I get the chance?"

"Yep." He tightened his hold. "Even if it's only a few days. There's no guarantee we will both live that long anyway."

"Don't say that." I faced forward.

"Why? It's true." He shifted in the seat next to me, keeping one arm around me. "I'll take whatever time I have with you and be grateful for it."

I shook my head and snapped the reins. The horse pulled the carriage down the dirt road.

After an uncomfortable silence, Nate asked, "How far have you gotten in Esther?"

"We read it through once a couple of weeks ago, why?"

"Why do you think it's in the Bible?"

"I don't know." It didn't mention God. "Okay, so why is it in there?"

"This is only my opinion, mind you, but I think it's an example of how important each one of us can be in God's plan."

"I'm not following you." I kept my eyes on the road.

"Esther was in a place where she could save her people. She didn't try to get there. I believe God allowed her to be in that situation. He knew she would have the courage to handle it."

I glanced at him. "It took courage to talk to her husband?"

"Back then, if you asked for an audience with the king and he was insulted—" He made a slashing motion across his neck. "Esther couldn't wait for him to come to her, so she took the chance that he would agree to attend her dinner."

"Oh, that whole fasting and praying thing makes more sense now."

He shifted on the seat. "You're probably wondering why I brought that up."

I jerked my head toward him and then, to avoid another accident, turned back to the road.

"I'm right, aren't I?"

"Yes. Tell me."

"Remember when Mordecai tells Esther that she was put there for such a time as this? If she didn't save the people, God could find another way, but she'd miss the blessing?"

I cocked my head. "Yes?"

He leaned toward me. "I believe you were sent here for a reason."

I pulled away. "To keep your blood line from dying out?" Where did that come from? I didn't much like the venom in my voice.

Nate either didn't notice or chose to ignore it. "Maybe, but I think there's something else."

I squinted at him. "What?"

"That, I don't know." He paused. "It's only a feeling. I've been praying about it."

What could I say?

For the rest of the ride, I stole glances at Nate and tried to think straight. He would make a wonderful husband and I was certainly attracted to him. But I couldn't stay here, so I wouldn't let myself fall in love with him.

Part of me wanted to pray for direction and part of me just wanted to get back to my old life. No, not my old life. When I got back to my time, I would definitely make some changes. I had already.

Chapter 24

I awoke with a start, blinking at the sunlight streaming in through the window. They must have let me sleep in today. I should've gotten out of bed, but I couldn't move a muscle. All the work, and standing for wedding gown fittings had left me a little sore, but that wasn't the reason I felt paralyzed.

Today was my wedding day.

I groaned and closed my eyes. For the past four days I'd been flip-flopping back and forth, trying to decide whether to go through with the wedding or run. I'd prayed about it, but a lot of those prayers were more the 'take me home before' than the 'tell me what to do' type. I kept coming back to the same problem. I didn't want to take vows I had no intention of keeping. But if I ran, where would I go?

"Please, God, tell me what to do. If you don't want me to go through with the wedding, provide me some place to go. Amen."

I sighed and swung my legs off the bed using the momentum to stand. I dressed in the flowered gown, saving my gray one and a new blue one for the wedding trip. Nate wouldn't tell me where we were going, only that we would be back by Monday. He knew I didn't want to be away from Lera and Jenny, and he didn't want to leave Ed with the whole work load for too long.

I went down for breakfast, expecting to eat in the kitchen. When I reached the dining room, I stopped short.

"Surprise!" Over a dozen women stood around the table, clapping.

Mattie hurried over to me and ushered me into the room. "We wanted to have the party for you yesterday but we needed an extra day."

I plastered on a fake smile and took Ed's seat at the head of the table. Jenny, Lera, and Lydia sat closest to me. Mrs. Kelley, the ladies from the quilting club, and several others from church occupied the other end of the table. I nibbled a doughnut and sipped tea, while everyone else chatted and presented me with several gifts to unwrap.

I peered at the presents. "You didn't need to. Nate's house is already set up."

"Nonsense." Lera forced a long narrow package on me. "You need a few things of your own."

I read the card. "These are from Lera and Simon." I unwrapped some nice white tapers and expensive silver candle sticks, held them up, and nodded toward Lera. "They're lovely, thank you."

The ladies gave me lace doilies, an apron, a few utensils I wasn't sure what to do with, and one huge box.

Mattie handed it to me, a big smile on her face. "It's from the club."

"Gee, I wonder what this is." I smirked as I slid out the quilt. "Oh!" My hand covered my mouth as I held up the most gorgeous bedcover I'd ever seen, white with brown and gold accents. They'd used the wedding ring pattern and the center square had our names and today's date. Tears ran down my face. "It's beautiful. Thank you." Mattie handed me a handkerchief, and I blotted my eyes. "You put a lot of work into this." I almost felt guilty for wanting to back out of the wedding.

"It wasn't a problem." Mattie waved her hand toward the

quilters. "We wanted to show you how much you and Nate mean to us."

Oh no. They hadn't given one to Lera. I glanced at her, trying to figure out if she was hurt, but she appeared a million miles away at the moment.

I'd been so obsessed with my own problems that I hadn't paid much attention to Lera. During my lessons with Caleb, I'd seen her every day, but her demeanor hadn't registered. Today, she seemed distant and guarded. She hadn't even fixed a plate for herself. Was she thinner, or was it my imagination?

After I'd opened the gifts, everyone chatted, each in their own little circles. Due to the lack of space, most of the women stood. This might be my last chance to make a friend I could run to. I recognized Mrs. Hodges and her granddaughter, Ida. I strolled over and opened a conversation, admitting to being nervous about the wedding, extremely nervous. Mrs. Hodges told me that was normal and then went on about what a good man Nate was. I couldn't argue with that.

Mrs. Kelley greeted me but I didn't try to connect with her. If I stayed with them, I might find myself on a mission trip out west. Moving around the room, I re-introduced myself to all the women whose names I couldn't remember, and hinted that I was having second thoughts about the wedding. They treated me kindly, but no one offered to help. Couldn't they see how desperate I was?

Jenny sidled up to me and whispered in my ear, "Having a hard time finding someone to take you in? Kind of last minute, isn't it?"

"I'm just making conversation." I turned my attention to Emily's mother without a hint of wanting to back out of the wedding.

Before Jenny could interrupt again, Mattie announced that it was time to get me and my dress to the church. She had planned for me to change there, to minimize the prospect of ruining my dress on the way. Good plan.

Everyone hurried to their carriages. Lydia and Lera rode together, which left me alone with Mattie. Something I'd avoided since my first day.

I settled myself on the carriage seat next to Nate's aunt. "Why did everyone agree to come all the way out here this morning, knowing they'll be coming back for the reception?" I scrunched my nose. "They could have given us the gifts then."

Mattie patted my hand. "Because they want to show you how much they care about you, dear."

From the buggy next to ours, Lydia called out. "It didn't hurt that they had dishes to bring for the reception. They took them to Nate's earlier."

I nodded, relieved not to add to their burdens.

"Besides, we don't often have the opportunity for a day-long party," Lera shouted as they drove off.

"Now, Cassie." Mattie flicked the reins and our carriage started rolling. "I know you're having second thoughts. That's normal. Don't worry though, Nate will treat you right."

"That's not what I'm worried about." I fiddled with my hands in my lap. "I'm afraid I'll mess up."

Mattie laughed and slapped her knee. "Well, of course, you will. So will he, but you'll work things out."

"But what if we can't?" I heaved a sigh. "What if I can't give him what he needs?"

"Oh, child. Don't you know? You are what he needs." Mattie winked at me. "I knew it before he did." She smiled and whipped the reins to get the horse to move faster. "If you ever get in a bad squabble, you just come running down the road. You're always welcome at my house."

I felt a glimmer of hope. "Thanks, Miss Mattie." Testing the waters, I said, "What if I panic today?"

"You won't. You'll do the right thing." Shot down. Maybe.

"What if the right thing is—"

"Whoa, Elvis!" The carriage popped up. "You've got to get us there in one piece. It's a big day." After she stabilized the carriage, she glanced at me. "What were you saying, dear?"

I squinted at her. "Elvis?"

"His original name was King, but Ed started calling him Elvis. He never told me why." She peered at the sky and then turned her attention back to the carriage. "Ed always had such fun naming the animals." She smiled. "But that's not what we were talking about. What was it?"

"Oh, uh, I can't remember. Must not have been important." The conversation wouldn't have led to what I wanted, anyway.

She nodded toward me. "Anytime you have a question, you come to me. I haven't been married nearly thirty years and learned nothing."

When we arrived at the church, Mattie took me straight to the room in the basement. Lydia and Lera had built a fire in the fireplace and already had the curling iron heating. A metal tub in the middle of the room sat waiting for the water to get hot. I didn't look forward to taking a bath with all these women present.

Thankfully, after Lera and Lydia poured the water into the tub, they all left to attend to the flowers and other last-minute details.

I submerged my head in the warm water. What if I didn't come back up? That would get me home all right. Just not to the twenty-first century. I popped out of the water, splashing some over onto the stone floor. At least it wasn't a carpet. I'd have to be careful when I got out. Maybe I could slip, hurt myself, and we'd have to call off the wedding? I shook my head. No, with my luck I'd break a bone.

I took a deep breath, and tried to focus on something positive. Nate's smiling face flashed through my mind. He always said to trust God. That's what I needed to do. God would provide a way out.

I clung to that hope through the drying off and clothing process, all Lera's ministrations on my hair, Mattie placing her pearls around my neck, and the kisses on the cheek from Lydia, Lera, and Mattie.

When I was ready, Ed came to get me. Lera and Mattie went ahead, Lera to be seated in the second pew and Mattie to the piano. Lydia, Ed, and I walked up the stairs at the back of the sanctuary and waited in the stairwell.

I gave Ed a pleading look. Don't make me do this.

He draped his arm around my shoulders and gave me a little squeeze.

After Lydia started down the aisle, Ed leaned over and whispered, "Have faith."

I bit my lip. "I trusted that God would get me home before now. That didn't work."

"That's what you wanted." He peered at me. "Have you bothered to ask what God wants?"

I stared at him. Was he was teasing? No, there wasn't even a hint of a grin on his face. How was I supposed to know what God wanted in a specific instance? I hadn't read the whole Bible, but I was pretty sure my situation wasn't covered.

"Don't you think this is unfair to Nate?" I whispered.

"No." He glanced toward the front where Nate stood. "He knows what he's getting into, doesn't he?"

I exhaled. "He knows everything I do."

Ed nodded. "There you go."

The wedding march began. Ed escorted me down the center aisle. I tried to smile, but in contrast to the genuine smile on Nate's face, mine must have looked forced. I wanted to run, but Nate knew what was going on. I hadn't tried to trick him. I'd tried to get him to call it off. Oh well, he was getting what he asked for.

When I arrived at the altar, Nate took my hand. I went on autopilot, repeating the vows, trying not to pay too much attention to them.

"I now pronounce you husband and wife." Pastor Kelley's proclamation startled me. I'd forgotten to talk to him about that. I had brought it up to Nate right after Lera's wedding, though.

"You may kiss your bride."

Nate enveloped me in his arms and planted a soft kiss on my lips. I leaned in, my hands trapped between us. The congregation clapped. When Nate released me, he escorted me down the aisle, and we waited in front of the church to greet the guests.

After all the guests had filed by us, a middle-aged man arrived with a huge camera on a tripod. He posed us in front of the church. He didn't need a flash, but we had to stand still forever. He took one picture of Nate and me and one of the whole wedding party. As I stood, my smile frozen in place, I wondered why most of the guests stayed to watch. When we headed toward the carriage, I found out.

Our friends pelted us with rice. Nate and I ran through the crowd and jumped into the back of the carriage. Mark got the horse moving before we were settled.

I grabbed the edge of the seat to steady myself. "I wasn't expecting that."

"Are you okay? Some of that stung." Nate brushed rice off his jacket and started to brush it off me.

"I'm fine, but I don't think I'll be able to get it out of my dress or my hair." I shook my head and a little shower of rice fell off into Nate's lap. "Sorry, I didn't mean to get you again."

"It's all right."

We continued brushing ourselves off, but neither of us said anything. It was one of the few times I'd felt uneasy being quiet with Nate.

Nate was the first to break the silence. "I've got a surprise for you. I'll show you after the reception."

"Why'd you tell me now?" I stopped brushing rice and gave

him the side-eye.

He smirked. "You're cute when you're annoyed. You know that?"

I pursed my lips. "So, you're going to annoy me, just to watch my reaction?"

"Maybe." He placed his arm up on the back of the seat behind me and motioned for me to lean against him.

I sat up as straight as I could until the carriage hit a rut, and I fell into him. He closed his arm around my shoulder and held me. I stayed put. After being held in silence for a quarter of the ride, I had to admit I liked it.

"Are you going to tell me where we're going tonight?" I craned my neck to see his face.

He grinned. "Nope. It's a surprise."

I faced the front. "You're just full of surprises today."

"So are you." His tone had softened.

"Me?" I looked up at him. "Were you surprised to see me walking down the aisle?"

"A little." His eyes twinkled. "But mostly, I was happy. I am happy."

He didn't ask how I was feeling. I probably couldn't have told him, anyway.

When we arrived at the house, Jenny, Lera, and Simon disembarked from Simon's closed carriage.

"Congratulations, you two." Jenny gave me an air kiss and Nate an overly friendly hug. I wore a smug smile because Nate didn't hug her back.

Lera gave me a squeeze and a real kiss on the cheek. "I hope you're very happy, Cassie." She shook Nate's hand. "You take care of her, hear?"

Nate nodded.

"Congratulations, you old scoundrel." Simon shook Nate's hand. "You got the prettiest girl in town."

I glanced at Lera, but she turned her head, and I couldn't

see her expression.

"Thank you, Simon." Nate stepped toward his cousin. "Lera, you look very lovely today, as always." He gave her a quick hug and then took my hand and led me off to greet some of our arriving guests. He'd handled Simon well. It was a good thing I hadn't said anything.

When I'd dared to think about the wedding, I'd always assumed the reception would be awkward. I was wrong. Nate held my hand most of the afternoon, greeting all the guests with me. The most awkward moment came toward the end, when Jenny screamed something unintelligible. Over the crowd, I could see her and Lera arguing. I'd started toward them to find out what it was all about when Mattie and Ed rushed over to us.

Ed pointed at the sun hovering toward the west. "You two better get ready to go."

"I'll have a picnic packed for you." Mattie nodded toward the front door, then disappeared through the crowd.

Nate ushered me into the house and led me to the once-empty master suite.

I stood in the doorway and gaped at an oak sleigh bed, an armoire, two dressers and a vanity, all matching. It was the most beautiful furniture in the house and it looked nothing like the dark woods in all the other rooms. There were even new draperies and understated wallpaper, very much my style.

Nate took my hand and led me to the closet.

I walked through into the bathroom. "You put an extra door in here? When did you have time to do all this?"

He grinned. "When you and the ladies were planning the weddings."

In the bedroom, I caressed the footboard. "How did you know? I would have picked this out."

"I'm amazing." He puffed his chest out and lifted himself to his full height.

I narrowed my eyes.

He relaxed his posture. "I asked Lera."

I sat on the bed feeling a little sorry for myself that I would only be here for a few months, if that. Then I felt guilty. "You didn't have to go to all this trouble."

"It wasn't any trouble. Ed already had most of it made." Nate sat next to me, taking my hand in his. He patted the mattress. "I wouldn't mind trying this out right now, but I think our carriage is ready."

I sprang up and stepped away. My sudden jolt of nerves surprised me.

"I'll go down so you can change into your traveling clothes." Nate started for the door.

I whirled toward him. "Wait, I can't get out of this dress by myself."

"I'll send Lydia." He stopped and turned toward me. "Oh, wait. I can help." He grinned as he sauntered to me.

I pointed to the fasteners down the back of the dress. "I can get the ones at the top and bottom, but I can't reach the middle ones."

"I can reach them all. Just stand still." He undid all the little buttons, but he took his sweet time. I tapped my foot through the whole process. When he finished, he turned me around to face him, gave me a quick kiss and strutted away.

As he was about to go out the door, he looked back. "If Aunt Mattie asks, Lydia helped you with the dress. And Aunt Mattie said to leave it on the bed."

"I know. She'll take care of it." I held my dress to myself and waved him off.

He blew me a kiss before he closed the door behind him.

After I changed, I took one more stroll around the beautiful room. He had gone to a lot of trouble. I took a deep breath and walked downstairs.

Nate waited for me in the empty foyer and held his arm out as I approached. When we stepped outside, our guests lined the walkway to the carriage, decorated with a variety of different sized cans, colorful cloth streamers, and a sign that read, "Just Married."

I squinted at Nate. "I didn't think this was the custom here."

He leaned in and whispered, "It's not. I'm pretty sure it was Ed's idea."

One glance at the broad smile on Ed's face confirmed it.

"Thank you ever so much." I jabbed Ed's shoulder as we walked by.

He tipped his fancy top hat. "Any time."

We climbed into the carriage, and Nate snapped the reins. As we drove off, we waved to Mattie, Ed, Lera, and Caleb. I didn't see Simon or Jenny. Why had Jenny and Lera been arguing, and why had Mattie kept it from us?

We clanked down the seldom-used road until we were out of sight. Nate stopped the carriage and started untying cans. I climbed out to help.

"Anxious to get there?" Nate squatted next to the wagon, peering up at me.

I folded my arms in front of me and scowled.

"Aw, come now. I was teasing." He untied strings from the carriage. "I thought you were curious about where we were going."

"I am. But we can't be going very far since we're coming back Monday." I lifted my chin. "I think I know."

"You do, do ya?" He squat-walked a few paces down the carriage and continued removing cans. "Where?"

"Atlanta."

Nate smirked. "We'll see about that."

I wagged my finger at him. "You can't change your mind just because I guessed it."

"No. I've already made the arrangements." He wore a cocky grin as he removed the last can.

Maybe I had guessed wrong. I started to pull off the sign.

He nodded at me. "I wouldn't mind leaving that one on, but if you want me to take it off I will."

I shook my head and climbed back into the carriage.

He whistled as he landed on the seat next to me.

I faced forward. "Nate, what was all that commotion?"

"That was a send-off, Ed-style." He flicked the reins, and the horse started to walk.

I glanced at him. "No, I mean with Jenny and Lera. Something happened that Mattie didn't want us to see."

He shrugged. "And you think I'd know about it?"

"Well, you did go downstairs earlier than me. And Mattie doesn't keep many secrets from you."

"She kept me out of the kitchen. Made me wait in the foyer for you."

I wanted to stew about it, but Nate's good mood was infectious. He kept asking me questions, taking my mind off the mystery. We chatted about the wedding and the guests other than Jenny. About halfway to Atlanta, we turned off the main road.

"Okay, so I guess I was wrong," I said, more curious than upset.

"Don't feel bad. There's no way you could have guessed this." Nate smiled wide.

We drove so far off the main road, I was afraid we were going camping for our honeymoon. Then we came to a clearing with a small lake and the prettiest log cabin. I'd say little, but it wasn't. It was about half the size of Nate's house with a wraparound porch on three sides, a wide section toward the lake. The deck must have faced due west as it looked straight into the sunset. I sat mesmerized while Nate unhitched Prince and led him to a small barn on the far side of the cabin. My skin prickled, probably due to the heat, but it brought me back to reality. Today had been more of a dream than a nightmare, but what now? I shuddered.

Nate sauntered from the barn, a smile on his face, and lifted me out of the carriage. Instead of going into the cabin, he carried me around to the swing on the back deck and then ran for the picnic basket. The moment he left, my muscles tensed. Why did I feel fine when he was with me?

After supper, we stayed in the swing, his arm around my shoulder, and watched the sun sink into the water, creating hues of purple and pink with a bit of gold mixed in. What a glorious sunset over the tree-lined lake. How could I have ever doubted the existence of God? The world had to have been designed by someone.

When the sun disappeared over the horizon, Nate took his arm from around me and started to get up.

I pulled him back. "That was breathtaking, something I've never taken the time to notice."

He took my hand in his. "I'm glad you liked it."

"Oh, I did." I pulled my hand away. The old knot formed in my stomach. "You timed this perfectly. I know what you're trying to do, but it won't work." I stiffened and slid away from him. "I'm still going back the first chance I get."

"Fine." He stood, lit a lantern, and carried it to the door. His mouth set in a firm line, he opened the door with one hand and held it for me.

I strode past him into a large room with a fireplace at either end. It had a small kitchen to my left and a living area to my right. I wondered where we would sleep until Nate raised the lantern, revealing the loft.

He pointed to a doorway near the ladder and handed me the light.

I walked in to find a working bathroom, much like the one in Nate's house. It looked new. "Whose place is this?"

"It used to be Martin's but it's ours now." He walked through the center of the room to the front door. "I'm going to get the trunk." Though Mattie had said it wasn't done, we'd packed together.

Nate brought the trunk in and dropped it next to the bathroom. "If you expect me to haul this up to the loft, you're mistaken."

It didn't take a mind reader to tell he was angry. So be it. I had never given him any hope that I'd stay.

I took my nightclothes and few toiletries out of the trunk and went into the bathroom. After a long lukewarm shower, I donned my new nightgown and robe. When I came out, Nate kneeled, brow furrowed, in front of the fireplace, pushing the ashes around with a poker. I stood there, not knowing what to say.

He nodded toward the ladder. "I'll be up in a little while." He hauled himself to his feet and shuffled toward the bathroom.

I climbed the ladder concentrating on not falling. Three quarters of the way up the whole loft came into view. Though the space was large enough for several beds, there was only one. I hesitated then continued to the platform, walked to the bed, and set my lantern on a small table next to it. Too restless to sit, I wandered around the room. Why did I do this to myself, to him? It wasn't fair. He might be able to start a love affair knowing it would end soon, but I couldn't.

My stomach in knots, I climbed back down the ladder. When I'd almost reached the bottom, I stepped on something other than the ladder rung.

"Ow!" He placed his palm on the small of my back.

"Oh, I'm sorry." I stepped up one rung. "I thought you were still in the bathroom."

"What are you doing?" He stood in my way.

"I thought I'd sleep on the sofa tonight." I swiveled my head toward him, nearly losing my balance.

"Go on back up before we both get hurt."

I hesitated, but he didn't budge.

"Go. We need to talk," he said.

Talking was okay. I couldn't get past him anyway, so up I

went. When I reached the top, I stood aside to let him up. He wore a white shirt that hung past his knees and was barefoot.

My cheeks heated. I'd never seen him without trousers.

He took my hand and led me over to the bed where we sat on the edge.

"Cassie, I'm sorry." He held my hand in both of his. "I didn't give you much of a choice . . . about marrying me."

I nodded and lowered my head.

He let go of my hand but leaned closer to me. "I love you. I'm not apologizing for that. I was hoping you'd give me, give us a chance."

"I can't." I stood, padded to the window, and gazed at the nearly full moon. "There's a hundred and forty years between us. Talk about an age gap."

"Actually, we're the same age," he said.

"Yes, but I don't belong here. We've been over this."

He walked over to me and placed a hand on my shoulder. "I disagree."

He turned me around to face him, took me in his arms, and kissed me. I kissed him back, but when I couldn't breathe, I pushed him away.

He started toward the ladder but stopped after a few steps and lowered his head. "I'll take you back to Mattie's in the morning."

"What?" I took hold of his arm, my heart racing. "I don't know how long I'll be here. I might as well stay with you until then. It'll be less embarrassing. For you, I mean."

Purposely gentle, he removed my hand from his arm. "No, I think it would be best to stop now. I'll go downstairs."

"Nate." I grabbed his arm again. "Why can't we just live in the same house as roommates until I leave? No one would know."

He pulled away and headed toward the ladder. "I can't do that, Cassie."

I plopped onto the bed.

"Until we got here." I peered at him. "I thought that was the deal."

His eyes bugged out. "How?" He threw up his hands and shook his head. "I'm sorry if I misled you." He took a deep breath and plodded away.

"It was probably my fault," I said in a low voice as he climbed down. I heaved a sigh and swung my legs up and under the covers. I lay there and listened to Nate fumble around downstairs. As I was about to drift off, I heard him climb the ladder.

He walked over to the side of the bed where I pretended to sleep, and touched my shoulder. "You awake?"

I didn't answer.

"I can't sleep on that little sofa." He paused, but I stayed quiet. I'm not sure why. Maybe, I wanted to see what he'd do. He walked around to the other side of the bed and crawled in, careful not to touch me. I rolled to my side, my back to him. He tapped me on the shoulder. "I knew you were still awake. You don't mind me sleeping here?"

"No, I don't mind." I'd go downstairs, but I fell asleep, instead.

When I woke up, I lay on my side and watched Nate sleep, noticing all the muscles on his bare back. He was nice to look at. And he treated me better than any guy I'd ever dated. If only he didn't live in the wrong century.

What if he could come with me? My heart quickened at the thought.

He rolled over and opened his eyes. A smile grew on his lips and then was replaced with a frown. "Morning." He sat up and swung his legs off his side of the bed.

I touched his arm. "Wait, can we talk?"

"Sure, but not here." He stood and picked his tan trousers up off the floor. He must have brought his clothes up last night.

As he was pulling on his undershirt, I sat up. "Nate, if you could, would you go home with me?"

He stopped with only one arm in a sleeve. "You'd have to support us for a while. I don't know how long it would take me to figure out a job I could do."

I shrugged. "Yeah."

"What would Todd say?" He peered at me while slipping his other arm in the sleeve.

How could I have forgotten about Todd? "That's a good question. We'd have to find a place to live."

He pulled his shirt down. "Our house probably wouldn't be available. It would either still be a museum or it might not even be there." He slipped his arms through his suspenders. "I get your point, though."

I blinked. "What point?"

"Leaving everything and everyone I know would be hard." His brow furrowed. "I'm beginning to see what a tough spot I've put you in."

I exhaled and leaned forward, hugging my knees. "Thanks for that anyway."

His eyes widened. "You really want me to go with you?" He walked past me to the ladder, stopped, and locked gazes with me. "I can tell you this. I'll pray about it. If that's what the Lord wants me to do, I will." Then he disappeared down the ladder.

I leaned back against the pillow and stared at the pitched ceiling while the magnitude of our conversation sank in. It was kind of hard to believe. I had a husband who treated me like a queen and loved me enough to follow me a hundred and forty years into an unknown future. That is, if he felt God leading him to. Shoot, it would have taken an act of God to get Todd to follow me to the next city. He never even used his own invention to come and find me. Wait, that wasn't fair. He might never have gotten my note.

"Okay, Lord. Tell me what to do." I sat up and bowed my

head. "Thank you for Nate. Please help us to be able to stay together. I love him. I didn't realize it until now." The tears rolled down my cheeks, but it felt good so I let them come.

I took a shaky breath. "You've allowed all this to happen to me. I was terribly put out at first, but now I'm glad I've had the privilege to come here. Thank you for everything I've gotten to experience. Thank you for all the people I've met, for Lera and Caleb, Mattie and Ed, Lydia, and Mark." I sniffed and wiped my eye with my knuckle. "Please help me to make the most of my time here or wherever I am." I opened my eyes and glanced at the window. "Oh, and I love you too."

A smile crept across my face. I felt both invigorated and sad. I had a new hope for the future, even though I had no idea what or where it would be. But I felt like I'd wasted most of my time here focusing on how to get back to 2010. I should have been learning all I could about the way of life, the people, everything. I should have spent as much time as possible with the people I loved.

I scrambled down the ladder to the main room, took my new blue dress, slip, and corset out of the trunk, and hurried into the bathroom. When I arrived in the kitchen area, Nate already had breakfast ready.

"I'm sorry, I was going to help," I said.

"No need." He handed me a plate of eggs and sausage. We sat at the table and began eating. He scarfed his food down without a glance in my direction. Probably not a good time to tell him my news.

"When did you bring food in?" I ate a bite of sausage.

"Caleb and Ed brought it a few days ago, when Ed finished the shower." He grinned. "They stayed over one night, and you didn't even notice."

"Mattie has kept me busy lately."

His expression sobered. "We can head back to Mattie's as soon as we finish."

"About that." I swallowed. "I've been doing some thinking and praying." My voice contained a note of pride.

Nate narrowed his eyes at me as he chewed.

I nodded and cleared my throat. "I've decided that you are right."

Nate choked.

I leaned toward him. "Are you all right?"

He tried to swallow.

I stood up and walked around the back of his chair. "Say something!"

He shook his head and put his hand to his throat. I reached both hands in front of him, made my left one into a fist, covered it with my right, and thrust my fist into his abdomen. A piece of sausage flew across the table.

He looked up at me, eyes wide. "Where did you learn that?" His voice was hoarse.

"Everyone knows it." I shrugged and strolled back to my chair. "The Heimlich Maneuver." I sat and glanced at him. "It's posted on all the restaurant walls."

"You saved my life!" He pushed his chair back and stood.

"Maybe that's why I was brought here." I shook my head. "No, I'm the one who made you choke."

He smiled and sat. "That's right." He leaned toward me and cocked his head. "You were trying to tell me something?" He scooted his chair in.

I took a deep breath. "I've decided to figure out why I was allowed to come here and to learn as much as I can while I'm here." I lowered my head. "I feel like I've wasted a lot of time."

"What does that have to do with going to Mattie's today?" He picked up his fork.

"You're right." I lifted my chin.

He held his fork out instead of taking a bite.

"I don't know how long I have left here, but no couple does. And you could be coming with me." I hesitated.

He gazed at me, leaning in.

I blurted, "I love you. I want to really be married to you even if it's just for a short time."

He dropped his fork and picked me up, chair and all. Chuckling, he let go of the chair and carried me to the ladder. "Okay, this was an oversight. I should have built a staircase."

I giggled as he put me down, and climbed the ladder in front of him. When we got to the loft, he picked me up and carried me to bed.

~

That afternoon, Nate asked if I wanted go for a swim in the lake.

I raised an eyebrow. "Did Mattie pack swimming clothes?"

He showed me his cheesy grin, then fished around in the bottom of the trunk and brought out a small package. "This is from Mattie."

I untied the string, unfolded the cloth wrapping, and held up a homemade swimsuit that looked a lot like my sports bra and running shorts. A giggle escaped me. She didn't have the right material for the bra, so she'd cut the back a bit lower and used hooks and eyes to fasten it. I could wear it under my clothing instead of my corset.

"Aunt Mattie said you didn't have anything to swim in, and she knew you wouldn't like what the other women wear."

"She's probably right. I'm sorry I laughed. It's actually pretty good." I held up the black shorts. "Do you think she'd let me wear it if the rest of the family were here?"

"Possibly. Try it on." He winked. "I want to see you in it."

I took it into the bathroom. "That's funny, I thought you'd want to see me out of it."

"That too." He chuckled.

I paraded into the great room, dressed in the new bathing suit, feeling sexier than ever. Nate ogling me didn't hurt. He didn't even make a pretense of looking away.

The next day and a half went faster than I would have believed possible. I lived in the moment, not thinking about going back, either to town or the future. We enjoyed each other's company, doing the few necessary chores together. Mattie and Ed came up in conversation, as did Lera and Caleb, Lydia and Mark. I purposely avoided talking about Jenny or Simon.

On Sunday morning, Nate read from the Bible, we sang a few hymns, and prayed together. Sunday afternoon was spent in the canoe on the lake, and Sunday evening we watched another sunset from the swing.

I sighed. "This is what I'm going to miss the most."

"What are you not going to miss?" He rubbed my shoulder.

"Nothing. I love this cabin."

"Don't try to cover it up." He curled a strand of my hair around his finger. "You were talking about going back to your time."

I bit my lip. "I didn't mean to. I haven't even thought about it since yesterday morning."

He dropped the lock of hair and leaned back. "So, are you going to answer my question?"

I snorted. "There's so many things I'm not going to miss. Let's see." I counted on my fingers. "Churning butter, wash day, riding in buggies. Have I told you about cars and paved roads?"

Nate drew me closer to him. "I expected you to say crinolines."

"I'm leaving those behind even if I stay."

He kissed the top of my head. "You thinking about staying?"

"I may not have a choice. No telling what Jenny will do."

Nate pulled away and slid a couple feet down the swing.

"Have you thought any more about going with me?" I slid toward him.

He draped his arm around me again and gave me a little squeeze. "I've been praying. No answers yet."

~

I woke up not wanting the weekend to be over. I started to dress in my gray traveling clothes, but Nate stopped me. He brought out my real running clothes and shoes. My eyes lit up.

"There's a path around the lake. It's about three miles long."

I squealed and clapped my hands. "I can go running before we leave?"

"Not by yourself." He grinned and held up a pair of shorts and a shirt that Mattie had no doubt made for him.

"You're not going to wear your boots, are you?"

Before I could get the question out, he held up a pair of Nikes. "Ed's. He and I are about the same size."

My jaw dropped. "He kept them all this time?"

"He hid them in the work room in the bottom of a trunk." Nate brought them closer. "They're still in decent condition."

We dressed and walked out to the path to warm up. Then I beat him in a race around the lake. He wasn't all that far behind me for someone who'd never run any distance.

"How often can we come here?" I stretched using the back porch railing for support.

"I was hoping to get out here every other weekend, at least in the summer. In the fall, we probably won't make it at all. Too busy."

"Winter?"

"Too cold. We'd have to huddle around the fire." He shifted and leaned over his other shin. "Maybe we will come in the winter."

"You didn't buy this place just for me, did you?" I peered at him as I reached for my toe.

"Of course not. It's about half way to Atlanta. We make several trips there a year." He bent the opposite direction. "Now we don't have to camp out on the way."

"That's good."

"Ed said it was a good investment."

This lake was a resort in my time and you had to pay dearly for frontage property. I was a little disappointed in Nate and Ed. Using Ed's knowledge of the future seemed like cheating.

"Ed told me he thought this might be a resort area one day." Nate winced. "But that was a long time ago. Before I knew he was from your time."

"Were you reading my mind?" The edges of my lips curled up.

"Maybe. Mostly, I was reading your expression." He rubbed his finger down my nose, and I batted his hand away.

~

The drive back wasn't nearly as fun as the weekend. It was hot and dusty, and the carriage seemed to hit every rut in the road. By the time we reached the house, I felt sore and irritable. It was supper time, I had no clue what we were going to eat, and I didn't feel like cooking.

I needn't have worried. Mattie appeared from the dining room as soon as we walked in the back door. "Supper's on the table." She greeted me with a kiss on the cheek. "I didn't think you'd want to cook tonight, Cassie. I hope I'm not intruding."

"Not at all." I smiled and squeezed her hand. "I'm grateful. I was wondering what I was going to feed him tonight."

What would I feed him the rest of the time I was here? I had no idea how to be the lady of the house. Until now, I'd been able to follow everyone else and do what I was told.

As if she'd been reading my mind, but maybe it was just my expression, Mattie patted my shoulder. "I'll be back tomorrow to teach you how to run a household. If we'd had the proper time to plan the wedding, I would have had you ready beforehand."

I quelled the urge to remind her whose fault that was.

Chapter 25

Bridal boot camp was the last thing I'd ever wanted to experience, but exactly what I needed. Mattie planned meals for me, taught me how to make them, and got me over my fear of the stove. All that while effectively evading my questions about why Jenny and Lera were arguing on my wedding day.

By the end of the week, I was able to function in my own kitchen, though I still had a healthy respect for the woodstove. I could also handle the washroom, the root cellar, and the cow shed. Mattie left me with a schedule for maintaining the house. Mrs. Jones would come in on Mondays, and Lydia would help me several mornings during the week.

However, my schedule would have to start later than I thought. I found out on Sunday that while Mattie was educating me the previous week, the rest of the family had been planning a surprise birthday party for her on Monday, which was also Independence Day.

Lera and Lydia showed up at the crack of dawn. We cleaned the house and cooked while Nate and Mark set up tables for the food and laid out blankets for the picnickers. Caleb and Ed had gone somewhere. Nate assured me we'd find out today what the two of them had been up to since the day of the bazaar.

At noon, Lydia and Mark went home for dinner, so Mattie wouldn't be suspicious. I seized the opportunity to talk to Lera alone.

"Lera, it's been a while." I gave her a peck on the cheek as she stood in front of the worktable in the kitchen.

She startled but then responded with a warm smile.

I strolled to the other side of the worktable. "I feel like I've been away for weeks. Did I miss anything?"

She shook her head, continuing to knead dough. "No, but we all missed you. Caleb wanted to visit, but Mattie told us you were busy." She glanced at me. "You look wonderful. I'm glad you survived the week."

"Me too." I laughed, and Lera giggled with me. This was as good a moment as any to ask the question that had been bugging me. "Lera, why were you and Jenny arguing at our wedding reception?"

She shrugged. "Which time? We're always arguing about something."

"Do you know what was going on in the kitchen?" I pulled a chair out and sat. "Nate said Mattie kept him away from here."

"Oh." Lera plopped the dough into a bowl, and slid it to the end of the table. "Jenny tried to bring some man to the reception, and I sent him to the kitchen." She stared at the bread dough in the bowl. "Jenny wanted to parade him through the reception, but he wasn't invited." She picked up a towel and twisted it. "Frankly, I was a bit relieved at the time. I thought she had a beau, but I haven't seen any trace of him since."

I felt both excited and sick. "What did he look like?"

"Oh, um, I can't remember." She waved the towel as if she was batting a fly away. "But she hasn't had any male companions since, except Simon."

It couldn't have been Tood. Lera would have remembered if he'd been a black man. Could it have been the same person who showed up at Lera's wedding? No, Jenny tried to keep that person away, so why would she bring him to mine? With no way of knowing today who Jenny had brought to my reception, I tried to banish it from my mind and enjoy the party.

~

Nate stood on the porch and held his hands high to signal the assembled guests. "Thank you for being here. Aunt Mattie thinks this is a family supper."

A murmur arose from the crowd, a few titters among them.

Nate cupped his ear. "Shh. I hear her carriage."

I surveyed the crowd of about fifty people, Mattie's friends from the church and quilting club. I'd been afraid we wouldn't have a good turnout because there was a big Independence Day celebration—complete with fireworks—in town that evening. But, if anyone could compete with that, it was Mattie.

Nate held his finger to his mouth until Ed said, "Maybe they're on the front porch."

When the door opened, everyone yelled, "Surprise!"

Mattie jumped higher than I had on the morning of my wedding. It was more fun to watch her, though it only took her a few seconds to get over the initial shock, and then she began working the room, or the lawn.

"She certainly has a lot of friends." I linked arms with Nate. "How does she do that?"

"She's lived here all her life, for one." He nodded toward her. "And she's always willing to help out a neighbor."

"Or a total stranger." I smiled. "I have to admit, she made me nervous at first, but I don't know where I'd be without her."

"Nor I." Nate gave my hand a gentle squeeze. He led me to Mattie, so we could offer birthday wishes.

After we'd greeted all the guests, I spotted Lera by herself and steered Nate to her. "Is Simon coming?"

She nodded without facing toward us. "He and Jenny are supposed to be here already."

"Aren't you worried?" I leaned toward her.

Lera stepped away, twisting the handkerchief she held. "They had some sort of business meeting. They probably got delayed."

"Oh? What sort of business?" Nate asked.

Her eyes blazed and her jaw clenched. "That is one thing I've yet to find out."

I reached my arm around Lera's shoulders and gave her a half hug. I didn't think Jenny was after Simon, but then what did I know? I prayed that Lera would figure out how to handle the situation.

A hansom cab pulled up to the front lawn. Most of the guests watched as Jenny and Simon stepped out.

Simon stumbled out of the carriage, faced the party guests, and bowed deeply. "I beg your forgiveness for being late. My niece and I had an unexpected business appointment." He wobbled over to Mattie, made a big show of kissing her hand, and slurred, "Please forgive me, madam, for ruining your birthday party."

"Not at all." Mattie blushed. "Come, have something to eat." She ushered Simon toward Lera and steered Jenny toward some of the eligible bachelors.

Nate and I walked with Lera toward her husband, but she waved us off and took him to the food tables.

As it grew dark, Caleb got more fidgety, especially when Mattie asked Ed to light the lanterns hanging in various places around the yard. Ed only lit one and gathered everyone around.

Caleb signaled someone out in the field. The person was so far away, I could barely see their light.

Caleb ran to Mattie. "Grandma, we've been working on this since spring. It was my idea." He skipped over to Ed. "Can I go help Mr. Brewer set them off, Gramps?"

"No, now that was the deal. He knows what he's doing." Ed laid a hand on Caleb's shoulder. "Besides, you've got something to do here."

"Set what off?" Mattie tilted her head.

The sky lit up with pink and white lights. Caleb and Ed

played their fiddles hurrying at first, to catch up with the display.

We all sat on the blankets and watched. It only lasted about five minutes, but it was my favorite fireworks show ever. It brought back some fond memories of Todd playing his violin for similar gatherings. The music was timed to the blasts, except when Caleb stopped playing and gazed at the sky. Ed got them started again.

Mattie beamed as she stood next to Lydia, but she watched Caleb and Ed more than the fireworks. Lera's face showed pride in her son, almost enough to erase the melancholy.

Chapter 26

I'd always assumed I would work outside the home after I got married, but I hadn't thought it would be literal. In the mornings, I went outside to milk the cow, gather eggs, and work in the garden.

Every afternoon, I saddled Mr. Ed and rode over to Lera's for Caleb's lessons. Mr. Ed was the only horse I could ride. Much as I hated to admit it, riding was faster than walking, and I needed the extra time for my chores.

While I was at the mansion, I kept my eyes open for signs of trouble between Lera and Simon. That's if I saw them together, which was rare. Simon wasn't there every day, and when he was, he usually had one or two associates with him. Every time I asked Lera if she'd found out what the new business venture was, she'd shake her head, her lips pursed. I wondered if it had anything to do with the thefts, but I kept it to myself, since there hadn't been any recently.

Every time I got the chance, I questioned Jenny about when she was leaving. She never gave me any helpful information and would avoid me if she could. I still thought about going home, but I didn't dwell on it as much, instead taking Ed's advice to live in the present.

One day melted into the next, and summer was over before I knew it. The noteworthy occurrences could be counted on one hand. Our state had been re-admitted to the union. Caleb read aloud a whole chapter from the book of Esther. Lydia studied Ed's books and announced to her dad and me that she wanted to be a scientist. Ed suggested she not tell Mattie right away.

For me, the highlight of the summer was the day I baked a cake that was not merely edible, but delicious. It meant I had finally mastered the dreaded woodstove. Of course, I hadn't gotten much else done that day. I was so determined for the cake to turn out, I sat by the stove and watched it bake, rotating it occasionally, since it was impossible to keep the heat even. Mattie and Lera could bake bread and cake and continue to do other chores, but I hadn't figured out how they did that. And my generation thought we invented multi-tasking.

October brought with it two torrential storms, two days apart. Everyone in the county worried about their crop. Nate and I enjoyed the first storm. We spent most of the day together, a large part of it cuddling in front of the fire listening to the rain.

During the second storm, Nate couldn't sit still and snapped at everything I said.

"Remember, Nate, you told me we could survive one bad year." I draped my arm over his shoulder. He stood and trudged to the window. I followed and gazed out at the downpour. "It doesn't look that bad to me."

"You're not a farmer." He stayed frozen in front of the window, as if he could will the rain to stop.

"I am now," I said, my voice barely audible. "I give up!" I threw up my hands and marched toward the kitchen.

"Give up what?"

"Trying to cheer you up." I kept walking.

There was a roof over the porch between the house and the kitchen, but the rain blew sideways. When I stomped through the kitchen door, my wet foot slipped out from under me. I tried to catch myself, but over corrected and stumbled forward right into the woodstove, turning in time to hit below my shoulder on my right arm. I yelped in pain, but the rain was so loud, I could barely hear myself. Even though Nate was in a sour mood, he would have come running if he'd heard me.

By sheer force of will, instead of passing out, I struggled to a chair, put my head down between my knees, and forced my brain to work. It went into high gear with thoughts about how dangerous this time period was and how I could die here before I had a chance to get home.

Finally, I cleared my head and said a quick prayer. I ripped the sleeve out of my blouse and walked to the sink, thankful we had running water. The sink was too wide for me to reach the burned part of my arm under the faucet, so I stepped to the hand pump we used as a backup if the windmill pump wasn't working. It took some effort and was a bit awkward, but I managed to pump cold water on my arm.

"What are you doing?" Nate sounded annoyed, but his tone softened when he reached me. "What happened?"

"The floor was slippery."

Nate took me by my good arm and led me out the door. The rain had let up a little, but all the cold water I needed came down right outside.

"Why didn't I think of that?" I showed him a sheepish grin.

"You look like you're about ready to pass out." He held on to me and made sure the cool water landed on my burn.

"I almost did." My knees still felt weak.

He took me into the laundry room, found a blanket to wrap around me, and helped me sit on a stool. "Stay put, I'll be right back." He took off for the small garden next to the house and came back with a familiar looking plant leaf.

"Aloe. Did Ed tell you about that?"

"We've been growing this for years. I'm not sure if it was Ed's idea or not." He squeezed the stalk and gently spread it on the burn, which was only about the size of a fifty-cent piece.

"Thanks, I think I'll live now." I smiled.

"Did you ever have any doubt?" He raised his brows.

I nodded. "For a few seconds." I don't know where they came from, but the tears started to flow. "I felt so alone. I screamed for help, but you couldn't hear me." I looked up at him. "Why did you come?"

He exhaled. "To apologize. It's not your fault that it looked like it was going to hail."

"Thank God." I met his gaze. "I mean that you came."

"You were doing fine on your own. But I do thank God you weren't hurt worse."

"And that it didn't hail?" I smirked.

He nodded, his expression grim.

Chapter 27

The sun shone for the first time in days. I lingered on the front porch, watching Nate and Ed lead a team of mules off to the fields. I'd love to be able to whip out my phone and capture the picture they made walking down the path through the knee-high grain, a slight breeze blowing the leaves of some nearby trees, green against the clear blue sky. When they disappeared over a rise, I started into the house to get to my own work.

A wagon careened through the side yard, team running fast, with a woman screaming at them. Jenny rolled to a stop in the mud in front of the house. She must have taken the shortcut through the woods.

She pointed at several large bundles in the cart. "You want to get out of here, you'll help me hide this stuff." She jumped down from the seat.

I sat on the porch rail. "Good morning to you, too."

She lifted a loaded burlap bag and carried it toward me. "Find a place in the house where no one will see it."

I crossed my arms over my chest. "I can't do that if it's stolen."

She glared at me. "It's mine, all right? Just hide it."

"No. If someone finds it, Nate and I will be blamed."

"Just say you were storing it for me." She walked past me

toward the front door, then turned back. "Have you decided you'd rather stay here?"

"Well, no, but—"

"Then take this." She held the bundle out to me.

"Wait. Why can't you hide it where you have been?" I stepped toward her, took hold of her shoulders, and turned her around so I blocked the door.

"This and the town hall are the only public buildings left in New Hope." She stood as close as possible with the package between us. "My contact at the town hall started getting suspicious a year ago. I buried these near Simon's place and forgot about them until the rain washed them up yesterday."

I planted my feet, my hands on my hips. "Why did you stop stealing last year?"

"What makes you think I was the thief?" She hit me in the chest with the package, forcing me to accept it. "Just hide these." She patted her drawstring bag containing the controller.

"Not in the house." I pushed her toward the edge of the porch.

She stepped around me. "What about the attic closet?"

"How'd you know about that?" I dropped the bundle between us.

Her sly smile returned. "The curator."

Hands on my hips, I said, "Well, if you've been talking to Adam lately, you should know they've been looking closer in the closets. It would be hard for you to get your hands on your stuff before the museum staff does."

"Where then?" She leaned over the bundle between us, her face inches from mine.

I stood my ground, not wanting to let her see how shaken I felt. "Why should I help you?"

"If you don't, you'll never get home." She clutched her bag and skipped away.

I marched toward her. "I don't believe you'll take me home

anyway. You could have several months ago."

"I told you, the job isn't done." She glanced toward the shortcut.

I stepped in front of her. "What are you really here for? Lera told me you have a business venture with Simon."

"So?" She leaned around me.

I tried to block her view. "You can't be playing time-cop. The longer you leave me here, and the more you do, the more the original timeline gets messed up."

"You have no idea what you're talking about." She stepped to the side and so did I.

My face heated. "Just because I wasn't in on the research doesn't mean I can't figure out a few things. I've had a lot of time to think about it."

Jenny gazed past me. "You've been too busy to figure anything out." She waved her arms. "You've been working, and making friends, and falling in love."

"You haven't given me a choice!" I backed up a step, clenched my fists, and closed my eyes for a moment.

She took a deep breath. "Where can I hide these?"

I was about to tell her where she could stick it when I carriage wheels sounded from out back. That would be someone from Mattie's.

Mind racing, I scooped up the small package still on the porch between us and pushed it at her. "Take the wagon to the carriage house, but stay out of sight until I take whoever that is inside."

I ran through the house and out the back door in time to meet Mattie and Mrs. Kelley.

"Good morning," I called, stepping down to the drive. "What a lovely surprise." I shouldn't have been lying to the preacher's wife, but I couldn't tell them they had lousy timing. "Please come in." I ushered them to the back door.

Mattie hesitated. "Don't go to any fuss. We can visit in the kitchen."

"It's no fuss." I hurried them through the pantry and dining room to the small parlor, checking through the front windows to make sure Jenny's wagon was out of sight. "Would you like some tea? It won't take but a minute." Before they could answer, or even sit, I rushed to the kitchen. Maybe they would chalk it up to nerves, this being my first non-family visitor.

I put the kettle on, then ran out to the carriage house to help Jenny get her rig inside.

As I closed her and her contraband in, I stage whispered, "Stay here. Don't let anyone see you."

"Don't worry." She wore a wicked smile.

I shut the door, raced back to the kitchen, prepared the tea pot and cups, and searched for something to serve with it.

After pouring the hot water into the pot, I ran back through the dining room, slowing to a walk before I reached the parlor. "The tea will be ready in a few minutes."

Mattie and Mrs. Kelley peered out the front window.

"Have you had a visitor this morning?" Mattie waved toward the road.

I gulped and averted my gaze.

"There's fresh wheel tracks out front," Mrs. Kelley said.

Why hadn't I thought about that? I cleared my throat. "Yes, as a matter of fact. Jenny came by this morning." She wouldn't normally have any reason to put her wagon in the carriage house. Why would she come here? "She was headed to Atlanta and just stopped in for a short visit." My heart pounded as I positioned myself between them and the window.

"How odd." Mrs. Kelley's brow furrowed.

"Oh, uh." I gestured wildly toward the window and the other side of the house. "She used the shortcut. She hadn't seen Lera and didn't trust the servants to tell her, so she stopped to tell me." I shifted my weight. "So, I could tell Lera. So, she wouldn't worry. I mean Lera wouldn't worry."

"No." Mrs. Kelley touched my shoulder. "I meant Jenny going to Atlanta alone."

"Oh, well, Jenny's a very independent girl." Mattie turned from the window and headed toward the sofa.

I could have kissed her.

"I'll be right back with your tea." I hurried to the kitchen.

I prepared a tray with a teapot, three cups and saucers, and a plate of the gingerbread I'd baked the day before. Leaving it on the worktable, I ran out to the carriage house, and opened the door a crack. "Jenny, you're on your way to Atlanta if anyone sees you." I started to leave and turned back. "Don't let anyone see you."

I ran to the kitchen, took a deep breath, picked up the tray and headed for the parlor to play the part of a perfect hostess. Of course, that wasn't possible given the construction grade gingerbread I served.

"What I really came to ask." Mrs. Kelley placed her slightly nibbled piece of gingerbread on her plate. "Would you be willing to play for the church Christmas pageant this year?"

I nearly choked on my tea. "Play what?"

"The piano." Mattie giggled.

"But you play for church." I narrowed my eyes at Mattie.

Mrs. Kelley glanced at Nate's aunt. "Miss Mattie has agreed to direct this year. But she told me you play beautifully."

I smiled and set my teacup on the end table, giving myself time to gather my thoughts. "Miss Mattie is too kind. Way too kind." I laid my hands on my lap. "And mistaken. She's never even heard me play."

Mrs. Kelley looked down her nose at Mattie.

"Oh, I'm sure she's heard Nate's opinion of my playing, which is where the error comes in." I winced. "I'm afraid Nate doesn't have much of an ear for music."

Mrs. Kelley smiled. "I understand, but you have two months to practice. Please think about it." She stood, patted my hand, and started toward the front door.

I bolted out of my chair and grabbed her arm, then released it. "I'll show you out, Mrs. Kelley." I headed toward the back of the house.

Mattie walked into my path. "Nell wanted to see the view from the front yard, Cassie. Some of the trees are starting to change color."

"Oh, it's still extremely muddy from yesterday. Maybe some other time." I stood between her and the door.

"Oh, yes. I remember that track out front." Mattie stepped toward me. "We'll just stay on the porch. Then, we'll go out the way we came."

I stepped out of the way and followed them to the porch, hoping they'd keep their eyes on the trees, not the track, because it went back around the house instead of to the road.

"It's lovely out here." Nell Kelley placed her hands on the porch railing. "It's so peaceful. But doesn't it get lonely?"

I shook my head. "I've felt lonelier in the city."

Nell nodded and headed toward the door.

Mattie followed us across the porch. "I never lived in the city, so I wouldn't know," she muttered.

I heaved a brief sigh of relief as they entered the house. Why did I care if they saw Jenny? But I'd already covered for her, and I didn't want to be found out. When I glanced down at the track, I realized I'd worried for no reason. The tracks made it look like she'd taken the shortcut here and gone on to Atlanta via the main road.

I led my visitors out the back door and helped them into their carriage, waiting until they were out of view before I went to find Jenny.

"Jenny, the coast is clear." I opened the carriage house door. The wagon was there, the team still hitched to it, but I didn't see Jenny or her cargo. Undaunted, I called out, "You can take your stuff and go now."

"What makes you think I'm taking anything?" Jenny popped out from behind one of the doors.

My hand flew to my chest as I jumped. "Because I'm not going to let you hide stolen goods on our property."

"So now it's yours?" She circled me. "It's already hidden, temporarily."

I clenched my fists. "Then put it back in the wagon and leave."

She stopped and faced me about half a foot away. "It's in the loft. No one will see it unless they look for it. Give me two weeks." She pointed at me. "Don't tell anyone or let Nate find it. If you can find the stuff after that, I'll move it."

I scoffed. "How am I supposed to keep Nate and Ed from seeing it for two weeks?"

"You'll think of something. If it gets reported to the police, I'll tell them you stole it." She sauntered toward the wagon.

I stared daggers at her, as if she'd break down. I'm not sure why I tried. She wasn't even looking at me. Finally, I gave up with a loud, annoyed sigh. "All right." I moved closer to the wagon and held up two fingers. "Two weeks." I had no idea how I would keep her secret. I pointed toward the door. "Now, go before someone else shows up."

She climbed onto the cart. "Right, I'm supposed to be on my way to Atlanta. Good one." She snorted. "I do have business to attend to. I'll be back in a few days."

I peeked out, then swung the doors wide, waiting for her to leave. When she didn't, I turned toward her. Jenny sat on the seat holding the reins, and the mules stood facing the back of the carriage house. I tapped my foot, and pointed toward the door with one arm, while holding the other on my hip.

She huffed. "Don't just stand there. Help me get this thing out of here."

My eyes widened. "You don't know how to back up?"

She scowled. "There isn't a gear shift, now is there?"

I stifled a laugh and walked to the front of the team. She hopped down. With both of us pushing, we managed to move the mules and the cart outside.

The only reason I'd helped was to get rid of her, but when she started toward the woods, I felt a pang of guilt. "Jenny, if you're really going to Atlanta, you'll need some supplies." I ran toward the kitchen.

She glanced back. "Don't be so naïve. If I go to Atlanta, it'll be in my car." She rolled toward the woods.

A while later, I heard a knock on the kitchen door. When it opened before I could get there, I thought it was Lera.

"The mules are tied up in the woods," Jenny said from the doorway. "You'd better take care of them the next two days." She walked around the house toward the front. I followed long enough to see her stride down the main road, straight toward the spot where I'd landed. When she disappeared, I shuddered.

~

The first chance I got, I told Ed he'd been right about Jenny stealing. I was in such a rush to tell him I didn't realize Nate was within earshot. He and Nate pestered me with questions until they'd heard the whole story. At least I didn't have to sneak off to take care of the mules. Nate brought them to the barn.

Jenny was not happy when she got back. She walked all the way to the wagon, and then had to come to our house to find her team. I couldn't help but snicker.

"Thanks for not moving the loot. Did Nate or Ed spot it?" Jenny stood outside the barn, holding the mules' leads.

I glanced toward the carriage house. "Of course. How could they not?"

Her brow furrowed. "They didn't call the sheriff?"

"They agreed to the two weeks, considering we have no proof. You should give the stuff back or turn yourself in." I put my hand on my hip. "How can you steal from people?"

She rolled her eyes. "I only took things they weren't using.

And I stopped when I had enough money. What's the big deal?"

"Someone could have gotten hurt from that fire."

"That wasn't me." She headed for the shortcut.

I called out. "It was because of you."

Jenny glanced over her shoulder. "How long was it before you blabbed all about me to your precious husband?" She led the mules toward the cart she'd left in the woods.

I ran after her. "Maybe he saw the stuff and asked me about it."

She snorted and continued.

I let her go. Why did I care what she thought?

For the next two weeks, I didn't see Jenny. When I went to inspect the carriage house loft, I was amazed. All her loot was gone. I searched everywhere on the property I could think of but didn't find anything. When Nate and Ed came in from the fields, I set them to looking.

Ed pointed to a circular cut on the plank floor section of the carriage house. "There's a hole here, but not big enough for all that stuff. If she did hide the loot here, I have to hand it to her. She did a good job." He scratched his head.

"And?" Nate tapped him on the shoulder.

"I'm just wondering if she had some twenty-first-century help." Ed pointed to the man-hole sized circle on the floor.

"Other time-travelers?" I asked.

"No. Modern tools," Ed said.

That would make sense, but it wouldn't do us any good to ask her about it.

~

It would have been nice if we'd had modern tools to help with the harvest. Despite the October storms, we got a decent crop and hired extra workers to help pick the cotton and bring it to the gin which was over the rise from the house. We still used the mules to turn the wheel, though Nate and Ed had been talking about getting a steam engine. They would have to move the gin closer to the stream, so they'd decided to wait a year or two.

Mrs. Jones and Lydia came in every morning to help me feed the workers and pack their dinner. During the harvest, Lera brought Caleb to me every afternoon, but there were several days that we picked cotton instead of doing lessons. Lera didn't come to the fields with us, but when we returned, she usually had a pie or some cookies waiting. She spent so much time with us, I got the impression that life in the mansion wasn't all she'd expected.

Mattie, Lera, and Lydia used most of our time together to persuade me to play for the Christmas pageant. As ever, I hoped I would be gone by then but I did start practicing.

Other than at church, I didn't see Jenny or Simon for several weeks and I didn't miss them. Every once in a while, I would think about going home. Sometimes it was a fleeting thought and didn't bother me, but other times I would dwell on it and start to panic. On the few occasions I prayed for God's timing, I received a peace I couldn't understand. I didn't know what the future held, but God did.

Nate was praying too. Every time I asked him if he'd made a decision about going with me, he would say, "Still no word."

271

Chapter 28

I stood at the worktable, neglecting my dough instead of kneading it.

"It's the last day of harvest, why so glum?" Mattie asked as she and Lera entered my kitchen.

"I bet I know." Lera took her apron off the hook next to the door. "She's thinking about Nate going to Atlanta tomorrow."

I scowled at her.

She pointed at me. "I'm right. You're just going to miss Nate too much." She laughed but not in a mirthful tone.

I narrowed my eyes at her. Was she jealous?

"Maybe she's not looking forward to being alone in this big house." Mattie stood in front of the stove, packing up leftovers. "Nate did hire someone to look after the animals, didn't he?"

"Yes. Mr. and Mrs. Jones and their boys will be in and out. I'll be fine." I sighed. I wasn't sure if that was a lie or not. Intellectually, I knew that they needed to go to Atlanta to sell most of the crop, but I wished Nate didn't have to go, or that I could accompany him. I began kneading the dough while Mattie and Lera cleaned up from our morning breakfast and dinner preparations.

"Now, don't you fret, Cassie." Lera took over with the dough. "You know they'll be back by Saturday." She smiled. "Besides, I can keep you busy this week. You can help me get ready for our Harvest Ball." She plopped it into a metal bowl and punched it down. "It'll be so grand. Bigger than the bash Simon threw last spring." She draped a towel over the bowl and stared at the floor.

Mattie crossed between us. "You mean the ball to welcome Jenny?"

Lera snapped her head up. "Yes, but this'll be better."

"How is Jenny, by the way?" I moved the dough over to the ledge next to the stove. "I haven't seen her in a while."

Lera meandered around the kitchen, tidying. "She comes and goes at all hours. I tried to talk to Simon about her, but he won't do anything. Won't even discuss the matter."

"If you ask me, he should." Mattie stood at the sink in the corner of the room. "People are going to talk. Her actions will tarnish his reputation."

Lera laughed. "Miss Mattie, Simon has a reputation for being rich. That's it."

"Lera!" Mattie clapped her hands to her cheeks.

"It's true." Lera twisted a dish towel, then snapped it down on the table and marched out.

Mattie and I exchanged glances. Then she walked over and patted me on the shoulder. "I don't think she's as happy in her marriage as you are, dear."

I nodded.

"Do me a favor and pray for her and Caleb," Mattie said.

"I already do."

She squinted at me like she could see through me. "You don't like Simon either?"

I turned my head from side to side. "I'm not exactly sure why. He just seems fake or something."

"That's it." She wagged her finger. "I can always spot someone trying to be what they're not. That's why I didn't like Lera at first." She clamped her mouth shut, walked to the end of the worktable, and wrapped leftovers.

Good. She hadn't been talking about me. Her little blunder confirmed my suspicions that Lera only acted the part of a lady. I stacked the wrapped food, ready to take it to the cellar. "I figured Lera was dirt poor growing up. She never mentioned family or anything before marrying John."

Lera picked the wrong moment to re-enter the room. She stood in the doorway, her face red and her eyes shining. How much had she heard?

"Lera, are you all right?" I asked.

"So, my dear, former mother-in-law and my best friend are gossiping about me." She strode toward me and grabbed a linen towel off the worktable, then twisted it as she paced.

After one trip back and forth across the kitchen, she stopped. "What did she tell you? Did she say that they took me in because they felt sorry for me?" She started pacing again. "Because I had to work in the fields from the time I was six, and still went hungry most days? Did she tell you that John only married me because he'd taken advantage of me?"

She stopped, looked me in the eye, and then nodded toward Mattie. "Well, the joke's on her. I took advantage of him. I knew they'd make him marry me. I went after Nate first, but he wouldn't tumble, if you know what I mean." She slapped her hand on the table and stomped toward the door.

My eyes went wide and locked on Mattie's. She pursed her lips but stayed quiet.

Lera continued to pace and wring the towel.

I found my voice first. "Lera, Mattie never said any of that to me. I guessed a little of it."

"Did you guess why I can't teach my own boy?" She snapped the towel.

I nodded. "You could always sit in on his lessons. Or I could teach you separately."

She shook her head, rubbed her hands down the sides of her apron, then turned toward Mattie and lifted her chin. "I'm very sorry, Miss Mattie. I don't know where my head is these days. I should have known you wouldn't be spreading stories, even if they are true." She opened the door and walked through. Just before closing it, she looked back. "You will come tomorrow to help get ready for the ball, won't you?"

"Yes, and think about my offer," I said.

"I'll just let myself out." She closed the door behind her.

I wasn't shocked at the information. It was the outburst that threw me. I peered at Mattie. "I've never seen Lera that out of control." I paused. "Or that honest, well, about herself."

Mattie reached for the teapot. "You knew she was raised poor?"

"I guessed. From the way she'd correct herself if she made a grammar mistake and from how she would cut herself off when she started to talk about her childhood." I checked my dough, but it hadn't risen yet. "Caleb told me once that his ma never read to him. I figured it was because she couldn't."

"You're very perceptive, Cassie." Mattie sat in the chair at the worktable.

The water was boiling, so I poured it over the tea Mattie had put in the teapot and brought it to the table.

"What do you think Jenny is up to?" Mattie drummed her knuckles on the table.

The subject change jolted me a little, but I shrugged and sat across from her.

Mattie leaned toward me. "I think she's made multiple trips to the future."

My jaw nearly hit the table. "Mattie?"

"I'm perceptive too." She sat up and winked. "I know where you're from, rather, when. I figured out a long time ago about Ed and got him to tell me about it." She wore a smug smile.

My eyes widened. "Did Ed tell you about me?"

"Of course not." She waved a hand in front of her face.

"And Nate thinks I believe you're Margaret."

I pursed my lips and shook my head.

She shook hers, too. "I should have known I couldn't fool Nate."

I bit my lip. "Yeah, did you figure out I wasn't Margaret when I said my parents were divorced?"

She beamed. "Oh, I knew before that."

"How?" I cocked my head, expecting to hear all the mistakes I'd made.

She pressed her palms on the table. "The way Nate treated you."

"What?" I sat straighter.

"Yes. He treated you like he'd never met you, not like you were his long-lost fiancée, with or without amnesia."

"Why didn't you say anything to Nate?" I lifted the lid off the teapot and replaced it because it didn't look ready.

"I liked you, despite the lies." She patted my hand. "I knew Lera had made up the story, so I decided to watch the two of you. Nate seemed wary at first, but then I could see him falling in love." She leaned back and smiled. "I knew it was for the first time. I'd never met Margaret, but the way he talked about you was completely different from how he'd spoken of her."

I furrowed my brow. "But how did you guess I was from the future?"

She chuckled. "I was suspicious from the beginning, but I knew for sure the day I caught you running."

"The clothes?" I peered at her.

She nodded.

I stayed quiet for a moment and then a chill went down my spine. "Do you know what Lera thinks about me?"

She rubbed her chin. "I'm pretty sure she hasn't thought about your past at all. You were a convenient tool to her."

Now I was confused. "But it was her idea to pass me off as Nate's fiancée. If she was interested in Nate—"

"She knew she couldn't get Nate. She also probably suspected Simon would be interested in you—"

I still didn't get it. "Yeah, so having me here was a liability for her."

"Not really." Mattie took a breath. "She was the most bothered by Margaret not showing up. For some reason, she was afraid it would tarnish her own reputation."

"Nate thinks you took it the hardest." I snapped my hand to my lips.

Mattie laughed. "Don't worry about it. Today must be the day for putting your foot in your mouth." She checked the tea and poured it into our cups. "I was upset when Margaret didn't come, but it wasn't because of the embarrassment."

I sipped my tea. "I know. It was because of what it did to Nate."

"I've always loved that boy like he was my own." She sipped her tea then held the cup between her hands. "I felt like, in another life, it was just the two of us."

I leaned forward. "Did Ed tell you that?"

"No." She looked me in the eye and smiled. "You just did."

I set down my teacup and placed my head in my hands.

She took hold of my hand. "Thank you. I'd often thought it. It's nice to know for sure."

~

That evening was both joyous and solemn for me. We were all together, celebrating the harvest, but I couldn't forget about Nate leaving the next morning. He kept glancing at me and touching my hand and my thigh under the table.

After the family left, Nate and I sat on the porch and watched the sunset.

"Nate, why can't I go to Atlanta tomorrow? I don't want to miss any time with you."

He grinned. "The way you hate wagon rides? Must be you're really going to miss me."

I stuck out my tongue.

He clasped my hand. "It's only for a few days. You'll spend most of your time over at Lera's, anyway."

I showed him my best puppy dog eyes. "What if I'm gone when you get back?"

"Don't say that." He stood and walked the length of the porch and back. "Is there any reason? Have you talked to Jenny lately?"

I shook my head.

He knelt and placed both hands on my shoulders. "I promise I'll be back in time for the ball, if not sooner."

~

Mattie and I waved goodbye to Nate and Ed as they drove away in two loaded wagons. We took the small carriage and set out for Lera's.

I craned my neck, straining to see Nate.

Mattie patted my hand. "Don't worry. He'll be back."

I faced forward and pasted on a pleasant expression, but I did worry, too aware of all the danger for him and me. I jumped at every little bump in the road. How had Ed survived here for thirty years?

I glanced at Mattie. "Did you know Ed was from the future before you got married?"

"Dear me, no." She snapped the reins. "I didn't know very much about him at all when I married him."

"So why?"

"I knew all I needed to." She chuckled. "I was in love. Plus, before Ed, I was headed for spinsterhood."

I laughed, but then remembered the other timeline. "You couldn't have been old enough to be considered a spinster."

Her brow furrowed. "I was twenty-one, which was very old for a single girl back then. I was also shy and homely."

I scoffed. "Miss Mattie, you don't look anywhere near fifty-one, and it's hard to believe you were ever shy."

One corner of her mouth curled upward. "I was, but that was before I met Ed and before I met the Lord. That happened about the same time."

"Tell me about it," I asked, before I thought about the consequences.

Her eyes twinkled. "A traveling evangelist came to town. I went to the first meeting and saw Ed there. I asked some folks about him, but the only thing they'd say was that he was new in town, looking for work.

"The second meeting, Ed didn't show up but the Holy Ghost did, for me anyway. I gave my life away that night, and I was on fire to collect as many other souls as possible. Ed was my first mission." She winked. "And it wasn't at all because he was cute."

I squinted at her.

She grinned. "The next night, I went to town early, found Ed, and dragged him to the meeting with me. He didn't seem to get much out of it. I did the same thing for the rest of the week. On the last night of the revival, Ed went forward. At the time, I thought it was true repentance, but through the years I've wondered if he'd done it just to get me off his back. More than likely to impress me, because we were married a month later." She turned and showed me her sheepish grin.

I debated asking her if Ed really did marry her for her money. Her family owned all that property, and he was in the same boat I'd been in with no saleable skills. Before I could dredge up the courage, we arrived at the mansion.

Lera greeted us from the porch. "Thank you so much for coming to help." She peered behind us. "Where's Lydia?"

Mattie handed the horse's reins off to one of Simon's stable boys, then smiled wide. "Lydia is in town with some friends, working on a mission project."

I bit my lip to keep myself from commenting. Lydia had told me in confidence that she would rather collect donations for unfortunate people than help prepare for a party to which she wasn't invited.

Mattie ascended the front steps. "I'm inclined to allow Lydia to spend as much time at church as possible." She sighed. "Maybe she'll become interested in spiritual things."

My guess was that she'd smuggled several of Ed's books with her and she'd be hiding in the church instead of out collecting donations with her friends.

Lera ushered us into the house, chatting about all the work left to be done. The foyer sparkled, but the pocket doors were closed, so I couldn't see the rest of the house right away. Lera led us through the main parlor, where several maids scurried around, dusting and polishing.

"You don't mind baking, do you?" Lera asked Mattie as she led us toward the detached kitchen.

Mattie's eyes lit up. "Of course, not."

I enjoyed working in the kitchen with Mattie and Lera. With Jenny and Simon away, it was a pleasant day. Memories from the spring before came to me. Had I only been here about half a year? Sometimes it seemed like years and sometimes only a few weeks.

During the trip back to Mattie's, she insisted I stay for supper, but she needn't have. I wasn't looking forward to spending the evening in that big empty house, and I certainly didn't want to cook for myself.

After supper, Mattie sent Mark to accompany me home. We took a lantern and walked, leaving the horse and carriage in Mattie's barn. I'd walk back the next morning before going over to Lera's.

Mark stayed silent while my brain worked overtime figuring out what to say. I asked him about farming and the harvest. He answered my questions with, "Yes, ma'am," and "No, ma'am." When I asked about Emily, his eyes lit up and he blushed.

I glanced at him. "Do you talk to Emily or do you just hold hands?"

"Both." He lowered his head.

"What do you talk about?"

"Lots of things." Mark stopped in front of the barn door. "I'll make sure Mr. Jones took care of the horses, then I'll go home."

"Thanks, Mark." I'd gotten a whole sentence out of him. I chuckled to myself and walked toward the kitchen door.

He stopped me before I could get inside. "Cassie." Mark took a few tentative steps toward me. "We talk about you, too. Well, Emily and her sister do."

I raised an eyebrow. "Oh?"

He stuffed his hands in his pockets. "They don't believe that you're Nate's first fiancée."

I exhaled. "Why should they? No one else does." I opened the kitchen door and motioned for him to follow. "What do they think?"

Mark set the lantern on the worktable, and we sat kitty-corner to each other. He made a couple of false starts before he said, "Eve, Emily's sister, thinks you were a friend of Margaret's. You swooped in after Margaret dumped him."

Interesting. I nodded and waited for him to continue.

He shrugged. "But she's jealous. She had her sights on Nate."

"Really?" Come to think of it, Nate did mention someone coming around hoping to bump into him. "Go on."

He snorted. "She thinks you stole Nate from her."

I narrowed my eyes. "But you don't?"

He shook his head. "Nate wouldn't have dated her if she was the last girl on the planet."

I cocked my head. "Why do you think that?"

"I know him and her." He cleared his throat. "She only wanted Nate because he's well-off."

I cringed, hoping he didn't see it. "So, what does Emily think?"

"Oh, she likes you. She thinks you're modern." He rotated his hat through his hands as he spoke. "She's trying to get her mom to let her cut her hair, and she only wears crinolines for formal events now."

I laughed. "I'm glad I'm having a positive influence."

He started to get up, then sat and leaned forward, brow furrowed. "There's something else you should know."

I held my breath.

It took him a few seconds to form the words, and he shifted his gaze away from mine. "There are people in town that think you and Jenny are up to something shady."

"Me? That's ridiculous." I tried not to show the guilt on my face. Had someone seen Jenny the day she'd hidden her loot? "Do they give any reasons?"

He shrugged as he stood and picked up the lantern. "Don't worry about it. It's just because you're both new in town."

I laughed, trying to sound mirthful instead of nervous. "She's not one of my favorite people." I stood and lit the lantern I kept next to the woodstove. "Good night, Mark. And thanks for the news."

He waved and headed for the barn. I secured the kitchen and went into the main house. As I climbed the stairs, I found myself praying for forgiveness and asking what to do about Jenny and her stash. I waited a while for that answer.

Chapter 29

I had fixed myself some tea and a slice of bread for breakfast, and was sitting at the worktable in the kitchen when Lydia rushed in. "Pa sent a telegram. I ran here as soon as we got it."

I jumped up. "What happened?"

She gulped in air. "They're on their way back. They're running a little late but will be here before the ball."

I plopped down. I'd spent the past two days trying not to worry and missing Nate more than I thought I would.

"Ma had another message." Lydia sidled over to me. "Mrs. Ramsey is in labor, and they asked her to help. She'll be there all day tending the older children and assisting the mid-wife. I'm to go to Lera's with you, work all day, and watch Caleb during the ball."

I stifled a laugh. "You look positively thrilled."

"Whoopee." She slumped on the edge of the worktable.

I finished breakfast, packed up my ball gown, complete with the lovely hoop, and joined Lydia in the carriage. She made me drive and heckled me most of the way. I didn't mind. She needed to vent.

I felt for her. She was much more interested in technology than society, a born scientist in an era where girls didn't have that option. Ed had been secretly encouraging her, teaching

Lydia and Caleb physics in the carpenter shop. Whenever I had a spare minute, I'd check on their progress. I could tell Ed was frustrated by the lack of technical equipment, but he had remembered how to make a potato battery.

Lydia pointed at a rock in the road. "Watch it. We want to get there intact."

"I thought you didn't care."

She kept her eyes on the path. "It wouldn't bother me to miss the ball, but I'd like to stay in one piece."

"Have you heard any of the gossip about me?"

She shook her head. "Where did you hear it?"

"Mark." I glanced at her.

She rolled her eyes. "Well, you can't trust much of what he says because he's getting it from Emily."

I squinted. "You don't think much of Emily?"

Lydia shrugged. "She's all right. A bit ordinary."

"Do you think he could find someone better?"

She pursed her lips. "Don't know. Don't care."

She and Mark didn't spend much time together, but I wasn't sure how she felt about him. It wasn't any of my business, but there wasn't much else to do, now that I had mastered driving the carriage. "Why not care? You two seem to get along."

"We tolerate each other."

I grinned. "You're not jealous, are you?"

"Ask him." She waited a few seconds. "Before, Mark was always jealous of John. But now, he's not happy about the time I've been spending with Pa."

I exhaled. "And I was worried Mark was getting more of your parents' attention."

She cocked her head. "Why would you think that?"

"No reason." I studied my lap, but she bent lower and looked up at me.

"There's a reason." She sat up. "And you'd better get your eyes back on the road."

I straightened and checked that the horse was still plodding in the right direction. "Okay, I have an older brother, so I know there can be some rivalry."

"Divorced parents and an older brother. Is that it?" She raised her eyebrows.

I nodded.

"Tell me about your brother." Lydia gazed straight ahead.

I shrugged. "Darren, your typical over-achiever. Good grades, athletic, popular. The whole package."

She blinked at me. "You had that, too."

I shook my head. "Just the good grades."

Her eyes went wide. "What's he doing now?"

I heaved a sigh. "He's running for Mayor of Philadelphia. The last I heard he had a good chance of winning."

She smirked. "Now who's jealous?"

I groaned. "I'm not. It's just that I'm expected to be at the election party, where I know I'll be ignored."

"You might not be able to get there." She faced forward again.

Lydia was right. I had no way of knowing when or if I would go back or what year it would be when I got there. What if it took me four or five years to get Jenny to send me back to the day I left? I'd have aged that much in a day. I shuddered. No wonder Ed didn't want to go back, now.

When we arrived at the Highland estate, we didn't see Jenny and Simon, but the servants' nervous demeanor told us they were at home. Simon's butler greeted us at the door, took the dishes Mattie had sent, and escorted us directly to Lera in the dining room.

Lera flitted here and there, alternating between barking orders, and doing things herself. She had silver out for Lydia to polish while I gave Caleb his lesson. One glance at Lydia's scowl, and I was thankful I wouldn't have to spend much time with her.

Caleb acted more distracted than usual during his lesson. We'd finished the book of Esther and were now reading John. After about an hour of struggling to keep him focused, I shut the book and announced it was time for a change of scenery.

Caleb jumped out of his chair and dragged me outside. He led me down to the barn, ran ahead, and then bounded back to pull me along.

"I got my own horse." He skipped in front of me. "Miss Jenny gave him to me." He showed me a wide smile as he pointed out the stallion. "His name's Lightning."

The beast was huge and looked mean. He shuffled in his stall, like he would bolt the minute it was opened. "You haven't tried to ride him yet, have you?"

"Naw, Ma won't let me. She says he has to be broken first. She's gonna get Nate to do it."

My breath hitched. "Nate?"

He bounced around me. "Yeah, he's broken a lot of horses. Elvis was wild when we first got him."

My muscles tensed. "Still, I'd rather she hire someone else."

Caleb pushed me.

I staggered a few steps back without falling, all the while staring at him in disbelief.

His eyes grew teary and his face reddened. "Miss Jenny's right. You don't think we're family anymore." He started to run off, but I caught his arm.

I pulled him to me and hugged him tight, then held him at arm's length, hands on his shoulders. "Caleb, I was just afraid for Nate. You know how scared I am of horses."

"Nate's not." He sniffled. "He can handle Lightning."

"Maybe so. But that's up to Nate. Even if he decides not to break him, I'm sure it'll be because of the horse and not because he's yours." I leaned toward him. "Do you understand?"

He nodded, then hung his head.

I let him go. He ran toward the stall while I stayed at a safe distance. Why would Jenny tell Caleb we didn't want him in the family anymore? And why would she give him such a dangerous animal?

I studied Caleb as he wandered through the barn toward the tamer horses, chastising myself for not paying much attention to him lately—other than as a student.

I approached him and rubbed his shoulder. "Caleb, do you like living here?"

"It's a grand house." He patted the nose of a brown horse.

"Yes, it is. But do you like it here?" I knelt next to him and turned him toward me.

He shook his head, and his lower lip trembled.

I leaned in. "Why?"

He shrugged.

I hugged him close.

He whispered, "I can't ever seem to do anything right, here."

"I know how you feel." I vowed to keep him in my prayers. After a moment, I touched him on the shoulder and ran. "Tag, you're it."

Caleb chased me to the other side of the barn and off toward the trees before he caught me. We both laughed, and I knew we were still friends.

~

I glanced around the spacious ballroom, festooned with fall floral arrangements and peach and ivory ribbons. "The room looks lovely."

Lera finished her last flower arrangement, stepped back, and surveyed the space. "I think the house is ready. It's time to make ourselves presentable."

I followed her toward the stairway, excited about the ball, and hoping Lera would do my hair again.

As we walked through the vestibule, raised voices sounded

from the hallway behind the stairs. I lingered hoping to catch bits of Jenny and Simon's argument, but they soon separated. Jenny scooted toward the back door, and Simon gave me a curt nod as he walked past me, out the front door.

I caught up with Lera on the stairs. "Haven't seen Jenny and Simon in a while."

Lera kept a neutral expression. "Neither have I. Simon's got a new business venture. In fact, after this weekend, he'll be staying the winter in Atlanta."

"Oh, no. I'll miss you."

"No, you won't." She pursed her lips, then relaxed them into a smile. "Caleb and I will be right here."

"You're not going?" My eyes bugged out. Nate had only been gone a few days, and I missed him.

She shrugged. "Someone has to maintain this monstrosity."

"I can't believe you said that." I joined her on the landing.

"Well, it is huge." The corners of her lips curled up, but the smile didn't reach her eyes.

We continued to her room in silence. I waited for her to close the door. "Lera, is there something going on?"

"A ball, silly." She laughed, but only for a second.

I kept eye contact.

She blew out a breath. "I'm not sure, but I don't trust Jenny. I think she's trying to come between Simon and me."

"But, she's the one that wanted you together." I sat on a stool and turned my head to hide my guilty face. It didn't work.

"Is there something you're not telling me?" Lera sat on a sofa next to the window.

Please, Lord, don't let me say too much. "It's just that, she noticed Simon was paying a lot of attention to me and asked me to encourage him to be attentive to you. It was a while ago."

"Apparently, she's changed her mind." She leaned her head back.

I stood and paced near the foot of the bed. "But, she's his

niece."

She scoffed. "Just like you're Margaret."

"How do you know she's not?" I whirled around to face her.

She pursed her lips. "It's obvious, isn't it?"

I shook my head, hoping she didn't know where Jenny and I came from.

She shrugged. "I overheard them a few weeks ago. Simon said something about why he should keep up the ruse, and Jenny said he still needed her."

"Do you think there's something between them?" I sat on the stool, facing her.

She looked down her nose at me.

"Stupid question?" I shifted on the seat. "I mean, do you think it's sexual?"

She nodded.

"Couldn't it be some kind of business arrangement?" I bit my lip.

She leaned back and gazed at the ceiling, as if she was trying to remember something. "Jenny has been trying to get him to invest in something new." She turned her attention toward me. "She said it would sell very well, what with all the thefts."

I tilted my head.

"Property Insurance. Like we need that here in New Hope." She rolled her eyes. "It's just an excuse to spend more time together."

The maid came in to tell her the bath was ready. Lera hopped off the sofa and hurried toward her lavatory.

"It may be just business. I know Jenny is all about making money." She might not have heard me.

While she bathed, I got into as much of my clothing as I could. Lera or the maid would have to tighten my corset. About the time I expected Lera to appear from the adjoining room, I heard her wretch. At least, that's what it sounded like.

I ran to the door, and one look at her confirmed my suspicion. "Lera, are you that nervous about tonight?"

"Of course not." She wiped her mouth with a rag and glared at me. Then she tightened her robe, wrapped a towel around her head, and shuffled past me into the room. "I'm pregnant." A corner of her lip flicked up. "I'm surprised you're not."

I shrugged. She didn't need to know I was purposely trying not to, until we figured out which time-period we'd end up in. I hoped we'd stay together, but that wasn't a certainty. "How far along are you?"

"About two months." She faced me, still toweling her hair. "Please don't tell anyone. You're the first to know, unless the maid has figured it out."

I stepped toward her. "Is that why you got so upset the other night?"

She dropped her towel and stood in front of the fire. "That's how I knew for sure. I was like that when I was expecting Caleb."

"Hormones." I picked up the towel and hung it on a hook near the fireplace.

"Huh?" She squinted at me.

"Never mind. When are you going to tell Simon?" I stood in front of her and glanced over my shoulder.

"I'm not." She began tightening my laces.

"You're going to have to tell him sometime." I gasped. "Ow. I won't be able to breathe."

"Sorry." She loosened the laces a bit. "I'm going to wait and let him see for himself when he comes back next spring. If he comes home." She finished my bodice and helped me with my crinolines.

"Why?" I kept still as she fussed with my skirt.

She sighed, fastened my skirt, and leaned against the four-poster. "If there is something between Simon and Jenny, I don't want to use the baby to keep him."

I peered at her. "But what will you do if he does take off?"

"I'll manage." She set her jaw and eyed me. "Now let's see what we can do with your hair." She led me to a chair near the fireplace.

I knew better than to continue the conversation while she curled my shoulder length hair with a hot iron.

I also knew to keep an eye on Jenny, that is, if she showed up.

Chapter 30

When the harvest ball began, Jenny and Simon were nowhere to be found. Maybe there *was* something between them. Lera greeted the earliest guests alone while I conveyed her last-minute instructions to the staff.

Simon arrived from the front door as I entered the ballroom. Lera scolded him with her eyes, but linked arms with him and continued to play the gracious hostess.

I mingled with the few early guests, trying to distract myself from my anticipation, but kept an eye on the door where a distinguished-looking butler in black tails stood waiting. Lera and Simon stayed in the pocket door opening between the foyer and the ballroom.

I spotted the Kelleys in the foyer and approached them. "Good evening."

"Good evening, Mrs. Bridger." Mrs. Kelley clasped both my hands in hers. "I'm happy to see you looking so well."

"Thank you." She could have noticed my stylish hair or my new gown. I plastered on a smile. "You look lovely—"

The door opened and Nate entered.

I ran from the pastor and his wife and threw my arms around him. He kissed me, picked me up, and twirled me around. If I'd been conscious of anything other than Nate, I might have felt embarrassed by the public display of affection.

When he released me, I glanced out the door. "Where's the rest of the family?"

"Aunt Mattie is still at the Ramsey's. Ed went over to pick her up. They'll be here later."

"What about Mark?" I asked, realizing the answer as I spoke.

"He's bringing Emily," we said in unison.

Nate handed his top hat and overcoat to the butler and escorted me toward our hosts. Lera was pre-occupied with the Kelleys, so our greeting was mercifully short, and Nate ushered me into the ballroom.

We danced several waltzes, but sat out the more complicated line dances. While eating food from the buffet, we chatted with Martin and Ida. Back on the dance floor, I looked up at Nate and bobbed my head toward the new couple. "Didn't expect that."

He chuckled. "An interesting match. I didn't see that one coming either." After a few more turns around the room, he asked, "Didn't Lera say anything?"

I shook my head. "She's losing her touch." I giggled, but my little joke fell flat.

Lera had been pre-occupied lately, but Ida was one of her best friends. How could she have not known or cared enough to pass on that tidbit? A niggling fear crept into my consciousness, but I pushed it out of my mind, determined to enjoy the evening with my husband.

Before the end of the song, I noticed Simon and Lera greeting Ed and Mattie. Ed glanced around the room as they headed toward us. I knew exactly who he was looking for.

"No idea where she is." I nodded at him. "Or what she's up to."

Ed jerked his head toward the corner of the room and walked away from the crowd. Nate, Mattie, and I followed. Out of the corner of my eye, I could see Simon sneak out of the ballroom toward the back of the house.

"Should we follow him?" I tilted my head in Simon's direction.

Ed shook his head. "He'll be back soon." He glanced at Lera. "It's Jenny I'm worried about."

I blew out a breath. "Yeah, I saw her arguing with Simon earlier, but she left before I could catch her."

"Nate." Mattie linked arms with him. "It's been an age since I've had a dance with you."

Nate bowed. "Would you do me the pleasure, Aunt Mattie?"

"I'd love to." Mattie smiled as they strolled toward the dance floor.

I raised my eyebrow at Ed.

"I didn't put her up to that." He leaned toward me. "Do you know anything else about Jenny?"

"Only that Lera's convinced she's after Simon, and she's trying to get him to invest in insurance." I chuckled. "That's a good one. Steal people's property and then sell them theft insurance."

"Sounds like Jenny." He held his arm out to me as several people crowded our space.

I accepted, and we strolled around the edge of the ballroom, nodding at people as we passed.

When we'd made it to a spot where there wasn't anyone within earshot, Ed whispered, "I think she's also been dealing in information."

I leaned close. "What do you mean?"

He scanned the room. "I met a business associate of Simon's in Atlanta. He says Simon's been hitting it big with his investments lately."

"That's good, isn't it?" I glanced toward the dance floor.

"For him, but it's also suspicious." He shook his head. "I just hope it doesn't attract the attention of the authorities."

I peered at him. "He'd have to hit really big for that, wouldn't he?"

"He's making a hundred times what he normally does." Ed smiled as I snapped my head toward him, my eyes wide. Then he frowned. "I just want to know, what's in it for Jenny?"

"There has to be something." I bit my lip.

He drummed his fingers on his thigh. "The fact that she's not here is making me nervous."

My breath hitched. "You think she's up to something, tonight?"

Ed's gaze darted around the room. "Or she's avoiding us. If she does show up, we need to talk to her."

I nodded.

"Still talking about Jenny?" Nate arrived at my side. He and Mattie were both breathing a little heavily.

I smirked. "Getting a work out?"

"I can still dance." Nate smiled and held his arm out for me.

He escorted me to the dance floor and held me close as we twirled around the room. My head rested on his shoulder when I saw Simon pull Jenny from behind the staircase. I scanned the crowd for Lera. She was talking to Ida and didn't appear to see them. Simon introduced Jenny to a guest, and made a bee-line to Lera who greeted him with what could have been a forced smile.

"Something going on?" Nate stopped dancing and followed my gaze.

"Simon just pulled Jenny into the room. Ed and I need to speak to her."

Nate released me, and I hurried straight to Jenny. On my way, I caught Ed's eye across the room and he headed toward me.

"Jenny Highland." I used my best southern accent. "I do believe it's been a coon's age." I addressed the man she was with, an older gentleman I didn't recognize. "I'm sorry sir, but I'm going to have to borrow Jenny for a while. I have news for her."

He bowed, and I whisked Jenny away before she could protest. Ed met us and we hurried toward the back hallway. I pulled Jenny into the library, where she'd detained me six months before.

As soon as Ed closed the door, Jenny stood in our way, hands on hips. "How dare you drag me in here like a common criminal?"

Ed and I looked at each other, eyebrows raised. I walked around her, and Ed stayed in front of the door.

I planted my feet and tilted my head. "Don't like it when the tables are turned, huh?"

She stalked past me, plopped into an oversized leather chair near the fireplace, and crossed her arms over her chest.

"We know something's up, and we want to know what." I strode toward her.

She clenched her jaw. "You'll learn exactly what I want you to and nothing else. Don't ask any more questions or I'll never take you home."

"I already gave up on that." I sat in the matching leather chair and faced her. "You don't have anything to bribe me with."

She glared at me. "You don't have anything on me, either."

"What about the thefts?" I leaned toward her. "All that stuff you stashed in the carriage house."

She raised an eyebrow. "Can you prove it?"

She had me there.

Ed approached and stood next to me. "Heard some interesting things in Atlanta."

Jenny leaned against the chair back and grinned at him. "Lots of interesting things going on in Atlanta."

"How did you convince Simon that you could help him with his investments?" Ed asked. "Does he know who you are?"

She met his gaze. "Do you?"

Ed nodded.

I looked from one to the other, not sure what they were talking about.

Jenny exhaled. "Simon only thinks I can see the future." She sneered. "He has no idea I'm from there."

"How did you convince him you were clairvoyant?" I asked.

She pursed her lips and rolled her eyes. "It wasn't hard. I just made a few predictions. I studied this time period before I came."

I shook my head. "Why help Simon?"

She scoffed. "To get him to let me pose as his niece. He's basically supporting me."

"Yes, but you've increased his portfolio about a hundred times," Ed said. "Why so much?"

She smiled wider and shrugged.

I furrowed my brow. "Where were you earlier, before the ball?"

She huffed, her eyes blazing. "I was trying to fix a problem you caused."

"Me? What did I ever do to you?" I pushed my weight to the edge of the seat and barely managed to keep from lunging at her.

"Never mind." She lifted her chin and leaned into the corner of her chair.

I softened my tone. "Lera thinks you're trying to steal Simon from her."

She laughed. "Why would I want him? Even if he wasn't—" She sat up straight. "He may be enamored of me, but only because of his financial gain." She heaved a sigh. "He's really in love with Lera."

I pursed my lips. "You might want to tell her that."

Ed pulled his watch out of his vest pocket, made a point of checking it, and slid it back in. "I think that would be a wise move." He stepped away from us and peered at Jenny. "So, how are things back in twenty-ten? Getting back to normal?"

"What is going on?" I stood and moved to the side so I could see them both.

Jenny jumped up and strode toward Ed. "You think you're funny, don't you?"

Ed frowned and shook his head.

Jenny pushed him slightly. "All that talk about not going back in time because history could change." She poked him in the chest, moving him back a step. "Both you and Todd. Well, you're the one who changed everything." She turned away, hands to her chest.

Ed stepped toward her. "I followed you to keep you out of trouble. How was I supposed to know you changed the year?"

"I bet you laughed like crazy when you figured out what happened to me." She wheeled around to face him. "You think it's all my fault . . .that I got what I deserved, don't you?"

He shook his head and placed his hand on her shoulder.

The door opened.

Ed jumped back as if he'd been caught in a compromising position.

"Oops, sorry to intrude," Martin said.

Ida giggled.

"We were about to get back to the party, anyway." Jenny rushed past them.

I followed her and Ed out the door, nodding to Martin.

"I got the feeling I missed something," I whispered to Ed in the hallway.

"Just confirming a suspicion." He reached into his vest pocket and showed me it was empty. "More than one."

I squinted. "Where's your watch?"

Ed grinned.

My hand flew to my mouth. "Jenny! When she was poking you?"

He nodded.

I stopped in a vacant area of the hallway. "Why so gleeful?"

"The sheriff should be here tonight." He glanced over my shoulder. "We have proof that she's a thief."

"I don't get it. Why would she try something like that, tonight?"

Ed frowned and shook his head.

Emily's parents interrupted us, and I didn't have a chance to ask about Ed's other confirmed suspicion. We entered the ballroom, spotted Mattie and Nate conversing with the Kelleys, and made our way through the crowd toward them.

Nate headed my direction, wearing a serious expression. "No more talk about Jenny. Let's dance."

I grinned. "You mean you dance, and I try not to step on your feet?"

He chuckled. "You're getting better. I'm an excellent teacher." He took me in his arms and we glided across the floor. The next song was a slow one, and Nate pulled me close. "I've missed you."

"Me too." I laid my head on his shoulder. The song was nearly over when there was a disruption at the door. Nate and I stopped dancing and turned toward Lera and Simon. They raced toward the butler, who tried to keep someone from entering.

Simon pointed at the door. "Go around to the back."

"That's where we take deliveries." Lera blocked our view of the unwanted guest.

"I was invited."

My eyes shot open wide. I knew that voice. Six months ago, I would have squealed and gone running toward it. But now, my feet were rooted in place, and a lead ball formed in the pit of my stomach.

"Cassie." Nate put his arm around my waist, holding me up. "What's wrong? Is that—"

I nodded. "Todd."

PAMELA G. BAKER

Chapter 31

"Cassie!" Lera called.

Startled, I peered around Nate. Todd, dressed in a vintage black suit, stood in the foyer, flanked by Simon and Lera. I hurried across the ballroom toward them, Nate right behind me.

Lera cleared her throat, her jaw clenched. "This gentleman says you invited him."

I shook my head. "Not to the ball."

Todd pulled away from Simon and peered at me. "I need to talk to you, Cassandra."

Lera glared at both of us. "Go around to the kitchen. She'll meet you there." She looked down her nose at me. "He's disrupted my party enough."

Todd hesitated.

"I'll meet you right away." I locked eyes with Nate, and we headed toward the central hallway. It wouldn't do any good to insist on going alone, and I wasn't sure I wanted to. As we strode through the ballroom, I scanned for Jenny, hoping she wouldn't follow us. She made eye contact with me but whirled around and flounced in the opposite direction. Good.

As we exited through the back door, Todd walked up to the porch between the house and kitchen. I glanced past him to make sure Jenny hadn't circled around behind. She wasn't in sight.

Todd held out his hands as he approached. "Sorry to barge

301

in, but I couldn't afford to wait any longer."

I squinted. "Wait?"

He grunted. "Jenny didn't tell you I was here, did she?"

I shook my head.

"Better come inside." Nate pointed toward the open kitchen door.

When we entered, three servants scurried off with trays in their hands. Only one old woman remained, stirring something on the stove.

"Is there another place we can talk?" Nate asked her.

"There isn't time." Todd tapped his foot. I'd never seen him this anxious.

We huddled near the entrance, Todd closest to the open door.

"There's going to be a fire. This whole house is going up tonight." Todd waved his hand, speaking fast. "I tried to tell the hostess, but she wouldn't believe me."

"Are you sure?" I asked.

"Adam showed me the newspaper clippings. He figured out your notes. He knows what's going on." Todd bobbed his head toward Nate, and his eyebrows rose.

"He knows too. You can say what you want."

"I don't know everything." Nate furrowed his brow. "Who's Adam?"

"The museum curator and town historian." I focused on Todd. "So why didn't you come back earlier?"

"I did." Todd raised his voice, his gaze piercing me.

My eyes widened. "The day of the wedding?"

He nodded.

I leaned in. "Why didn't you insist on seeing me, or come back?"

"You'd just gotten married." Todd glanced away. "Jenny told me you didn't want to come home. She said you didn't want to see me."

"I wanted to say goodbye, at least." I touched Todd on the upper arm while Nate held my other hand.

"There was another lady that didn't want anyone to see me," Todd said.

"Aunt Mattie," Nate and I said together.

Todd scoffed. "Yeah, she didn't want to see me tonight, either."

I narrowed my eyes. "Tonight's hostess kept you away from the wedding?"

"Yeah." He nodded.

"Lera." I blinked. "But she said she didn't remember what you looked like."

"She probably didn't want to talk about it," Nate said.

"We don't have time for this." Todd stepped away and waved his arm toward the house. "The fire!"

"Do you know what time the fire started?" Nate asked.

"The article said during the party." Todd cleared his throat. "For all her efforts, Jenny hasn't been able to change much."

My breath caught. "Is that what she and Simon have been arguing about? She wanted to cancel the party?"

"That's what she told me."

I tugged Todd's sleeve. "How much have you seen of her?"

"Sporadically over the last several months."

"Months?" My jaw dropped.

He shifted his weight. "Yeah, it was two before I realized you were missing."

I raised an eyebrow. "Because of the email?"

"You appeared to have moved out."

"Jenny." I pursed my lips. "How did you find out I didn't?"

"Your brother came looking for you."

I snorted. "Only two months?"

Todd jiggled his leg. "She sent your family emails, too, saying you didn't want contact. He finally decided enough was enough."

I bit my lip. "You didn't find my notes?"

"After your brother showed up, I started looking around the museum. We found the letters, and later, Adam caught Jenny behind the carriage house."

I stepped toward him. "Did you catch her with the antiques?"

He nodded.

"Where did she hide them? She wouldn't tell us."

He glanced out the door. "She dug under the section with the wood floor."

"Ed and I looked there," Nate said.

"She brought back some modern tools, dug a deep tunnel, and made a wood box under the carriage house. You could easily have missed the small hole at the top." He shook his head. "I suppose I should have known she'd gotten the start-up money illegally."

I furrowed my brow. "How?"

"She didn't have an identity." Todd glanced toward the main house. "How else could she have gotten money? At least at first."

"What do you mean?" Nate asked.

"Now, she has an income from a trust fund Simon established for her. She used some of the money from the stolen antiques to get forged identity documents."

"Why didn't she have an identity?" Nate asked, parroting my thoughts.

"She said Ed messed up the timeline." Todd waved his arm. "He'd caused her ancestors not to get together."

"Simon and Lera!" I gasped. "That's why she wanted to make sure they got married." I paused. "So how is she even walking around?"

"Not sure." Todd shook his head. "Maybe because she was outside the time stream when it happened? When she got back, nobody knew who she was, and none of her family existed." He shrugged. "That's what she told me anyway. It took her awhile to convince me she'd been my assistant."

"Why didn't you go back to before Jenny left the first time and stop her?" My cheeks burned. None of this would have happened.

He checked his wristwatch. "I'll tell you later. Right now, we need to get all those people out of the house."

My shoulders tensed. "How are we going to do that? They won't believe us. And the party has just gotten started." I bobbed my head toward the house. "They're expecting to be here until the middle of the night. Wait. How did it start? We could keep it from happening at all."

"They never figured out how it started, or even where." Todd stepped outside. "We have to evacuate."

Nate started out the door, ran back, and gave me a quick kiss. "I'm sending Ed to get the fire hose. I'll be back. You might want to say a prayer." He dashed off.

I lowered my head and prayed for help. When I finished, I looked into Todd's surprised eyes. Inspiration hit. "Todd, do you still play the fiddle?"

He cocked his head. "Yes, but I don't have one with me."

I grabbed his hand and led him outside. "Go around to the front lawn. I'll meet you there ASAP. Be ready to play."

"What are you going to do?" He squeezed my hand then dropped it.

"Move the party outside." I ran into the house, and took the back stairs two at a time. Nearly out of breath, I knocked fast and loud on Caleb's door.

Lydia opened it, a frown on her face. "What's the matter?"

"Caleb, bring your fiddle. And bring your grandpa's old one, too."

Caleb grabbed the fiddles, and I pulled him out into the hallway. "You come too, Lydia."

"What's this about?" Lydia followed us down the hallway,

one fist on her hip.

"You'll find out." I marched them down the central staircase. When we reached the open pocket door connecting the foyer to the ball room, I stopped, took a deep breath, and summoned my best public speaking voice. "Ladies and Gentlemen, may I have your attention."

Lera glared at me, but no one else noticed.

"You won't want to miss this," I said, louder this time. A few people turned toward me. "In a short time, there will be unique entertainment on the front lawn. Please join us. It's a beautiful evening. Why stay inside all night?"

Lera approached, red faced.

"Todd knows what he's talking about," I whispered and started toward the door, leading my procession.

As I left, Lera said, "Please do step outside for a short while."

I ran ahead and introduced Caleb to Todd. Caleb stared for a moment. I was afraid he would refuse to play with a black man. He made a few song suggestions, and Todd shook his head.

I prayed that this would work and tried to arrange everyone on the lawn as far away from the house as possible. When I approached Caleb and Todd, they looked at me, fiddles ready. I nodded at them, and they played a lively tune.

After most of the guests started clapping and tapping their feet to the rhythm, I headed back inside to see if anyone was still there.

Nate ran into the ballroom from the back. "I was worried—" He glanced around. "Where is everyone?"

I gazed past him. "Outside on the lawn. I just came in to see if we had any stragglers."

Nate bobbed his head toward the orchestra.

The leader scowled.

I strode to him. "Sorry about that. You need a break anyway."

He pursed his lips and gave me a short bow.

Not a good time to encounter a cranky musician. "If you would, please come outside. We may need your assistance. I don't think they have a large repertoire."

He huffed, then turned toward the other players.

I tried again. "I need to keep everyone outside as long as possible. It's a surprise. I'm sorry I didn't get a chance to tell you earlier. It's for Lera."

All eight musicians stood.

"It looks like we have a deal." The leader sighed. "What do you want us to do?"

"Bring your instruments and be ready to entertain outside?"

They all agreed and followed us out.

On the way, Nate whispered in my ear, "That was brilliant."

I pointed upward.

He smiled. "Keep praying."

"Did Ed already leave to get the fire extinguisher?"

"Yeah, he took the shortcut, but it will still be a while." He set his jaw in a grim expression.

An out-of-control fire was still a possibility, but I felt better with everyone outside. Except the servants. I stopped on the veranda and did a one-eighty.

Nate pulled me to him. "Where are you going?"

"To tell the servants."

He ran with me.

"You're invited outside in front also," I called as I hurried past a couple of waiters.

They looked at me like I was crazy.

"Please serve the guests out on the lawn," Nate said.

The waiters walked toward the front door, and we continued through the house, ordering servants to the lawn. When we got to the kitchen, the same old woman was there, still cooking.

Nate looked directly at her. "You're needed on the front

lawn with everybody else."

She lifted her chin. "No, sir. I's needed right here."

"Please, you have to come outside," I pleaded.

"I know where I belong." She folded her arms over her chest. "I know you be up to something, but I be staying put."

"You have new orders. Please come with us," Nate said firmly.

"My orders come from above, and they ain't changed." She sat in a chair next to the stove and hummed a slow tune.

I prayed about what to do, then glanced at Nate. Without a word, we walked up to the woman, each grabbed an arm, and escorted her out of the kitchen. Either she'd gotten the same instruction we had, or she had a better sense of smell, because she walked around to the front of the house without a struggle. We found her a chair and went back to make one more sweep. We were about to enter the front door when we smelled smoke.

"It's starting." Nate pulled me off the porch.

He signaled some of the men standing toward the back of the crowd, and we ran around the house. Nate pulled water buckets from the area around the well. I went to the barn and gathered all the containers I could find—several buckets and a few pots. Lydia, Mark, and Martin appeared. I handed Mark and Martin the buckets and told Lydia to go get more help.

Lydia planted her feet, hands on hips. "I can carry water just as well as anyone else."

"Here." I shoved a pail at her. "I'll go get more help." I hurried away. When I glanced back, she held a bucket for Nate to fill.

As I approached the lawn, I scanned the crowd for Lera and Simon. Lera danced in a line with the musicians and most of the guests. Before I could get to them, Simon veered toward the house, which now had smoke coming up from somewhere near the center. I hurried to intercept him. He brushed me off and ran onto the porch. Lera chased him, but she had to pass me.

"Don't." I caught her and pulled her back as flames shot up toward the starry sky.

"Simon!" Lera wailed. She struggled against my hold. "Where is she? First, she tried to steal him. Now she's killed him."

I held onto her. "You don't know Jenny started it."

She took a breath. "She's been missing since we came outside. And I overheard them talking about a fire."

"Who? Simon and Jenny?"

She nodded.

"Did you hear any details?"

"Does it matter now?" She glared at me, trying to pull out of my grasp.

I tightened my hold, and scanned the crowd. The last time I'd seen Jenny was when I went to the kitchen to meet Todd. How long ago was that? It seemed like minutes and hours at the same time.

Come to think of it, Jenny was probably over a century away.

The music stopped. Everyone either stared at the fire or ran for water. I held onto Lera until she overpowered me and trotted toward Caleb who stood with a group of old men discussing how the fire could have gotten out of control so fast and the chances of putting it out.

"Even if Ed brings that newfangled contraption of his, this house is too big."

"Fire's covering half of it already. Can't get close enough. If he could get up over it—"

Caleb sprinted away, followed by Lera and me. He ran to the barn and grabbed some rope and a few flat pieces of wood that looked like they were the beginnings of a new swing. We tried to ask him questions, but he ignored us and scrunched his face in concentration. He took off again toward a toolshed. Lera and I looked at each other and shrugged. He was staying away from the fire. That's all that mattered.

I walked outside and watched the daisy chain. They had enough people to keep the fire from spreading away from the house, but not to make progress dousing it. It seemed like an age before Ed arrived with a group of men and a full water bag.

They brought the wagon as close to the house as possible, positioned the hose, and applied pressure to the bag. It made a slight dent in the flames at the front of the house, but didn't come close to putting them out. Ed signaled his crew, and they rode off in the direction of a nearby stream. To my surprise, Todd was with them. Nobody said a word about his color.

Several minutes later, they were back with another load, having about the same effect. The next time they arrived, Caleb ran to his grandpa carrying the boards, rope, and something metal I couldn't quite distinguish. I stood on tiptoe, but the crowd around Ed and Caleb was so thick it was impossible to see what they were doing.

It wasn't long before one of the younger men, holding the nozzle of a hose, rose into the air on Caleb's contraption. At first it looked like they'd thrown the rope over a tree branch, but I could hear a metal squeal. Caleb must have found a pulley, which they'd attached to the tree limb. The young man squirted the top of the fire and got more of it under control, but they almost dropped him.

"This works better, but we need someone lighter and a way to get closer to the fire," Ed said as the team started off toward the creek.

Caleb dashed off toward the toolshed. By the time Ed's team returned, everybody chattered about Caleb's invention. It impressed most of the crowd, and several people volunteered to use it. Caleb was too young, so who would they select?

Lydia stepped in front of the wagon as they arrived. "I'll do it, Pa. I'm light."

I ran over to her. "Lydia, I thought you were on the bucket

line."

"I heard about the lift." She raised her chin, her eyes shining. "I can do it, Pa."

Ed hesitated until the fire popped. He heaved a sigh. "All right."

Lydia ran toward Caleb.

Ed raised his arm and called out, "Be careful."

Lydia sat on the board, holding the hose, while they hoisted her. This time the pulley was attached to an L-shaped pole mounted on the rear corner of a wagon which was closer to the fire.

Caleb supervised the use of his invention from his post next to the water wagon.

Lydia was much closer to the fire than the young man had been. As she aimed the hose, she called to me, "Don't worry. Nate is still filling buckets."

Slightly relieved, I searched for Mattie and ran to her. Lera joined us. We huddled together, holding our breaths as Lydia got closer to the fire. Mattie murmured prayers, and I prayed silently. Lera stared at Caleb, who stayed put near the water wagon.

If they saved any of the house, it would be the front corner closest to where we stood. As far as we knew, Simon was the only person still inside. It would be a miracle if he came out alive.

When water wagon went for another load, Lydia stayed on the seat, suspended from the second wagon and they swung her as far from the blaze as possible. At the first sight of the water wagon, the men would hoist Lydia and swing her into place to avoid wasting time. Lydia leaned down and grabbed the hose from a man on the wagon. Though Lydia seemed to take it in stride, my stomach clenched each time she did it.

While Lydia was lifted in place for her fourth or fifth go, Jenny galloped in on one of Simon's horses. She leapt off and marched straight to me, her face red. "Where's Todd?"

I pointed toward the wagon returning from the stream. She ran toward it, and I followed, Mattie right behind me.

"I thought she was back in her own time," Mattie whispered in my ear.

I glanced over my shoulder. "So did I."

Before she reached the wagon, Jenny yelled, "Todd, what did you do?"

Todd checked his watch. "Stay here. We'll talk later."

"I told you there was no stopping this fire!" She clenched her fists. "We can't change anything!"

"We can try," Todd yelled from the wagon.

Jenny stomped her foot and folded her arms over her chest.

Mattie and I walked back to watch Lydia and the rest of the crew fight the fire. For all Mattie's fear, I could see pride on her face as well.

Everyone in the crowd worked to combat the blaze. Mattie, Lera, and I all helped press the water bag, while the crew that hauled it out of the creek rested.

Lera had invited Sheriff Hill and Dr. Smythe to the party. Between turns hauling water, the sheriff asked questions, trying to investigate. Dr. Smythe stayed busy making sure no one over-exerted or got too close to the smoke.

Through that long night, I watched Jenny, wondering why she was still there. She hounded Todd every time they came back from the creek. He would check his watch and keep going.

By the time the fire was nearly out, everyone looked exhausted. Nobody, except Jenny, had been a spectator. She stood at the back of the crowd, her expression alternating between anger and hopelessness.

The crew headed out for what could be the last time when Jenny ran up to Todd. I couldn't help but overhear.

"We need to go," Jenny whined. "You're going to get us all stuck in this God-forsaken place."

"There's still time. Simon could be alive. Don't you want us to find him?" Todd jumped down from the wagon, followed by Ed. It left without them.

"It doesn't matter!" She screamed and ran toward the fire.

Mattie, Todd, Ed, and I ran after her.

Jenny waved her arm toward the ruins. "Don't you see? It's all wrong. We can't do anything to make it right. Not with all the constraints you put on your machine."

I glanced at all the people who knew nothing about the time machine. Most stared, mouths open. They probably thought she was crazy. Likely, they were right.

Jenny trotted toward Lydia and Caleb. "Ed was the only one who changed anything. These two shouldn't have been born." She pushed Caleb, and ran to Simon's horse. Caleb stumbled, but wasn't physically hurt.

Sheriff Hill intercepted Jenny before she could mount. He brought her back, handed her over to a deputy, and nodded at Ed. "For her own protection."

Then the sheriff grabbed Todd's hands and pulled out handcuffs.

"You can't arrest him!" I yelled at the same time as Jenny.

"He's got the only way out of here," Jenny screamed.

The sheriff ignored her and fixed me with a glare.

I took a deep breath. "What is he charged with?"

"Arson."

"What?" Todd and I yelled together.

Todd wrenched his arm out of the sheriff's grip and shook his head. "I warned everyone."

"That's the point. You were the only one who knew about it." The sheriff cuffed Todd and started dragging him away. "Probably our thief, too."

Ed and I looked at each other. What could we tell Sheriff Hill?

"Wait!" Ed strode toward the sheriff, stopping him with a

hand on his arm. "If he set it, why would he warn us?"

"Conscience got him?" Sheriff Hill slumped. "I don't know."

"I don't think Mr. James started the fire." Ed scoffed. "And I know he's not the thief."

The sheriff sneered. "How do you know that?"

"Because she is." Ed pointed at Jenny.

The sheriff dropped Todd's arm and squinted at Ed.

Todd started to run, but stopped when Ed shook his head.

Ed turned to the sheriff. "Jenny stole my pocket watch earlier this evening. Check her. She's probably still carrying it."

Jenny showed us her sly grin and handed over the drawstring bag.

The sheriff rifled through it.

I gasped as an image of Jenny in the library flashed into my mind. "I think she's wearing it here." I placed my hand on my bosom.

The sheriff threw out an irritated sigh, and asked his deputy to search Jenny. The man kept hold of her but shook his head.

Sheriff Hill, Ed, and Mattie all peered at me. Did they want me to retrieve it?

I held my palm out to Jenny. "Come on. Hand over the watch."

She smiled and raised one eyebrow. "How positive are you that I have it?"

Taking a deep breath, I pulled the ribbon on the front of her blouse, reached in the top, and fished out the pocket watch.

Ed and Mattie wore smug smiles while Sheriff Hill looked impressed. He reached for the watch.

Jenny huffed and pointed at Ed. "He gave it to me."

Mattie lifted her chin. "I gave him that watch."

The sheriff un-cuffed Todd and told the deputy to keep Jenny in custody.

Jenny batted her eyelashes at the sheriff. "You believe them and not me?"

"I've known them much longer," Sheriff Hill said. "And nobody in this town would give away a gift from Miss Mattie, especially Ed."

Ed cleared his throat. "I also have reason to believe she killed my son, John."

The sheriff nodded, still watching Jenny. "Always thought John's death was suspicious." He turned toward Ed. "Him being a champion rider and all. We'll investigate."

The water wagon rolled in, and everyone, except Jenny, and the deputy charged to hold her, went back to work.

Lydia sprayed the fire from her perch on the hoisted seat. Jenny came running toward the water wagon, the deputy limping after her. Todd jumped down from the wagon, and she pleaded with him again.

This was getting old. I leaned over to Mattie to make a comment and nearly missed what happened next. I wish I had.

The deputy took hold of Jenny as Todd shook his head and held his hands up, turning back toward the fire. Jenny stomped her foot, pulled away from the deputy and ran, pushing Todd. Todd fell against Caleb who hit the man holding Lydia in the air. He fell, letting go of the rope, but not before Lydia was swung toward the wagon. Lydia hit her back hard on the edge of the wagon and fell to the ground in front of it.

Several men ran to Mattie's youngest, lifted her, and carried her away from the fire as Ed shouted not to move her. Doctor Smythe rushed over and tended to her with Ed advising from behind.

Todd commandeered the water wagon, and they headed out for another re-fill. The bucket brigade kept going, able to get closer to the house with each toss.

I looked up in time to see Lera walk toward the rubble. I ran over and held her back. "Wait until the fire is out!" I yelled.

"He could still be alive!" She struggled against me.

"Yes, and you could still get yourself killed." I stopped and gaped.

Nate, black from the soot but otherwise intact, carried a body over his shoulder.

Both anger and relief mingled in my mind. If he was going to risk his life, I was glad I didn't know until it was over.

I let go of Lera and rushed to him. "Simon?"

Nate nodded.

I peered at the body. "He doesn't look burned."

Nate shook his head. "We found him in the grass, just off the kitchen steps. He must have crawled out the back door before the fire spread across to the kitchen." He took Simon to a grassy area and laid him on the ground.

I checked for a pulse. It was there, but faint. "He's still with us." I touched Lera on the shoulder. "I'll go find Dr. Smythe." I narrowed my eyes at Nate, pointing at all the soot on his face. "You scare me like that again, and you're going to need a doctor."

He grinned. "Yes Ma'am. You stay with Lera. I'll get the doc." Nate ran toward Lydia.

Lera sat with Simon's head cradled in her lap, stroking his hair, and murmuring to him. "Don't leave me, Simon. I'm so sorry for yelling earlier." She leaned in closer.

I knelt next to her. "Is he talking?"

She put her finger to her lips and lowered her ear toward Simon's face. He pointed to his chest. When she sat up, Lera held a Bible.

"What did he say?"

"Jenny tried to take this earlier." She held the large black leather book out to me. "It has the only known record of his family history. He thinks she was trying to protect it. She knew about the fire."

Nate brought the doctor, and Lera turned her attention toward the examination.

I scanned the area for Jenny. She stood with the Sheriff, his deputy, and Todd. Todd wasn't under arrest again, was he?

I walked toward them, Nate right beside me. "Jenny knew about the fire, too."

"Apparently, we have a couple of prophets here," Sheriff Hill said.

"I can explain everything." Jenny struggled against the deputy's hold.

"No, she can't." Todd checked his watch again.

The sheriff stared at Todd and then Jenny. "Somebody better start talkin'."

"He's got something of mine." Jenny pointed at Todd.

Todd and I exchanged glances. I hid my hands behind my back and moved closer to him. Without drawing the sheriff's attention, Todd slipped his remote to me and pointed at Jenny.

"That's a lie." Todd lunged toward her.

The sheriff and deputy scrambled to keep them apart. I ran to Nate and hugged him, trying to look scared, which wasn't difficult, while I slid the remote into his back pocket.

"What did you do with it?" Jenny screamed, pawing at Todd. "You idiot. You could have done so much with that machine, but with all your limits, you made it useless. Worse. Now we're both going to get stuck here."

Sheriff Hill squinted. "What machine?"

Todd shrugged. "I don't know what she's talking about. I'm not sure she knows."

"You're lying." Red-faced, Jenny pointed at him. "You made it impossible to go back to a time before I left, so I couldn't undo anything. I lost my whole family! My life! She's lost hers too." She pointed at me. "We're all going to be stuck here."

Sheriff Hill motioned toward his deputy. "Take her into town. I'll send the doc in when he's finished here."

"No." Jenny shook her head. "All I was trying to do was set

things straight. Lydia, Caleb, Mark, and John shouldn't ever have been born."

Ed jabbed a finger close to her chest. "Were you going to kill them, too?"

"John got in the way of what should have happened." Jenny pushed Ed away. "It was an accident. I was trying to get him to leave Lera."

She continued yelling as the deputy hauled her away, but I couldn't understand the rest of her rants.

"It looks like you may have been right about John, Ed." Sheriff Hill bobbed his head toward Jenny. "If I can use the confession, I may have both the thefts and John's murder case solved." He turned to Todd. "You're free to go. Don't get in any trouble."

Todd checked his watch. "Don't worry. You won't see me around here again."

The sheriff tipped his hat and walked away.

"Wait!" Todd jogged toward him. "If you let me take Jenny, I can make sure she never shows up here again."

The sheriff shook his head. "Sorry, she's dangerous, both to others and herself."

Todd returned to us while the sheriff caught up to Jenny and the deputy.

"Does that mean you still have time to use this?" Nate handed Todd the remote.

"Barely," Todd said.

My heartrate increased. "Why don't you have much time?"

"I set a limit." He checked his watch for the hundredth time. "I'm shutting down the machine when I get back. I didn't want Jenny to try anything slick to get me to stay longer. If I don't leave within fifteen minutes, I'll be stuck here."

I clasped his jacket sleeve. "You can't get to the machine in time!"

Todd held up the device. "This is a different remote. I can

leave from here." One corner of his mouth quirked up. "Matter of fact, that's why she came to get me. Hers won't work anymore. Couldn't trust her."

"Why didn't you just go back to before anyone left and shut down the machine?" He hadn't answered my question earlier.

Todd shook his head. "I couldn't. I'd put limits on it."

"Why?" I asked.

Todd exhaled. "The first time I used it, I went back a few days, saw myself, and both of us freaked." He chuckled. "Because of that, I limited it to outside my own lifetime. And when we go home, it has to be at least to a minute after we left."

"What about not being able to go back any further than you've already gone?" Nate asked. I was impressed he remembered that detail.

Todd shrugged. "Never did figure that one out." He peered at me. "Are you coming? It can carry up to three people. You could both go."

A surge of hope hit me, and I peered at Nate. He bowed his head for a second then smiled at me. His expression said yes! I wrapped my arms around his neck. Thank you, Lord.

Ed tapped me on the shoulder. "Lydia wants to say goodbye."

We snapped back to reality and ran to Lydia. Why hadn't I gone to her earlier? We found her lying on a blanket over the drained bag in the back of the water wagon. Mark and Mattie knelt beside her. She looked pale and her breathing was fast and shallow. Mark closed his eyes and squeezed her hand. Mattie sobbed and prayed.

I glanced around for the doctor, but he wasn't in view.

Nate and I knelt across from Mattie and Mark.

Ed jumped on the back of the wagon.

I touched her forehead. "Lydia, you were so brave. I'm sorry this happened."

"Nice knowing you," she said, so softly I could barely hear

her.

I forced a smile. "Don't say that. I'll see you again."

"Ma says, no." She showed me her wicked grin, if a weak version. What did that mean?

I squinted at Mattie.

Mattie sniffed. "Doc told us to make her as comfortable as possible."

"But she needs treatment." My stomach knotted as the doctor approached. "Why is she having a hard time breathing?"

"I think she has some internal injuries, but I can't do surgery here, and she won't make it into town." Dr. Smythe studied his feet. "I'm sorry, there's nothing I can do." He stood on the ground near the wagon, but his voice sounded like he was farther away.

I turned toward Ed, expecting him to do something.

He gazed at Lydia, a tear in his eye.

They'd all given up. I couldn't believe it. I scooted to the edge of the wagon, and grabbed the doctor by his lapels. "You have to try."

"Half a mile on these roads will kill her." Dr. Smythe pried my fingers off him. "And the pain will be unbearable."

I closed my eyes, not wanting to accept this. "Too bad this had to happen here," I muttered. "In my time—"

My eyes met Nate's, and I knew we were thinking the same thing. He helped me down, we raced back to Todd, and pulled him over to the wagon.

"Todd, do you think your hospital could save Lydia?" I asked.

"I don't have a—oh, the one in town?" He sat on the end of the wagon and looked Lydia over. "I could go straight to the hospital." Todd locked eyes with me. "But then I wouldn't be able to take both you and him."

Nate and I peered at Ed and Mattie.

"We've got five minutes," Todd said.

"I don't think she's going that fast," Mattie said.

I touched the end of the wagon. "No, Todd's device. It's on a timer."

"Oh." She and Ed exchanged a long meaningful look.

Mattie caressed her daughter's forehead. "Lydia, go with Mr. James. Promise me you'll study your Bible."

Lydia nodded.

Mattie peered at Todd. "Please take care of her."

"For me." Ed shook Todd's hand.

Todd pulled his controller out of his jacket pocket and pushed buttons. He peered at me. "You coming?"

I hesitated, tempted, but Nate squeezed my hand. I shook my head, tears in my eyes.

"Thought not." Todd fiddled with the gadget.

How did he know, when I didn't until a second ago?

Todd glanced behind us. "Can all of you stand over there?" He pointed to the wagon parked between us and the few firefighters and party guests that were still on the property.

Mattie gave Lydia a hug and slid toward the end of the wagon.

Ed held Lydia's face in his hands and kissed her forehead. He got to his feet slowly, helped Mattie down, and up onto the other wagon.

Mark, Nate, and I gave her quick pats and hugs, then jumped down and climbed up to form a line shielding Todd from the rest of the crowd.

Todd pushed another button, and his time machine appeared out of nowhere. Mark and Mattie gasped. Lydia's eyes lit up as much as was possible in her condition. Todd picked her up and stepped onto the contraption.

We waved and said our goodbyes. Mattie blew kisses. I could tell she wanted to jump to the other wagon and give Lydia one more hug, but there wasn't time. Todd pushed another button, and they started to disappear.

"Wait!" I cried. They became solid again. "If you didn't think you could change anything, why warn us about the fire?"

"Jenny couldn't change anything. I thought I should try, this time." Todd grinned. "Besides, the newspaper reported a mysterious Negro stranger saved most of the guests at the party."

"You didn't change anything from that report?" I asked.

"In the article I read, both Lera and Simon died, as well as a few of the guests." He stood straighter. "I'd say we changed quite a bit."

"Does this fix Jenny's problem?"

"Who knows? I could go home and find her at work." He pulled out an old, folded piece of paper. "Almost forgot. Adam also found this in the museum."

Nate jumped off the wagon, grabbed the paper, and brought it back to show me.

I gasped at the vintage photo of Nate and me holding a newborn.

"It didn't have a date," Todd said.

I smiled. "I knew you weren't a mind reader."

"Can't leave it here." Todd stretched out his arm.

I handed the picture back to Nate who gave it to Todd.

He chuckled and pushed the button. Todd, Lydia, and the machine disappeared.

I felt numb as we climbed down from the wagon. Probably from the physical and emotional exhaustion. Everyone looked drained.

Mattie smiled through her tears. "Well, I have a hundred and forty extra years to pray for that girl's salvation." She clasped her hands together. "I'll be in heaven when it happens. And what rejoicing there'll be that day."

I couldn't help but laugh as I wiped a tear from my face. Lera came over to find out what was so funny. I nearly panicked. How would we explain Lydia's disappearance?

"Lera, Lydia's gone," Mattie said.

Lera closed her eyes. "I'm so sorry, Miss Mattie."

"Don't you worry." Mattie patted Lera's shoulder. "We were laughing because I finally have hope that we'll see her again in heaven."

Ed pulled Mattie aside. "You could see her here, too."

Mattie tilted her head.

"But Todd is dismantling the time machine." No point pretending I hadn't heard him.

Ed's eyes twinkled. "Lydia has a few ideas of her own. With the technology she'll have available, I wouldn't be surprised to see her one day."

Mattie shook her head and chuckled. "That one is definitely yours." She pulled Ed back toward the rest of the group and approached Lera. "How're Simon and Caleb?"

"Caleb's fine." Lera exhaled, a wan smile on her face. "Simon's going to make it. It'll take a while."

"You can stay with us, until he gets on his feet again," Nate said.

Lera gave him a quick hug. "Thank you. We'll be out of your hair as soon as we can rebuild. I don't think it'll be quite as grand." She showed Mattie a small smile. "Mansions are overrated, anyway."

As Nate, Ed, and Mark carried Simon to the water wagon, Mattie and I watched Lera gather up Caleb who'd fallen asleep on the ground.

"I'm going to miss my girl," Mattie said.

I touched her shoulder. "We all will. But you made the right decision."

She looked me in the eye. "*You* made the right decision. Thank you." She gave me the fiercest hug I've ever had. We clung to each other for a while. When we pulled apart, my eyes were watery, but Mattie's were dry.

"Tomorrow." She nodded at the sun peeking over the horizon. "Today, I'll take some food to Jenny in the jail." She led me to Nate's carriage. "We'll find her a good lawyer. Maybe Nate can help. He always wanted to study law."

I stopped and gaped at her. "Mattie, she killed John."

She wagged her finger. "Now, remember. Innocent until proven guilty."

I backed away. "She confessed."

"I forgave whoever did that a long time ago." Mattie wiped her brow with a handkerchief. "Jenny is practically family, and she needs our help." She gave me a long look. "Why do you think your circumstances are so different from Jenny's?"

I shrugged. "Because, I didn't go to twenty-ten to find I didn't exist?"

She shook her head. "Think about it, what do you have that she doesn't?"

I must confess, the first thing that popped into my mind was Nate, but I knew that wasn't what Mattie meant. I prayed to know the answer she wanted, and nearly fell over when it hit me. "My faith?"

She squeezed me in a one-armed hug. "And who better to go see Jenny with me. You can share your faith with her."

My shoulders tensed so much they nearly touched my ears. "But, but. I'm just learning."

She led me toward the carriages where the rest of the family waited. "Don't you worry." She tapped my upper arm. "I'll be there with you, and the Holy Ghost will give you the words."

I lowered my shoulders, but still felt uneasy as we loaded everyone in the carriages and headed for home. Caleb and Simon slept in the back of the water wagon, but due to space constraints, Lera rode in the back of our carriage. We stayed quiet for the first half of the ride.

Exhaustion warred with adrenalin. I shouldn't try to make sense of anything in this condition, but my mind wouldn't stop. How could so much have changed in so little time? I resented Mattie for insisting I visit Jenny, but that was the least of my worries. I was also slightly annoyed that we were going to have house guests indefinitely. I wasn't mad at Nate for offering, just for not talking to me about it first. He'd learn. Still, that was minor. Why would God leave me here?

Nate's shoulder touched mine. "I thought you'd be asleep by now."

I flashed a tired smile. "Too much going through my mind."

He nodded. "Yeah. Keep praying, Cassie."

I closed my eyes. "God, why? Where are you?" That little lightbulb popped into my head. He hadn't left me, and I chose to stay. He could use me and bless me here.

My eyes flew open wide. The day of the bazaar, when I'd had that feeling I'd be going home, we'd gone to Nate's house. I'd actually been headed home just as we were now. How wild was that?

Lera leaned in from the back seat. "Cassie, did you notice Ida and Martin? Now there is a match I could never have imagined."

I smiled at her. "I'm not as worried about you, anymore."

She giggled. "When do you think we'll see Lydia again?"

I bit my lip.

She clicked her tongue. "You all think I'm too dense to see what's been going on? I know Ed, Cassie, and Jenny are from the future and that's where Lydia went. I'm not stupid."

"Never thought you were." Only that she was oblivious.

Nate glanced over his shoulder. "Well, now that it's out in the open, I doubt we'll see Lydia soon. If she comes back, she'll come for something important and then leave."

"Lydia really does belong in the future." I shuddered. Did I?

Nate draped his arm around me, reminding me I belonged with him. An unbelievable peace washed over me, and I leaned into his embrace.

What did the Bible say? Peace that passes all

understanding. I still feel it, at least on most days.

Author Bio: Pamela Baker feels called to write suspense and speculative fiction from a Biblical worldview. She began by writing skits and one-acts for her church drama team, and had the privilege of watching one of her plays performed at a homeless shelter in Atlanta. Her flash fiction stories have appeared in Spark flash fiction magazine, and the print anthologies Stella's Secret Sonata and Bolero at Breakfast. More short stories can be found on her website: https://pamelagbaker.com/ and in her newsletter: https://mailchi.mp/514e09a1e16f/adventures-in-writing

Born in Corning and raised in Addison, New York, she earned a degree in Electrical Engineering in Bridgeport Connecticut, then moved to New London to work at Electric Boat. After marrying a sailor, she lived in a suburb of Charleston SC and worked at Charleston Naval Shipyard. Since 1994, Pam and her loving, supportive husband, Gary, have called Warner Robins Georgia home. She was a software engineer at Robins AFB, and they raised two daughters. Now, she shares her office with rescue dog, Petra.

An avid reader, she also enjoys performing in community theater, singing in her church choir, and traveling via ships, planes, trains, and automobiles in that order of preference.

Social Media: Facebook: https://www.facebook.com/pambakernovels Instagram: https://www.instagram.com/pamela_g_baker_writer/

Twitter: Website: https://pamelagbaker.com/

Pinterest: Goodreads: https://www.goodreads.com/user/show/1035095-pamela-baker

PAMELA G. BAKER

.

Made in the USA
Columbia, SC
23 October 2024

44457564R00183